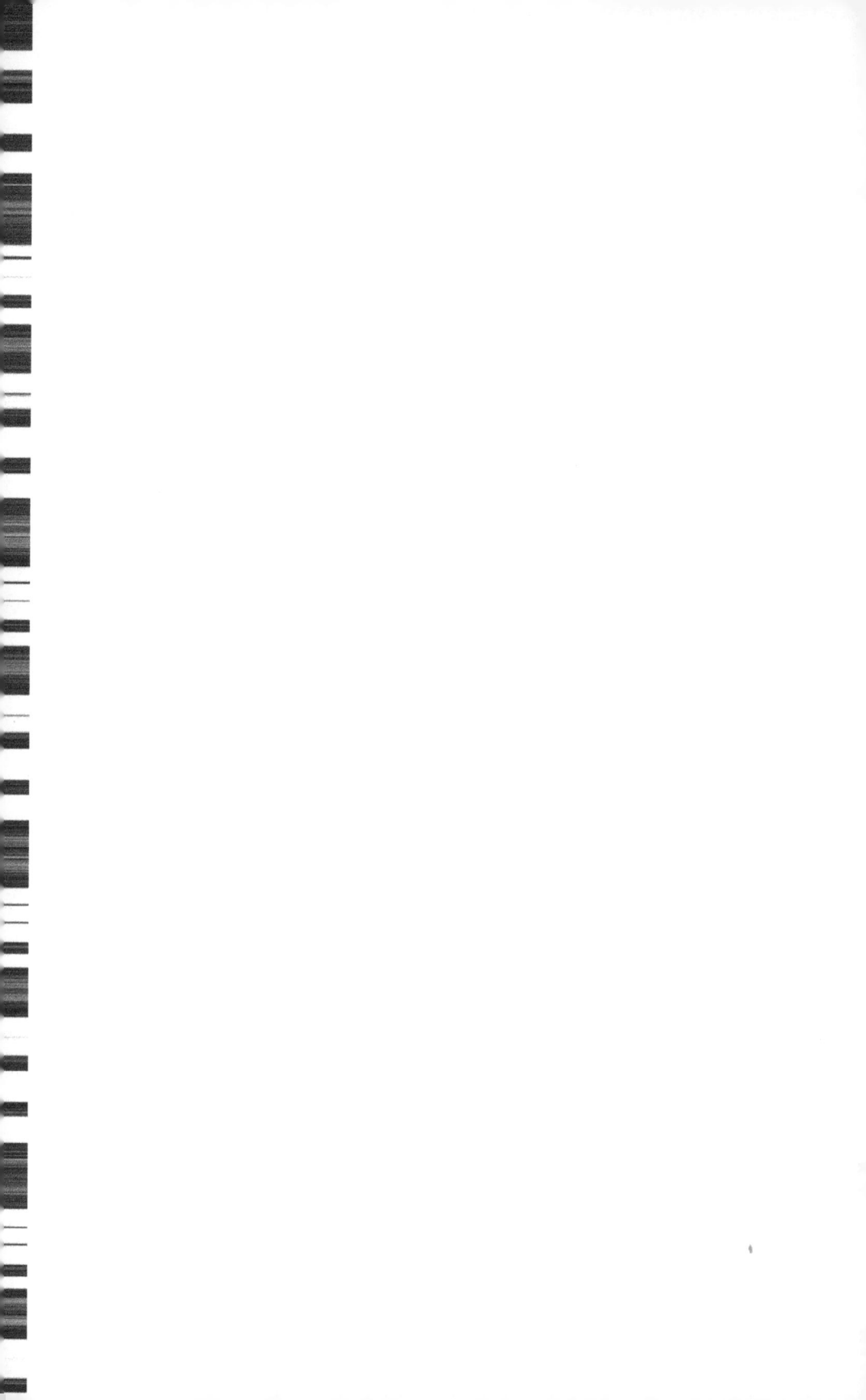

THE BOUNTY OF BLOOD AND NAILS

THE BOUNTY OF BLOOD AND NAILS

N K BROWN

This book is a work of fiction. Names, characters, places, and incidents either are products of the author's imagination or are used fictitiously. Any resemblance to actual events or locales or persons, living or dead, is entirely coincidental and not intended by the author.

THE BOUNTY OF BLOOD AND NAILS

CITY OWL PRESS
www.cityowlpress.com

All Rights reserved. Except as permitted under the U.S. Copyright Act of 1976, no part of this publication may be reproduced, distributed, or transmitted in any form or by any means, or stored in a database or retrieval system, without the prior consent and permission of the publisher.

Copyright © 2026 by N K Brown.

Cover Design by MiblArt. All stock photos licensed appropriately.

Edited by Lisa Green.

For information on subsidiary rights, please contact the publisher at info@cityowlpress.com.

Deluxe Hardback Edition ISBN: 978-1-64898-579-9

Paperback Edition ISBN: 978-1-64898-537-9

Digital Edition ISBN: 978-1-64898-538-6

For Nikki and Sheena, looking forward to the day when our books are on the shelf together

CHAPTER ONE
TOFFEE AND TAROT

It was almost time.

The final night, the crescendo, the climax. The other charlatans would be turning up the fires, pouring out the charm, increasing the danger, the difficulty, the disbelief. I had to remain stoic. Isolated, yet approachable. Alluring, yet aloof. They didn't *need* to know what I could see, yet I appealed to them, like a whispering siren. A craving. An urge. An itch.

There was only one I needed to satisfy tonight.

I shivered as night rose around me. The air thinned, laced with a refreshing chill as the last of the sun's color bleached from the sky. One by one, fairy lights popped to life. Green, amber, purple, silver, all small fiery splotches of color suspended from spindly wires looping between the stalls. A gentle breeze rumpled the cloth in front of me, evoking the small tinkling of bells that hung weighted at the edges of my table.

The gentle twang of a harp filtered through the calm night. A few isolated notes of a violin chased after it, attempting to warm the pre-magical atmosphere. The wooden sign suspended above my stall creaked in the breeze.

A low whistle snagged my attention. I placed the tarot deck upon the velvet cloth and brushed the deep hood from my face, allowing a glimpse of the stall across the aisle to the left. The candy man grinned, dimples puckering his cheeks. I didn't know his name, nor age—somewhere in his mid-twenties surely, but the high-waisted tan trousers and star-studded suspenders made him appear twice that age. Or perhaps transported in time from a century ago.

I wasn't doing anything to subvert the stereotype either. Black cloak with scarlet trimmed hood. Sleeves that dripped down past my hands allowing only a flash of red nail polish and multiple silver rings to emerge as I tapped confidently upon the chosen card, eager to bestow my knowledge of the future upon the lucky client.

Candyman ran his hand around the gold-rimmed edge of the floss machine. Cotton candy swirled around his finger, interlacing like a fat pink chrysalis. He slowly brought his finger to his lips, maintaining eye contact, sucking the chrysalis into his mouth. I knew what he would taste like later. Sugar and caramel and a hint of rum—kept in a not-so-secret bottle under his stall. I swear that when I looked away, he would dab himself with the candy floss like sticky cologne, knowing that it would make me kiss him harder, that it would entice my tongue to caress his skin, my teeth to nip in all the right places.

Though tonight, there would be no fun for either of us.

I let the hood fall back across my face. The music picked up, a thrum of excitement charging the air from a crowd of people I couldn't yet see. If I was successful, there would be no time to lose myself amongst the bags of sugar, the mounds of sweets, the warm, roving hands of Candyman. If she came and it worked, I would have to dissolve into the dawn, putting as much distance between myself and the Collectors as possible.

Sweat prickled my palms, threatening to slide down my skin and pool upon the velvet tablecloth. I forced my breathing to deepen, my lungs to expand past the point of recoil.

From under the peak of my hood, I caught sight of the first eager footsteps rushing the aisle. The grass lay trampled, blades permanently bowed from the weight of passersby this past week. Yet, for the last six days, she had not come.

She must tonight.

My heart ticked like a bomb, speeding toward the deadline. Sixty days it had taken me to find this one. She was reclusive, a shadow. I didn't know what she'd done, but I wasn't surprised they'd ordered me to track her down. Her bounty was impressive. If I could be as stealthy as her, we'd both disappear into the ether, no tracts, no guilt, transformed into legacy.

Candyman handed a large paper bag stuffed with toffees to a small girl. He bent over the stall, deftly flicking the top cube into the air and snapped his teeth shut around it. He winked as the girl giggled, her mother affectionately patting her braided hair.

So that is what he would taste of later. Cinders and treacle. I swallowed, holding his gaze which had floated not-so-innocently to mine until he turned to the next customer, a broad grin lapping at his cheeks.

The music hung thick now in the air, twined with shouts and laughter. From my right, the swoosh of a lit torch rippled a wave of heat toward me. Marianne didn't only eat fire, she commanded it, molding it into shapes like smoke rings from a cigar. Some of the magic here was real, parlor tricks, really. Just enough to make people part with their money, but not enough to be arrested.

Sweat trickled down my spine. At least now I could blame it on the heat in the air.

Once the first rush of visitors subsided—those who instinctively knew where they wanted to go or were dragged by small children—the timid arrived next. These were innocents, virgins to the fayre. They'd come for a specific reason. Perhaps to catch the eye of one of the performers, eagerly hoping to be chosen as a volunteer to levitate ten feet into the air before being caught by the toned biceps of the magician. His shirt sleeves rolled up, winding ink crisscrossing his flesh.

On more than one occasion I'd seen his tattoos morph into the mirror image of the person he wanted to tempt backstage. How could one resist when your face was clearly visible etched permanently upon his body? It was fate of course, and so one did not resist.

My first client was here. It wasn't who I needed to see, but I doubted

I'd be lucky enough to escape so early. She was a young woman of nineteen or twenty. Her cheeks were flushed, and she gripped the arm of a young man, tugging him toward me. She would never have ventured this far by herself, and yet, the eagerness in her eyes told me I was who she'd come to see.

Shame I was a fraud.

I gestured silently to the bench in front. She sat carefully, scooping her long skirt beneath her, the bells tinkling seductively as she rustled the tablecloth. The man stood behind, one hand on her shoulder. The sinews popped from his hand; his fingers almost clawed, but he stopped short of releasing that pressure onto the bare skin of her neck.

I riffled the tarot cards in my hand. The deck was pristine, the pattern on the back that of a simple silver skull upon black, the kind you could purchase anywhere. The satin cloth and silver ribbon binding them also looked new, like I'd exchanged them for a handful of pennies a week ago when the fayre opened.

A trained eye would see the con, could smell the treachery a mile away. I could scrunch the deck, bend the edges and yet wasn't this whole place one large trick? A parallel realm an ordinary being could wander into for only seven nights per year and be transported into a land of magic and fun and frivolity. One where they could step out of their ordinary, meagre lives and succumb to their dreams. Or so the proprietors would have you believe.

"Are you sure, my dear?" The man's face stretched tight. His mouth was obscured beneath a manicured moustache. "We have talked about your disposition toward the supernatural at length. Have you forgotten?"

I flattened my palm and raised my hand toward him. My nails wanted to extend, the gift coursing through my bloodstream like poison.

"Oh yes, honey," she answered. "It's only a bit of fun. I won't take any of it to heart, I promise." Her mouth curved downwards as she spoke, her dark eyes beseeching.

They all wanted the same reading from me this week, *will I marry the crown prince?* No one was so bold as to outright say it, but it was written in the singe of heat on their cheeks, in the coil of hair they twined nervously around a finger. But not this one. She needed something else.

The man tutted and fumbled in his waistcoat for coins. He withdrew two coppers and dropped them into my open palm, returning the pounds and gideons that were ostentatiously brandished amongst them back to the pocket.

I nodded, tipping the coins into my cloak and returned my hand to the tarot. I tapped the skull on the uppermost card as my thigh knocked against the table leg, silently cracking a vial of incense. The perfume seeped out, infusing the air with a faint shimmer. The young woman's eyes widened, her chin lifting as she inhaled deeply.

"That's my nana's smell," she whispered. "Roses."

The man above her said nothing, everything he wanted to utter explained in the twitch of his mouth and the tightening of his hand upon her shoulder. If she wasn't so enraptured by the aura, she would be able to feel the bruises pooling beneath his fingertips, blemishing the smooth skin beneath.

I turned the first card over. The Grim Reaper. It was my favorite to start with. Everyone knew someone who had died or was dying. That was life.

"You have lost someone whose wisdom meant a lot to you." The crack in my voice was not intentional. I needed to get a grip on my emotions.

Another pulse ricocheted through my veins as the magic struggled to escape.

She inhaled sharply. Her hand pressed to her breast, but not over her heart. Her fingers rested on a gold brooch shaped like a butterfly pinned to her green dress.

I turned the next card face up revealing two entwined skeletons with empty sockets gazing at one another, bony arms encircling barren ribcages. The Lovers.

Her face faltered. She stared at the card, her knuckles blanching as she gripped the brooch.

"You see," the man interrupted, pulling her back from the table, "it's us. Now, let's go."

I turned over the next card, pushing it in front of the others and toward her. A man dangled upside down from a spiral pillar, his legs entangled with a serpent, a crown of thorns encircling his head.

"What's that one?" He lowered his head, squinting at the table.

"The Hanged Man."

He choked, jerking backward. He grabbed the woman's shoulder again to half-drag her from her seat. "Come on, we're leaving."

When he released her and turned to straighten his waistcoat, I slipped the final card across the table. The woman took it, glancing quickly at the picture and the inscription before slipping it back face down.

"You know what she would have said," I whispered. "Because that's what you believe as well. Trust your instincts."

She swallowed, her eyes wide, cheeks drained of color. She bestowed a small smile upon the man as she delicately took his arm, as if suddenly repulsed by the thought of touching even his clothing. As they walked away, she turned back to me and nodded. My chest tightened as my breath paused on the inhale. Good. No one should be trapped by another.

I reined in my emotions, crushing them beneath years of well-trained lies. The air thinned again as the cool breeze drained the incense.

Perhaps there would be time to linger when the fayre closed, and the patrons had departed. We could all finally be ourselves. I did love toffee, probably more than the small caramel droplets Candyman kept in a bowl for melting. Maybe tonight I would line the small candies down his chest, arranging them like stars, before using my tongue to trace swirls and patterns and galaxies as they melted from his body heat...

There she was.

Everything stopped. The dragon of fire Marianne shot into the air paused, a great tongue of jade flame cauterized from its mouth. The jaunty spring from the bow of the violin froze on the strings. The clouds of pink candy floss strangled the white stick.

Then the breath whooshed from my lungs, adrenaline igniting my body as the world revolved once again.

She was here.

I'd studied every inch of the small portrait I had been given when assigned this task. Ingrained the details onto the corrugations of my mind while traveling through wood and dale, skirting cities and plowing through barren countryside.

As I closed in and navigated the labyrinthine streets of this town, I imagined every conceivable change of hair color, added wrinkles or frown lines, each blend of fabric she could opt to wear. I had questioned the baker, the tailor, the midwife, all in a roundabout, casual tone, painting an amicable smile on my face while secretly probing their answers for the minutiae.

Dully, she was as expected. Mid-forties, brown hair streaked with gray, thick glasses perched upon a straight nose. Her clothes were average—well-pressed, but clean. She hid her wealth in the diamond necklace that peeked out of her frilled collar and the pointed shoes inlaid with golden thread and satin bindings which serpentined up her ankles.

What had she done? And, more importantly to whom? Maybe it was better not knowing. Then I was just doing a social service—for a hefty fee. The chase had been fun, the funneling of the hunt heart-pounding. But the kill? I may not be directly slitting her throat, but I was handing over the knife. My stomach flipped, the sweat beading upon my palms.

I flicked the top card at her. It fluttered on the breeze, dying at her feet.

She stooped to pick it up, turning toward me with a cock of her head as she considered what I could deign to offer her. I raised my face, allowing the color from the fairy lights to fall upon me as the hood lifted, unmasking the shadows. I gestured toward the empty bench.

Don't run. Don't flee. I don't want to have to chase you.

She moved closer, a smirk stretching her lips. "That was a silly little trick." Her voice stretched, the sarcasm snagging the attention of passersby. "Is this my likeness?" She twirled the Death card in her fingers.

"A warning," I said.

She didn't believe in the power of the deck, for her fortunes were not told in fables and fairytales. She would sit just to prove a point. To prove how ridiculous this was.

The crowd grew steadily around her, magnetized by her scorn.

My heart hammered and my mouth dried. The hood flapped back over my face as she settled herself, elbows planted upon the velvet cloth, the bells cackling wildly with the movement.

Don't leave.

Don't hate me.

"I don't need a fortune read," she said. "What else do you have?"

I pulled the tarot toward me and positioned them perfectly square at the edge of the table. I held out my palm hoping she wouldn't notice the sheen of congealing sweat.

She extracted a dainty coin purse from the depths of her outfit and handed over one copper. "You can have more if these fine folk are impressed." She waved her hand, inviting the hovering people closer.

A small throng had gathered. It wasn't surprising. She was well known, respected, and feared. It had been difficult getting anyone to talk about her, to reveal even the smallest morsel of information. Once they sniffed where the conversation was going, they rapidly scurried away. Being tantalizingly close for such a long time had been half the fun. They were as curious as I was about the woman underneath.

I reached under the table and pulled up a velvet-draped divider. It was a foot high and the same width with an ebony cloth attached. She watched me intently as I reached across and gently lowered her left arm. I moved it to the side, palm down, fingers splayed. I slid the board along the table and into the crook of her arm, arranging the cloth over her left shoulder so she seemed to melt seamlessly into the fabric.

Next, I flopped out a doll's arm. Stuffed, pink and plump, perfectly proportioned to her own body size. I slid the severed end under the cloth, positioning the hand and unpainted nails exactly like her real one.

Candyman's eyes lingered on mine through the packed bodies as they jostled for a better vantage point, but the flirtation had gone. His brow furrowed, a fleeting look of worry marring his features until my view of him was engulfed by the crowd again.

If this went wrong, I would need access to all his hidden rum. Gorging on sugar and drinking myself into a stupor would be a good swan song for my life thus far.

I tugged the two strands of silver ribbon out from under the tarot. I ran each length along the fake arm and her real one simultaneously. Her brow furrowed, a small crinkle of disgust burrowing into the skin above her nose.

"Do you feel this?" I asked.

She huffed, her eyes darting to those closest before answering, "Of course I do."

I stopped stroking her real arm but continued to slide the ribbon up the doll's arm. "And now?"

She scoffed again. "Yes."

A small murmur arose from those watching. The woman stilled, her blue eyes narrowing on me.

I nodded. "Very well."

Returning the ribbons to the corner of the table, I scooped up a handful of fire jacks from an alcove underneath. Marianne had kindly lent me a few dozen at the beginning of the fayre, in return for a doctored reading of ill omens when her ex-wife visited.

I cracked one of the jacks between my fingers, tossing it quickly into the air as a small ball of white-hot fire cracked into life. It hovered for a split second before sizzling into ash and drifting toward the table. I shifted in my seat, pressing my thigh into the table leg where another aroma waited. This would release the charred scent of burning flesh, raising the air temperature by a few degrees with it.

I took another jack between my fingers and squeezed, dropping it quickly onto the doll's arm. As it landed, I cracked the vial with my leg, the noise lost amongst the woman's shriek.

She gaped at the fake arm and the charred circle marring its pink wrist. The crowd tittered. Whispers of, "Did you really feel that?" and "She's part of the act." I waited until they quieted and took another jack to her real arm. She couldn't see over the screen, hadn't even noticed my arm move to the side as she stared transfixed at the black stain on the doll's arm.

I cracked another and rested it on her real hand. It ignited, a brief ripple of heat firing into the crowd. They drew back, some gasping, a few honks of nervous laughter, but the woman did not move.

She frowned at me, then swiveled to assess the crowd. I reached out to tug on the fake arm. "Sit still please." As if I'd pulled her physically, she turned back and settled. The crowd gasped again.

I pushed the remaining jacks aside, willing the tremble in my fingers to cease and pointed toward an elderly lady to the right of the woman. She wore an elaborate jewel-spattered hat, braided with ribbons and flowers.

"A pin, please." She extracted one, a fine specimen, two inches long with a diamond head.

I started on the woman's real hand. Gently, the pin sunk into the flesh between her fingers, skewering her to the velvet table as if she were a butterfly. She made no sound, nor even flinched. The crowd was silent, sensing the finale, their eyes wide, muscles tensed as they hung on every little movement.

I pulled the pin out slowly, a smear of blood coating the barb. Moving toward the fake arm, I gently prodded the flesh of the forearm. The woman jumped. I did it again, and she flinched. Hovering the pin just above the fake skin, my eyes locked with hers beneath the hood.

My right hand crept toward her real arm, nails silently extending. Power coursed through my body, pooling with a tingle in my fingertips as I dragged my nails down her arm, the jagged ends biting into her flesh.

She didn't move an inch.

I fought to stop an exhale of relief as the magic rushed out, my body yearning to lay limp as if exsanguinated.

A young boy popped up beside the woman and crammed himself next to her on the bench. "What's going on, Ma?" He shoved a pink and green swirled lollipop into his mouth and stared at the fake arm with my pin hovering over it, before peering past the barrier.

My stomach twisted. She had a child?

It was too late, but the real question was, would it have stopped me?

I smoothed the blood away using the velvet tablecloth and tugged down her long sleeve. Unfolding the cloth from her shoulder, I returned the barrier beneath the table and lowered my head. The audience broke into applause.

In a daze, the woman cautiously wound her arm in as if the nerves had all come loose. Coppers rained onto the table, bouncing off one another until the excited voices turned away to see what other wonders the fayre held.

Midnight had barely struck, but I was done.

When I pushed the remaining fire jacks toward the boy, he pocketed them gleefully. I waited until his mother had fully roused herself and shepherded the boy away before tugging down the wooden sign above my stall. Candyman was obscured again in the rush of customers who had left my performance, blocking my last view of him. I scooped up the coppers, left the tarot and other equipment, and headed toward the far end of the field.

Once the grass began to tickle my knees and the colorful glow from the fayre had dimmed to an ashy firelight, I doubled over and retched.

When there was nothing left in my stomach, I straightened, wiping my mouth on my sleeve. The woods bordering the field were thick and almost impenetrable, but I had scoped out my retreat already. Picking my feet high along a narrow game trail, I made for the other side, a distance of only a few miles if I stayed true.

I didn't know how much time I had before the Collectors came. They wouldn't snatch the woman at the fayre, it would be too public. On her way home, perhaps? Maybe they had a shred of decency left and would wait until she'd tucked her child into bed, sparing him the eternal nightmares. It would be better to wake and find her vanished than the alternative.

This, I knew firsthand.

The wood pressed in around me, brambles snagging on my cloak and razor-thin spiderwebs caressing my face. Where were the night creatures? The hooting owl, the mouse rustling through the fallen leaves? Even the bats were not silhouetted against the dark clouds.

I ignored the acid roiling in my stomach, the ever-deafening roar in my ears to turn back and spend the night in the warm embrace of Candyman. Safely tucked up amongst people and far away from the darkness that lurked everywhere else.

A twig snapped like bone from just ahead.

Is that why the animals had fled? The Collectors were already waiting?

Crunch.

I tried to submerge the screaming of my subconscious mind, the instinct for self-preservation and pushed through toward a small clearing.

A figure emerged from the shadows on the other side.

CHAPTER TWO
THE DEVIL IN DISGUISE

"Take a seat, Tam." The figure lowered her hood and waved a gloved hand toward the ground at her feet. "You look terrible. You've been working hard, yes?"

I ground my teeth, cutting off the retort that bubbled back. I obeyed, settling myself along the bony spine of a fallen tree. "Why are you here? I've barely finished. You can't possibly need me to go again?"

I tried to force myself to focus, to keep my head clear for the incoming conversation. What I would give to be huddled up beneath Candyman's stall right now. It would've been better had I failed, at least then she wouldn't have an excuse to come for me so soon.

Siobhan giggled in her trademark, tinkling laugh. Girlish, silly, *innocent*. It made men and women swoon at her feet, but I knew better. My handler always got her way. If I pushed back, she found a way to punish me. The targets kept growing more difficult to find. Almost impossible.

She would make sure to suddenly appear when I'd reached my lowest—waist-deep in a peat moss bog with an assassin's blade biting into my jugular or when a rival bounty hunter captured my prize seconds before I arrived. She'd present an ultimatum, try to coerce me into giving up and ceding myself to her.

I'd not fallen prey to her yet, but I'd come close.

Catching me now, seconds after I'd finished with my mark, when the blood still crusted my fingertips, should not have come as a surprise. The timing was perfectly executed on her part.

"But my dear, you've been so successful, no?" She pushed a golden curl behind her ear, her latest color transformation designed to match today's beauty standards. Once, she even modeled herself after me with snake-green eyes and wild brown hair. When that didn't sway me, she shed that skin and moved on. She was ancient, of that I was certain. She hadn't aged a month in the two decades I'd been bending to her will.

At the moment she emulated the romantic women from oil paintings. Voluptuous, sensuous, cherubic. She pouted rouged lips, fluttering her lashes at me.

"Your Collectors have been asking after you again. My dear Tam, I'm not sure how long I can keep them waiting. They must see you. They yearn for it. Can you not sense it?"

I kept the disgust far from my face, the memories chained down in the furthest recess of my mind. "I try not to hang around. I have a job to do."

"Mhm, quite." She tugged off the velvet gloves, biting the tips of her fingers one by one.

I sank back against the shadows of the forest, wishing they'd engulf me too.

She took her time, looking down at her polished nails, the color flickering from pink to green and back again. "If you really don't want to be tied to them anymore, there is a way out. You only need to ask, my dear. Accept my invitation to join me. I've only offered this once in my lifetime, so you are honored, no?"

"And what happened to them?" I already knew the answer. Her constant flitting in and out of my life, learning my habits, molding my personality came at a cost to her too. A weakness, just one. It was all the leverage I had, so I kept it close to my chest, but it was all I needed.

"They were not as strong as you, my dear. You're heartless, cold, manipulative, all the qualities I admire. Especially when that person is firmly under my control. Although, I do sometimes have my doubts. It is natural, I know. I was human once upon a time, but that's why I check in on you so often." She caressed her bare finger down my cheek. The touch was downy-soft, ticklish, sending warm chills snaking directly into my core.

I leaned away from her. "I'm fine. No need to come again."

My stomach spasmed. *Not now*. Acid crept back into my throat, and I swallowed it down.

"You're not wavering on me, are you? My protégé suddenly spouting a conscience?" She tsked, sucking air between her straight teeth.

The sound dragged me back to the fayre and the small boy sucking on the swirled lollipop. His messy hair flopped over his eyes as he glanced back and forth over the barrier between his mother's hand and the doll. I shook the image away. It wasn't like there hadn't been people to witness before.

No, not people, a *child*. Not much older than I was when...

My stomach lurched. I forced my hand away from my belly and dug my nails into my palms. Why wouldn't it settle?

"No. It's the adrenaline, that's all," I said.

The come down always took a few days, especially when there were no outlets nearby—inns, ales, company. My thoughts idled back to Candyman. He could have made me forget everything by now.

"Mhm." She leaned over me, wafting lily of the valley perfume, and my eyes dropped to her breasts before I could stop myself. Blush heated my chest and painted my cheeks despite my best efforts. She was toxic, and I should have known better.

She giggled again, covering her mouth with a delicate hand. "Well, my dear, as you are so keen to avoid distractions and return to work, I have come with a special assignment for you. A gift, if you will. For we all know, you are my favorite, yes?"

I groaned before I could stop myself. *Favoritism*. The time between hunts had been steadily diminishing over the past few years. Every time I turned down her advances, she reappeared in my life faster than before.

"Oh no," she cooed. She lifted my chin, her fingers molding to my skin, leaving her mark. "You will love this one, I promise. I had to pull many, *many* strings to get this for you. In fact, if you fail, there is a whole queue of suitable candidates already waiting to take your place." Her thumb circled under my jaw. "Shall we say six weeks to completion?"

I swallowed. The ball of saliva audibly scratched its way down my dry throat. If she was giving me a time frame, she suspected it would take at least double that amount to succeed. She would be there hovering, salivating, just waiting for me to extend the deadline, the favors dangling from her outstretched hands like iron shackles.

I managed to nod.

"Superb, my dear." She withdrew from my face, her scent embossed upon my hot skin. "Of course, you must remember that such an important bounty comes with immeasurably high stakes. You've already used up your one failure, leaving me with no wiggle room. If you don't succeed, Goddess forbid, then you will be moved along in your role. Promoted, if you will." She blinked at me; her round blue eyes entrancing. "Sounds wonderful, no?"

No, it did not. It was a death sentence. For more than just me. I nodded, unable to force my lips to curve into a smile.

"A little warning to go alongside all I have given you so far, my dear. They are clamping down on magic, more so now than ever before. The perpetrators are being rounded up so those with your gifts can be cherry-picked out of the barrel. Due to this, blood magic is becoming increasingly rare."

"What happens to them?" I'd heard rumors at the fayre of performers disappearing or suddenly retiring. The tricks had been toned down and the magic dulled but unease had cloaked the air.

I'd never met another who harbored blood magic like mine. Siobhan probably kept me far away from anything remotely resembling a comrade, afraid I'd ask questions. But there must be more to my skills than hunting and embedding the trackers.

"Most are returned if found to harbor just cheap elemental magic or trickery. The others? Well, I hope you never have to find out. So the need for discretion, to keep our little operation fully staffed, is most important. And it's not just in the North, though the walled town you're heading to is one of the worst for concealment, second only to the queens' territory.

"You're a dying breed, one that is being actively exterminated, and I would so hate to lose my little pet in such a manner. Don't look so surprised, my love." She pouted and fluttered her extended lashes, incorrectly reading my expression as fear and not curiosity. "There's always something being coveted. It used to be seers, then mediums, and now it's dark magic. Blood magic. It's a tale as old as time."

As old as you are then. Thank the Goddess I said it in my head and not out loud. Although she knew what I was thinking. I could see it in the twitch of her lips.

She closed the distance between us, but I didn't pull back, refusing to cede my airspace. It was a narrow line, but she liked that I walked it.

"Well, here you are." She withdrew a small portrait from the pleated folds of her skirt, a trail of glitter impregnating the air behind it. "He will be easy to find, and the position is all set for you once you arrive. All you need to do is get in, be discreet, and I'll find you when you're done. So, really, you should try and look more grateful my dear, shouldn't you?"

She'd removed the only parts of the bounty I enjoyed. Given me a stationary target, well-known, impossible to miss. She'd completely eliminated the hunt and the chase, leaving me with only the kill. All I had to do was get in and get out without being noticed? A shiver wriggled down my spine. It would never be that easy.

"What position am I taking?"

"Oh no, no, no." Her red lips split into a grin, her perfectly straight teeth too bright for the grim night. "That would be far too simple, don't you think?" She placed a heavy coin purse on the fallen tree beside me and backed toward the far end of the clearing in the way she had come, and the way she knew I needed to go. "But you know where to find me if you need help, don't you, my dear Tam? And of course, what I would just *love* in return."

She raised her palm and blew me a kiss. A puff of lily-sweet scent glided past my lips and coated my mouth. My stomach churned again.

I looked down at the picture in my hand and my heart stuttered. I knew him. Even through the miserable gloom and the rough edges of the glitter, that face was unmistakable. Everyone in the country knew him—Prince Bellinor, the only child of the queens. He was supposedly perfect. Not just in looks, but with a soul of pure diamond. Humble, generous, and more ferociously guarded than the Goddess's pearly gates.

That's why she'd given me six weeks. It would be six weeks spent dodging the gallows, wriggling my way out of a charge of high treason. If I were to be arrested, would Siobhan save me? She'd know about it, maybe even orchestrate it. Hidden amongst a distant stone circle, she'd wait for me to utter her name with my dying breath, begging her to save me.

If that was her plan, she'd be waiting a long time.

Although, she could equally just let me die, as punishment for every time I'd rejected her advances. She must have quite a tally going by now. Maybe she'd wait until I descended the brimstone ladder into Hell and snatch me from the very front of the ragged line of people and bind me to her in the nonexistent realm she'd inhabited for eternity. I shuddered. That would be worse than death.

I pocketed the coin purse and threw the portrait into the woods.

CHAPTER THREE
SEVERING THE ILLUSION

The journey north took me three days on horseback. Siobhan had ruined my mood with her appearance and the long trek over empty moorlands ate into a huge chunk of my imposed time limit. If that wasn't enough, I had to pay for a horse out of my earnings.

The coin purse clinked in my pocket as the mare plodded up and down the dales. Twenty-five gideons, although a pretty generous sum, was already almost half gone. Five for the horse, five for food, a skin of water and hardy wool-lined clothing, then a further five for a myriad of small knives and a leather thigh holster. If I'd been attacked en route, they would have done me little good against the spears and sabers of the Moors people, but I felt safer knowing they were all strapped within easy reach and invisible to an onlooker.

Mist rose amongst the brown gorse and purple heather like specters clutching at the ground, desperate not to be dragged up into the skies. Permafrost leeched into the soil, causing the heavy hoof falls of my mount to crack like ice. I stroked the soft brown fur of her neck, inhaling the sweet smell of hay from her mane.

"We'll stop for a rest soon, Siobhan." I patted her gently. "I'll get you the finest lodgings in the city." I smiled to myself, content with my choice of name. I'd thought it amusing to imagine riding Siobhan until she collapsed, having her be unable to keep up with me. *Me!* But then I realized I actually quite enjoyed the horse's company, her soft whinnies and faithful companionship. Also, she had stubbornly refused to get involved in any of my jokes, which was very sensible. Being trapped between a devil and a human when you were only a beast was a very unsafe place to be.

Just as the cold finally penetrated my marrow, congealing the very essence of my core, the edge of the city arose from the mist. I wrapped my numb fingers around the worn leather reins and urged my horse toward the serpentine path leading up to the wall.

From a distance, the wall looked like any other, a dull expanse of gray that bisected the countryside. Up close, it was magnificent.

Stones of every size and shape, ranging from ebony to silver to gray were stacked baklava style like an expensive pastry that had been shipped from far overseas. Where there should be springy moss and signs of weathering, glittering facets of diamond sparkled, translucent and radiating light like the wall harbored its own lifeforce. A soul.

I whistled and Siobhan the horse snorted her approval.

We continued to the top of the path and halted at what I hoped was the gate. It looked like every other section of the wall, except for a small rectangular hole where a set of suspicious looking eyes peered out.

"Three gideons to enter Prince Bellinor's land." A gloved hand appeared in the slot where the eyes had just been. The fingertips poked through the fabric, bitten nails and worn skin chafed to a shiny red.

"Three?" I rarely ventured north. In fact, the last time I was here there was no wall, but it wasn't three, that much I knew. Probably one, at most. The temples, seers, and blind faith in omens that increased with every footfall up the country usually had me scurrying back to the warm, free lands of the South. I'd falsely assumed their piety would have made them more hospitable to strangers. Maybe Siobhan had told them to up the fee, that they could keep the excess for themselves. She had sway *everywhere*.

The hand remained, fingers twitching in impatience.

"Fine." I dug out the coins and returned the depressingly empty purse to my pocket.

The hand was sucked back inside the dark hole, and the slow cranking of a lever began. The gate opened just enough to allow us through, then snapped shut. I dismounted and tried to take a step toward the gate person, but my thighs locked, fire sparking up my back. I grabbed onto the reins and stared at my useless legs.

"Long ride?" The woman who operated the gates came forward and offered me a hand. With difficulty, I straightened. Every muscle in my body screamed hellfire, even my skin pulsed in irritation. "The chafing's the worst, lass."

I grunted.

"Usually, I advise travelers to avoid bathing for a few days but in your case, you may want to grit your teeth and brave it." She wrinkled her nose.

I grunted again.

"Stables are a mile to the east alongside the wall. There is no riding within the city, mind. Taverns are everywhere so take your pick and the market will be setting up shortly."

I took a shaky step, the feeling returning to my extremities like knife blades. "Did I already pay you for all this information?"

She laughed. "We set the toll depending on whether we like the look of the traveler or nae."

She pointed down the central street which shot straight as an arrow toward a large castle in the distance. Houses were crammed down either side like the parting of hair on a head, leaning toward each other over the road. Wooden signs flapped in the breeze and lines of dripping washing hung suspended between them.

There was an unsettling familiarity about it. The street was the same, the shape of the houses, the faint freshness of the moors in the air, but since the prince had claimed this land and barricaded the inhabitants inside with his wall, the town I once knew had mutated. I felt it in the quiet lingering in the vacant side streets and in the moss infiltrating the seams of the houses.

"Castle is down there. Prince already has a new lady of the court mind, so don't get your hopes up."

"How often does he get new ones?"

She shrugged. "There is some kind of curse on them poor women. A few have disappeared, some *supposedly* returned to their towns in the dead of night never to be heard from again." She lowered her voice. "The last one was found in such a state, the body couldn't be identified except for the tiara of rubies and diamonds impaled in her skull."

I grimaced. "A gift from the prince?"

"Aye. The Goddess has her reasons."

Excellent. If he had faults after all, and the image spread throughout the rest of the kingdom about his generosity was fictitious, this would be a breeze. If he was being targeted for something he'd done by having his ladies of the court murdered, and the people were blaming the Goddess instead of him, there would be scope for blackmail. I could lure him out. How could he not be directly involved in something like that?

"But you need to keep your eyes open, lass," she continued. "There's been other disappearances, all young women, rumored to harbor magic."

"What kind of magic?"

She raised her brows, her hat jumping up her forehead. "Does it matter? All's illegal up here. The prince is more lenient than most, although don't let gossip like that travel down South to the queens."

"Are they linked? The prince's murdered fiancées and the local women?"

She shrugged. "If I knew that, lass, I'd have a pretty penny by now and be living out my life on the coast somewhere, not freezing out here manning the gate."

I gathered the reins under the horse's chin and turned her toward the narrow path that ran alongside the stone wall, my mind brimming with information.

"Before I go, did you set the high toll because you liked the look of me? Thought I was rich enough to pay?" I gave her my best smile, which unfortunately involved my cracked lips bleeding.

She chuckled. "Aye, lassie. I thought you'd be able to pay, but I doubt it's your own hard-earned money you're touting." She eyed my old cloak and scuffed boots, raising her eyebrows again at the pristine flaxen pullover underneath. "That cashmere?"

It was a little flashy, but if I was about to spend the winter in the North, I'd be damned if I had to wear only sheep's wool.

My smile widened. "Whore or criminal?"

She patted me on the shoulder. "I have no preference. Both'll find plenty of work up here." She returned to a small three-legged stool by the gate and resumed her vigil of the moorland beyond.

Good. I could play both roles easily.

Siobhan, the horse, seemed quite content with her new lodgings as I passed over the reins—and the rest of my coin purse—to the groom before winding my way to the castle. I stuck to the main street knowing I'd get lost in the random crisscross of alleyways that made up the perimeter.

The castle was monstrous. Like the wall, the stone was injected with glittering diamonds. The alcoves and speared turrets concealed toothy gargoyles, while long slits lined every side where arrowheads could be notched and poised ready to fly for an assailant.

Guards flanked the towering main doors, sabers dangling from their belts, the hilts carved from translucent gemstones. The pair at the door said nothing as I approached. Both women had their dark hair severed from their faces, tight cheeks drawn into identical superior expressions. I had no doubt they would impale me the moment I raised my hand to knock.

I continued walking the perimeter, eventually spotting the servant's entrance. Another guard had been posted here, closely scrutinizing the face of every person that scurried up to the small door.

I slotted in behind a woman carrying a basket stuffed with bread. My fingers twitched and saliva pooled in my mouth as the aroma wafted over to me. Perhaps she'd let me have the parchment they were wrapped in? I would lick the condensation off, rolling the flavors around in my mouth as I savored every drop. My stomach growled audibly, and the woman rolled her eyes at me and moving the basket out of reach before returning her attention to the guard. He ushered her through, and I stepped to the front.

"Business?" the guard barked.

Yes, what a great question. "I have come..." What had Siobhan said I was doing? I can't say to assassinate the prince, to infiltrate his private quarters and to upend the entire queendom. "To see about...a job." That sounded right.

The guard rested his hand upon the diamond hilt of his saber. His uniform was neatly pressed, all a rich, sapphire blue. It would probably make just about anyone look dashing and handsome. Who didn't like a side of power with their latest exploit?

He cleared his throat, and I returned my eyes to his face.

"I have a job," I said. "Here. To start, now." Goddessdamnit what was wrong with me? I blamed Siobhan—the devil not the horse. She'd stolen my free time, forced me straight back into work when I needed to blow off steam and purge the previous hunt from my system.

I wished Candyman was here for a few hours. He'd be packing up and traveling to the next location, collecting whichever women or oddities he came across on the way. Oh, what I'd do to be back there, left to my own devices, blown like a will-o'-the-wisp whichever way the wind gusted. It would definitely not be this far north.

"Stay." The guard held up his hand as if I were a dog.

I started, snapping from my musings. I glared at him, cursing the thrill of submission that shot through me.

He returned a few minutes later with a tall reedy woman. She wore a light blue pinafore with a classic white apron and matching cap. Surprisingly, her humble dress was complemented by a rather astonishing matching set of diamond-laced ruby earrings and necklace.

"You are the new lady's maid?" Her nose twitched as she inhaled my musty horse-sweat-countryside odor. "Tam?"

"Yes, ma'am." Maid. *Maid*! If it wasn't degrading enough to be bound into this awful contract and forced to do Siobhan's bidding, now she'd sent me to clean up shit and tuck little rich girls into bed at night. Maybe I should just give myself to her now. Would it be worse?

"You're a little old for a maid, aren't you?"

"I am only twenty-eight. I think experienced is a better word."

Unimpressed, she continued scouring my body with her dark eyes as if she could magically clean me just by willing it. "Perhaps it is better this way." She folded her arms and cocked her head.

"Why is that, ma'am?"

"You're tough looking. Unapproachable."

I was, in truth, quite flattered and so remained quiet in case more compliments came along.

"Also, forgettable. The prince won't be interested in you, and the lady of the court won't be jealous."

Was that still good? Technically, I did need to blend in and disappear, so yes, I'd accept that as well. I smiled and waited for the conclusion to her musings.

"Are you armed?"

"Armed? I'm a maid." She held my stare, and my body wilted. Siobhan would *love* this woman. "Yes, I am."

"Good. Keep it hidden."

She turned and pushed open the small side door. I followed quickly, cataloging the locations of my knives as I scanned the corners, ceiling, doorways, and anywhere that looked remotely secretive.

We passed through a bustling kitchen into an endless cramped corridor. As the kitchen doors swung shut behind us, life stilled, severing the illusion of a bustling, vibrant household. No people, no noise, just emptiness.

Small passageways flitted off at irregular intervals and a dark hole sporadically appeared in the wall. The feeling of being watched clung to my body like a shadow, but when I turned my attention to it, trying to make a set of eyes appear in the gloom, nothing happened. My fingers twitched toward the knife at my thigh.

"Your room is here, adjoined with the lady of the court." She stopped outside a plain wooden door. "You have the lower area, and she has the upstairs suite. Inside, there are clothes and a bath, which you must take immediately."

I grunted my acceptance. I did stink.

"If you need me, my room is next to the kitchens or you can ask for Matron, but there should be no questions, no trifling concerns, and no accidents. Your *one* job is to guard Lady Lilyanna."

"I'm her babysitter, not her bodyguard."

She ignored me. "Do not leave her side. Do not leave her alone for a moment and for Goddess's sake,"—she bent to whisper in my ear, her voice almost inaudible—"*never* leave her alone with the prince."

She snapped erect again, brushing invisible dirt, or perhaps my odor, from the front of her apron. "Go and bathe. Your posting begins now."

CHAPTER FOUR
WHISPERS IN THE WALLS

The bath hurt as much as I anticipated. Hot, soapy water scalded all the sore areas as if wielded by Siobhan herself. The uniform, I quite liked. It was the same dark sapphire that the guards wore, but in a close-fitting sweater that rose to my neck and dropped to mid-thigh with snug, velvety leggings.

The only things out of place were my scuffed boots, but they hadn't gifted me with new shoes. These hid a small knife in the seam of each one anyway, so I kicked the grass and mud off as best I could and ventured up the spiral staircase toward Lady Lilyanna's room.

There was no lock on my side of the door, nor hers when I cracked it open. The walls here seemed thinner than below, not deep enough to hide a person, but I still felt something watching me. Everywhere I looked, the shadows would shift as if harboring a soul of their own, obscuring their occupants.

I stepped into the large lounge. It was at least three times the size of my dungeon below with two separate doors leading to adjoining rooms. A huge fire blazed in the hearth, diamonds sparkling in the ornate moldings. Large stained-glass windows distorted the town beyond, the houses contorted into colorful mounds of melted wax. Plump purple chaises and thick rugs were artfully scattered throughout the space. Hopefully my job didn't include maintenance of this place but only of its occupant.

The clouded marble floor echoed my footfalls, amplifying my tread, no matter how quietly I tried to walk the perimeter. There were no tapestries on the walls, nor paintings. Not a drop of warmth or personality bled into the decor. No flowers hung limply in vases, though the lingering odor of roses threatened to gag me.

I sniffed at the window. Perhaps they were outside? Concrete was smeared in the window lining, barring all scents, breezes, and sounds from the descended fog of evening. I scratched at it with my nail and moldy flecks sprinkled to the floor.

A door opened, and a young woman of about nineteen peeked her head out. Her hair was disheveled, blonde mats caked to her skull and a lingering floral odor surrounded her that choked to the back of my throat. She clutched a robe to her breast, the cream silk drooping down over her shoulders. I wasn't sure if she was in trouble or if I'd interrupted something.

I coughed. "Are you Lady Lilyanna?"

She nodded, glancing quickly around the room and up at the ceiling before scurrying over to me. Extending a hand, she tugged the robe tighter with the other as it slipped. "You must be my appointed maid. Welcome."

I shook her damp hand which smelled strongly of flowers like she had jumped in a vat of rose water. "Are you in trouble, miss?"

"Trouble?" Her face paled, and she glanced at the ceiling again. I followed her gaze, seeing nothing except the diamond-encrusted ceiling sparkling like the night sky. "I suppose I have found myself in quite a precarious situation." She hoisted the robe higher and tossed a clump of hair over her shoulder. "You're a bit old, aren't you?"

I bit back my retort and smiled. "Consider me your big sister." Who has been forced to wait on you hand and foot like an infant.

She smiled back, a hint of color returning to her cheeks. She really was beautiful and innocent. Innocent enough for me to immediately like her. Maybe having a kind-of-sister for a few days would be entertaining. Different, anyway. Siobhan had been my only constant for so many years, I sometimes forgot not all relationships involved being dragged into other people's games.

"I wish to take a bath," she said.

"Alright." I stood there waiting for her to leave so I could snoop around the room and inspect the ceiling thoroughly.

"I will need you to run it for me."

I blinked. "Would you also care for me to wash your hair and coordinate your outfit afterward?"

Relief broke onto her face. "Oh, yes. I'm so pleased you arrived when you did." She took my arm and led me toward the door she'd emerged from and into a very large marble bathroom. "As you can see, I began the process myself, but the water wouldn't run hot and then the oils were too pungent. I didn't know what I would do if the prince suddenly summoned me like this."

Water had sloshed down the sides of the bath and pooled on the floor in oil-slicked puddles. Towels were randomly flung about to cover the spillages, all now sodden with a faint pink sheen like diluted blood. An almost extinguished fire crackled and popped in the hearth as water dripped into it from the mantle above.

What had she done in here? It looked like she'd been fighting a bear. With rosewater.

I sighed. I wasn't a real maid, but I could at least properly draw a bath.

Once the sunken tub filled and a mild lavender steam wound its way into the air, I placed a new towel upon a small stool and backed toward the doorway with a gesture for her to start.

"Where are you going?" Lilyanna dropped the robe into a puddle of water and cautiously stepped down into the bubbles.

"To find you something to wear, I guess."

"You can do that afterward. I will need you to wash my hair and then braid it. Can you do a reverse twist knot? That would look the most impressive for when I dine with the prince tonight."

I didn't answer. She would be lucky if I managed a simple plait. Was that my job for the next six weeks? I glanced longingly at the door before moving to the bath and plopping myself down in a dry patch. "Do I need to wash Your Ladyship as well?"

She giggled. "Lilyanna is fine. You can call me Lady Lilyanna when we are at court."

She lowered her head back, and I kneaded the water into her hair, working the mats loose with my fingers. She hadn't confirmed whether she wanted me to wash her or not. Surely, she could manage that task herself since she'd lived nearly two decades on this earth. And if I did lather her down and she didn't want me to, I'd probably be fired. Or hanged for inappropriately touching the prince's new toy.

"And what am I to call you?" Her eyes closed as she leaned back into my hands, murmuring contentedly.

"Tam is fine."

I added a small amount of soap. The prince would thank me if he didn't have to dine with a walking floral arrangement. The pungent odor of rose still clogged the room.

"I arrived earlier today." Lilyanna's eyes remained closed and her face relaxed. "I was informed that I would be given a maid when I arrived, so imagine my shock when I was told you were delayed."

"You poor thing."

She moaned again as I ran my fingers down her scalp. "Yes, quite. Anyway, it was an arduous journey to get here. The lands to the West are incredibly rugged, which is why they're so well protected. We mine mainly gold out there, second only to diamond, of course."

She leaned forward and with a reluctant sigh, I began soaping her back.

"So, this match will do wonders for my town. I never thought it would happen. It was read in my tea leaves when I was twelve and repeated every year on my birthday. But all these years, the prince has been inviting new ladies to be in his court, I didn't know if it would ever happen. He's such a charmer, I don't know how anyone could resist the invitation."

"Haven't all the previous ones been killed?"

"Oh Goddess, no." She raised her arm, and I worked my way down toward her hand. "Well, some have died, that is true. But none of their deaths were the prince's fault." She offered me her other arm. "Just wait until you meet him, Tam. He's enthralling! And not just because he's beautiful, he's also so kind. They say his heart is made of pure diamond. What a match we will make!"

I doubted the prince would be worthy of her. He did have a reputation for being extremely generous, polite, and educated, despite the less savory rumors also circulating. He treated his staff and his people very well. Butter wouldn't melt in his mouth, or so they said. I didn't believe it. I'm sure it eventually curdled like everyone else once you'd been with it long enough. He'd been targeted for a reason.

I had no intention of getting to know him before I killed him. Goddess forbid I actually *liked* him, too.

I sat up on my knees, cracking my aching back. "Do you want to soak a little longer or shall I get you a towel?" This dinner couldn't come fast enough. What if I could access the prince straight away? I could end my task within a day and abscond into the night on Siobhan—the good one—before anyone came looking for me.

"Yes, I am done. Thank you, Tam," she said. I grabbed the towel, and she stepped into it, allowing me to swaddle her in a cloud of fluffy white. "You will be there throughout dinner?" The smile slipped from her lips, her light blue eyes suddenly intense.

"Yes, I will be nearby."

"No, I want you right there." She grabbed my arm, her manicured nails imprinting upon my flesh.

What was I supposed to say to that? I didn't want to stand in the corner and watch people eat, pretending I was nothing more than a realistic statue. I needed to scour the castle, find the easiest ways in and out, scurry around with my head down. Isn't that what maids did? But the fear widening her eyes sent chills skittering across my skin.

"For propriety's sake of course," she added.

"Of course." I flashed her a smile with more confidence than I suddenly felt.

She released me, hugging the towel close to her body again. Instead of glancing at the ceiling, she briefly eyed the hearth and shivered, gooseflesh erupting over her bare arms.

"Get dry and I'll find you dinner wear." I pushed her from the bathroom and steered her toward the unopened door which had to be the bed chamber. "Then I'll attempt to braid your hair."

I suppose I could use dinner to my advantage. Maybe offer to help serve the prince, and I could 'accidentally' trip and scratch his arm. Or maybe we were supposed to prostrate ourselves before him and in a show of false modesty, he'd say, "No, no," and offer his hand. As I rose to my feet, my thumbnail could dig into his palm, lost amidst the pressure of the grip. But it had to be deep. And it would sting. He couldn't know or I'd be in shackles within seconds and unwittingly find out what actually happened to those with blood magic the royals had been rounding up.

It would remove the variables if I could do it straight away. It wouldn't be ideal not to know the layout or the habits of the staff, but then they too wouldn't know me. A failed hire that only lasted a day. Then I'd swipe a few valuables on the way out, using the profits to bury myself in ale and meat pies at a local inn before fleeing south again. If it only took me a day instead of the imposed six-week deadline, even Siobhan wouldn't be waiting for me. I could taste true freedom.

As I pulled the door to the bathroom shut behind me, a groan vibrated through the air directly above. I snapped my head to the ceiling but found only my own face, reflected and monstrously distorted by the diamonds.

A chill tiptoed down my spine.

CHAPTER FIVE
THE BRUSH OF A THOUSAND CRIMES

EVERYTHING LOOKED THE SAME.

The castle housed a labyrinth of identical gray stone hallways and shadowed recesses. Sconces burned sporadically, creating a fine sheen of smoke that clung to the ceiling.

"The dining chamber must be downstairs. Have you seen any stairs?" I asked.

Lilyanna gripped my arm. Her skirts swooshed behind us, snagging with an occasional rip of fabric on the rough floor. I'd grabbed her the first dress I could find, not thinking through the color choice of shiny bronze which rapidly collected dust as we walked, fading to a dull, burnished taupe. It wouldn't matter, there was a whole brand-new wardrobe in her rooms gifted to her by the prince. She could throw it away after dinner and help herself to a dozen new ones.

"I haven't been out since I arrived." She glanced over her shoulder before continuing. "But when I was escorted to my rooms, I didn't go up any stairs. The corridors slope upward, I think."

"Why didn't you arrive with your own guards or maid?"

"They brought me to the castle but were allowed no further. I was informed I'd be assigned whomever I needed when I got here." She answered my unspoken question, "Something about not wanting an outsider to become familiar with the layout, you know, in case the match didn't work out." I grunted, and she added, "For security. It makes a lot of sense if you think about it."

Tap-tap-tap.

I stared at the walls, searching for the cause of the noise.

Lilyanna opened her mouth to continue, but I cut her off with a raised hand. We walked in silence for a moment, but the sound didn't recur. Her constant babble of conversation was ruining my concentration. How was I supposed to memorize the route and think about my real mission with her blathering on?

In reply, the magic stirred in my blood with a dim knocking of its own, preparing to be unleashed. That must've been what I'd heard. It was distracting, and if I didn't tamp it back down, it would become a full-throated scream within my blood vessels before long.

At the beginning, before Siobhan forced me to override the impulses with her own unique teaching style, the magic would ooze from my fingertips. Sometimes slow, black, and sticky, but other times spurting fresh and arterial. Any hint of power up here would have me thrown in jail until I could be exsanguinated or publicly hung. Maybe even packaged up and sent back to the queens, or however the prince decided to deal with magic in his town.

I took a deep breath and forced the swell of magic to ebb. As it faded, my mind cleared. I stopped, swiveling my head in an attempt to assess if we were going up or down. The temperature plummeted as we entered a new corridor. The way ahead was gloomy with thin smoke pooling on the ceiling, reaching down with small tendrils to snag passersby. The stone floor morphed into gnarled floorboards in an obvious division.

"This is ridiculous." I slapped the wall, instantly regretting it as pinpricks of pain lashed up my arm. The magic bucked, seizing onto my outburst. "This can't be right. Let's go back the way we came and try again."

"Don't worry, Tam." Lilyanna patted my arm. "You'll get use to the layout."

I grumbled my reply. I was not a tour guide, nor a chauffeur, and here I was trapped in this rat maze of a castle. I couldn't even see my reward at the end of it. I should be free right now, as free as I could be, doing who or what I wanted. I kicked petulantly at the wall, the boards under my feet creaking, and the magic throbbed against my temples in response.

Slam! A loose stone plunged from the ceiling, ripping between us. I pushed her away and leaped back. Another fell directly in front, a cloud of darkness billowing out. Dust coated my mouth and choked my throat. I coughed, dragging Lilyanna back by the elbow until the air cleared again.

We stood in stunned silence.

"I don't think this is the right way," she deadpanned. "The castle is sending us a sign." She gave one shrill giggle before dissolving into a coughing fit.

I clapped her on the back until she'd righted herself. "At least you can see the bright side of this place." I smiled, gently brushing dust from her shoulders when a foul odor wafted up. I pulled my face away. "You stink."

"What!" She spun around, frantically dusting herself. "I'm supposed to meet the prince."

I caught her mid-twirl and picked large chunks of something black and rotten from her blonde hair. Did that come from the ceiling? I glanced up at the hole, now obscured as smoke from the sconces seeped in.

A chill breeze swished through the corridor, dispersing the pile of dust beneath the hole in the ceiling. The two stone tiles had fractured, perfectly aligning themselves with their identical counterparts on the floor, forming a raised divide where the stone ceded to wooden floorboards.

I returned my attention to Lilyanna. "Come on, I'll fix you up on the way." We moved in the opposite direction. "Hopefully he'll have a long, old-fashioned table and won't be able to smell you from way down there."

I swatted at her skirt, dislodging more particles, and she pushed my hand away, lifting her chin. "Not funny."

"It kind of is."

The corner of her mouth twitched.

We rounded a corner and immediately faced the dining room. The large oak doors were flung open with warm candlelight blanketing the expansive stone floor. She straightened, somehow losing both the playfulness and strength in her expression. In the blink of an eye, she was the young, helpless woman who couldn't even draw herself a bath.

Is this what the prince wanted? Or who she thought he'd want? Beauty aside, he'd picked her for a reason, and she'd traveled all this way, being unable to keep any familiar comforts or personnel.

I flicked a final piece of ash from the end of her braid, and my hand lingered on her arm a beat too long, keeping her in the hallway. No, I had a job to do. Get in and get out. I didn't need to be a pawn in someone else's game. The magic thumped inside my head again, and I ushered her inside.

Prince Bellinor rose from his seat and gestured for her to sit beside him. He wore a grave-black velvet suit, with a matching waistcoat and bowtie. There were so many hidden layers to his clothing, he looked like one of the holes in the wall, where spying eyes could emerge at any moment. Chestnut brown hair and matching irises completed the perfect image. I tried my best to hate him, to paint him with the brush of thousands of crimes, but his smile at Lilyanna was so genuine, I couldn't.

He even had dimples, for Goddess's sake.

My stomach growled as my eyes roamed over the laden table in front of them. An entire suckling pig was skewered in the center, its crisped skin dripping with fat as the aroma of sweet pork melted into my pores. Oh, Goddess, what I would do to sit at that table and stuff my face right now.

I backed against the wall, slotting in beside a burning sconce and one of the prince's guards. It looked like the first time Lilyanna and the prince had met in person. They kept the conversation neutral, discussing the weather and local trade, but there was an edge of flirtation in the lingering glances and the way the prince offered to pour her wine. He could have snapped his fingers, had me or another servant come and refill her glass, but he did it himself.

Lilyanna fumbled with her napkin, her attention dropping to her lap. In the pause of conversation, the prince glanced over at me with a coy smile that made my stomach drop. Oh my, was he beautiful and that was such a wicked, wicked glint in his eye.

If his ladies of the court were being murdered or ousted, perhaps there were other factors at play? A jealous woman? A hateful guard? Maybe the same person had arranged his bounty purely for revenge when their plan to have him arrested or dethroned for the murders failed. I mean, Goddess above, if he smiled at anyone else like he'd just done to me, I'd completely understand.

I shoved the thought away. I wasn't supposed to care. It didn't make a difference in what I had to do. Get in, get out. How many times did I need to repeat that until it stuck?

To remind me of my duty, the magic thrummed to life in my veins. My nails stretched, trying to elongate from my fisted hands. It knew the target was close.

I took a deep breath, willing my body to behave and filled my nose with the mouth-watering scent of the feast. My stomach grumbled once more.

"When do we eat?" I hissed at the guard standing next to me.

Prince Bellinor had two personal guards, both handpicked and both understood to be completely loyal. In other words, deadly.

"Who are you?"

"Miss Lilyanna's humble servant." I bobbed a subtle, and obviously insincere, curtsey.

His black eyes took the liberty of roaming up and down my body in response. Dark stubble peppered his chin and cheeks. My face warmed as I imagined it scratching my neck as his mouth meandered down my body the same way his eyes were.

What was wrong with me? Perhaps Siobhan had cursed me at our last meeting.

My hand fell to my hip, and I angled my body toward him. "I know, I too am most surprised by my prowess. But you know..." I waited for him to supply his name.

"Clement." His attention returned to the dinner in front.

"Clement, I have many other talents as well."

He choked, earning himself a glare from the other guard standing on his left. She pressed against the wall, her bodyweight tipped back upon it, but her hand remained glued to the hilt of the saber at her waist.

Prince Bellinor rose and strode round to the other side of the table, his polished boots echoing on the stone floor. Clement's attention snapped back to him, and my muscles locked as the prince passed Lilyanna. He plucked a bottle of wine from a diamond-studded bucket. Ice clinked against the glass and droplets of condensation slid down the slides, sparkling in the flickering candlelight. Silence descended upon the dining room as he filled her glass with blood-red wine, each glug of liquid echoing up to the domed ceiling.

Clement cleared his throat again, fixing his gaze upon the prince who returned to his seat. "Don't try that on anyone else or they'll cut your head off. Distracting a guard is a crime."

"Well, you shouldn't be so easily distracted."

He tsked, and I turned my attention back to the table with a sigh of relief. Lilyanna looked happy sitting there, barely nibbling at that mouth-wateringly delicious feast. No trace of the doubt or fear like she'd shown in the bathroom lingered on her radiant face. She'd probably just been nervous. Her hair looked quite good as well. If she were a pony at the fayre, she'd win first prize for that braid.

I leaned around Clement to speak to the other guard. "And who are you?"

"Bryn," she said, without bothering to look at me.

Knowing when I certainly wasn't wanted, and which of the two was marginally more accommodating to my presence, I focused back on Clement. "So, we're probably going to be spending quite a lot of time together, and you're now my only friend here. We should get to know each other better."

His cheek twitched as he bit the inside of his mouth. "You have no friends here. You should leave."

"Can't." I forced my voice to be light, but the whisper rose in pitch. "Bound to my duty, I'm afraid. As you are, my friend."

I ignored the side-eyed look he shot at me. His fingers drummed over the sparkling hilt of his saber. He glanced at the ceiling, then at the hearth before settling back upon the prince who laughed at something Lilyanna said.

An echo of the moan I'd heard in the bathroom stirred, coming from the far side of the room. The fire drooped before blazing again and the hairs on the back of my neck rose. Clement's suppressed shiver told me he felt it too.

"What's in the walls, Clement?"

If he was surprised by my question, he didn't show it. Minutes passed as we watched dessert being served on translucent plates. Pops of yellow and pink and gold leaf surrounded by the hypnotizing scent of burned sugar.

I thought he was going to continue ignoring me until eventually, he said, "Everything."

My mouth dropped open. Questions shoved to the front of my tongue, jostling for position. Prince Bellinor stood to help Lilyanna to her feet, signaling the end of dinner.

"You can eat in your room," Clement said. "Don't leave your post or forget your place."

I bristled. Did he think he could get away with talking to me like that just because he thought I was a maid? I clenched my fists, the magic pounding against my fingertips like a pulse. I had to focus, or it would control me. When had it even surged? It must have crept up while I was distracted, an insidious entity within my own body.

I bit the inside of my cheek. I knew I needed a break after the fayre. Siobhan was testing me, seeing how far she could push before I snapped. At this rate, not far.

I tore my glare from the side of Clement's face and stalked toward the prince whose hand still swallowed Lilyanna's. I would do it now, get it over with. My vision tunneled.

Before I could get within touching range of the prince, Clement blocked my path with his arm outstretched in front of me.

"What are you" I spluttered.

"You can't get within three feet of the prince," Clement said. His other hand gripped the hilt of his saber, knuckles white.

"Well, that's"

Lilyanna interrupted. "Tam, I have had a wonderful dinner but now I am so very tired. I think we should head straight for my rooms."

I slapped Clement's arm as Lilyanna joined me, but he didn't move. His face was set, features stony. An uptight, immovable wall. Already in position on the prince's other side, Bryn nodded, and they moved in unison with him toward the doors.

A three-foot rule? That was ridiculous. Stupid Clement. I bet he just loved enforcing that, muscling people out of the way. He probably had a marked strip of measuring leather that he whipped out and rolled toward the prince's feet to stake the boundary.

My breathing settled. It was fine. I could do it tomorrow. A good night's sleep would help me control my power anyway. We followed, but as soon as we left the dining room, the passageway was already empty. No footsteps, no rustle of clothing, no distant closing of a door. Where on earth had they gone?

"I wonder if we should get ourselves a pair of guards for moving around the castle." I swiveled left and right, hesitant to strike off in the wrong direction again.

"You're my guard." She patted my arm fondly like you would a puppy. "And I have faith in you."

I grimaced at her. Freeing the small knife from my boot, I palmed it, unable to stop myself from looking at the ceiling once more. "Then I'm sure we'll sleep well tonight, my lady."

The fire in my small hearth popped and crackled, its glow keeping my face warm despite the thin covers. Wind howled outside, muted by the thick stone walls. Hail peppered the pane like knuckles rapping on the glass, keeping me wide awake.

I stared at the dancing flames, trying to ignore how they threatened to take me back to the night of the storm. The slam of shutters against the windows, the scream of the wind...I needed to get out of here, to return South. The unpredictability untethered me.

Chill laced the air when I slid out of bed and into the shadows, gooseflesh crawling up my skin. The castle was too quiet, too still. Worry pitted in my gut.

Last time I'd ignored sensations like this, my world had ended.

I crept up the winding staircase. The metal dug into my bare feet, my toes curling around the treads for support. The door into Lilyanna's room creaked open and thick, soupy air washed over me, leaving a sheen of moist sweat clinging to my skin.

Her hearth had extinguished, despite the large windows being bolted shut. Faint gray smoke perforated the air like burned flowers. I'd stoked it before retiring to bed, and added three fresh logs to the kindling, certain it would last well into the next morning. Having made enough fires for survival, it was second nature. Maybe the castle's wood was tainted, veined with mold or blight.

Despite the humidity, I shivered. Magic unfurled in my bloodstream, stretching into my tingling fingertips, preparing for defense. My heartbeat accelerated.

Soft squelching followed my footfalls as I padded to Lilyanna's bedchamber, the soles of my feet clammy on the tepid marble. Her door was tightly shut, no light flickering beneath the threshold.

My hand rested over the carved diamond knob. Was I being paranoid? I'd heard no one enter or leave as I'd tossed and turned downstairs. If I snuck into her room in the middle of the night, she'd scream and wake the whole castle.

I pressed my ear to the door, straining to listen over the whoosh of blood in my ears. Seconds passed, melting into minutes. I should go back to bed. I needed to be rested and fully alert to make sure I tagged the prince without detection.

The magic stubbornly surged, refusing to retreat, my fingertips on fire.

Something heavy collided with the floor inside the bedchamber, thumping onto the stone.

I flung the door open, the wall shuddering as it struck and bounced back. Lilyanna lay frozen on the floor, her entire body rigid and lifeless. I yelped and dropped to my knees, grabbing her shoulders and violently shaking her. She moaned, then fell silent again.

I pressed my fingers to her neck. Her pulse bounded and the exposed skin on her chest and legs flushed red hot as if she were feverish. Her body trembled, and she whimpered softly like a terrified animal backed into a corner.

I scooped her into my arms as best I could and hauled her onto the bed. The sheets were still smooth, not even a wrinkle marring the cool white silk. Her eyelids fluttered open, the mewling noises immediately severed.

"Tam?"

"Hey." I pulled the sheets up and tucked them around her slim frame. "You fell out of bed. Was it a seizure? An episode? I bet they have a doctor nearby."

She blinked slowly, barely able to stay awake. "You feel them watching, don't you, Tam? Their whispers linger in the walls like echoes. Repeating over and over."

I brushed her forehead. "There's nothing there, it's just the storm." I forced my voice to be calm, to sound certain. Her skin cooled, the feverish sheen receding. "I'll go and find help."

She shook herself, forcing a shallow smile. "It was just a nightmare," she whispered. "It only needs to be me and you, Tam. No one else. Don't mind me, forget I said anything."

"A nightmare?" Had I overreacted? If I ran through the castle screaming for help because she'd just had a bad dream, they'd fire me on the spot. Then I'd lose access. Telling a stranger about voices in the walls, that I wasn't entirely sure weren't there, would not be helpful either.

I smoothed a wayward lock of her hair, plucking it out of a hardening pool of sweat on the pillow. "Okay, a nightmare."

She murmured agreement and nestled deeper into the covers. "I haven't fallen out of bed since I was a young child."

I sat on the edge of the downy mattress, her body rocking toward me slightly with the weight. "Well, if it keeps happening, I'll get you some crib bars. Although, they'll probably be made from diamond and so sharp they'll impale you."

She closed her eyes again, face softening.

"But then problem solved, I guess."

Her soft breaths warmed the space between us.

"Lilyanna?" I tutted softly and crept up. How could she fall back to sleep so easily? The soles of my feet stuck to the floor. Small particles of grit or something sharp slipped between my flexed toes on the hard stone. Crouching down, I ran my hand across the floor and a clean streak of gray appeared, leaving my palm blackened. Shining faintly in the dull twilight, a large patch of stone lay surrounded by thin dust. It fit perfectly with Lilyanna's silhouette where she had fallen, but how had she not disturbed the ground around? And where did it come from?

The only dust I'd seen so far was when we got lost on the way to dinner. Everywhere else was spotless. Maybe they only cleaned where they thought people would see? Or perhaps they literally swept everything under the bed. I hardly saw any staff, except in the kitchens, maybe this was the best they could do?

I suppose it could have arisen from the fireplace or become exposed from under the bed by a wayward draft. I squinted up at the thick window. No breeze stirred and the rim was cemented shut like all the others. Condensation pebbled the inside of the pane, trickling down and pooling on the floor in a slick oily puddle with flecks of black dust swirled through.

Distorted through the moisture, a grotesque carved face leered at me. Its deep eye sockets glinted in the sparse light, the diamond cores burning as if they were alive. Gnarled hands curled around the window frame, its long, pointed nails extended toward the glass.

I shook myself and stood up. That gargoyle must always have been there, I'd just not noticed it before. I cursed whoever designed this room for their lack of drapes. Backing toward the door, I kept one eye on Lilyanna to make sure she didn't wake and one on the gargoyle who's head inched around, following my retreat.

I chided myself again and willed my heart rate to return to normal. Quietly closing the door behind me, I headed over to fix the fire with hopes this would be my last nighttime ramble for a while.

CHAPTER SIX
THE LABYRINTH

BREAKFAST HAD BEEN LEFT OUTSIDE THE MAIN CHAMBER OF LILYANNA'S ROOM with a curt knock. When I went to retrieve it, the corridor was deserted once more. I declined her offer to join after I'd laid everything out and slipped outside under the pretense of finding more tea.

In the light of day, the walls were even more stark. Devoid of any homey touches, the dim light from the sconces neither warmed the air nor the atmosphere. The flagstone floor was swept clean and the corners free of spiderwebs. I'd heard no one moving about last night. I'd hardly slept, what with listening out for Lilyanna and chiding myself for every second that slipped past when I should be resting so I would be refreshed and able to formulate some kind of plan today.

There had to be staff somewhere. Maybe I'd find them in the kitchen. Matron must run such a tight ship that the help was stowed neatly away, neither seen nor heard. I'd hoped the castle would be bustling, full of people watching and listening discreetly—the kind I could barter with. The prince had to have secrets stored here somewhere.

I turned the corner expecting to see the dining room, but another identical passageway stretched before me. How was I supposed to memorize the layout when everything shifted? I should get some twine to thread my way through the labyrinth, marking the nearest exits. I stopped and rubbed my eyes. Maybe the floor plan was mapped in my subconscious, and I just had to relax.

"What are you doing?"

I started. Clement stood in front of me, a heavy frown on his face. I suspected it was his default look. That, and irritation.

"Going to the kitchens. This place is a maze. It's like the walls move."

He scoffed. "You think the walls move?"

I pursed my lips. Was it too late to make a joke out of it? He'd not appreciate it anyway. It'd just bounce straight off his immaculate uniform and puffed chest.

His gaze floated over my shoulder. He paused, hand sliding to the saber by his side. Before I could turn, he grabbed my arm and tugged me down an intersecting corridor. It was so narrow, he had to tow me behind him. I jerked my arm away as we emerged back within the wide aisle that led to Lilyann's chambers. Or at least I think that's where we were.

I squared up to him even though I was at least a foot shorter. Heat splotched his neck, and his hand clasped the hilt of his saber. He leaned forward, speaking in an angry whisper.

"Why are you out by yourself? You do know women are going missing. I have enough to do without patrolling your whereabouts as well."

"Just from in town, though. I'm safe within the castle, right? Only the prince's fiancées have mysteriously met their ends within the boundaries you so rigidly patrol, my friend." Goddess save me but winding him up was delightful.

He hissed through his teeth, lowering his face toward mine but didn't answer my question.

"Am *I* in danger, Clement?" I repeated.

He pursed his lips, fingers drumming an obnoxiously loud rhythm on the diamond hilt at his waist. "Stay with Lady Lilyanna. That's your job."

"But that's not an answer. Stop speaking in riddles and tell me."

"You're supremely irritating," he growled. *Thrum-thrum-thrum*, his fingers relentlessly struck the diamond.

"*I'm* annoying?" It took every ounce of self-control I had to not rip the saber from his hands to stop that infernal noise.

He stared at the ceiling, but whether hoping a slab would fall directly onto me or him, I didn't know. "You've been here less than twenty-four hours. You arrived late, and you seem to have no idea what you're doing and are incapable of doing the one job you've been told to do." He pointed at Lilyanna's door down the corridor.

I opened my mouth to retaliate, but Clement was staring over my shoulder again. He stiffened.

The prince strolled down the corridor, the Bryn on his heels. "There you are Clement, you read my mind. And, Tam, isn't it?" The prince smiled at me, dimples popping.

Why did he look so perfect? He was the spitting image of his portrait, not a flaw to be seen.

"Tam? Yes." Heat itched across my chest and stained my cheeks. "That's right, Your Highness." I dipped into a half-curtsey, half-bow. Why was my tongue so thick and my throat so dry?

Clement grimaced behind the prince, and the Bryn arched an eyebrow.

"Please never do that again, Tam," the prince said with a gentle laugh. "And not only because I have no idea what you were trying to do. Grovel? Spasm?"

Even my ears burned as I tried to mold my face into a neutral expression.

"I don't wish to be treated like royalty, it's why I left my mothers' dominion and set up here by myself."

I nodded. I needed to scratch my neck or fan my face. The embarrassment was cooking me from the inside out.

"I like to treat my staff like family. My mothers hate it, of course, which, along with this tempestuous northern weather, means they rarely visit." He shrugged and his smile widened. "And I have no plans to change."

Okay, this was good. Maybe that would mean he would be easier to access. It would certainly make spending time around him while chaperoning Lilyanna far more enjoyable as well. My marks were usually conmen, criminals, and embezzlers. I never asked Siobhan for the details of what they'd done but their secrets spilled out eventually. None had been innocent.

Acid crept up my esophagus, spurred by my wildly thumping heart. How was I to mark him, to physically destroy his life? Was he supposed to deserve it?

I shook myself. It didn't matter. It never mattered.

The prince gestured for me to walk, and I led him the few paces down the corridor toward Lilyanna's door. Clement kept himself inserted between us, enforcing his stupid three-foot rule.

"I've come to give Lady Lilyanna and yourself a tour of the castle. I heard there was some trouble finding the dining chamber last night?" the prince said.

That must have been what they were laughing about at dinner. "Yes, the layout is a little confusing."

"The castle knows where you need to go. Sometimes when I find myself quite lost in an unexplored section, I just ask the walls for guidance and a passageway simply opens up before me, squirreling me back to the start."

Was he messing with me? Clement had been adamant I'd been seeing things, but the prince was now insinuating the castle was magical? Surely that went against every law in the queendom. I wanted to call him on it but also didn't want to offend him at the same time. This was not a problem I usually had.

"That's useful," I said. Goddess strike me down, what was wrong with me?

He gave a noncommittal reply, and Clement widened his eyes, subtly shaking his head. I ignored him.

"I'll go and get Lady Lilyanna ready." I dashed inside without knocking and shut the door. I pressed myself up against it, nothing holding me there but confusion.

"Where did you go? It doesn't take that long to find tea." Lilyanna paced the floor, leaving a large gap between herself and the hearth every time she passed.

"I got lost. Again. But the prince found me, he's outside and wants you to join him." I tugged on the neck of my sweater, still hot and flustered. He was unnervingly handsome up close.

"You were *alone* with the prince?" She stopped circling.

"Well, not alone. The guards were there, obviously. Although there would be nothing wrong with that surely. It's not like I sought him out while your back was turned."

She pursed her lips.

"Well, you're dressed, so shall we go?" I waved at a half dozen discarded boxes scattered over the floor. Hats, furs, shoes, all manner of finery pawed through and left. I didn't know what she was looking for, but it'd fall to me to tidy it all up later.

She huffed. "It's *Lady* Lilyanna. You need to address me properly when we're in company."

I groaned, not bothering to hide my eye roll.

She twirled to face the door, her skirts buffeting my legs and pointedly waited. I groaned again, stepped around her and opened the door. I was halfway into a mock curtsey when I remembered who was standing on the other side.

The prince raised his brows, lips quirking as I stood to the side, and he reached for Lilyanna's hand.

"You look beautiful as ever." He kissed her hand gently and then wrapped it around his arm. "I hope you've found something amongst the gifts I left to please you."

"Of course. I'm happy with everything you've chosen."

I shook my head, knowing he had to have seen the mess in the room she left behind. I would've been happy with even one of the silken wraps or cashmere lined gloves. At least he was trying to make her feel comfortable.

They fell into step down the corridor with Clement and Bryn slotted in behind them. Without enough space between their bodies, I was forced to trudge along behind.

If only I could take the prince's arm as well. How easy it would be to stumble and dig my extended nails through the sleeve of his jacket. Maybe I would enjoy walking beside him first though. It wouldn't hurt to take at least one lap around the castle. It wasn't every day that I was allowed this close to royalty, even if he didn't act like it.

Lost in thought, I tripped over my own feet and almost crashed into Clement's back. He gave me his now familiar irked expression and continued walking.

"I hope your maid is working out for you," the prince said to Lilyanna. "She was highly recommended. Royal postings, tenured service, it really was quite an impressive list of credentials."

Lilyanna didn't answer right away. My body clenched. I needed to do a better job of distancing myself from her. She was already suspicious that I'd spent a second of time alone with the prince without her knowledge, despite my protestations it was an accident. If she didn't see me as a friend, she wouldn't see me as a threat. Although that idea was ridiculous. I needed to start weaving some lies about these fabricated credentials in case Lilyanna questioned me later when deciding whether to have me fired for her misplaced jealousy.

"Yes, we get on rather well. It was a perfect decision, my prince."

I rolled my eyes at her sycophantic tone. Had I sounded like that?

"Good," he replied. "I wish for you to be comfortable and at home here while we get to know each other. You are free to wander around the castle or the gardens. It is a luxury that even now I sometimes take for granted. My mothers kept me on a tight leash as I was growing up. You probably never heard a single word uttered about me and it was not because I was a model child." He gave a rich laugh.

"As soon as I turned eighteen, I left the South and claimed our ancestral home. Over the past ten years, this town has gone from a tiny trading post to the richest municipality in the queendom. But the best part is escaping those chains, also known as my so-called *royal duty*."

I nodded along behind them. Why was I listening so intently? And why was I smiling? Goddess no, I needed to get a grip. This is not what I was supposed to be doing. I hadn't noted a single corridor or which direction a window faced this entire time.

Lilyanna's hand on his arm was light, her fingers coiled softly around his sleeve, but there was a steeliness to her spine, and her body tilted ever so slightly away from him. She looked like I did the day I realized the truth about Siobhan, what she wanted me for, and why she'd spent so many years grooming me.

She'd presented me with a new bounty one day—a 'devilish challenge', she'd said. I recognized the man instantly although I'd kept my face blank. Jealousy swarmed through me at first.

She'd never known I'd seen them together, her and her previous 'favorite'. She'd trained me too well and trusted me more than she ought. She knew I'd accept any challenge and any bounty without question, even if it was one of my own people.

After I'd scratched him, leaving him to the mercy of the Collectors, she'd offered me his position. But it was as clear as a dead-end road. That was not where I would end up. If I ceded myself to her whims and followed her through the realms, she'd never make me an equal partner. She'd turn on me the second I stopped worshipping her and grew bored.

She didn't know the balance of power shifted that night, and she never would. I knew what she wanted and would always make sure to keep it just out of her reach. If there was any hope in ever wriggling out of this cursed deal, she needed to want me, to crave me, to know she couldn't possibly exist without me. At that point, a bargain could be struck.

Lilyanna walking in front of me now, carried that same hesitancy, a resolve that pinned her shoulders back and forced her stride to synchronize with his. She didn't want this, and more importantly, she knew something I didn't.

A light breeze tickled my face, uncoiling wisps of hair from my messy bun. An awareness shivered through me as clearly as if someone were screaming my name. The ceiling above was bare with no cracks or loose slabs. I ran my fingertips along the wall. No dust, no cement, and certainly no breeze from outside.

Another gust slithered past, belching muggy, stale air. Neither guard flinched, even when the cuff of Clement's trousers tremored. Lilyanna was the only one who reacted, but even her slight shudder was rapidly replaced by a forced straightening of her shoulders. As if suddenly struck with the urge to concentrate where she was going, her face turned away from the prince, but she continued her attentive nods and murmurings to his monologue.

We rounded a corner, and the temperature normalized, the familiar faint scent of roses perfuming the air. Everyone continued as if nothing had happened. Perhaps it hadn't? Castles were supposed to have drafts. I dragged my hands down my face. I needed to sleep. Or drink. Maybe flee? Anything rather than being trapped here.

"Clement," I whispered. He kept walking. "Clement!" I poked his back.

Grudgingly he turned, falling back a few paces. Bryn pursed her lips but moved to the center of the corridor covering for him.

"Oh, you'll be fine for a minute." I flapped a hand at her. The biggest danger within this barren cage was me. "I want to know where to go—"

"Away from me."

I snorted and clamped my hand over my mouth. His eyes twinkled in response, a momentary lightning of his rigid expression. Oh, Goddess help me, he was handsome when he wasn't being a dick.

"No, where to go outside of the castle. Where can I take Lilyanna, somewhere to let off steam, see the town, have some fun?" I wanted to find out what she knew, or if I was being paranoid. Why was she here and what did she want? She would be more likely to tell me the truth when we couldn't be overheard. And a few strong ales would break her down nicely.

"She cannot leave the castle."

"What?"

He frowned at me, any warmth that previously shone from his eyes now scrubbed clean. He was back to his irritated expression. "Her parents signed a clause before sending her here. It was part of the agreement."

"Does she know?"

"Yes. And I've already told you why. Women are going missing, and she's safer here in the castle with you to accompany her." He looked between me and the prince, itching to reclaim his position. Then he glanced at me, his face softening. "Although…"

He hesitated as we locked eyes. My heart jumped, and my stomach bottomed out. This was a good man. Too good for me. Irritating, yes. Arrogant, also yes. He was handsome but rugged, honest but cautious. And here I was trying to destroy the prince and probably take down the entire town with me.

"…the Diamond Nightingale does a decent meal, ale, and…other things." He shrugged. "If you have time one evening and find someone else to sit with her."

Heat swirled in my lower abdomen, dancing its giddiness through my bloodstream. That was an invitation I could get behind. Perhaps he was not quite so straitlaced after all. I could truly befriend him, use him to pave my way to the prince, and perhaps learn some incriminating secrets along the way. Maybe even more about the clamp down on magic. Clement must be privy to a lot being so close to the prince. If he trusted me, he'd let me get closer and bypass that stupid three-foot rule he seemed to love upholding.

It could even just be physical. If it went further than drinks, it could be a replacement for the days of fun I'd had to leave behind with Candyman at the fayre. An excited shudder ran through me, and I grinned at him in reply. Yes, this could work.

"You really want to take me out?" I asked. "I got the impression you hated me, my friend."

"I don't love that you call me that," he replied. "But it's really a way to benefit all of us. You can get your quirks out"

"Excuse me?" I tried to look offended but suddenly every filthy thought I'd ever had crowded into my mind with Clement squarely involved.

He looked momentarily horrified as his dark eyes widened. "I mean your rudeness..." My eyebrows shot up, but he doggedly continued, "And your fumbling when around the prince. You know..."

"Are you always this good at conversation? You'd think a royal guard would have better social skills for peace-making, conflict resolution, charm."

"I can show you my skills."

His face was expressionless as he held my gaze and Goddess help me if a bloom of warmth didn't grip my body, tingling all the way into my toes. The tips of his mouth lifted, the smallest crinkle appearing around the edges. I stared at him open-mouthed until he turned away and assumed his regular position, barring me from the prince while my thoughts gleefully danced around.

I rolled my shoulders. My muscles seized, aching as I forced them to relax. I must have been keeping them raised. Maybe that was why Lilyanna looked uncomfortable. It could just be the castle, not the prince. He'd been nothing but hospitable so far, but this place was not exactly warm and welcoming. He probably left a much finer palace behind down South to come up here and live his free life.

The prince and Lilyanna halted outside her room. I forced myself in beside Clement, ignoring their superficial conversation, my mind already firmly planted on this inn with a pint of frothing ale in front of me.

"Tam?"

Clement elbowed me, and I snapped to attention. "What?" When I realized it was the prince talking, the blush returned with a vengeance.

He smiled, his dimples popping. "Do you think you can navigate this labyrinth now?"

He swept his arm wide, and the silk of his shirt rustled against his honed chest as it stretched. Why was I noticing that? I was going to need more than one drink at this rate.

"Yes, they were suspiciously easy to navigate today." It was kind of the truth. I had paid very little attention but even so, the dining room, ballroom, library, and gardens all appeared where they were supposed to be.

"Good." He kissed Lilyanna's hand again and held open the door for her.

Clement bent to whisper in my ear as I passed. "You probably weren't paying attention before. It's not like the walls move or anything."

I swallowed my laugh and hurried in after Lilyanna. I glanced quickly at the prince, thanking him as I passed. His face had hardened, his smile fixed. He didn't say anything further as he closed the door behind me, but I caught sight of the look he shot at Clement, and my muscles seized again as unease gripped me.

CHAPTER SEVEN
A CLOUDBURST OF ASH

AFTER OUR TOUR, DAYS PASSED WITHOUT US SEEING THE PRINCE. WE SPENT THE time cooped up in her room playing checkers. Meals were laid out for Lilyanna in the dining room and when nobody else joined her, I sat in the prince's chair with my feet upon the lacquered surface, polishing off everything she didn't want.

The only route I learned led from our chambers to the dining room. Whenever we tried to take a different path or see another area of the castle, the twists and turns of the corridor would shepherd us right back to where we started. Every time I thought I had the layout memorized, a new wall would appear to sever my view and corral me back to the start.

The only thing I now excelled at was being a maid.

Hair, check.

Drawing a decent bath, check.

Listening to state secrets from Lilyanna and hearing all about life in the Northwest, check.

But even my very amicable company did nothing to stop the drain on Lilyanna. She screamed my name multiple times throughout the night, waking me with a heart-pounding jolt each time. I ended up dragging my quilt upstairs to nestle outside her chamber.

Sometimes she would still be asleep like on the first night, but clawing at a pillow over her face, her screams muffled. Other times she would shoot out of bed, swatting at an invisible garrote that hung from the ceiling.

"It's driving me insane," she said on the third night, the dark circles under her eyes more pronounced by the day. She was seated in front of an ornate mirror watching me release the silken blonde strands of her hair from the twist. "I can't sleep properly. I'm hearing things that aren't there, seeing things even when I'm awake."

I rubbed her shoulders, nodding in agreement. They were driving me mad too. Neither of us would last the remaining five weeks at this rate. "I can try and find you a doctor, maybe get a sleeping draught made."

"No. I want to be prepared, be fully alert just in case..."

I agreed with her there. I didn't want to let my guard down either. "Then why don't you leave?" I ran the comb through her hair, the lingering scent of rosewater coating the bristles.

"I am in love with him. It is my duty." The brush snagged, and she winced as I tugged it out. "Besides, you shouldn't be listening to my rambling. I'm just homesick. This place is different, that's all. It's interfering with my sleep pattern."

I grunted.

A rustle caught my attention, and I snapped my head to the door, gripping the comb as if it were a blade. A small scrap of paper was thrust under the threshold.

I picked it up, still clutching my comb-dagger. The prince's blood-red seal congealed the fold. I tore it open, scanned it, and passed it to Lilyanna. "It's nothing, he just wants to see you tomorrow for a fencing lesson."

She clapped her hands, the worry erased from her face even though the ashen sheen remained. "Excellent. Perhaps he had business to attend to and now he's back. I'll make sure to tell him how much I missed him, but that I appreciate he's a busy man with a town to run."

"You do that." I ushered her toward the bedchamber.

She sniffed at the note before pressing it to her breast. Before I closed the door, she whispered, "You'll be out here though, won't you?" The paper slowly shredded under her nails despite the smile she plastered onto her face. I knew she wanted to glance at the ceiling, and it took every ounce of strength in her body not too.

"Yes, Your Ladyship, I'll be sleeping right here."

From my position on the floor, my ear pressed against the small gap under her door, I knew that even despite my assurances, it would take her hours to finally succumb to sleep. Every rustle of the silk sheets, every spasm of her body as she jolted awake on the cusp of dreaming, speared through me like I *was* her.

I'd only known her for a few days, but I'd never spent so much time with a single person before. One that wasn't Siobhan anyway, but even she would disappear when she'd had her fill of me. It had to be the castle. There was an energy, a presence churning in the air that I couldn't quite place, and my need to protect Lilyanna from it was overshadowing my real duty.

A dull moon climbed in the sky outside, muting the stained-glass window so only jagged shards of gray and black could be seen. The castle *seemed* to be asleep. The air was heavy, the silence thick, but a shiver trembled down my spine like someone had dragged their nails across my flesh.

The second my eyes closed, a giggle erupted from above me. I lurched up and tiny feet scrambled away, small motes of dust falling from the ceiling. A rat? A child?

My heart pounded in my ears. I ran my hand down my thigh checking for the dagger secured under my nightgown. I removed a carving knife I'd taken from the dinner table as an added precaution from under my pillow and crept toward the hearth.

The fire had completely extinguished even though I knew I stoked it before laying down to sleep. The embers were hot, the air shimmering above them, but no smoke filled my nostrils. A black ash handprint with splayed fingers was clearly visible on the white marble, as if someone had been reaching out of the fire.

I stared at it; my body frozen. Lilyanna's bed creaked from the adjoining room, rousing me from my thoughts.

Of course nothing had reached out of the fire, I'd been here the whole time. It had probably been there all day. I needed to sleep, not toss and turn at every imagined sound, frying my nerves. Fires popped all the time, didn't they? The ash must be from that—like a cloudburst upon the floor.

I scrubbed the stain away and relit the fire with kindling. Once it roared, I stepped back and surveyed the room. The dust had stopped falling from the ceiling, the air warming again, but a sliver of light cut across the clouded marble from the door that led down to my room.

It creaked open as I nudged it with my shoulder, the carving knife held before me. Each step of the metal staircase groaned beneath my weight, shifting as I descended. The fire flickered in the small hearth. I hadn't tended it since arriving, as I'd been sleeping upstairs, but despite this, it never faded. Unlike the one in Lilyanna's room. My bed was still made, the floor freshly swept, untouched as a vault.

Except the door at the end stood ajar.

This was ridiculous. Maybe this was why Siobhan had given this bounty to me. If everyone else turned tail at the slightest sign of the supernatural, I'd be employed for the rest of my mortal life.

My bare feet were silent on the cold floor. I edged the door open and slipped into the corridor. The light from the small fire in my room licked up the walls, illuminating the hewn stone. The shadows at the edges of my vision transformed into gaping mouths and sinewy limbs, slowly creeping toward me. I forced them away, swinging my gaze back and forth to oust them as they reached...

There was nothing there. I should return to bed, barricade the door. Maybe it had swung open in a draft?

I grasped the door handle ready to flee back inside, but another giggle bubbled down the corridor. It echoed, ricocheting off the stone.

It wasn't inside the walls this time.

I let out a breath and raised my knife, following the shaking tip down the corridor. Not trusting myself to navigate the turns back to my room, I chased after the fading laughter.

The air chilled as I walked as if I had plunged into icy water. My heart trilled, my chest constricting further with every shallow breath. The smooth stone beneath my feet morphed into wooden slats, the deep-set eyes of the wood following me as I walked.

A creak whispered behind me, and I froze. Turning slowly, the shadows parted to reveal an empty corridor that sloped gently upward. Was I underground?

I crept toward a circular hole in the wall where a ray of moonlight squeezed itself through. I pressed my face against the rough stone, a gust of dank night air puffing against my eyeball. Lone footsteps were approaching, their heels level with the peephole. With every step, a silver spur jangled softly on the person's boots. The sound pierced through me, excitement merging with the dormant magic in my veins. It was him. I knew it. The Sheriff.

The one that got away.

Bounty hunters were allowed one failure, and he was mine. Another failure, and the deal I was forced into would be revoked with punishment meted down the line from the Collectors to myself. A fact Siobhan loved to remind me of.

I tapped the stone with my nail, fixated on his spurs. If he was here, I would find him. But where would he go? I'd heard no reports of a sighting in almost a year, but it wouldn't be long before the town criers would be screeching his appearance up and down the streets if he were discovered. Then all the bounty hunters in the land would descend to claim my victory.

The clink of the spurs faded into the night. I knew him. I'd studied him, hunted him, chased him all over this Goddess forsaken land. He would go to the seediest inn he could find, hole up for a few days while he worked a mark before vanishing again. According to Clement, that place was the Diamond Nightingale.

This time, I would do things differently. I would become his mark. He would come to me. But first, I had to make him want me, make him think that I was valuable and that he'd lucked out.

I had to go now. If I could tag him and seed the trackers under his skin, he'd never be able to escape. The Collectors would pursue him through any realm and find him in even the most remote locales. Then I'd be square again with Siobhan. Better than that, I'd have an advantage. She would actually owe *me*. I'd have caught the mark no one else could.

A thrill of excitement raised the hairs on my bare arms. Luck like this never befell me. I could quit this awful castle, barter for an extended time off, leave the prince, Lilyanna, and Clement with his stupid three-foot rule...

Before I could move, a hand clamped down over my mouth.

My scream was muffled, knife clattering to the floor as another hand dug into my wrist, impinging the nerve. I kicked and hit shin, but the hand didn't loosen. I thrashed, getting just enough purchase to bite down on their fingers. My teeth ground into bone.

"Goddessdamn you!" The man spun me around, his arm pinioning my chest against the wall. Clement's face moved barely inches from mine as he hissed, "Do not bite me again."

I snapped my teeth and glared at him. "Then let me go."

He leaned closer, his taut body aligning with mine and heat rushed off him, warming the air around us. His breath panted into my face, filling my senses with traces of pine and polish. He hissed in a barely controlled whisper, forced out through gritted teeth, "What are you doing in this part of the castle?"

This part of the castle? I processed the chill, the wooden floors, the accumulated dust. This is where Lilyanna and I had strayed on the first night before being turned around.

"A midnight stroll." I tried to sound airy and casual. I'd been caught snooping many, *many* times before, it came with the territory. My words usually saved me but today my body betrayed me. My voice wavered, heart pounding beneath the corded muscles of his forearm, and he knew it. I wasn't about to tell him I'd followed imaginary voices down the corridors, nor that I suddenly felt like the castle had led me down here.

"What are *you* doing out of bed so late?" I asked.

"My job."

Something changed in the atmosphere around us. I couldn't place it, couldn't hear anything but Clement felt it too.

"Go back to your room. They sense you're here and even I wouldn't be able to protect you." He loosened his grip, and my lungs dragged in oxygen, but he remained uncomfortably close, his torso pressed against mine.

"From what?"

He swallowed, his eyes flickering to my lips before settling back upon my own. "You can't leave her unguarded. Go. Please. I've said all I can."

He hadn't really said anything. He knew something too. Everyone in this place was keeping secrets. If I'd been allowed to hunt the prince in my own way, I could've found out what was being hidden before I jumped feet first into the middle of it all. Siobhan was testing me. She must know. Or maybe she didn't, and her reach didn't extend quite as far as she wanted. Either way, I didn't want to find out what inhabited this castle the hard way.

I nodded, and he stepped back. I scooped up my carving knife, the handle ice-cold. The blade had notched where it struck the stone, fractures spiderwebbing through the metal. He took it from me, wincing as he touched the handle and pocketed it as he strode away, rubbing his hand down his tunic afterward. The wood creaked beneath his boots, swallowing his body long before the sound.

A door snicked shut, leaving me in silence.

If his room was nearby, then shouldn't Prince Bellinor's be as well? The guards would likely be standing sentinel outside or on alert in adjoining rooms if the prince wanted to maintain his image of normalcy inside his own home. Maybe that would be my way in. If this area of the castle was banned, my presence could go undetected. If I could only slip past Clement's sharp ears first.

Although, if I found the Sheriff and quickly, I could bargain with

Siobhan and avoid having to destroy the prince at all. Lilyanna could find herself a new maid, marry the prince, and they'd all live happily ever after in this creepy castle while I spent all my hard-earned coppers inn-hopping my way south. Back to normal.

I sighed. My breath misted in front of me, spiraling like dragon's steam toward the ceiling. An awareness prickled the hairs on my neck. Even the walls had fallen silent. The castle pulsed expectantly, and I was the fly caught in the center of its web. For the second time that evening, I felt like I'd been deliberately lured down here.

I turned and fled.

CHAPTER EIGHT
THE ONE THAT GOT AWAY

I FLICKED THROUGH THE CRUMPLED NEWSPAPER AS I WALKED LILYANNA TO THE fencing room. Why had they shunted the story of the missing woman all the way to the back? I scanned each headline, my elbow irritatingly jostling Lilyanna with every turn.

She tripped over my foot and grabbed my arm to steady herself. I stopped while she unwound from my body, smoothing her gold tunic with an air of nonchalance.

"You should be concentrating more on your job and where we're going," she huffed. "These floors are most uneven." She eyed the sconces flickering high on the walls. "And the walls could crumble at any second."

I folded the paper and tucked it under my arm. I scanned the ceiling for any loose slabs or cracks. "Okay, job done. Shall we go now?"

She glowered at me but took my arm and let me lead her onward. The castle did seem to be behaving. Even though the daylight barely penetrated the infrequently spaced narrow windows, the corridors were wide and straight. But it was as though we were being corralled, it knew exactly where we ought to be heading.

What a ridiculous idea. I shook my head to clear it, trying to infuse my clogged mind with sane thoughts. I was just tired. Even if there was magic here, it couldn't have a mind of its own. Someone had to be in control.

"I don't feel like ending up like those other women." She spoke lightly, but her nails gripped my sleeve, piercing my skin.

"His fiancées?"

"No, the ones from town. I won't be dying like his fiancées, I've told you. I've seen my future at the castle, but those murdered women are still worrying. There was no talk about them in my premonitions and to have another occur only last night! I've barely been inside this town for a week, and the grisliest events are unfolding."

"Oh, the tea leaves. Right. They only dictate your likelihood of marrying the prince, not of unfolding current events."

She drilled me with a glare.

"Anyway, did you read it?" I waggled the paper at her.

"I scanned it at breakfast. The prince had it open. I presume that's where you lifted it from?"

"I'm not a thief, thank you, but yes, I took it when he left. You were too busy describing how wonderful he is in painful detail to notice. I ate a few of those apple pastries at the same time."

The corridor sloped gently downwards, a rare glimpse of the brackish sky opening above us through an elongated window. How did they live all day trapped between these walls? And Lilyanna had sworn not to ever leave. I'd have to find the gardens and force her to enjoy some fresh air, as much for my sake as hers.

"There wasn't much in it," she continued. "Another woman gone, no body. They suspected there were links to magic, that someone is killing women who specifically harbor blood magic, but so far there's been no clear motive. Or at least, not one widely shared so anybody could be next."

The murders of the town women and the prince's fiancées had to be linked. One person with access to the castle doing them all. If they were after blood magic, they could be coming for me next. Or they could just take me out to clear the path to Lilyanna. My skin pebbled as a chill snaked through me. "Are they sure she was murdered?"

"The prince told me at breakfast his guard had gone to investigate and will be bringing back more information. He said I was safe here within these walls." She glanced again at the ceiling, her eyes tracking back and forth.

"Which guard did he send?"

She shrugged. "I don't know. The sullen one maybe? The one with the beard."

"His name is Clement." I flushed. I don't know why her description of him bothered me, it was surprisingly accurate.

"Yes, that does sound right," she mused.

The Sheriff could be involved. He was prowling around just last night, skulking through town but murder wasn't his forte. Ferreting out secrets and using that information for his own gain was much more his style.

He would be far easier to lure than the prince, and he may have useful information about the women and if they were targeted for their magic. Blood magic was the rarest of all, and highly prized by sorcerers and priestesses. But how had they been captured? They should have lived their lives in quiet fear of discovery, keeping their gifts a closely guarded secret. If anyone would know the answer, it would be the Sheriff.

I dropped the paper outside the heavy doors of the fencing room. Sensing we'd arrived, Lilyanna straightened her shoulders and tossed her head into the air. All her twitchiness morphed into a demure, sultry smile. It would have been amusing had her nail marks not been indelibly imprinted onto my arm, tattooing her anxiety onto my flesh. She patted some color into her wan cheeks and strode into the room as I held open the door. I nodded, impressed with her focus.

The acoustics of the room muffled my tread as I headed for Clement. Hunting trophies lined the walls, pelts, antlers, and taxidermized animals speared on diamond hooks. I avoided eye contact, knowing their beady gazes would reappear in my nightmares otherwise.

The sleepless nights had finally caught up with me. I swayed into Clement, standing like a human totem beside me. He glanced at me in surprise but didn't shrug me off. I leaned in closer, propping my weight against his muscular side.

Did he just flex his bicep? I snorted, disguising the noise with a loud yawn.

"How do you stand so still for so long?" I groaned.

The prince parried with Lilyanna, both wielding long sabers that flashed under the glow from the candelabra. The *click, click, click,* of blade upon blade was putting me into a trance. He remained silent, maybe he was still irritated about last night?

"Are you ignoring me, Clement? Come on, it was only a little nibble."

I nestled deeper into his side, letting his body heat envelop me. I yawned again, earning me a tut of disapproval.

"I told you to stay in your room. To never leave her side," he muttered.

"Yes, I'm sure if the roles were reversed, you'd have no problem sticking to her," I said, and he frowned down at me. "You're not very subtle, my friend. Can't keep your eyes off her."

"I'm not watching *her*." He reddened beneath the dark stubble and resumed focus on the two figures dancing round each other. "Not the way I watch you." The admission came so quietly I almost missed it.

He couldn't possibly mean it like it sounded. I studied his closed-off face, the dark circles under his eyes. Just for a moment, I forgot he was a royal guard and realized he was just a man. One with secrets, a hidden truth that encompassed his entire being. And I wasn't making his life any easier. He did have to keep watching my every move, but thankfully, he didn't know the real reason why.

I turned with a sigh to watch the couple sparring. Lilyanna was remarkably good. If the prince had any thought about letting her win today, that had gone up in a flaming pile of shit. She was the one who quite obviously kept dropping her defense to allow him the odd point. I loved it.

"And don't call me *friend*." Clement gently pushed me off him, his hand lingering on my arm a beat too long. "I'm doing my job."

"Of course, I don't blame you. When you're just grunts like us, you've got to take any perks offered."

He growled, a deep feral sound from deep within him that sent chills of pleasure coursing through me. He could move away, stand on the other side of the room like Bryn, but he didn't.

She'd very clearly made a beeline across the expanse of blood-red marble in the dining room this morning when we'd entered, all because I'd casually asked her how her day had been going so far. She'd once again taken a position as far away from me as possible. She caught me looking, smoothed back her already perfect hair cinched into the neatest bun I'd ever seen, and turned away. She propped one leg back against the wall, her hand falling to the hilt of her saber. Maybe she was embarrassed that she had nothing interesting to say to me, and it wasn't that she found me irritating. Either way, there was one less person between me and the prince. I just needed to befriend Clement to gain access.

"Bryn doesn't like me then?" I asked.

"She thinks you're a distraction."

"Oooh, what kind of distraction?" I whipped my head back toward where she was studiously ignoring us.

He laughed, quickly stopping himself. He cleared his throat. "Not the good kind."

"And what do you think?" I nudged him.

He caught my elbow and placed my hand back by my side. "She's been here a long time. Well before me, and we both trust each other implicitly. To do this job, you have to." He let go and resumed his focus on the prince. "So, let us work."

I sighed and dragged my hands down my face. My skin was clammy, and I knew there were dark circles etched under my eyes too. I'd managed to cover most of Lilyanna's with an oily moisturizer I'd found in the room, but I didn't want to smell of literal roses all day. Why the prince was unable to find anything with a different scent was beyond me. That cloying, sweet odor made me nauseous, but was it enough of a reason to sentence him to death?

My head dropped onto Clement's shoulder again. I sniffed, rolling my cheek so that it pressed against the soft sleeve of his tunic. Goddess, he smelled good. Refreshing, like pine. My mind wandered into the woods, soft pine needles cushioning my feet, the wind glancing against my skin.

"Did you just smell me?" Clement asked, his lips twitching.

"No," I scoffed. "It's just nice to smell something other than roses." I straightened and focused intently on Lilyanna's offensive posture, tracking her lunge across the training floor.

"So, you did, then?"

I could hear the smile in his voice, the swallowed chuckle. My cheeks burned as I ignored his perusal of my face, but I kept my side aligned with his, refusing to move away.

Prince Bellinor pulled back, the point of his sword dropping to the floor. Sweat dripped from his brow and a grimace replaced the cute dimples. Lilyanna in her cropped leggings and gold tunic waited patiently, not a hair out of place. She shot me a small smile, her blue eyes shining with enjoyment before resuming her modest, patient visage.

I needed the prince to lose his temper and to show the dark side that he must keep hidden. Those previous women didn't murder themselves. Could he really be innocent? It'd be easier if he were involved, then I'd be doing a great service to the public and not committing treason just for a heavy coin purse.

One of the brackets on the wall guttered. There was no breeze here. The walls were stone, the floor marble and the large window cemented shut for the winter like all the others. I blinked and righted myself, pushing away from the wall I'd leaned on instead of Clement. My magic sent a sharp pulse through my system in response.

If it was one of the staff and not the prince to blame, then I'd need to get Lilyanna out of here as well. Maybe that's why the guards took their jobs so seriously. Even the prince needed saving.

Finally, they both sheathed their sabers.

Lilyanna ducked her head in a curtsey, but he pulled her to her feet. "Nonsense, my lady." He bowed low before collapsing to his knees, prostrating his arms in front. "You clearly wiped the floor with me."

She giggled, her eyes darting to me in delight. I raised my eyebrows and smiled. The prince pushed back to his knees and extended his hand. She gently pulled him up, then twined her arm around his as they walked over to us. They looked like such a perfect couple, maybe they could truly make this work. Be happy, or whatever it is people tried to do in relationships.

My magic boomed again, louder, stronger, making me flinch.

A large ewer filled with pungently sweet lavender water sat in the center of a small folding table. Purple petals hung suspended in the liquid as the prince poured two glasses. For once, I was thankful not to be included.

Prince Bellinor turned and gestured to the room. "This is my ancestral home. My mothers rarely make the trek up here anymore and this place fell into quite a state of disrepair. There are still areas of the castle that are quite dangerous to wander through."

He didn't look at me, but heat prickled my chest. It was like he knew I'd been roaming the corridors last night and was gently warning me from doing it again. To confirm, Clement elbowed me.

"But that's also where I found some of these valuables," the prince continued. "All these beasts are hundreds of years old. They came with the castle, and I didn't have the heart to throw them out."

I followed his gaze, skimming over a huge buck mounted to the wall, a towering black bear wedged into the corner and a skein of geese suspended in flight along the far side. Maybe if I released the bindings on the bear, it would topple forward at just the right moment. Its large, rough pads could come down directly on the prince and in an effort to save him, when I dragged him out from underneath, I could 'accidentally' scratch his arm. I'd be a hero and back squarely in Siobhan's good graces. She may even delay forcing my partnership with her if I proved too valuable on the ground.

He took a few paces across the floor and lifted his glass toward a semi-circular fountain in the corner. The bust of a rearing horse extruded from the stone wall above, water running down its white mane and pooling in the basin at its feet. "The kelpie would lure travelers, appearing like an innocent, gentle horse. They would climb on its back and be stuck fast to its hide where it would then return to its loch and drown them."

I wrinkled my nose. That's what it felt like in this Goddessforsaken castle.

From the corner of my eye, the light shifted. The nearest sconce quivered before toppling from its alcove directly where Lilyanna stood.

Clement lunged for her, and they both fell forward. Her glass shattered on the stone, small sprigs of lavender floating in the sticky water. Flames danced down her back, catching the gold tunic. I grabbed the ewer and sloshed it over her while Clement patted the rest out. He helped her to her feet before the prince swooped his arm around her waist, whispering soothing words in her ear.

I put the jug back on the table as Clement stalked toward me.

"Why weren't you paying attention?" he hissed.

"I was. I was listening to the story."

"That's not your job. You're supposed to guard Lady Lilyanna, not listen to the prince brag about his hunting exploits."

"Well, I was obviously paying more attention than you because that's not what he was talking about."

Clement gritted his teeth, lowering his face toward mine. "Do I need to tell you again—"

"Well, my friends." The prince clapped Clement on the shoulder, and he backed away a step, freeing my airspace. "Now that we both know how interesting you find my topics of conversation..." He winked at me. Clement's cheeks pulled taut beneath the dark stubble, a faint blush coloring his neck. "How about we return to more pressing issues."

"Is it an omen?" Lilyanna's voice trembled.

The prince turned to her, his smile tight. "Lilyanna, my dear, this castle is very old and very temperamental. Do not take any of its quirks to heart, there will be plenty of time for you both to become acquainted."

"Both as in Lilyanna and me, or the castle and her?" I asked.

"All of the above, Tam."

"Your Highness, a word?" Clement asked. The prince nodded, and they stepped to the side. "She needs to leave," Clement said, not bothering to lower his voice and jabbing a finger toward me. "She's not doing her job. There's going to be an accident, and there are already many whispers circulating about the mysterious deaths. It'd be better for everyone involved if one of your personal guards looked after Lady Lilyanna instead."

What was his problem? It was like he'd been waiting for an opportunity to kick me out. He dropped his defenses every now again, drawing me closer, even flirting with me, in his own restrained way, but it was all an act. Well, I could do that too, I'd had years of practice keeping people at arm's length, but I needed to stay physically close now. If I were forced out of the castle, I'd never be able to get near to the prince again.

"No! I can do it," I called.

They both turned to me. The prince bore a half-smile, amusement dancing across his face while Clement's jaw tightened, a muscle ticking beneath the thick stubble.

Eventually, the prince walked back over to Lilyanna and gently took her hand. "What do you think, my love?"

The pause she took made my stomach somersault. Maybe she hadn't forgiven me for the non-existent flirtation with the prince when I'd met him in the corridor.

"She has to stay. I only want her." She brushed at her side and winced. A strip of charred fabric fluttered to the floor. "I'd like to return to my rooms." Her smile was weak, her face ashen.

I stepped forward to help her, but Clement blocked me again.

"What are you doing?" I hissed and sidestepped him, but he flung out an arm to keep me back.

"It's quite alright, Clement," the prince said. "I will escort both ladies back to their rooms." He held out his other hand to me.

Clement froze. His arm remained flung across my chest, his body between us. Did he really think I was that dangerous? I had only bitten him a little bit last night after he had disarmed me first with practiced ease. Maybe he thought it was my fault accidents kept befalling Lilyanna, and that bad luck may mar the prince as well. Whatever the reason, it was clear he didn't trust me. I fought back the burn in my chest, trying to ignore how much it stung. At least it had been confirmed that any softness before was just an act, a way to pass the time. He didn't want me here, he didn't even like me. Why did that hurt so much?

The silence stretched.

Clement refused to move. His teeth remained locked together, gaze fixated on the floor.

The prince shrugged. "As you like." He winked at me, dimples reappearing in his cheeks. "My guards do take their jobs a tad seriously."

"As they should," I said.

"Yes, quite. Don't worry, Tam. We will have plenty of time to become acquainted"—Clement's body shifted further in front of me—"I heard you are like a big sister to my dear Lilyanna."

Did she tell him that? I'd been privy to their every conversation since arriving here. They never discussed anything other than trivial events. Lilyanna spoke at length to me about her family, her friends, her country, but never breathed a word of it to him. Or had I missed it? My insides iced as my stomach clenched.

I grunted a reply. He turned, and they walked arm in arm from the room, both guards following at a respectable distance. Clement glared at me over his shoulder whenever I tried to sneak past and catch up. I rolled my eyes and stomped along behind him, studying the walls for new holes as I went.

The prince kissed Lilyanna's hand when we stood outside the door to her chambers. "You will join me tomorrow for dinner, my love?" His eyes were green today, but they had been brown before. Perhaps the tunic he wore altered the color? "I have a wonderful surprise for you."

"Of course. It would be my pleasure." Her smile seemed genuine. Small creases formed beside her full lips and wrinkled the skin beside her eyes, but tension coated her face. Maybe just from the lack of sleep or the constant paranoia from noises and eerie breaths in the castle?

He held the door open, and she passed inside. I moved to follow, but he reached for my arm to draw me back. Once again, Clement got in the way.

Prince Bellinor gave a low chuckle. "I only wanted a word. You may stand between us if you must."

Clement's jaw flexed, but he remained there like a barrier. Goddess, he was infuriating.

"I will be sending Lady Lilyanna and yourself a little gift tomorrow. I would like you both to wear them to the dinner."

"Am I invited then?"

He chuckled. "You will be present, yes. You are practically family to her, and I'm sure a close confidante by now."

A cool breeze swept through the corridor, raising the hairs on my arm as if a tarantula were tiptoeing up my skin. Clement nudged me toward the door, keeping himself angled between us.

"Until tomorrow, Tam," the prince said. "Take good care of my dear Lilyanna. She is priceless."

The door snapped shut behind, and my breath left my body in a gust. I turned to the hearth to check if the fire was stoked and gave the ceiling a cursory scan. Lilyanna hovered in the doorway to her bedchamber and tilted her head for me to follow.

Her bedroom was as large as the sitting room. A huge four-poster bed with a carved wooden frame was pushed against the stone wall. White silk sheets were pulled taut, the diamond-encrusted edges glittering in the low light from the wall sconces. Tapestries covered the walls, their thick weave muffling all sound. Whenever I entered, I was torn between feeling comforted and trapped.

"Lilyanna, I think you should leave."

"Shhh." She pressed the bedroom door tightly shut and pulled me over to the dresser. She sat atop the velvet-lined stool and gazed ahead.

I stood behind her and slowly unbraided her hair. "You know it's not right here," I whispered, eyes meeting hers in the mirror.

"It's my duty."

"*Duty*. Goddess, do I hate that word now." I ran the comb through her hair, loose coils transforming into a gentle wave.

"Tam," she chided, "language. Don't forsake the Goddess's name, it's bad luck."

I grunted, narrowly avoiding rolling my eyes.

"You do know why I was invited here? To be his match?"

"Something about gold."

"Diamond controls the whole country. It's the purest gemstone ever born from the Earth and only here, inside Bellinor's walls, can it be mined. The legends say there's an infinite supply gifted directly by the Goddess to the prince. That's why he's so generous, spreading the wealth throughout the city."

My hands stilled, but she gently touched the comb for me to continue.

"Legend also says the prince has a heart of pure diamond and that's how he keeps replenishing. He spreads himself to the population when they need it."

She shrugged. "Either way, diamond controls everything. It sets the price for gold, silver, or iron. Provinces that join his see the price of their resources skyrocket. Combining say, diamond and gold, would ensure my town in the West was always provided for."

"There are other ways to make deals rather than marrying someone."

"It is an honor," she said, too loudly.

I put the brush down.

"Keep going. You can practice your braid for tomorrow's big dinner." She scooped up a handful of razor-sharp diamond-encrusted pins from the top drawer. "Matron left these after she'd cleaned the room. Said they were a gift from the prince."

I separated three strands of her silken hair and began to weave them together. "Have you seen Matron's jewelry? The rubies alone should have cost a fortune. What do you think the prince was buying? Silence? Loyalty?"

I placed a sparkling pin between the layers, watching her neck muscles tense, the pulse in the hollow of her throat briefly standing distended before she forced herself calm again.

"Rubies are the stone from the outskirts of the queendom. Harvested only from a windswept island in the North Sea. Their price has always been high due to the cost of the lives lost climbing the cliffs, scrambling amongst the scree, and fighting the black-tipped waves to bring them ashore."

She paused, fighting a shudder as I gently placed another pin.

"The princess of the isle was here barely six months ago. As a wedding present, the prince had gifted her a ruby studded crown. When she was found, the crown was so deeply embedded in her skull that the bone had fused with the crystals, red on red, as if it were part of her."

"Then why in Goddess's name are you here, Lilyanna?"

"I intend to live."

"Me too," I muttered.

My mind returned to those black boots and the jangling clink of spurs. The Sheriff had led me on a merry dance round the entire queendom, vanishing into thin air whenever I neared. I knew everything about him, from the women he favored to the jewels he stole. The only thing not told to me was why he had been targeted, which one of the many jilted women glaring at his retreating back had struck a bargain for his capture.

If I finally took him, I could let the prince go. I liked that he'd moved away from the queens to set up his own life, created a pocket of freedom even if it was in this cursed castle.

Then I'd persuade Lilyanna—kicking and screaming as I tied her like a sack to my horse and hand delivered her back to the West—that marriage was not in her best interests, that those ridiculous tea leaves were wrong and remaining in this creepy hellhole would have her buried in a golden casket before the year expired.

She smiled, more a flattening of her full lips than a curve. "You can take these out now." She flung the pins from her hair, not waiting for me to do it. Thin golden strands hung like twisted nerves from the metal.

"How have there not been wars over these women? I've heard

nothing of these events until recently, and I spend a good deal of time listening to gossip. Were they linked to the other murdered women; the ones supposedly killed for their magic?"

"The other women I don't know." She rose and walked me to her door. "But news of the ladies of the court was kept quiet because a deal has always been struck that could not be refused."

"How do you know?"

"Us outlying towns talk more than people think." Her face remained light, her hand resting upon my arm, soft and warm, but a steeliness formed inside her. "I'm going to get out of these burned clothes and lie down for a while."

I nodded.

She wouldn't leave willingly, and she knew much more about this situation than I did. I too was bound by a contract, my life dedicated to a cause I hadn't chosen. The risk of death was always there, but I wasn't surviving just for myself.

Lilyanna was a martyr, not a hero. Exactly like me.

CHAPTER NINE
THE ART OF SEDUCTION

Now I had two bounties at once. And neither of them was going to magically appear in Lilyanna's room while we idled the day away playing checkers. I left her behind after asking an unimpressed Matron to watch her, ignoring the irritating flicker of worry in my gut and headed out.

The market was easy to find. I followed the cries, calls, and raised haggling voices, my nose upturned as the wind carried the scent of roasted chestnuts and blackened swedes. After spending days trapped in the gray stone castle, I had to hover in the alleyway until my eyes adjusted to the colors.

Carts laden with sprouted cauliflower and bushy lettuce formed a meandering path while crates of potatoes and blood-red radish stacked ten high teetered over the crowd. People milled around, some with wicker baskets looped around their arms, others with pockets stuffed with wares. The scene was so similar to the one from my childhood, a pang struck my heart. Only then I'd been the one dragging a sheep on a fraying halter over the cobblestones or carrying as many chickens as would fit in my arms. Not for the first time I wondered what had become of our abandoned smallholding. Someone would have destroyed it as the wall ran straight through the land, but did they pillage it first? Were any of the items in the market heirlooms of my past?

Young children surrounded by a bubble of raucous energy sat cross-legged against the front of the houses, dice and sticks thrown on the ground in front of them. A small pile of coppers sat ferociously guarded in a scrawny girl's discarded hat.

Look at them closely, my dear. Siobhan's voice whispered against my skin, tickling the top of my ear. The memory as clear as if she were standing with me now. *One of them is a cheat.*

Siobhan had taught me how to read micro expressions on someone's face, a shift in body posture or an almost imperceptible alteration in voice pitch. To start with it was easy. When we were at market and my nerves shot, my stomach growling, she'd move us to the side and stand close, one hand kneading my shoulder, her fingers never wavering, her support unbroken. She'd toss a gideon in one hand, my reward if I guessed correctly and enough to last me a month.

I watched for a few minutes before it became clear. The youngest of the group threw weighted die. They wobbled on the edge before tipping in the wrong direction. The group cheered in unison, color warming their pallid cheeks. The boy grabbed the die and cupped them in his hands, ready to throw them again. Secretly imprinting his thumb on the numbers he wanted to fall next, he transferred a magnetic magic marker. The rest of the group muttered excitedly, unconcerned and unaware.

I could easily tell them, just a casual sentence dropped in passing. Siobhan would say, *It doesn't matter. You got your answer and now you move on. It's simpler that way, no guilt.*

I pressed back against the wall and tugged the hood of my cloak over my face. If the boy remained this adept, his luck would continue. If he were truly clever, he'd switch back for the regular pair hidden in the pleat of his trousers just before the group's suspicions fell on him. I wonder what other tricks he could do with that rare magic?

My blood magic was only good for one thing, a fact Siobhan had made crystal clear when she'd transferred the thread to me. But I'd made it work and carved out a life for myself. I'd been infallible until the Sheriff came along.

I rested my foot on the stone and scanned the crowd back and forth seeking the anomaly. A true chameleon, he'd blend in with any and every crowd until he'd found what he was looking for and transform into what that person wanted. I'd let him figure me out later, when I was ready. Eventually, I found him.

The Sheriff roamed through the towering aisles. I wasn't close enough to hear, but I knew the *clink, clink, clink* of his spurs would be rattling through the air. A brown peaked hat and woolen cloak completed his ensemble as if to appear as though he'd trekked from the Highlands to sell his own wares and was just casually browsing his fellow countryman's stalls.

He blended in so well, I couldn't make out any defining features, except his boots. But it was him. He carried himself with the air of a ghost. No one noticed him and yet, they instinctively gave him a wide berth.

What was he doing here?

He paused by a crate of stacked potatoes and peered down at the produce, but his eyes remained fixed ahead. I followed his gaze, and my heart jolted. Clement stood in his usual wary pose—hand on the hilt of his saber and eyes rapidly scanning the market—with Bryn his mirror on the opposite side. The prince had his back turned, perusing a stall of scarves and gloves. His thick, satin suit of charcoal flowed down his lithe form, distinct against the hard line of Clement's sapphire blue tunic.

My gut twisted, adrenaline snaking through my thighs. Was he after *my* bounty? Siobhan had said others would be lining up if I failed, but this wasn't his style. He flourished at blackmail and seduction, not cold-hearted stalking. He liked to play with his food before eating it, not swallow it whole.

As long as he wasn't after Clement.

I shook myself. What was wrong with me? It didn't matter. It shouldn't matter. Clement shouldn't matter. He'd made it abundantly clear he didn't trust me, so why was I still thinking about him? If anything, the Sheriff removing Clement would make my job easier.

Regardless of the Sheriff's plan, I would get to the prince first.

I kicked off the wall, flicked down my hood, and skirted around the market, popping back in again so that the Sheriff would have a direct eyeline to me. I sidled up to the stall, inserting myself between Clement and the prince. I'd barely rested against the table when Clement grabbed my arm and spun me around.

"What?" he said, keeping my arm pinned, my body flush against him while he positioned the prince safely behind him. "*Tam,*" he groaned. The short knife on my thigh jabbed against his leg. He shook his head slowly and pushed my cloak aside, his warm hand running down my hip. But he lingered, his fingers gently squeezing. Something sparked between us like a flare of magic as he plucked the knife from the holster and pocketed it. I shouldn't have liked it, shouldn't have submitted, and yet I offered no resistance.

He kept the grip on my arm, his face lowered to mine. "Why have you left your post?"

"I haven't really." I tugged weakly to free my arm, but both my body and mind were quite content to allow him this little bit of control. Or perhaps a lot more, under the right circumstances.

"Yes, you have. Your one job is to guard Lady Lilyanna."

"Oh, calm down." I yanked my arm free. "She's with Matron. I tried to bring her with me, but she reminded me about that stupid contract not allowing her outside without the prince."

"Yes, it's dangerous."

I rolled my eyes. "*I'm* out alone."

"Good."

I barked a laugh. His lips quirked.

"Anyway, it's a good thing I'm here, because I'm currently saving your fine ass."

He folded his arms across his chest. "What?"

"I'm doing your beloved job for you. I'm protecting you."

"You're distracting me."

I smiled coyly and fluttered my eyelashes. He raised his dark brows, the rest of his face unflinching.

"There's a man following you. He's been watching for at least an hour, trailing you around the market. He's very hard to spot, so don't beat yourself up about it. He's practically a ghost."

"Do you know him?"

"I know many, *many* people, Clement." My smile widened as he pursed his lips. "But I can tell you, I also saw him hanging around the castle the other night. You know, when I accidentally bit you."

"Yes, I remember." He unfolded his arms, a hint of warmth loosening his muscles.

"He's looking for a weak spot. He thinks that may be you."

Clement growled.

"Joking!" I squeezed his bicep. "You're actually very strong."

He swatted me away, a crinkle appearing around his mouth.

"But I am looking out for you, in my own way. Maybe one day you'll trust me."

He grunted.

"You're a man of many words today, my friend."

As soon as his gaze ripped from mine to sweep over the market, chills raked over my skin.

He sighed. "I'm working."

My attention settled back on the prince. He stood watching our exchange, dark eyes shining and a faint smile tickling his lips. I nodded in greeting at him, which was better than the weird curtsey-bow thing I'd done before.

"So, Tam, now that you've joined us." The prince spread his arm over the stall behind him. "What do you fancy? Trinkets, jewelry, clothing?"

"I've not come here to shop," I said. Clement elbowed me. "But thank you."

The prince turned and dragged his fingertips over a pair of fur-lined gloves. "I'll find something else for you then." He turned and winked.

I blinked, momentarily silenced. Was he flirting with me? Or just being nice? Surely, he wouldn't really buy me something in front of his guards and all these people. Whispers would circulate very quickly.

He turned back and trailed his hand over a collection of glittering figurines. I raised my eyebrows at Clement for help, but he chose that moment to scan the crowd over my head again searching for the Sheriff, his jaw set and body stiff.

The prince rattled a few gideons in his fist and handed them to the stooped man behind the stall. He plucked a palm-sized butterfly from the table and held it out to me. "Here."

I hesitated. The magic zoomed to life within me, my nails automatically sharpening. Wasn't this what I wanted? What I needed? Perhaps I could tag him right now and be done.

Clement snatched it from him, inserting his body between us.

"Oh, for the love of the Goddess, Clement," I hissed. "You've taken my knife, now what do you think I'm going to do?"

He thrust the butterfly at me.

"I'll give this to Lilyanna." I craned my neck around him to look at the prince.

"Don't *you* like it?" the prince asked.

Why was he looking at me so intently and why, oh why, was I blushing? "Oh. Well, sure." I studied the figurine. The body had been molded from solid gold, cross-hatched with small hairs made from a fine blade. The wing segments were each a different gemstone—ruby, sapphire, silver, and emerald. The spiked antenna shimmered in translucent diamond. "But I usually prefer gifts that have a dual purpose." I tossed the butterfly into the air. "It's not heavy enough to bludgeon someone with." I ran the pointed antenna down Clement's bicep before he pushed me away. "And it's not sharp enough to sever an artery."

"Alright, that's enough." Clement physically turned me around and marched me away. "Go back and do your job. Stop messing around."

"I like messing with you, friend."

"I'm not your friend." He gave me one final shove and returned to the prince.

"Thanks!" I waggled the butterfly in the air.

From the shaded corner of the market, the Sheriff watched the exchange. His eyes never left the flashing gemstone as I tossed it high into the air again before pocketing it and heading back to the castle.

I had his interest.

Later that evening, I dragged the butterfly out and placed it onto the checkerboard before Lilyanna.

"What am I supposed to do with it?" She reached with the tip of her finger toward one of the antennae, as if she were a princess drawn to a spinning wheel needle in a fairytale.

"I dunno. Put it with your collection of sparkly things?"

"Ouch." She pulled her finger away from the butterfly, sucking on the end. She glared at the figurine. "Listen, Tam, I need you to run an errand for me tonight."

She cast one last irritated look at the butterfly before stalking toward the bedroom. She returned holding a straw doll, its yellow hair limp and straggly. She placed it on the checkerboard face up, although it had no face, nor any features.

Lilyanna held up two hairpins—one gold, the other diamond. She eased each one into the doll's chest, forcing aside the fibers until only the tips of the pins remained like engorged ticks.

I grimaced at the doll, certain I would not like this favor.

"It's the lunar festival tonight. All over the North, towns will be lighting huge bonfires and sacrificing effigies to the Goddess. As I'm not allowed out of the castle, I need you to go in my place and offer this for me. It's a token to ensure the match between the prince and me succeeds."

I prodded the doll with my finger. The tips of the pins scratched against the smooth checkerboard as the doll rocked.

"Listen, Tam, I need to do everything in my power to make this happen. You don't understand the weight of expectation on my shoulders. So many people are depending on me." Her voice hitched, and she took a deep breath. Calm washed over her face again, a perfect mask of deception.

Oh, I did understand. I had a sudden urge to tell her, to come clean and unburden myself for the very first time. It wasn't only Siobhan depending on me, but the Collectors. If I failed, a whole line of consequences would ensue like the strings of fate not only being cut but set on fire, spreading to those nearest. But then the prince winking at me in the market pushed to the forefront of my mind, and my stomach fluttered. I didn't even know what he'd done and for the first time, I actually cared. Especially if success meant I'd also damn Lilyanna and all her people. What a decision. Did I even have a choice?

Steeling myself, I pulled my hands into my lap and nodded. "So, I just throw it in?"

"Yes." She clutched the edge of the table, body leaning toward mine, and her hair spilled over her shoulders. "It's all a secret as well. Everybody covers their face and goes alone or in pairs. So no one will know you're carrying that for me."

Maybe the prince would be there too, hidden amongst the crowd. He could also be unguarded. Heat rose in my cheeks as I remembered my half curtsey, half bow monstrosity that I did last time I was alone with him and his attention was on me. I'd probably just simper like an idiot.

The Sheriff could also be there. It was exactly the kind of event where he would lurk, watching people throw in their secrets, ready to pounce.

"What shall I do afterward?"

"Come straight back," she said.

I rolled my eyes. "First, I'm your sister but now when you want something I'm your slave."

She pointed at the inert checker counters sprawled over the tabletop. "It's not like you're working overly hard now, is it?"

She arched a brow over twinkling eyes, and I wrinkled my nose. Maybe she'd never had a maid who talked to her before. Maybe no one talked to her. They probably all scurried around meekly doing their jobs, eyes cast down, uttering one-word assent to any questions. I kind of liked being around her too, although I would never tell her that.

"Looks like I'll be having another sleepless night." I stared out the thick window. The distant houses merged in a sea of dreary taupe-like melted candles. I sighed. "I wish I had my knife back."

Lilyanna nodded. "Yes, I wouldn't mind one myself."

Her face paled, hands still clawed from gripping the table. Long, sinewy tendons stood erect in her forearms, disappearing under the green silk of her cropped sleeves. She forced herself to relax, prodding at the butterfly again. She would have been far happier with a weapon as a gift from the market, not piles of fancy clothes and stacked boxes of hats, but that was the impression she was giving him. He thought she'd like that butterfly.

Unless he had meant to give it to me?

The fire spasmed, skittering shadows across the bare walls toward us.

"I forgot. I'm not supposed to leave you," I said.

She pushed herself away from the table, smoothing her new dress. "This is more important. I'll be perfectly safe." She folded her arms over her chest, barely concealing the rash of gooseflesh that puckered her skin.

I moved to the fire and added another log. The marble hearth sparkled, not a speck of ash marring its surface. I shivered. It was like it was waiting for me to leave.

"I'll ask Matron to sit here for a few hours again," I said.

She huffed in reply but uncrossed her arms, a hint of warmth trickling back into her face. I didn't have the heart to tell her that I doubted Matron would be a match for whatever lived inside these walls.

CHAPTER TEN
EFFIGIES

It was a perfect night for burning effigies.

Not that I'd ever participated, nor even heard of this ritual before today. The sky was cloaked, the moon barely a sliver. People scurried down the cobblestone street with hoods pulled low or scarves tied as masks around their lower faces. Hoar crystallized into my cloak as I walked, grating together with a faint crunching as the folds tangled with my legs.

If only I'd asked the prince for gloves at the market, but it would take too long to tug off each finger while trying to access the magic if I happened to run into the Sheriff. Or the prince, I suppose. If I saw him and he was alone, misgivings aside, I'd be a fool not to act tonight. I shook myself, patting some feeling into my face against the bracing cold.

I shouldn't have written the prince off entirely, not yet. And why? Because he had dimples and a cheeky smile? Because he almost bought me a gift? Because I didn't know if he was guilty? None of it should matter. I had no intention of being with a prince for Goddess's sake. My cheeks tingled as I patted them harder. I needed to get rid of this stupid weakness or I'd accidentally throw my own token into the bonfire instead of Lilyanna's.

Halfway between the castle and the distant gates, the bonfire blazed, flames dancing wildly in the center of the main street. Crates from the market lined the edges with tall stones hemming them in to prevent stray sparks from igniting the houses crowded on either side. The thin washing lines had been removed, or disintegrated, giving the smoke an uninterrupted escape into the heavens.

One by one, solitary figures crossed to the fire. Some knelt, others bent their heads in worship while a few just stopped and stared into the shimmering heat. With each offering, the fire would gutter, then roar as it surged upward swallowing the token before settling again.

A stooped woman made her way to the front. The sparse crowd hung back to watch and catalog the offering. She threw a handmade rattle into the flames. The wood ignited easily, and a scrawled name etched in the wood glowed white along the handle before a rush of heat blanketed the crowd. The fire glowed green so quickly I would've missed it if not for the image burned onto my eyelids when I blinked.

"Magic, my dear." Siobhan's voice whispered directly into my ear. I jumped, snatching at my blown-back hood. "You should be careful with that...thing you are about to offer." She took the doll from my hand using only the tips of her gloved fingers. It dangled by the solitary strand of straw-colored hair, the scalp bulging under the pressure.

I snatched it back. "Why do I need to be careful?"

She wiped her hand on her cloak—a beautiful ermine-lined velvet monstrosity that swamped her entire figure. Before she could answer, or more likely, change the subject, two castle guards bearing diamond-encrusted sabers jogged around the fire. Their heads swiveled in unison, feet unnaturally loud against the crackle of the fire. They stopped where the woman had barely been seconds ago. I scanned the crowd, catching a faint glimpse of a stooped back disappearing down a distant alley. The guards muttered to each other before melting back into the shadows.

"Prince Bellinor is rather clever," Siobhan said. "While appeasing his superstitious population, this fire is also rigged to flare when contacting trace amounts of magic. He won't be that interested in the green flare, but yours, my dear...well, I'd just love to see what fireworks true blood magic emits, especially as powerful as yours."

No one else approached the bonfire. Quiet murmurings passed between strangers as dolls, toys, and gifts shuffled in cold hands.

She could be lying. Everything she ever told me was wrapped up in lies and riddles. I had no magic on my skin, and I hadn't used it in over a week. People had still come out alone regardless of the fact there was supposed to be a murderer around town. Maybe everything was just rumors she'd planted, bubbling over in a small town, and Siobhan was making me follow through on a bounty of someone truly innocent because she wanted to test me.

Or just because she could.

"Did you send someone else after my bounty?" I asked.

"Oh no, my dear." She reached out to adjust my hood, tugging me toward her as she did. Her perfume replaced the dense smoke in the air, and I inhaled deeply despite myself. "That's better," she cooed. "Although I do love it when you're angry." She kept a grip on my hood, forcing my head to remain angled toward hers. "I'm afraid someone else must have sent them, but a rival? How fun."

"It's not fun. It's the Sheriff." I pushed her arms away, turning back to watch the fire.

"The Sheriff. You're only failure, right?"

I stayed quiet.

"Mhm. Well, you know two others were unable to catch him before you, and I had to lose both of them because of it. Just imagine if you fail on this bounty as well. I'll have no choice but to bump you to Collector. Of course, you know what that would mean for your current ones. Such an interesting, desperate bargain they caught you up in, no? Tell me, have you made amends yet?"

I pursed my lips. The magic stirred in my veins, pushing toward my shaking fingertips. If I wasn't careful, it'd ooze onto the street like blood.

"Then I could hire the Sheriff as *your* bounty hunter," she continued. "Now, what a wonderful tangle of fortune that would be. Reminded forever of your failures."

"I'm going to get rid of him." Sticky heat welled under my nails, and I thrust my hands into my pockets. The whole fire would explode if Siobhan was right about the magic trap. She knew she did this to me. I forced a deep breath. "It's an embarrassment to you as well that he's still out there, and you couldn't fulfil *your* promise to the client."

She edged closer, the soft folds of her cloak tickling my legs. She turned her head, brushing the edge of my hood aside so her breath warmed the curve of my ear. "There's nothing that can embarrass me."

I tried to swallow, tried to move away, but it was too difficult to stop the blush arcing up my neck. Not when I had to stop the magic seeping from my fingers as my body relaxed and to coordinate my legs at the same time.

"At least tell me what the prince did. Who arranged his bounty? Is he involved with the murdered women?"

"Oh, I can't tell you that. I don't like interfering too much in the lives of mortals, it's rather tedious." She withdrew from my airspace, my body slackening as if she'd been holding me upright. She patted my arm. "That's why I have you, dear. Now, off you go. It's your turn, yes?" She nudged me forward.

Two other figures moved toward the fire at the same time. I grabbed the doll by its foot and flung it high into the flames as both other people did. The bonfire whooshed, growing a foot all around as it devoured the offerings. The orange glare flashed crimson before sparks screamed into the air, spiraling like a trebuchet's grenade toward the midnight sky.

I was already backing away, the space where Siobhan had been moments before now empty. Heavy footsteps pushed forward, but I didn't stop to watch. Tugging my hood down low, I skirted the crowd and melted into the nearest alleyway. It snaked left and right, disorientating me within minutes.

I slowed my pace, glancing behind me. The thick smoke belched into the sky to my right, but houses crowded either side leaving no openings to emerge back onto the central street.

My shoulders caught on a wooden shutter which thumped back

against the house. I spun around. My mind leaped back to the night of the storm—the night it all began.

Shutters flapped against the sidings, concealing the splintering of the door, the vibrations from the footfalls...

I froze.

A figure hovered in a sliver of light from the neighboring house, a scarf wrapped around his throat and lower face. His hair shined with a rich chestnut glow where it peeked out from under the hood of his cloak.

Not the Sheriff. The prince.

My heart pounded. This was it. A perfect opportunity. Feelings aside, there would be no witnesses. I could escape any number of ways through this rat maze of alleyways, but it still had to look like an accident. Otherwise, I'd have to kill him too, and that wasn't my job.

My stomach turned as blood splattered over the kitchen floor, muted by the lashing rain...

Not now, not now. I forced myself back to reality, chest tight as a sickly swell of nausea climbed up my throat.

This was it. My best chance. I had to get out, leave this town to flee the memories. I lowered my hood and moved toward him. "I'm so glad I found you, my prince. It's dark and creepy out here tonight. I was only out doing an errand for Lady Lilyanna and got turned around." I stopped a few paces away.

He took a step forward, angling himself so I was pressed back against the wall. The light fell on his back, encasing his face in shadows.

"Where are your guards?" I asked.

My hand twitched toward my thigh. It was still bare. I grasped for the magic instead, priming it, pumping it into my fingertips, but it slunk deeper within me, further and further with each swipe of my will. My heart thudded. What was happening?

"Sometimes I like to shake them, experience a little freedom." His voice was low, strained through the wool scarf. "They'll be here any second, though." He lowered the fabric and inhaled deeply. My skin chilled. "What shall we do to pass the time, Tam? It's not often we're both allowed this close to one another unprotected."

He pressed forward, his chest now inches from mine. The brick wall snagged on my cloak and the distant smoke melted into the air, leaving only his form towering above me.

Movement from the far side of the alleyway caught my attention. A flash of light upon silver spurs. He had to see this, it was the temptation I needed. One of the two of them had to die.

I steeled myself, leaning closer to the prince. His lips parted, his breath warming the space between us. I reached again for the magic, but it stayed hidden, coiling deep inside me.

My breath hitched as he closed the gap. I should pull away, this was too close, too real, but my body was trapped, anesthetized, as he hovered so close I could almost taste him.

Panicked footsteps echoed down the alleyway, the distant clink of spurs fading as they grew louder. Two guards rounded the far corner and even from this distance I recognized Clement's lithe form. The hold snapped, and I slipped away from the prince, tugging my hood back up.

I darted around the corner, hurrying back in the direction I'd come, wiping my mouth as I went. We'd come so close to kissing, I could still feel his breath condensed on my lips. Why had my magic failed me? I flung out a hand to steady myself on the wall as my head spun. I'd gone too far. I wasn't in control, my head wasn't in the game. That must be it because it had never happened before.

Mt stomach twisted as I remembered it was Clement who had almost caught us. Of all people, I did not want him to have seen. I forced my feet to move again. The alley spit back onto the main street, and I ran toward the castle, my cloak flapping around my legs. And oh, if Siobhan had seen me? I stumbled, slapping my thighs angrily to force the weakness out. Goddess above, she'd have flayed me alive and thrown me onto the bonfire.

The castle gates sprang into view, the sentinel gargoyle watching my every move as I darted underneath and toward the servant's entrance. I had to find the Sherriff. My magic would work on him. It had too. But the prince? I grasped at it again, trying to draw it back from the depths. It didn't feel like it withdrew because my heart wasn't in it or because I wasn't concentrating. There was an uneasiness to it that curled ribbons of nausea through my stomach. It was like it was hiding.

Scared.

I walked through the castle unseeing, mildly surprised when I arrived at Lilyanna's door without any detours. Matron whisked past me without so much as a goodnight. She'd kept the fire stoked, even more thoroughly than I usually did. The flames roared, consuming the entire hearth, and blackening the marble ledge above.

I settled down outside Lilyanna's door and tugged my duvet down from the chaise. I stared into the fire until my eyes unfocused, the dancing figures blurring into a whirlwind. A shadow passed over the room, licking at my skin like silk, and I blinked when the familiar market scene from my childhood appeared.

Bales were piled around the edges, wisps of loose straw chased by the wind tumbled across the packed dirt floor. The stalls were bare, crushed against the edges of the square. The same people who attended week after week gathered around a central stage. The plinth was newly erected. The wood slats creaked in the breeze, the coils of rope hanging from the beam were pristine, the waxed edges shiny against the matt of the gray sky.

I froze at the back, my feet unwilling to get any closer. Despite the distance between me and the stage, I had a direct view like the crowd parted just for me.

Five people were herded toward the gallows bound by rope like a line of waddling ducklings. Each hesitant footfall was magnified by the silence, the crack of the stairs snapping through the thin air. Ropes came down and were tied securely at the nape of their necks. They all looked the same. Terrified.

"One of them is innocent," Siobhan breathed.

Bile shot into my throat. "Then why aren't you helping them?"

She patted my arm, sliding into position behind me. Her face lowered, and she pressed her warm cheek against my clammy one. "They haven't asked my dear. Choose wisely, for if you get it right, you'll be rewarded, and I'll let the innocent one go."

I swallowed and scanned the faces again.

"Oh, and one of them murdered your parents. See if you can tell who. Don't get it wrong or they may walk free instead. Perhaps then you won't miss a detail so important again, will you?"

I'd replayed the night my parents were murdered over and over in my mind. I had missed things, all the signs of their panic, their preparation at hiding from the oncoming foe. The door had not just been latched but bolted. Knives were removed from the kitchen and placed under pillows. The shutters crashed against the windowpanes in the storm because they'd been pulled closed, instead of their usual position lying flat against the walls.

At any time, I could've realized and stayed awake to help keep guard. It didn't matter that I was a child, just one more person defending our home could have made all the difference. And so, I absorbed every droplet of information Siobhan fed to me like a leech, willing it never to happen again.

I focused back on the five people. Three men and two women. The first had his face upturned, pleading to the Goddess. Not him. The next two had their eyes closed, swaying in the gusting wind, their bodies relaxed. They'd made peace with the decision—not them. The next woman trembled, chest heaving, eyes fixed on a small knot of silently weeping people in the crowd, but there was a rigidity in her spine and in the way she planted her boots. She wasn't sorry.

I stared at her, unable to tear my eyes away. It must have been her.

Eventually, I choked down my sob and focused. The last man had tears streaming down his face, carving white lines in the dirt. He kept his chin high, stubbornly refusing to meet the pleas of the woman in the crowd directly in front of him. He didn't want her there, didn't want her to suffer, didn't want her to think he was guilty.

"You've chosen?" Her words brushed against my cheek.

The gallows creaked as the large wheel turned, and the floor began to open.

I nodded toward the man at the end. Siobhan pulled back, lips skimming my hair, her hand remaining on my arm.

The last man's face morphed into chestnut coiffed hair and a flash of dimples before my eyes. I'd nodded toward the prince, decided to save him. Decided he was innocent.

The floor collapsed and all five people plunged into the opening.

A ripple passed over the crowd. The woman at the front dove under the stage, golden hair flashing in the sickly sunlight. She flung herself around the prince who had smacked into the dirt floor, the rope uncoiling from the beam. The other four swung in the breeze above.

Siobhan turned me around, and we walked from the market. "They'll say the Goddess saved him. He'll be forgiven of his accused crimes."

Relief weakened my legs, and Siobhan's arm tightened around my waist. "So, I chose correctly? It was the woman who was the murderer, right?"

She giggled. "We'll never know, my dear. But that's half the fun, is it not?"

I dragged myself back to the present. The marble floor was cool beneath me, the flames burning high in the hearth. Maybe my magic had faltered because it was protecting me. It knew I wasn't fully committed. The clear night, the effigy, the hunting of magic, not to mention Siobhan's presence.

Yes, Siobhan. It was her fault.

She was testing me to make sure I wanted it enough. She had dragged me back here to my hometown when I'd spent so many years avoiding any association with the North and now, she was making me confront my memories, forcing my hand.

But did I want to destroy the prince? Shouldn't I find out if he was guilty before I added another tally to my list? The Sheriff was certainly guilty, he'd left a pile of bodies and heartache in his wake. He was the easier option, the one with less collateral damage.

I tugged the thin quilt up to my chin and kept focused on the hearth lost in thought until I finally fell asleep.

CHAPTER ELEVEN
THE GUISE OF A GIFT

LILYANNA AND I WERE LATE FOR BREAKFAST ONCE AGAIN. I THOUGHT I'D HAD THE route memorized, then somehow, we ended up taking the long way, passing through corridors we both swore we'd never seen before. But in a castle packed with identical slate gray walls and blurry high windows, everything seemed the same anyway. Goddess above, did I hate this place.

I sidled up to Clement who didn't even bother greeting me before his scolding. "You left your post again last night."

"Is that why you look so pleased to see me today? I bet you've been planning your verbal chastisement for the past few hours. Did you even get any sleep, or were you thinking of me all night?"

His hand moved to his saber. The obnoxiously boring rhythm of his fingers drummed into the silence.

I sighed. "Lilyanna made me, alright. I'm sure you obey orders you don't approve of all the time." He still didn't respond, just kept up that infuriating tapping on the diamond hilt. "Anyway, you took my weapon away. How am I supposed to guard her when I'm unarmed?" I wasn't about to mention the knives in my boots because he would whip those away in a heartbeat if he knew.

"Knives won't do you any good here." He finally glanced down at me, the smallest trickle of softening cutting through his dark stare. "The only thing that will is listening to my advice. Or leaving. Preferably both."

I grunted and focused back on the breakfast table. They couldn't even eat that much food between them. Lilyanna pecked at some things, but it was such a waste. If I were unleashed, I'd demolish everything from the smoked fish to the tomato tartlets.

The prince noted Clement and I had stopped talking and cleared his throat. Previously, he'd been silent, scanning an open paper in front of him. "I need to remind you, my dear, to stay inside the castle. There are still worrying developments occurring in my town. I have the best people hunting for the culprit, but I'd hate to have you put in danger." He directed his comment to Lilyanna, but his gaze attached to my face. "Only your maid is allowed out on errands. But, even so, I'm still concerned about both of your navigational skills. It appears that finding your way to and from the dining room still seems to be a little tricky."

She laughed. It was an easygoing, light noise, but I knew her better by now. Her shoulders stiffened, and she remained focused on her plate, pushing around small pieces of hash.

Was the prince irritated with me? We'd come so close to kissing. There was no doubt that was his intention. I didn't suspect people usually rejected his advances, and I'd literally turned tail and fled.

A knock sounded at the door, and Clement strode over. He had a brief conversation through the gap with Matron. Her ruby and diamond necklace caught the candlelight as she spoke, reflecting like dripping blood across her throat. He nodded and closed the door.

"My prince," he said. "There was a man seen loitering around the castle. He tried to enter via the servant's entrance, saying he wanted to speak with you and had information about the murders. Matron sent him on his way, and said he should contact the detective in town who will inform me if there is any merit to his advice."

The prince nodded. "I agree."

"And just so you know, it was the same man from the market. A newcomer to town. It could be nothing, maybe just trying his luck, but I'll have the castle guards stay on alert in case he returns."

My heart thumped against my ribcage. The Sheriff. It had to be.

The prince returned to his paper, and Lilyanna to pushing food around her plate. I shifted my weight, adrenaline firing through my body. I couldn't let him leave. He needed to see me, to know that I could get him access to the prince or at least had secrets to spill. He wouldn't be able to resist an opportunity like that.

"Clement," I whispered.

He frowned at me.

"I forgot to go to the kitchens and ask for afternoon tea to be sent up. Lilyanna sent me out the other day, and I got lost and completely forgot."

"Not surprising."

I ignored him. "Cover for me. I'll be back quickly, presuming I can find my way."

"No. I'm not going to cover for you, Tam. It's your...Tam!"

I slipped away and was out the door before he could finish. I hurried toward the kitchens and thankfully the corridors behaved themselves. The room was deserted as breakfast service was over. I snatched a stray teacake from the counter and swallowed it whole as I pushed through the servant's entrance.

The wind tore into me, slicing through my sweater and leggings. I kept my head down but my senses tightly focused as I hurried toward the gate. He would be lurking somewhere, observing who went in and out, cataloging faces, memorizing the castle routine. It's what I'd do, what I'd done, before Siobhan severed all the fun from my job.

I scowled, my concentration lapsing for only a second, but enough that I walked smack into the Sheriff.

"Oh, I'm sorry." I pushed off him, wishing I'd had the foresight to compel my magic to fire.

"Not your fault." His voice was smooth and low, exactly what I'd imagined after all this time. He took a step back, glancing toward the guard posted at the servant's door. "You look freezing. You shouldn't be out in this weather without a cloak." He wore the same peaked hat and wool cloak he had in the market, both pulled so tightly together only a sliver of his face was revealed.

"Yeah, I know. I was heading out to find it. I left it at the Nightingale, the inn in town. But it's probably best I borrow some outerwear and get it later."

Above us, the gargoyle hovered. Its face creaked toward me in the wind, the sunken diamond eyes sharp and alert in the stone face. The Sheriff didn't notice. Or perhaps the gargoyle always swiveled, silent as a weathervane.

Instead, he looked over my shoulder again, his body tensing. "Well, I may see you there. I needed a good recommendation for where to spend my night and to do so in the company of such a fine woman would be a treat."

I should've been flattered, but I doubt I was any more tempting than the hundreds of other women he'd been with. The guard posted at the door strode up behind me and I turned, knowing that as I did, the Sheriff vanished, the dull clinking of his spurs dying on the wind. The gargoyle above creaked back to stare through the gates toward the town.

Before the guard could speak, I hurried back inside. Hopefully, breakfast hadn't finished, or Clement would be even more irked than before. But it didn't matter, I had a date with my target. I'd been closer than ever before. Just so long as he didn't spook between now and this evening.

A sharp knock came at the door, and a note was kicked under the threshold. Clement was presumably still mad at me. Shame that it gave me a thrill of warmth whenever I thought of his hard eyes and perfectly tensed body. Irritation suited him down to a T.

Neither of us moved.

"You want me to get that, Your Ladyship?"

"Ouch." She pulled her finger away from the butterfly, sucking on the end.

I laughed and retrieved the note. *Dear Tam, I hope this is more to your liking. Your friend,* followed by an indecipherable signature. I shook the paper in case something else magically fell out and eventually opened the door. A petite blue box tied with a velvet ribbon was shoved up against the wall. I brought it inside.

The ribbons pooled to either side with the smallest tug at the bow. Lilyanna and I knelt over the box as I lifted the lid. A flat circular object with diamond-encrusted fob and buckle was sunk into a velvet pillow. The cap was solid gold, a small indentation present, which opened when Lilyanna lightly pressed it, revealing a glass face and quivering hands.

She cooed, but I sank back onto my heels, my hands clenched in my lap.

"Is this from Clement?" It was just like him to send me a passive-aggressive gift. "This is a timepiece, right? Because I can't get you anywhere on time."

"It's not for telling the time." She gently lifted it out, her lips slightly parted. "It's for direction and these are incredibly rare."

"Well, he's still an ass. Insinuating I can't navigate my way round this stupid place. Why don't you get one?" I glared at the compass in her hand, not wanting to touch it.

She patted my arm. "Because I have you." She placed it back on the velvet pillow and took the note from my hand, studying the writing. Her face hardened only for a flash, but it took great effort for her to smooth the frown lines embedded on her forehead before she spoke. "It's not from Clement, it's from the prince. That's his handwriting." She sniffed the paper and wafted it toward me. "And his scent."

I gagged at the strong rose odor.

She handed the note back, her face carefully plain. "There's more on the back. He wants you to go to his chambers at sundown. He says, 'it's east'."

"Why?" I glanced at her, but she ignored me.

She reached for the compass again, turning it over in her hands, the glass surface flashing in the firelight.

"Lilyanna, don't even think about it." I tore up the note and threw it into the hearth. The paper caught instantly, glowing skeletal white before vanishing in flame. "Why don't you come as well? You can tell him how much you like your gift. The butterfly. It's probably worth way more than this, and he handpicked it for you himself, I saw him. This was probably just an afterthought, a taunt for my inability to ferry you around in here."

My stomach twisted as I remembered how close we'd come to kissing last night. That was probably what he wanted to talk about. Matron had insinuated as much when I first arrived, though she'd thought he wouldn't be interested in me. In that moment in the alleyway, I'd wanted to kiss him. My mind had emptied, my mission totally erased, but something wasn't right.

I shivered as the sensation returned of my magic fleeing, hiding deep inside my soul and leaving me empty. I pushed it away. I didn't need yet another weakness, but I did need to locate his room. I'd wished that just the other night.

Perhaps the goddess of fate was helping me after all.

She dropped the compass back into the box. "No, I should be getting to bed." She turned and strode toward the bedroom, swiping the butterfly from the checkerboard as she went.

I sighed and lifted the compass to buckle it to my waistband, tugging the sweater down so that the fabric covered the flashy diamond fob. I might as well get this over with, then I could work on soothing Lilyanna's ego.

I glanced at the glass face when outside her room, but the delicate hands did nothing except quiver. So, I walked down the barren corridors keeping straight until the stone floor ceded to wooden planks and the temperature plummeted.

As I walked, soft scratching followed overhead. Glancing over my shoulder, a thin trail of ash billowed from the ceiling, coating the floor in a perfectly straight line. A trail of breadcrumbs illuminating my way back? There was no way I would trust in following it. It would be easy for it to suddenly veer down a corridor, or for the walls to switch positions and con me into descending into the belly of the castle.

Burned orange light flickered beneath a door up ahead. The wood frame stood as plain as every other here, and yet, I instinctively knew it was his. The magic slunk deeper, hiding away in the furrows of my body. I shoved my hands under my armpits, biting back a shiver and kicked at the door with my foot.

The prince opened it and ushered me in with a small bow. I made it about a foot before freezing, my body locking into position. Some inner warning blared inside me. Clement and Bryn materialized at the prince's elbows.

"Thank you for coming, Tam. I assumed you found my note?" He wore a black bathrobe, his chestnut hair wet and tousled. Steam rose from his body as if he were a supernatural being. The rose scent subdued, a moist, unplaceable aroma having taken its place.

I nodded.

"I had to postpone dinner this evening as I had a most pressing engagement. I wish for you to extend my apologies to the Lady Lilyanna."

"Alright. You could've said that in your note as well."

Clement inched taller, sucking in his stomach muscles. I tried not to look at him. Tension rolled off him in waves, threatening to infect me too. A small kernel of disappointment solidified in my stomach. I wished he'd given me the gift.

The prince grinned, his dimples popping. "Where's the fun in that? Besides, I wanted to see if you liked your present." His eyes dropped to my thigh, probing beneath the hemline of my sweater.

I brushed back the fabric, tugging out the compass so the gold case winked in the glow from the fire. "I do, actually."

"Good." He clapped his hands together. "And do you know how to work it?"

Heat crawled into my face, coloring the tips of my ears. "Yes."

He smiled. "You need to activate it with a tap from a specific stone. The castle is lined with basaltic rock mixed with slate, so you'll have a constant supply so long as you stay close. And now you know where to find me as well!" He waved an arm behind him.

My skin prickled. Had I wondered that out loud the other night? I'd been close when I'd stopped and saw the Sheriff out of the window, but I didn't get the same tug as I did tonight. Perhaps he hadn't been in his room.

Clement cleared his throat, a frown etched onto his face. The prince noted his expression and laughed, clapping him on the shoulder. "My regular guards have the night off for their monthly debauchery. They're keen to get started, and I do believe I am keeping them."

I snorted before I could stop myself, clamping my hand over my mouth. I couldn't picture either of them doing anything remotely risqué. *Debauchery.* I snickered, and Clement drilled me with a glare. Goddess-damn me, but he was so sexy when he was irritated. Perhaps he'd take that attitude into the bedroom. Throw me over his knee, give me a light spanking...

Clement snapped his fingers in front of my nose, and I jumped, wiping the disgusting grin from my face. His dark eyes glinted only for a second, but it was enough to send heat pulsing through me all over again.

"Okay, well, enjoy your evening, everyone." I ducked my head and backed away. "I'll smooth things over with Lilyanna for you."

Clement escorted me to the door and said in a low voice that sent tingles feathering up my thighs, "The offer is open to you as well, Tam. If you're open to *debauchery.*"

I hurried back down the corridor, unable to resist throwing a smirk back at Clement. Aiming straight, I ignored the smear of ash along the floor. Tempting as Clement's offer was, this would be the perfect night to find the Sheriff. The guards were off duty, and the prince was holed up in his room. Lilyanna was shut in her own bedchamber in a fabricated huff. No one would know if I slipped out of the castle.

Most importantly, no one would be able to pin the crime on me.

CHAPTER TWELVE
THE FIRST SCRATCH IS THE DEEPEST

I SQUASHED MY BEDDING OUTSIDE LILYANNA'S DOOR AND THEN CRAMMED ONE OF the plump armchairs in front as well. It wasn't much of a barrier, but it'd have to do. Hopefully, Clement wouldn't be at the tavern tonight, or he'd spend the time admonishing me about leaving my post.

More importantly, I'd need to make sure no one recognized me or could associate me with the Sheriff.

My cloak had been freshly washed and hung from a solitary hook on the back of my door. It smelled faintly of roses, but still enough to make me gag. I slipped out and headed toward the kitchens.

The castle wasn't fully silent. An energy hummed below the surface, the air thick and expectant. The walls were behaving tonight, no noises, no obstructions. It was as if the castle knew I would be returning and was content with allowing me passage to the outside. To freedom.

The penetrating cold air of the street hit me full in the face as I slipped out of the servant's entrance. The guard paid me no attention as I huddled inside my cloak with the hood low and my hands wrapped around my body for warmth. My worn boots were silent as I padded down the cobblestone street, glancing up at the creaking wooden signs as I passed.

Every other house was a tavern of some kind. The first had a smoky-red glow to the window, a lipstick smeared sign reading *'women only.'* Another had thick, mottled glass. The shapes inside were distorted, but strangely erotic as they glided around, merging into one another. A faint, seductive beat vibrated the floor as I passed.

The Diamond Nightingale was disappointingly plain. Like every public house I'd ever visited, the windows were dirty and smeared and the sign above clung on by only one hinge. But the comfortably familiar smell of wood smoke, rich ale, and meat pies lingered in the air. My mouth watered.

A few meager coppers bounced around in my pocket amid the collection of small silver rings I had worn at the fayre. I slipped one on, tugged my hood lower over my face, and pushed open the door.

The roaring heat from the fire swarmed around me, rowdy conversations and the chinking of glasses suddenly booming into life. Games of dice were in full swing on the rickety central tables, men and women perching on the edge of long benches, craning their bodies over the die, their arms hovering ready to snatch their winnings.

Dice was a game of luck. I'd grown up playing and had lost years of earnings failing at it, until I realized that even luck could be forced.

I kept my hood over my face and walked to the bar. A glass with strong, brown ale was plonked in front of me, the liquid swishing up the sides, and I slid two coppers back across. Leaning against the rough countertop, I surveyed the room.

The Sheriff's boots were the most notable thing about him. He changed his face regularly—hair color, beard, moustache, skin tone. I knew most of his disguises, but most importantly, I knew his addiction. The one thing he could never turn down. Information.

If I'd played it right in the market by setting myself up as the prince's mistress, then he would be seeking *me* out tonight. There was no need to admit it had almost really happened.

I twisted the silver ring on my finger. It was heavy and irritating, causing my fingers to spread further than was natural. A cheer went up from the closest table. Three die each showed only one spot. A woman noisily raked the collection of coppers and oddities from the center of the table, scraping them into the gaping mouth of her purse.

The players shuffled around the circular table, a lithe man taking position at the head. His dark beard crawled down his neck, a full day's growth coating his chin and cheeks. His eyes were bright, posture relaxed, and underneath the sapphire tunic, a perfectly honed torso waited. My pulse accelerated, my body flushing both hot and cold.

Clement.

He scooped up the dice, cupping his hand around them and blew. They rattled, clinking together before he threw them across the table. While his eyes followed their tumbling progress, I slipped away from the bar and squashed myself into the far corner.

His back tensed in a brief reminder of his usual erect posture and for a split second, I thought he'd sensed me. Then he sighed, stooping with relief. A few patrons around the table whistled. A young man sidled closer, his hand resting lightly upon Clement's shoulder.

I lowered my face into my drink, unable to stop myself from glaring at that man's hand. If he knew I was here, would Clement turn his attention to me? Perhaps have me blow good luck onto the dice, a faint blush painting his cheekbones beneath that enticing stubble as my lips brushed his knuckles and our gazes sparked...

No. I had to behave. Clement found me infuriating, or so he said. He'd probably flee back to the prince, ratting me out for leaving my post without setting anyone to watch Lilyanna. And I had a job to do.

The dice were scooped up, returned, and in the brief pause while odds were calculated and purses weighed, the *clink, clink, clink* I was waiting for sounded. I clenched my fingers around the half-empty drink, the silver ring scratching the glass.

The Sheriff carried a void around him. I'd never gotten close enough before, but I'd heard the tales. He didn't smell of anything, didn't particularly look like anyone familiar, but if he let you near, people were sucked in. Once you penetrated that inner circle, you were bound. A kind of magic perhaps, or just well-crafted charm.

My knuckles blanched, and I rested the glass on the narrow table in front of me as sweat condensed on my palm.

"Quite the night." The Sheriff eased himself onto the bench beside me. He crossed one leg over the other, the silver spurs flashing in the firelight.

There was no need to be subtle. He'd spotted me the moment he entered the room, a dog on a scent. It's what I did.

"Can I get you a drink?" I moved toward my pocket, but he gripped my sleeve. His thumb slid over my wrist, massaging my pounding pulse.

"No need to be nervous." His fingers slid down my hand, and he tapped the ring on my finger. "Unless you're being watched?"

Clement threw the dice again and hissed low. The man's hand dropped from his shoulder, and Clement moved to the side as another took his place. He glanced toward my corner, and I flicked my attention back to the Sheriff, but his gaze burned through my hood.

"Husband?" The Sheriff leaned back against the wall, his arm resting on the window ledge with his body still turned to me. His blond hair was long and tied at the nape of his neck, face pale, but full. Not the look of a man who had been running from half the bounty hunters in the country for years.

"Brother-in-law," I whispered.

"He's not particularly good at dice."

"He doesn't know how to gamble."

The Sheriff's gaze snapped back to me, one side of his mouth tipping up. He leaned forward, his other hand swiftly moving aside the folds of my cloak to rest on my thigh. "Does he always watch you this closely?" His gray eyes moved back and forth between mine. The gap between us narrowed and his breath washed over me—tasteless, odorless, an unknown.

"He likes to remind me of my duty." I gulped down the rest of the ale, grateful for the giddy rush of warmth that bloomed under my skin.

The Sheriff's hand slid up my thigh, squeezing my loosening muscles. "He wishes you were his."

I shrugged. My face was still turned, my clothing unidentifiable.

Clement shouldn't recognize me, but still, my gut twisted. "Is he looking?"

"He can't take his eyes off you, but that's half the fun." He winked. "Two more, I think." He strode to the bar, his shoulders pulled back, confidence palpable.

I kept my face turned to the side, but I knew Clement clocked his every step.

The Sheriff handed me another ale, and I buried my face in it, cursing the blush rising up my neck.

He turned back to me, angling his body so I was partially hidden, his hand returning to my upper thigh. His fingers stroked small circles as he talked, creeping tantalizingly higher. "So, I noticed that the prince buys you gifts?"

My answer was incoherent as he gently brushed my crease. My body pulsed in anticipation.

"How many women does he have on the go?"

"He's currently unattached," my reply was slightly breathless. "So, as many as he wants."

"And your brother-in-law doesn't like that."

"He doesn't like a lot of things."

His fingers swirled again, and I took another deep drink.

"They're very tight-lipped at the castle. It's good to find someone who will talk. This town too, it's full of secrets."

"The murdered women? Were they linked to the deaths of the prince's fiancées?" Did I sound too eager? My head lightened as the ale sloshed through my system.

"If you're worried about your position in the castle, that is, you should be safe. All the women had something in common, either wealth, or rare jewels, or magic. However, when the prince was banished up here by the queens, there were rumors of one too many bodies piling up that even the palace couldn't sweep under the rug." His fingers continued to circle, tearing my focus from his words.

"That's not what the prince told me," I said. "He'd said he left to forge his own path, to escape his royal duties." Had I fallen for it? For him, so easily?

"I can imagine. I have a lot of ready information, and I'm always eager to trade, but I need access to the prince."

So, he was after my bounty. I should be furious, at least territorial, but his hand was so warm, his fingers so enticing. Perhaps the Sheriff wasn't telling the whole truth. He obviously had an ulterior motive.

I leaned in, expecting to taste the ale on his breath but only mine lingered between us. "And what do *I* get for all this information?"

The Sheriff grinned. "I'll show you." He took my hand and lifted me to my feet. He strode toward the back of the inn, and I followed, my palm sweaty in his. I kept my head turned away from the game in the center of the room. Would Clement notice?

The Sheriff dropped my hand, and I wiped it on my cloak as we entered the hallway. Spurs clinking, he climbed the wooden stairs to the third floor. Running one hand along the floral wallpaper as we rose, he hummed a jaunty tune, never once turning back to check if I followed.

He knew he had me.

Maybe Clement wouldn't care. He'd just think I had found my own entertainment for the evening. As long as I made it back before he could check on me, it would be fine. He wouldn't see the aftermath, and I couldn't be blamed if I was tucked up back in front of Lilyanna's door staring at the gaping hearth. I shook the nerves from my system. I couldn't let the mere sight of him unsettle me. He was probably only watching my movements out of professional curiosity. It was his job to know everything going on in or around the castle, which extended to me.

The floorboards creaked, the aisle undulating slightly beneath my feet. The Sheriff stopped at the first open door and held it open. As I moved past him, he leaned into me, pinning me against the frame with his hot body flush against mine.

"Your brother-in-law works at the castle too?"

I nodded. "Prince's personal bodyguard."

His lips closed on mine, groin hardening against my stomach. "I live for challenges like that," he whispered, freeing my mouth for just long enough to hear my moan of agreement.

He rolled me around the door frame and flattened me against the wall. The door snicked shut, its lock snapping into place. He tore open my cloak, and I tugged the tunic over his head, throwing the fabric into the corner. He worked his mouth down my face, my neck, my chest, his hands roving under my shirt in perfect synchrony.

Goddessdamn was he good. He was a professional. No wonder someone wanted retribution. I freed his belt, an assortment of knives clanging to the floor and my ring caught against the light hair on his chest as I moved upward.

"Sorry," I panted. "I should take this off. Wouldn't want to scratch you."

He grasped my wrists and held them above my head, pressing me back against the wall. "Keep it on."

Good as he was, I had a sudden image of Clement in front of me. He'd take his time, working his way systematically through every pleasure point in my body. A welcome heat pushed lower into my abdomen.

The Sheriff regained my focus, tugging the rest of my clothes off and letting my undergarments pool on the floor by my feet. I stood with the gummy wallpaper molding to my back, dim moonlight illuminating my naked body while he stood back. His gray eyes travelled slowly down my breasts, tracing an invisible line to my stomach, my skin tingling as if he were running his tongue across me.

His erection throbbed, and he took himself in hand, stroking slowly while his gaze penetrated every inch of me. Heat pulsed between my legs, wetness seeping down my thighs.

Sometimes I *really* loved my job.

"I can taste you from here." He licked his lips, moisture beading on the slick surface.

"I'd rather you tasted me here." I tilted my hips, arching my back to allow him full view of me.

Lust shone in his eyes, his face breaking into that mischievous grin that I'd followed around the country. He had me. He wanted me, but it was my turn first.

He grabbed my hips, lifting me up and onto him. I wound my thighs around his waist, sinking deep upon his shaft. His mouth covered mine, swallowing my moan. I threaded my fingers through his hair, my nails tingling as I gently scratched his scalp.

Not enough to bleed, not yet.

He thrust harder, my back pounding against the wall. Magic swirled through my veins, setting my nerves on fire.

I was losing control.

Pressure built deep within me, my senses numbing to everything except the heat, the sweat, the pleasure.

He took my breast in his mouth, working my erect nipple between his teeth, and I was done.

I was his.

I threw my head back as he dug his teeth into my skin, sucking and tugging while he speared me deeper. I screamed as the fire within me burst, clinging onto just enough sense to realize I'd dug my nails into his back. There was no hesitation this time as my magic released.

He pulsed inside me, matching my intensity, oblivious to the blood trickling down his sweat-soaked skin. He leaned against me, my body still wrapped against his with the wall supporting us both. His panting breaths were sticky on my neck, his fingers still clutching my thighs.

Eventually he carried me to the bed. We both lay sprawled on top of the tatty cover, neither of us wanting to burrow beneath the sheets amongst the stains of hundreds of others. Within minutes he was asleep, a soft snore rocking his body.

How does this happen? I'd never understood how someone could sleep in front of another, especially a stranger. I ran my finger down the smooth contour of his face, traced the curve of his damp lips. He was so vulnerable like this.

I smiled.

The magic inside me dimmed, my muscles loose, my body deliciously achy. How long could I stay? Perhaps I too could sleep. Trust him just enough. As long as I awoke before him, it would be okay.

Maybe he was waiting for me to rest. What would he take for his token other than the free information? Maybe a lock of my hair? Or perhaps he would snoop through my pockets to find some kind of memento that would allow him to track me later. He may just be planning to use Clement as his source. Blackmailing the most influential party involved would be a smart move.

Although, if it was blackmail he was setting up for and that's why he wanted access to the prince, perhaps the prince *was* involved in the murders. If he was running from a mounting pile of rumors from the South like the Sheriff had said, perhaps he couldn't help himself but to continue up here. Maybe the Sheriff hadn't been hired by another party but came the old-fashioned way, by following the evidence trail. But any proof of those claims was about to be destroyed by the trackers I'd unleashed into his system. I'd need to either believe the Sheriff, a known criminal, or continue believing in the prince, who hadn't shown any signs of hiding a darker part of himself.

I spun the fake wedding band around my finger, watching the steady rise and fall of his chest. The blond hair trailing down his stomach darkened in the gloom. Perhaps Clement had a similar trail? Pure black. Pure power. As dark and dangerous as his eyes.

The faint tinkling of a bell sounded. An innocent set of chimes caught in the wind but a reminder that the Collectors would soon arrive. They'd sense I'd implanted the trackers and released my magic.

I couldn't see them. I'd successfully avoided them for almost two decades. It was hard at first, especially when I was young. They'd bound me to this life, used me in their deal with Siobhan, but I still wanted to see them. Wanted to relive my life, their lives, to return to what we had before magic and death swallowed us. But my spite over what they'd done, and my lingering common sense, always moved me on before they arrived. It was better that way.

I rolled out of bed and dressed swiftly, taking one of the daggers from his belt on the floor and slipping it into my thigh holster. I pulled the cloak back around me and dropped the hood. The Sheriff had not moved. How long had I lain and watched him? Twenty minutes? Thirty? An hour?

The door whispered shut, the floorboards creaking as I crept back downstairs. The inn was still in full swing. Dice clinking, drinks being poured. The fire crackled, filling the room with smoke and cloying heat.

I passed quickly. There was no suspicious glare from Clement as he monitored the stairs and no sign of his tapping foot as he stood vigil in the hallway waiting to pounce. He must have already left. My shoulders sagged. Goddessdamn me, I was weakening already.

Friends, just friends. Or at the very least, he was just a method of access for my bounty. Maybe he hadn't recognized me after all, which was a good thing, so why did a rush of disappointment cause my shoulders to slump? In fact, it was lucky he'd gone back to the castle in case Lilyanna needed anything. If he asked where I'd been, I could pretend I had wandered to the kitchens to get a snack and got lost, leaving her side for barely a moment. He had no proof to the contrary anyway. I nodded to myself, purging any feelings of sadness.

As I walked back to the castle, I rubbed my fingertips. The Sheriff's dried blood fell like snow upon the cobbles. No evidence. No association.

No guilt.

The guard let me in without any questions, and I returned to my room. The door was still closed, the fire burning in the hearth. I tossed my cloak on the bed and ascended the spiral stairs to Lilyanna's room.

The temperature shifted as I opened the door. Subtle at first, a cool breeze rushing out, but as I stepped inside her room, the air froze my breath. White puffs of cloud illuminated the darkness before me.

The fire was out, its embers not even smoldering. I crossed quickly and grabbed more wood from the pile to thrust on top. How had it burned through so quickly?

Once it lit and I had blown the cloying, black smog up the chimney, I sat back on my heels and turned slowly around.

A winding trail of soot like a tail or dragged limb, marked a path from the hearth to Lilyanna's open door. My bedding and the chair had been thrust aside, both covered with sooty smears.

I jumped up, freeing the stolen knife from my thigh and leaped for her room.

CHAPTER THIRTEEN
THE CHOKER

Lilyanna lay flat on her back, arms cinched by her sides and her legs extended like she was in rigor.

I ran to her side and shook her, eliciting a small rattle as air wheezed through her clenched teeth. The silken sheets were wrapped around her body so tightly her chest barely moved. The edge dug into her neck, bruises mottling the pale skin underneath. Her lips were tinged blue, a solitary globule of saliva crusted to the edge of her mouth.

I shook her again. "Lilyanna, wake up!" Where was the end of the sheet? It appeared fused to her body as if she'd made the cocoon herself and would stay in there until she rotted.

Pushing my fingers as far under the sheet at her neck as I could, I sliced with the knife, the fabric ripping easily with the pressure. She gasped.

I shook her again, slapping her chest. "Wake up!"

Her eyelids fluttered open, her pupils obscuring the whole eye. She coughed, her body shuddering under the sheet.

"Hold still, I need to unwrap you." I rolled her onto her front, finding the seam and shook her out.

"What are you doing?" she murmured, her voice hoarse.

"What in Goddess's name are you doing?" I helped her into a seated position and scooted her back against the wooden frame. English ivy was carved into the headboard, its tendrils almost pulsing in the weak light. "You were literally dying. Didn't you feel yourself trapped?"

She rubbed her throat. Angry red slashes encircled her neck, the flesh between storm cloud gray. "I was dreaming." She pointed a trembling finger toward the carafe of water on the dressing table. I filled a glass for her and she sipped, wincing as the cold water sloshed down her tender throat. "The prince and I had just married, and the price of gold skyrocketed. My province was flourishing and to celebrate, they sent me a gown woven from pure gold. It wound from my neck to my ankles, hugging my body, reminding me of the joyful future to come."

"Well, I can tell you it would not have been a joyful ending if I hadn't burst in." I took her empty glass, refilled it for myself, and drained the water in one gulp.

Lilyanna turned toward the dark window, the thick pane blocking even more light than usual. "Do you think it's a sign?"

"Yes. Yes, I fucking do. I don't know how much more obvious you want it to be. How many accidents can you have before you realize something is out to get you? Squashed by chunks of the ceiling, burned alive by a sconce, or choked to death in your own bed. It's a sign. Get out." I gasped for breath, my heart hammering.

"Maybe." She stroked her throat, her eyes finally meeting mine. "Will you sleep in here for the rest of the night?"

"Oh." I looked at the tangled bedsheet, the carved vines on the headboard and the ashen-faced young women propped up like a doll. "Well, I don't think it would be appropriate…"

"It's an order."

I snorted. "I don't think you can order me around."

"It's your job."

"I just saved your life."

She slid down until her head rested upon the matching white pillow, her blonde hair matted and wild and pointed to the space beside her.

"I won't be able to sleep." I filled another glass of water. The adrenaline had ebbed, the magic in my veins completely disappeared, and my body screamed to rest. It wouldn't begin to regenerate until the morning. Although, I did prefer the emptiness, the solitude and the calm left in its wake. I sighed. "Do you need me to tuck you in as well, Your Ladyship?"

"Seeing as you're already up, I doubt it would inconvenience you greatly."

I grunted and flapped the sheets over the bed. It settled like a starved ghost, clinging to her form. I slid in beside her, keeping my arms firmly wedged on top of the covers and the cold surface far from my neck.

Lilyanna rolled onto her side and leaned toward me. "Since we're having a sleepover, I have so many questions for you. I want to know everything about you, Tam, and I'll tell you everything about me. It'll be so much fun!"

I grimaced. "I don't think—"

"I'm joking." She laughed softly, but it caught in her throat, and she coughed in my face until the fit had passed.

"We'll talk about this again in the morning." A heavy silence fell between us. "Okay, goodnight then." I turned back and fixated on the ceiling. Lilyanna's rhythmic breaths tickled my neck with warm air almost instantly. Every inhale produced a delicate wheeze, but at least I knew she was still alive. Perhaps I could slip out when she fell into a deep sleep and resume my position on the floor by her door.

I turned back to her, propping myself onto an elbow and studied the smooth contours of her face. What was she doing here? I hardly knew her, yet I couldn't bear to hear about her grisly murder spouted as idle gossip in town. If I left her, that would surely happen. When had history ever changed? None of the prince's fiancées had made it up the aisle so far. She knew this. What was she playing at? How could she believe that effigies and tea leaves would lead her to succeed when every other woman failed?

I sighed softly, the weight of responsibility settling onto my soul. Was this what it was like to have a little sister? Did I just have to sit here and watch her make a fatal mistake?

I edged away from her, but she grunted, flinging an arm out and over me. Men never gave me this kind of trouble when I wanted to escape their beds. Clement, however, would probably be quite watchful. I bet no one ever slipped out of his bed without him knowing. *Stupid Clement.*

Night took forever to fall away. The windowpane eventually clouded gray, the pre-dawn light unable to penetrate the thick clouds that congealed overnight in the sky. I scanned every inch of the ceiling, alert for even the smallest scratch, but the castle slept soundly.

The kitchens should be alive by now, pots clanking, grease sizzling on the stove. Matron should be marching up and down the corridors, dusting shadows and shaking out rugs, but this room was a vacuum. The only sound was Lilyanna's soft breath. Even the storm building outside and the rain lashing against the stone walls were deadened.

I wriggled out from under Lilyanna's warm arm and padded toward the lounge. Once out of the bedroom, a sharp rapping sounded on the door. I crossed over and opened it to a very irritated-looking Clement. His fist was still raised, caught mid-knock, and he looked as if he were about to muscle shoulder-first through the door.

Perhaps it was worry instead that lined his face and clawed his hands into fists?

"What do you want?" I said.

"Good morning to you, too." He exhaled slowly, running his hand down his face. The wrinkles across his brow and the sag to his cheeks remained. His stubble was even longer today, it wouldn't be long before I could twine my fingers through it. He eyed me too. "You look awful, Tam."

I groaned and went to shut the door, but he shoved his foot in the way. His now familiar pine scent washed over me, but it was mixed with sweat. Was he nervous?

"Didn't you get any sleep?" he asked.

"I slept like a dog." I folded my arms, not ceding my position in the doorway.

"You mean with one."

I scowled. So, he did know. Heat itched up my neck and stained my cheeks. "What do you want?" I nodded toward the items crammed under his arm, two boxes and a rolled-up newspaper.

He extracted the paper and tossed it at me. "Page two."

I opened it with a crack and flipped quickly. A handsome man gazed demurely out from amongst the text. The black and white image didn't do justice to the long blond hair he had pulled back in a ponytail, nor the slim frame hidden beneath a tailored jacket. The caption read: *Prolific Lothario, dubbed 'The Sheriff' found brutally murdered in the town of Bellinor*. My stomach seized. My eyes locked upon the words.

Clement reached forward and gently took the paper back. "I'll summarize for you. He was found alone in a room at the Diamond Nightingale early this morning. His body had been shredded. His entrails...disemboweled. There was so much damage that the cause of death could not be ascertained."

Acid crept up my throat. At least the scratches were hidden.

"I didn't do it," I said.

"You were the last to be seen with him."

"I was here all night." I swallowed. I clamped down on my thigh muscles, trying to stop the tremors that fired through me.

"Do you want to read the preliminary coroner's report? They're having a special doctor brought in who deals with this level of torture to confirm. As head of the castle guards, I attended the autopsy so I could be prepared to issue a threat warning for the prince."

"I don't want to know." I sucked in air, trying desperately to dilute the vomit swirling at the back of my throat.

"Tam." His voice softened. He leaned closer, his hand gently tipping up my chin. "Look at me." I swallowed down another mouthful of bile. "I know you're lying."

"I didn't do it!"

"I saw you there last night, with *him*. And in the market, you were the one to warn me. I know you know him." He shook the paper at me. "But there is no mention of that and there never will be. Why do you think I'd tell?"

I didn't answer.

His thumb stroked my cheek, and he sighed. "If you're in trouble, if you're next, tell me."

I pulled out of his grasp. "There's nothing to tell. I wasn't there."

I'd paid my debt. I'd done my part. I just had to keep it together until I could find Siobhan—who usually found me anyway—and wheedle my way out of tagging the prince. Even if the Sheriff was right, and he was involved in the murders, or hunting those with my kind of magic, it really wasn't my problem. This was why I should have kept out of it and why I should be halfway across the country on my well-deserved break. I shouldn't be responsible for assassinating the crowned prince for Goddess's sake.

I gritted my teeth. I should've called for Siobhan straight away last night, but then those murderous sheets distracted me. Lilyanna would go too now that she'd been almost strangled—I'd make her—and we could leave this creepy-as-fuck castle behind us.

"I wish you would trust me." Clement's hand balled into a fist; his muscles locked tight. "Aren't I your *friend*?" He infused the word with such a girly intonation that I snorted, pulled from my stampeding thoughts. He relaxed an inch, a shadow of a smile tugging at the corners of his mouth.

"Is that all you want to be, Clement?" He froze again, his dark eyes glued on mine. Tension warmed the air between us and my stomach twisted for a different reason.

"I think you might be a little more than I can handle." He swallowed, his teeth crushing his lower lip. The distance between us narrowed. "Besides, I would like to keep my intestines inside my body."

I pushed him away, noting how firm his chest was despite myself. "Goddess damn you, I didn't do it."

He grinned and my heart lurched. "Here." He handed over the two small boxes. Both were wrapped in a golden ribbon and surprisingly heavy. "It's for the dinner this afternoon. Specially requested by the prince."

"I'll give them to Lilyanna when she wakes up."

"The smaller one is yours."

I rattled it. "I don't wear jewelry."

"You wore a wedding ring last night." I gaped at him. How did he notice everything? "And it's from the prince. It's not a request." He rocked back on his heels preparing to leave. "Also, just a warning, Tam, it's going to be weird."

"Why?"

He shrugged. "Any time the guards and the servants"—I scowled at the word 'servant' in reference to me—"are invited to a celebratory feast, rather than just watching from the edges, it's awkward. Just..." He took a deep breath, his head cocked to the side as he scrutinized me. "Try to go unnoticed by the prince, okay? For all our sakes?"

"I'm not sure I can—"

"And next time," he turned to leave, his voice floating down the corridor, "maybe you should take me up on *my* offer of a night out. You'd get into less trouble."

"I'm not in any trouble," I yelled after him.

"Yet."

I rolled my eyes at the empty hallway. I closed the door and peeked my head in to check Lilyanna was still sleeping and hadn't overheard. The sheets lay flat where I'd left them and her soft breathing, broken by an occasion wheeze, was consistent. Outside the thick window, a stray ray of sunlight broke through the swirling clouds and tickled the gargoyle's face. It shifted, its hollow eyes staring directly at me. I shivered and backed away, leaving Lilyanna's door ajar.

I freed one of the small knives from my boot and hurried down the spiral stairs to my unused room. The fire crackled softly having barely burned through any of the kindling I'd set yesterday. Pressing my back to the door and using the edge of the hearth to block my body, I speared the tip of the knife into my wrist.

"Siobhan," I whispered.

A fat drop of blood rolled down my arm. I dabbed at it with my sleeve before it could spill onto the floor. Beside me the fireplace stuttered, and I pressed further into my recess.

"Siobhan," I hissed louder. Where was she? I'd found the Sheriff and completed my bounty. She must know by now the Collectors were dispatched and a name permanently crossed off her list. If she would just hurry up and appear, I could sweet-talk my way out of setting up the prince's murder and then beg Lilyanna to leave with me. At the rate she was going, it wouldn't be long before she was killed too.

Seconds ticked by, dragging into minutes. The fireside beside me devoured the kindling, suddenly ravenous. My heartrate accelerated and sweat dripped down my spine.

She wasn't coming.

A gust of stale air rushed down the chimney and the fire went out. Smoke coiled, creeping around the hearth and toward my hiding place. I bolted for the stairs, keeping my thumb pressed over the wound on my wrist.

Siobhan had left me here, abandoned me in this cursed castle. If I wanted out, I'd have to murder the prince and do so before Lilyanna suffered the same fate as all the others.

CHAPTER FOURTEEN
THE CHOSEN ONE

Lilyanna and I were the last to arrive for dinner that afternoon. She paused before the large carved doors of the dining chamber, her fingers fluttering over her neck.

I slapped her hands away. "Stop fiddling with it. It covers the marks perfectly, but it won't if you manage to break it before we even arrive."

The prince's gift to her had been an elegant choker constructed of three rows of golden satin ribbons with small twinkling diamond crystals between them. It stretched from her collarbone to just beneath her chin, perfectly obscuring the angry red slashes from the twisted bed sheets.

My wrist jangled as I reached up to smooth back a strand of blonde hair that escaped the knot I invented for her. My gift was more subtle. A simple gold bangle with a diamond clasp. It weighed more than it should and kept bashing against my wrist whenever I moved, sending small jolts of irritation through me.

"Alright, let's do this," I sighed, opening the door and ushering her through.

I wore my usual uniform of a sapphire sweater and black leggings, so no one paid me any attention as I scurried in behind Lilyanna. She, however, was ravishing. Her midnight blue gown was so dark it looked black except when it caught the flickering candlelight. Shards of diamond were sewn into the bodice and trailed down the flowing skirts like moonlight sparkling off ocean waves.

I smiled. I needed to get her out of this place as Siobhan wasn't going to save either of us, but she could at least enjoy herself first. She really was remarkable. Quite at home dressed up like royalty and equally talented when parrying with a razor-sharp saber. Unfortunately, she was stubborn as a mule, and it may well be the death of both of us.

The dining table was laden with steaming platters of meat and vegetables. My mouth watered as I caught sight of roasted lamb shanks, the bones pared and shining. Fresh mint jelly I hadn't tasted in years lay in a small dish beside the lamb, its surface reflecting the expansive candelabra above in a peppered green hue.

The prince rose and kissed Lilyanna's hand while I remained fixated on the feast. He turned to me and held out his hand for mine, a roguish smile on his face. A golden waistcoat peeked out from amongst the dark double-breasted suit, a diamond pin in his lapel. A picture-perfect gentleman.

My nails flexed automatically. Clement didn't usually let me get this close. How easy it would be to deliver a scratch to the small band of flesh between his thumb and finger when he gripped my hand. But could I then sit through dinner? What if the Collectors descended on the feast, stirring up every guard in the castle and town? I'd never get away. I'd be held, questioned, and probably hung alongside Lilyanna just to prove to the queens they were doing something.

The prince's hazel eyes, flecked with gold today, bored into mine. An invitation? A challenge? Something had shifted between us in the alley at the lunar festival. A creeping unease filtered down my spine.

I reached for him, my nails unsheathing like a tiger. My heart pounded as my vision tunneled upon his hand. The magic stirred, barely a flicker traveling through my veins. Shouldn't I find out if he'd really done anything first?

The Sherriff's face materialized before me. Not the perfect image from the newspaper clipping, but one where he was sprawled on a filthy bedsheet. Deep gouges dripped blood from his back, pooling with serum and slick mucosa from the trail of intestines cascading onto the floor.

I jerked my hand away just as Clement appeared in front of me, grasping my arm and tugging me toward the table. "You can sit next to me."

"But—" I looked back. The prince had taken Lilyanna's arm and was leading her to a chair, a flicker of amusement on his face.

"Clement," the prince called. "Lilyanna's dear sister can sit on my other side. That would make for quite the fun night, don't you think?"

Yes, a second chance. I forced my breathing to deepen. In response, the magic slunk deeper, out of reach. Why did this keep happening around him?

The Sheriff's face swam into view again. My body flinched, suddenly cold as if doused in freezing water. This had never happened before. Then again, I'd never stuck around to find out what happened to those I'd marked. I should have known. Deep down I probably always did. The Collectors side of the bargain was far worse than mine.

The magic tingled, reminding me it was still with me, that I could do this, but I'd have to focus. It wanted to attach to determination and power, not uncertainty. This was no time to develop a conscience. If I could tag the prince at dinner, I would. Otherwise, I'd go and grovel for forgiveness from Siobhan and use my trump card to buy myself a few weeks until I was dragged under again.

Clement narrowed his dark eyes at me when I remained mute. I shrugged, unable to remember if I'd been asked a question.

"If those two are sisters," he said, "then we must be brothers, my dear prince. And so, I will sit on your left."

The prince chuckled. "And it begins! These really are my favorite gatherings."

Clement dragged me toward the head of the table, firmly planting himself between me and the prince. I slipped into the high-backed chair, forcing my mind to empty and the magic to bide its time.

I sucked in a deep inhale of the juicy aromas floating by. "You've had quite a few of these gatherings, or so I've heard." I directed my comment at the prince, plucking a large lamb chop from the transparent diamond platter in front of me.

The prince chuckled. "Yes, that is true. And it seems like you have not been invited to many, judging by your lack of table manners."

Clement elbowed me, and I dropped the bowl of buttered carrots I was tipping onto my plate alongside the lamb.

"I am joking! Eat!"

I pulled a face at Clement and resumed heaping my plate full. Matron was seated opposite me and Bryn beside her. My other side remained empty, giving me plenty of room to drag dishes across the table to my area.

I dipped my lamb in the mint jelly, barely able to stifle a moan as it melted in my mouth. The meat was deliciously tender and cooked perfectly. When was the last time I'd eaten like this? Siobhan's fluttering eyelashes came to mind, reminding me that it had been when she'd last asked me to join her. She'd taken me on a private tour of the southern castles, casually slipping all the deals I could be making into the conversation, the lives I could control, the freedom I'd have. I just had to give up every shred of dignity and incinerate every last one of my morals. Her apprentice. I snorted. She wanted a lot more of me than that.

The prince raised his goblet. "A toast." I lifted mine while the others did the same. "I do so enjoy these annual gatherings. They are much more delightful than the ones my mothers used to make me sit through. And seeing as we have two new faces joining our unusual family," he gestured to Lilyanna then to me, "I thought this would be the best way to celebrate." He drank and we followed suit. "Let's begin. Ask me anything. I would love for you two to be comfortable in your new home."

I shoveled a forkful of honeyed parsnips into my mouth. When I came up for air, I asked the prince, "So, why do your fiancées keep dying?"

Clement choked on his wine. Lilyanna bit back a grimace, her fingers fluttering to the choker wrapped around her neck.

Clement gripped my knee under the table and lowered his face to mine. "He's still the Goddessdamn prince, Tam. Behave."

The prince's smile was taut. He pushed food around his plate, head tilted. Lilyanna started chatting about trade routes between their cities, but his focus remained lasered on me and Clement.

"It's a valid question," I hissed back. "And you won't let me close enough to find out."

"For good reason."

I rolled my eyes, and he groaned.

The prince's fork chinked against the plate, and I looked up. "Do you need someone to cut up your food for you, my dear prince? There's plenty of help around the table."

Clement kicked me.

The prince put down his fork and grabbed the large carving knife. He held my stare, the room suddenly silent around us, before plunging the knife into his lamb, holding it like a spiked head. He tore off a large chunk with his teeth.

I snorted and Lilyanna giggled. Even Clement managed to smile.

Matron opposite me angled her goblet of wine at Clement. "I agree with the young lad."

I turned to Clement and mouthed 'young'? He pushed me away.

She tipped her goblet so it now pointed at me. "You do still need to learn manners. We need all the help we can get around here, and I know you're able to do it, girl." *Girl?* I snorted again, eyeing the now empty wine goblet and the single curl of gray hair that escaped her white cap and hung around her face. "You practically sing your respects to me." She poured more sweet red wine into her goblet from the carafe and grinned at me.

She was grinning at me? Clement was right, this dinner was weird, but amazing. "That's because you practically ooze authority, ma'am." I pressed my hand to my heart. "And I'm a *teeny* bit afraid of you."

She nodded into her wine and hiccupped.

"What about me?" asked the prince.

I shrugged. "You'll get there."

He threw back his head and roared with laughter. Clement gave me an exasperated look, but he couldn't hide his smirk even beneath the thick stubble. Matron's words from our first meeting about being forgettable and Clement's repeated warnings to stay under the prince's radar trickled to the forefront of my mind. A bit too late for that.

I glanced at Lilyanna who smiled politely. She cut a tiny piece of potato and pushed it onto the back of her fork, her attention disproportionate to the task at hand.

As if sensing the shift, the prince scraped back his chair. We all stopped and focused on him. He held out both hands toward Lilyanna, palms open and empty. Then he closed his fists and spun around, the tails of his jacket flying out behind him. When he reached her again, he dropped to his knees with a flourish and held out a ring.

"Lilyanna, my love, let us make this official. You are my chosen one."

My stomach clenched. This is what she wanted, what she thought she needed. But had it sealed her fate? I needed to get her out of here, to drag her with me. I'd accompany her back home to tear up that stupid contract and be on my way.

I shook my head hoping she'd see, and Clement kicked me again. I glared at him before painting a smile back on my face.

I wouldn't let anything happen to her.

Lilyanna threw herself at him, draping her hands around his neck. He kissed her with such surprising intensity that I was almost jealous for a second. The dimples popped in his cheeks and his eyes came alive as he beamed at her. He really did seem to be in love with her. Maybe he would leave with her if I could get them both out of here and away from the city?

Although, without the threat of the murderous castle hanging over us, I could concentrate solely on my mission and see if he was really guilty before I acted. He'd done nothing but be welcoming and kind thus far with his behavior that of a normal, innocent man. Maybe that's why Siobhan sent me? She wanted to see if I'd obey her, even if the assignment was grossly unfair.

The Sheriff's warning echoed in my ears. There must be some truth in the rumors about the prince for him to risk coming out of hiding and travel all the way up here, and there was still the reaction of my cowering magic to consider.

Distracted, I twisted the bangle around my wrist, the smooth gold cold against my skin.

"Do you like your gift?" Clement asked.

"Yeah, I do."

"I picked it myself." I stared at him, and he blushed. "I mean, the prince sent me for it...I...Look." He turned my wrist over and pressed on the diamond clasp. A needle thrust out of the gold, its tip a rusted green. "It's not as effective as that kitchen knife you stole, but the venom on that needle will incapacitate a full-grown man." He pressed the clasp again and the needle sucked back inside the bangle. "Or kill someone of your size."

"Wow. Well, I like it a lot more now." His thumb brushed my wrist, sending tingles up my arm. "Don't you think you should've told me first though? A little dangerous if you ask me."

He chuckled, the sound rushing as coils of warmth through my body. "I think you can handle it. And as you seem intent on doing everything I tell you not to, I thought you may need the extra protection."

He was worried about me? That was novel. "Thank you," I mumbled. "So, are you happy that I'm still here, or are you still plotting to have me thrown out?"

"I'm growing used to having you beside me."

"What a lovely sentiment."

He kept his fingers loose around my wrist, his grip soft but firm enough to keep me from pulling away. "You're different."

I sucked in a breath. "This just keeps getting better and better. Please go on."

He grinned. "And that's what I like about you. You're the only one here who openly speaks their mind. I find it...interesting."

I should have rolled my eyes or tutted, but the way he said it, with a hint of color brushing his cheeks, made warmth bloom in my chest. He squeezed my hand and leaned in closer. For a second I thought he was going to kiss me, before the prince loudly cleared his throat and Clement swerved.

He gently replaced my hand on the table, and we both sat and listened to the conversations around us, neither of us really paying attention. My sole focus was the closeness of his thigh to mine, the faint scent of pine I was coming to recognize on instinct as his, and the growing pressure that hummed in the air between us.

Clement cleared his throat. "Does Lilyanna like her gift?"

I stared at the gold choker. How perfectly it obscured the grooves carved into her flesh. Clement had chosen it? Clement had chosen it.

I shivered. "It's a perfect fit."

CHAPTER FIFTEEN
BLOOD MAGIC

Lilyanna and I walked arm-in-arm behind the prince. As usual, Clement and Bryn flanked him, their shoulders tight, backs straight. The prince had dressed all in black, pristine layers of velvet and silk draped over his body in perfect proportions. He carried himself taller, his presence larger than before.

We moved toward the old section of the castle where the stone floor ceded to wooden planks and the temperature turned glacial. The ground outside rose higher in the rectangular windows, partially covering the thick panes, then half-obscuring them before fully blocking the daylight out.

I shifted Lilyanna further into the center of the passageway and away from the sconces which leaned out from the walls, billowing toward us as we passed. She tugged the neck of her sweater up to her chin, its white wool covering the bruises but accentuating the pallor of her cheeks.

The prince stopped before a narrow, single door and addressed Lilyanna. "Thank you for accompanying me today, my lady." He bowed his head, lips tight, but his eyes sparkled.

Bryn twisted the diamond knob and pushed open the door. Stale air rushed out, the rose scent that permeated everything unable to bloom down here.

"You may not enjoy what you are about to see, but it is essential business when running a city. We are all, of course, doing the queens' work, and you will be joining me in that venture soon."

He offered his hand, and she reluctantly unwound from my arm and placed her fingers in his. He raised her hand to his lips, gently kissing her knuckles. She lowered her head as a smile crept upon her face. The prince's eyes darted to mine, a grin flashing briefly before he resumed focus on her. A chill shot through me.

They walked through the narrow door with Bryn following. Clement blocked my way as I moved forward.

"Move. Don't you dare think you're leaving me outside while she's in there alone." I swatted at him, barely even appreciating the tense muscles under his tunic.

"Calm down, you're coming in, he wants you there." He glanced over his shoulder before hurriedly whispering, "I'm begging you, Tam. Stay quiet. Don't do anything."

"What? Why?"

He looked behind him again. "Because you'll look guilty."

I folded my arms. "I haven't done anything. I told you." Indignation swirled inside of me. Why was he always lecturing me?

He forcibly uncrossed my arms and gently held my hands by my sides. "I believe you." His dark eyes were earnest, pleading as they darted between mine. "But the others won't."

I pulled my hands from his and twisted the gold bracelet around my wrist. My finger absentmindedly landed on the diamond clasp, and I trapped it against my skin. My pulse throbbed beneath the needle, the magic in my blood tiptoeing around the obstruction.

I frowned. What was he involved in? What did he know? He kept going to great lengths to warn me about something; to tell me to leave. He even gave me the bangle to protect myself. But all this without telling me why. It was infuriating.

I nodded. "I'll try."

I pushed him aside and hurried after Lilyanna. He let out a frustrated groan behind me as he followed.

Though my body screamed at me to run, I forced my feet to keep moving evenly. From the look on Lilyanna's face, she was trapped in the same dilemma.

Two carved benches ran in a circle around the room bisected at four points by a narrow aisle. In the center, the floor fell away into a rank void. Sweat, rot, and decay belched from the opening. Except for the void, the room was well lit. Hundreds of candles lined the edges and hung from the ceiling. The wicks were different colors—crimson, midnight blue, bruise green, but the heat crinkling the air above the flames was a mirage. Only chills laced their way through the air.

A handful of people were seated, one with a quill and parchment balanced on their knee. I hadn't seen the prince invite any of the townsfolk into his castle so far, so he must be making a point about something.

I crept up alongside Lilyanna and we perched at the back, our weight solely in our feet, ready to bolt at a moment's notice. The prince circled around to the opposite side while Clement and Bryn walked down the aisles on the right and left. They all stopped at the edge of the darkness.

Clement's hand feathered the hilt of his saber, his fingers drumming a tune which matched the pounding of my heart. Bryn smoothed back her perfect hair, keeping her body devoid of emotion.

The door snicked shut behind us. Lilyanna and I spun around, her hand locking with mine. I realized too late that I should've sat on her other side so I could access my knife. I pulled one of the small blades from my boot with my left hand. Resting it back in my lap, I closed my fingers around it and forced the whirring adrenaline in my body to calm.

A priestess glided slowly over the floor. Her long, sheer robes matched the prince's midnight black ensemble. A thin layer of diamonds clung like gauze to the fabric, making her shimmer in the multi-colored glow from the candles. The crystals absorbed each hue as if it were their right.

She wore no veil, a sparkling diadem wound into her pale hair instead. Lilyanna's hand tightened around mine as she realized the same thing. This was not a Goddess sanctioned blessing we were about to witness.

The priestess moved down the aisle in front of us and halted, making up the fourth point. A rumbling began and the floor shuddered as a platform emerged slowly out of the darkness. It creaked to a halt, the circular stage smaller than the pit, floating like an island lost at sea.

Three people huddled back-to-back in the center. Their clothes were damp, stained with black and brown smears. No shackles bound their bare feet or shaking hands. They blinked in the candlelight, faces contorted by shadows and fear.

The prince cleared his throat. His face was carefully bland, posture alert but relaxed. Even so, his eyes gleamed. "You are here for the savage murder of a citizen." I sucked in a breath. "He was found at an inn within the walls of *my* city." He paused, casually hooking one hand into the waistband of his black trousers. "And why, might you ask, is the prince getting involved in one murder? Especially when I have a team of seasoned professionals to manage trivial incidents like this."

Clement and Bryn remained unmoving, but an awareness brushed through me as if Clement was urging me to sit still, to stop my foot from tapping upon the floor.

"Because blood magic was used." The prince's tongue darted out, moistening his lips. "But of course, I am nothing if not fair. First, we must prove it."

He lifted his head and nodded at the priestess. His gaze lingered on me and Lilyanna. I forced my knee to stop jiggling, and she dug her nails into my hand while keeping the rest of her body perfectly controlled.

The priestess withdrew two long silver rods from inside her robe. I'd never witnessed divining rods used for their true purpose. At the fayre, they were used to seek water, ale, or adulterers all for the enjoyment of the crowd. It would have been a death sentence to use them to seek blood magic, especially when so few of us harbored it.

My own magic slunk deep inside me, crawling into the furthest crevices it could find, lining every furrow. My blood chilled as it left, vessels constricting to conserve energy, a tingle squeezing through me.

Placing both rods in one hand, the priestess loosened her grip, allowing their weight to tip forward, the points wavering freely in the air. Magnetized, Lilyanna and I leaned forward simultaneously.

We both flinched as the divining rods caught the scent, jerking into action. The two rods wavered, crossing over one another with a dull twang.

I willed them not to settle.

Not to spin around and point at me.

The three people on the platform remained mute. Why weren't they fighting? They weren't even trying to defend themselves. They hadn't been involved. They were probably just unfortunate enough to have stayed at the same place that night.

The divining rods twitched again, unable to find a focus.

I peered closer at the woman facing us. Her eyes were wide, opened in a silent scream, yet her body moved not a muscle. A small glob of spittle dribbled from the corner of her mouth, black as tar. Creases lined the clothes over her biceps and around her waist as if she were being forcibly held. The two men behind her sat in identical positions, their chins unnaturally tilted as if something had a grip on their hair.

Was the castle protecting them by forcibly keeping them silent?

Or condemning them?

I swallowed. They shouldn't be blamed. I could tell them I was there that night, that I'd not seen anything, or perhaps that the Sheriff had made many enemies from other cities—which was true—and that his assailant would have immediately left. Something. I had to do something.

The rods swung again, crossing over each other, the pace now frantic.

I shifted, forcing myself to stand and Lilyanna dragged me down, the bones in my hand crushed under her grip. "No, Tam."

From the side of the pit, Clement's attention snapped to me. His mouth parted slightly, warnings gathering on the tip of his tongue.

"I need you," she whispered.

My eyes fell to the bruises creeping over the neck of the sweater like poison vines. She would be dead within a day if I left, or if I were thrown into the pit with the others. The castle was trying to claim her and nobody else would protect her.

Bile edged into my throat as I forced myself to remain sitting, useless, *guilty*.

The priestess lowered the rods.

We both slumped in relief. Lilyanna loosened her grip on my hand. Blood pounded back into my fingertips, poking at my skin like fiery pins.

"Not enough blood magic has been found," the prince said. Was he disappointed? His thumb remained hooked in his waistband and his weight tipped down one leg. "Although you have all been seen boasting about your powers, doing tricks and spells to profit from your cons. I should send you down South to the queens." For the first time, the three people squirmed, fighting against their invisible bindings. "That is the law, as you know. Anyone caught doing magic needs to be thoroughly assessed."

Lilyanna leaned forward, her gaze pleading. The prince glanced at her and smiled. The dimples reappeared in his cheeks, his face lightening under the glow from the candles suspended from the ceiling.

"But I have built a reputation for being fair and what would my beautiful future wife say if I turned you over without concrete proof of the deception?" He chuckled. "You are to be exiled instead. Go where you please. My guards will escort you to the gates tonight. I only ask that you do not renege on my kindness and ever return."

Lilyanna nodded enthusiastically as if accepting for them. I inwardly thanked the prince, my body sighing with relief.

The woman on the bench huddled over the parchment scribbled furiously, the quill scratching loudly.

"Send a message to the townsfolk," the prince addressed the writing woman. "We are still hunting for the culprits, but we will find them. Our town has the finest resources in the queendom and justice will be served."

Lilyanna sprang to her feet and pulled me up. "Let's go, Tam."

I turned to follow, my mind automatically seeking out Clement. He was my beacon. I had to search beneath the stoic exterior, but the warning shone clearly from him. He remained tense, nervous, his nostrils slightly flared. Why wasn't he happy? Would he prefer they were executed for something we both knew was my fault? Or was it something else?

I let her drag me out of there. No one moved behind us as we left. I only hoped that once the door closed, the prince would be true to his word and release them.

I sat and listened to Lilyanna gush about how lenient and generous the prince was for the rest of the afternoon. I didn't fully disagree, but I definitely did not approve of his theatrics. We didn't need to be there to witness his trial, and yet, the whole thing seemed to have been orchestrated just for us. He could have given a statement to the papers, or had the priestess assess the prisoners in private.

Would he keep looking for others? Maybe Clement would finally break, sick of seeing innocents dragged down into the castle dungeons and spew my secrets. He had many secrets of his own hidden deep in those dark eyes, but would mine slot easily into the gaps? Add to the weight of his burden?

I stared out of the thick window in the lounge as the night sky morphed to purple. I nestled deeper into the chaise, enjoying the plump cocoon before I'd be forced to lie between the murderous silk sheets in Lilyanna's bed again. The houses lining the central street melted into distorted shapes. Their edges blurred with faint lights burning sporadically in a streaky haze up to the dark line of the wall in the distance.

Four figures crossed under the gargoyle beneath the window and left the castle perimeter. I bolted upright and pressed my nose to the cold glass. The middle two were the men from the trial. Their tattered brown clothes and shuffling gait indicated being recently tied up and not yet able to fully stretch their bodies. The accompanying figures wore the sapphire blue tunics of the guards, both gripping one of the men by the elbow.

Despite the darkness and the blurry window, it was clear the woman was missing.

I swung off the low chaise and darted to my room. Lilyanna was safely in the bath, away from all flames and bed sheets. The hearths were stoked and the ceiling surprisingly quiet like all the spectators had slunk to another part of the castle.

I ran down the metal staircase, my heart thumping in time with my feet. Would they have kept her in the dungeons? Maybe something happened after we'd left, and Prince Bellinor changed his mind about releasing her.

In two strides I passed through my small room and threw open the door. Reeling backward, I clutched at my chest. "What in the…bloody hell, Clement."

"Sorry." He looked anything but sorry as his lips twitched. He filled the doorway, hands on either side of the frame completely blocking my passage. "Where are you going, Tam?"

I straightened, my hands falling to my hips. "How in the Goddess's name did you know?"

His dark eyes danced in reply. "I know you pretty well by now."

"No, you don't." I didn't care if I sounded petulant. I needed to wipe that smug look off his beautiful face.

"The prince was going to send her to the queens regardless of the outcome. She'd been flaunting her magic for months. She knew the risks. When she was caught, it was inevitable."

"But he said he'd let them go. That nothing was proven."

"You were there, you saw the rods. Magic was in that room, it just couldn't be localized."

I drew in a breath. Was he telling me the truth? He'd known I would go searching, and if I found out something had happened, I'd blame myself, who wouldn't? He'd been very quick to make sure I knew she was separated from the Sheriff situation but guilty, nonetheless. Who was he protecting, me or the prince?

"What's going to happen to her?"

"I hope you never find out." He dropped his hands from the frame and reached to pull the door closed. "Goodnight, Tam."

A key clicked in the lock.

CHAPTER SIXTEEN
SOUL SEARCHING

The prince came to the rooms to spend time with Lilyanna in the morning, and I stood in my usual place beside Clement. He was smart enough to know I was furious and smarter still to keep his thoughts to himself. As he left, he shot me an apologetic smile, which had the irritating effect of thawing my frosty posture. He then made an overly dramatic scene of closing the door without turning the key in the lock again. Such an ass.

Lilyanna and I played checkers and twiddled our thumbs, awaiting a summons for dinner or some other orchestrated activity. I gave it an hour before I left her reading by the window and slipped out.

I stalked toward the kitchens, still irritated at being locked in all night. I needed to find the missing woman, to find out what was really being done with her. She had enough magic that the prince didn't release her with the others.

The castle ran with a skeletal staff. The only place I ever saw people was the kitchens, where baskets of goods were deposited, deals bartered for, and tailored clothes left. No one ever ventured further, so, if gossip were to be found, that would be where.

The slate floor in the kitchens had been swept and cleaned, a faint twang of polish masking the ever-present rose essence. The chef kneaded dough in the center, small flakes of flour spinning in the air around her.

I sidled up to the table. "Do you have any of those meat pies to spare? Lady Lilyanna would like to keep some close by so that I don't have to keep shirking my other duties and running down here multiple times a day. They're her absolute favorite, she swears they're the finest in the queendom."

The chef continued to work the dough, slapping it upon the wooden table. Her brow beaded with sweat; her plump cheeks flushed. "You mean *you* don't want to have to keep running down here bothering me, aye lassie."

I ran my finger through a trail of flour leaving a deep slash. "You know me so well."

She harumphed, flipping the dough and continuing her unbroken rhythm.

Nails scrabbled faintly across the ceiling, the hair on my arms rising as a chill whispered past. In the corner of the room, spots of ash dribbled down the walls and formed into a tumorous mound on the floor.

"She tells me they are a favorite of some of the locals," I said. "But no one else can replicate them without using magic. Is there a lot of magic in town?"

"Tam!"

I froze, my spine erect, muscles seizing.

"If it isn't you again." The prince strode inside the kitchens, mimicking my position across the table with one hand resting on the wood. Only mine was clawed into a fist and his rested delicately in the white dregs of flour.

"Wants some of the small pies, Your Highness." The chef kept her eyes on her work, the dough slapping and squelching as her knuckles drilled into it.

"Oh, I'm so sorry, Tam. I should've told you," the prince said.

Clement moved to stand by my shoulder, his hand resting featherlight upon the small of my back. His presence seeped into me, a foreign calm battling against the burning irritation. Didn't either of them have better things to do?

The pile of ash in the corner dispersed as if it had never fallen.

"I've had to request that all my staff turn their attention to the upcoming wedding feast. So, there will be nothing going spare for the next week or so." He dragged his forefinger through the flour dust and winked at me before licking the tip clean.

Clement's hand pressed firmer against my back, but my nails unsheathed. Without warning the magic surged, unwilling to be placid any longer and latched onto my irritation.

"However, you are always welcome to dine with me." The prince pushed off from the table and headed toward the corridor. "Alone, if you want." His lips curved. Spots of white flour embedded into the cracks like pus.

"You're breaking my table, lassie," the chef chided. She swatted at me, and I declawed my hand, leaving behind deep gouges in the wood.

Clement shot me a look before he left. Did he know what I was looking for? He could have warned the prince and orchestrated this little coincidental trip. But no, he usually found me alone to keep his warnings private.

The castle might know. I eyed the corner which sparkled, ash-free in mockery.

But it wouldn't stop me.

I couldn't get out again until that evening.

I'd spent the remainder of the day watching the sun sink painfully slow and planning my next move. I wanted to find out where the woman was being held. If she had blood magic, even traces, I needed to know what they were doing with her and why. Something or someone in this castle was involved and it wouldn't be long before they came for me.

"Lilyanna, get your cloak. We're going for a nighttime stroll."

She clutched the thick woolen material to her chest and grimaced. "Why?"

I groaned and took the cloak from her, flapping it around her shoulders and cinching it tight. "The prince mentioned something about seeing the stars. He said it's rarely clear here in winter and tonight there are no clouds." I pushed her toward the door. "And something about wishing on a star, or equally stupid, I wasn't really listening."

"The wishing star!" She bounced out the door immediately peppy. "Tam, you know what that means, right?"

A flutter of guilt skimmed through my veins. "No, tell me."

She looped her arm through mine. "Oh, I will."

I steered her down the corridor, surreptitiously scanning for any movement or noises. I never saw any staff in the corridors, except for Clement, and this was the only time I was thankful for the eerie vacancy.

"The Plough is most visible at this time of year. The different points, as I'm sure you know, represent wisdom, strength, and protection. The cup at the end is the portal through which people are known to pass into the spirit world after death and..."

The floor sloped gently downwards, the already dark windows squeezing more and more light from the corridor. I was so used to feeling my skin prickle from the eyes always on me that I couldn't help the flood of gooseflesh when I realized the castle was not watching tonight. It was peaceful, slumbering. Dead.

"...then on crystal clear nights, the wishing star can be seen bisecting the entire plough. It shoots directly through the center and if you're lucky enough to witness it and attach your wish, it fires straight through to the afterlife, directly to the Goddess."

Maybe the castle was exhausted after using all its energy for another task, like watching me. I studied the ceiling—no ash, no scratching. I shivered.

Our feet passed onto the boards of the old castle, the rough wood groaning beneath us. I dislocated a sconce from the wall and held it out, forcing a way through the shroud of darkness that had fallen.

Lilyanna went silent. She pressed closer, her nails digging into my arm. A plain door appeared at the end of the corridor just within reach of the torchlight.

"Where are we going?" she asked.

I clamped my lips together.

"Tam?" She halted, folding her arms and planting her feet.

"Okay, fine." I moved behind her and pushed her toward the lone wooden door. "We're not going to see the stupid stars. It's cloudy. It's always bloody cloudy here." She opened her mouth to argue, and I cut her off. "I'll find you something else to wish on."

"No, I'm not going back in there." She grabbed the door frame, blocking me with her body.

I reached under her arm and twisted the knob. The door swung open with a groan as stale air and rot strongly laced with blood gushed out.

"Look. You can go back to the room by yourself and stare at that Goddessdamned hearth by yourself or come with me."

She ground her teeth. "This is not what I signed up for. You were supposed—"

"I didn't sign up for this either," I snapped. I slid the dagger from my holster and shoved it at her. "Here."

She stared at it for a second before rocking it back and forth in her palm, weighing it, familiarizing herself with the heavy hilt. A flush of warmth forced away the chills. I bet she was more adept at wielding that thing than I was.

"What about you?" she asked.

I stopped and grabbed my small blade from my boot. "Don't worry, I have more where that came from." I threw the knife in the air and caught it, unable to stop my grin.

She snorted. "What are we doing?"

I moved her to the side and entered the circular chamber we'd been in just yesterday. "We're going to free that woman." She looked at me blankly. "The one from the trial. I saw the men being released, but they kept the woman and when I tried to find out why, Clement locked me in my room."

"Clement did?" Her eyes narrowed and even in the gloom I could see her suspicion.

"He had nothing to do with it. With the woman, I mean. He said the prince detected magic on her after we left, and she wanted to stay at the castle to atone rather than being sent South."

She pressed her lips together.

"Oh, just leave it, it's not him." Heat prickled my chest and itched its way up my neck. "Something links these murdered women, and the prince's ex-fiancées, you of all people should want to find out what it is. And if it is blood magic, they shouldn't be killed for something they have no choice in."

"Blood magic has been hunted since the dawn of time," she replied. "Only recently have the queens outlawed it. And, I agree, it's not fair, but when have the royals ever done anything not directly for themselves? Except for the prince, he's generous and forgiving and"

I elbowed her. "Focus."

"Fine," she said. "It started slowly, the perpetrators rounded up in secret, but now the search is more desperate. It's had a domino effect on all our towns up here because people are afraid to use any type of magic. So, the soil is less fertile, the mines more dangerous." She rolled her shoulders back. "It's why I'm stuck here. It's the only lifeline we can see." She gripped the knife tighter. "Let's go."

We moved slowly toward the central pit, our footsteps echoing around the circular room. The smell of blood, sweat, and excrement belched from the crater. Lilyanna gagged and turned her face away. I leaned over the edge, holding my breath, inching the flame out. The light barely penetrated four feet into the darkness when its flame swooshed and guttered. I yanked it back.

"She must be down there. I can't see a thing, but it stinks." I said, trying to avoid the fumes emanating from the pit.

"Yeah, I know." She wiped her eyes, her skin moist and clammy in the fire's glow.

I swirled the torch again. A flash of silver winked back at me in the darkness. I crept around the pit, holding the torch low until it caught upon the rungs of a wooden ladder, sparkling diamond hinges bolting it to the wall.

"Absolutely not," she said.

I ignored her. Thrusting the handle of the torch between my teeth, I lowered myself over the edge of the pit. The ladder creaked but held, the treads worn and thick, allowing my fingers to grip securely. "'Den stay in 'da dark," I mumbled.

I descended quickly and the ladder immediately vibrated above me as she followed, her cloak swinging dangerously close to the naked flame.

The air choked as we lowered, thick, humid, and cloying. It coated my skin in a moist sheen. I couldn't close my mouth around the wooden handle and the reek swirled in, lining my tongue and plunging down my throat. As soon as my feet sank into the sticky floor, I ripped the torch out and covered my mouth with my sleeve. Lilyanna did the same, her stomach convulsing as she heaved, but she kept it down.

She nudged me, and I lifted the light, simultaneously wishing it were brighter and snuffed out completely. The walls of the pit were hollowed from earth, smooth and towering, ascending into nothingness above us. As the flame alighted on its surface, gouges, nail marks, and teeth marks stretched upward, outlining furrows that were darker and slimier than the surrounding walls.

We both stepped forward, edging around the chamber while keeping our backs away from the wall. My heart hammered, pulsing in my ears, pulling my focus. Lilyanna kept a vise-tight grip on my arm, her head swiveling constantly.

The light caught on the edges of a door hewn from the earth. I ran the flame up and down searching for a handle. Deep divots dented the wood, but it remained flush with the wall. I kicked it, achieving nothing. Lilyanna squeezed my arm, and we moved on. Another three doors lined the pit, each spaced like the aisles within the benches upstairs. All had no handles, no windows, no give. All were locked.

"Let's go. We tried." Lilyanna tugged on my sleeve again. She still held the dagger clutched to her face with a handful of her cloak to smother the smell. The diamonds burned in the torchlight, glowing orange and yellow like a silent fireplace.

My magic, which had lain dormant, stirred. It stretched through my body in a languid prowl, tugging my shoulders to the right.

"This way." I edged toward the center of the pit. My feet stumbled over the raised ledge of the platform, and Lilyanna crashed into my back. My hand dropped from my mouth and the unmistakable odor of fresh blood speared into my nostrils.

Lilyanna whimpered, glancing repeatedly over her shoulder, but the torchlight barely illuminated the dais, the rest of the pit swirling with shadows. They danced and wriggled, always just out of reach, pulsing as if with their own lifeforce.

Ash piled over the platform in an unbroken swathe, thick enough it covered my boots. Where the three people had been bound yesterday, now only a large box remained. The panes were all made of glass, impregnated with diamond veins that weaved down the joints.

Inside lay the woman.

Her body was limp, limbs splayed, her neck twisted. Skin the color of powdered snow peeked out from underneath soiled clothing. Congealed clots of blood stuck to the inside of her elbows, jugular, and inner thighs. No blood had spilled on the floor of the box, the walls, or the ceiling, but she'd been exsanguinated.

And there were signs of a struggle.

Ash handprints with clawed nails and stretched fingers covered every inch of the glass, streaking down the joints.

The box rattled.

We both jumped. Lilyanna stuck to my side like a second skin. Another thump and a fresh handprint marred the glass directly in front of us. "What?" I pointed at the mark, words sputtering on my tongue.

"Her spirit is sentient," Lilyanna whispered. "If the body is not laid to rest, the spirit will seek revenge."

"On whom?"

"Anyone it contacts, unless it's controlled by a higher power. It'll be bound to the location where it was separated."

"The castle?"

She nodded. "The castle."

"Stuff like this doesn't happen down South, just so you know." I freed my other knife, dropping my cloak from in front of my face again and trying to breathe through my mouth to mute the stench.

"It does." She readied the dagger. "You just don't believe in it."

The box lurched, rocking onto its edge before crashing down in a cloying swirl of ash.

"Come on." We both went for the joints, the blades skittering over the glass, unable to find purchase. I flipped the knife and slammed the butt against the glass. On the other side, the handprint pushed back. "Can we bury her when we get her out?"

Lilyanna rammed the butt of her dagger into the glass with a dull thud. Not even a single spiderweb crept through the surface. "It's probably too late," she gasped, "but we won't know until she's out."

I raised my fist to slam it against the side again when a distant noise snagged my attention. I hushed Lilyanna, and we both lapsed into utter stillness. Footsteps.

"Someone's coming," I hissed. "The prince or the priestess, coming back to finish the job."

"Or Clement."

"It's not Clement." My stomach twisted at the thought.

"He locked you in your room last night so you couldn't do exactly this."

"It was to keep me safe. Probably."

She tugged my arm. "Look, we tried. We need to go."

"Can't we save her soul? Just one more try, I owe her."

She dragged me from the dais, her dagger biting into the flesh of my bicep. "You don't owe her anything. Why would you think that?"

I didn't answer, too tangled in my own guilt.

"Never mind. We're about to join her if we're found down here." She snatched the torch from my hand and flung herself toward the ladder.

I followed, mouthing, *I'm sorry*, but darkness had already swamped the platform.

CHAPTER SEVENTEEN
CHECKMATE

THE COURTYARD WAS THE WORST PART OF THE CASTLE.

Manicured bushes and spiraled trees led toward a large central fountain that stood drained and exposed for winter. Fresh, frost-tipped air swirled around the space, allowing the tantalizing experience of freedom. The gargoyles craned their necks from the turrets and the high wall laced with jagged diamonds glittered from all sides, slick and deadly. A constant reminder of where I was.

I leaned against the castle, tilting my head back so that the wall fell from view and only the fat, gray clouds were visible lumbering across the sky. Lilyanna and the prince strolled the perimeter hand in hand, their voices hushed and excited. He wanted the wedding in two weeks, which was likely a good thing seeing how Lilyanna may not make it that long. As if in agreement, the long membranous tail of the gargoyle above my head floated into my eyeline like an arrow shot through my moment of freedom.

We hadn't spoken a word about last night. Lilyanna regained her composure a lot quicker than me, forcing the memories into whichever distant part of her mind she stored her trauma. I remained down in that pit, lost amid the rocking glass and smeared handprints.

"This is my favorite time of day," Clement said. "When we're both standing here together."

"Mine too." My stomach fluttered. I was beginning to look forward to waiting beside him, watching the mind-numbingly boring courtship between Lilyanna and the prince. He made it more than bearable, keeping my heart pumping and my body flushed with warmth. He was safety, comfort, familiarity, and despite Lilyanna's views on the subject, I trusted him.

I hated myself for the weakness.

His hand brushed mine. "Because you're actually doing your job, behaving yourself, and I get a sliver of worry-free time."

I groaned. "Do I really make your job that much harder?"

"Yes."

"And do you still find me irritating?"

"Yes."

I snorted. "But the most important question is, do you trust me now?" A faint twinge of embarrassment fluttered my chest like I really cared about the answer.

"Yes," he answered without hesitation.

Strands of my hair snagged on the stone as I turned to look at him. Despite the softening of his mouth, tension strummed down him like a taut bow.

"You need to leave the castle, Tam." He kept focused on the prince's meandering progress. "If you won't do anything I say, please do this."

"I need to make Lilyanna leave." My hand rose to my neck as I stared at the amniotic-colored skin that poked out of Lilyanna's high collar. "She's an innocent caught up in"—I waved my hand up toward the hovering gargoyle—"all of *this*."

What would happen if she ended up in that box? If I left, there would be no one to protect her.

Clement fell silent, waiting until the prince and Lilyanna were at the far end of the courtyard. They both sat on a low bench half-obscured by a holly bush, its red berries plump and glistening against the gray stone.

"You're not a very good judge of character." He turned to look down at me. "Especially for a maid that moonlights as an assassin."

I frowned. "That's not—"

"She's almost got what she wants."

"Yeah, but at what price?" I held his stare, cursing how beautiful his dark eyes were up close. I'd barely have to move an inch, and my lips could be pressed to his.

"Seriously, Tamara." I flinched at my real name, drawing back. "I'll get you out, no matter the cost. The other day could have been a completely different story. You may have been the one on trial and I…" He shrugged, frustrated.

I folded my arms across my chest and ripped my gaze away. The prince and Lilyanna were circling back toward us.

"Why is it just me you want to get rid of?"

"You're the only one who doesn't want to be here." His hand skimmed down my side, coming to rest on my hip.

"And you?" I turned back, softening in his grasp. Just the lightest contact of his fingers against my skin and my mind cleared, my body blossoming to life.

"It's my—"

"If you say duty, Clement, I'm going to draw this sparkly dagger, drag you into the center of the town, and challenge you to a duel."

He tipped his head back and burst out laughing. "I'll have you on your back in seconds."

I leaned into him, moving with the tightening of his fingers as he drew me closer. "Promise?"

He grinned.

"And what are you two laughing about?" the prince said. He and Lilyanna stopped in front of us, his arm slung around her shoulders. Her eyes were bright, smile full, but there was a wariness in her expression.

"I challenged Clement to a duel."

Clement's arm fell from my waist and hovered over his saber. Bryn appeared on the other side of the prince, cutting me a withered glare.

The prince ignored them both. "Well, go easy on him. It's hard to find staff that lasts around here."

"Mhm, yes." I nodded. "And—"

Clement clamped his hand across my mouth before I could say 'women.'

"No, Clement." The prince angled his body toward me, trapping me in his aura. "Let her speak. I do enjoy Tam's questioning."

It was now or never. Clement could huff in irritation as much as he liked.

"What happened to the woman prisoner? She didn't leave with the other two."

The prince raised his eyebrows. "You do manage to ferret out information, don't you?" He glanced at Clement, and my insides froze. "More came to light after you both left. She decided to stay with us, to atone for her crimes here at the castle rather than journeying South." His arm tightened around Lilyanna's shoulders. Her collar pulled away from her neck, exposing the marks under the pressure.

"Crimes? But—"

"Practicing magic, flagrant magic, is a crime. She may not have committed the act she was blamed for, but her actions condemned her all the same."

"So, she's still alive?"

The question hung as mist between us, painted on the cold air.

"No." His smile faltered. "There was an accident, and she took her own life. In the stressful events of the day, she wasn't fully searched and had a hidden knife." He patted Lilyanna's arm soothingly even though she hadn't flinched.

"But—"

"It really wasn't Clement's fault, Tam." His cheeks relaxed, the dimples popping as his smile casually returned. "He's been distracted lately."

My mouth fell open. I swiveled to Clement, but he wouldn't meet my gaze. His jaw was set, a muscle pulsing underneath the ever-lengthening beard.

"Shall we go back, Tam?" Without waiting for an answer, Lilyanna wriggled out of the prince's hold and linked arms with me. My body moved numbly alongside hers. So many thoughts swirled through my jumbled brain, contorting with the rapidly rising anger.

The wind chased us inside, forcing us through the wide doors into the castle before instantly dying as we crossed the threshold.

"Lilyanna, you know that's not true. It's...we..." There had been no blood, no marks, no evidence. She'd not killed herself in that box.

"Please, Tam. There are some things you have to let go."

As if in agreement, the stone walls groaned, mortar dribbling to the floor. The sconces on the wall pulsed, drawing us onward and back into the belly of the castle.

Our eyes met briefly before we both sucked in a deep breath and wound our way back to her rooms.

I was getting better at checkers. Not because I wanted to, but due to the lack of anything else to do. Dinner was cancelled once again, so we'd eaten in Lilyanna's room and now sat across from each other, bent over the small brown and white pieces.

Dusk had already fallen outside the thick window. The deep purple air leeched into the flicker from the candles we'd stationed around ourselves, having automatically moved as far from the hearth as we could. Even if it meant aligning ourselves with the freezing stone wall.

"What do you see in the prince?" I pushed one of my brown pieces forward, the carved ridges sinking into the grooves of my finger.

"I mean, he's handsome, generous, a prince." She jumped one of my abandoned pieces, the cream tile clacking on the board. She piled it up with the others she'd taken.

"Sure, but is that what you want?"

She laughed, her eyes never leaving the board as she stubbornly stayed three moves ahead of me. "It's fate. I told you it's been read to me in my tea leaves for years. Now I'm here, it's all coming true."

"Being strangled and burned was in the tea leaves?"

Her mouth twitched. "I can see your attempt to look out for me." She moved forward, exposing a rift down the center of her pieces. "Thank you."

I pushed my piece toward the opening, realizing my mistake as soon as I'd let go. I huffed back into my chair and folded my arms. "Am I supposed to dote on the prince as well once you're married?" She jumped one, two, three of my counters, never once looking up, her tongue wedged between her lips. "You know, choose his outfits, brush his hair. Am I tied up in your dowry?"

She jumped the final piece, the cream circles outnumbering the brown four to one. "When I marry the prince," she noisily raked my counters into a pile, "and we eventually have children, you'll have so much more to do, you won't even have time to complain." Her eyes met mine, face lit by candlelight. "How will you ever cope?"

I barked a laugh. "Maybe I'll get myself a maid."

She waved a hand at the massacred checkerboard. "Or a tutor."

A flurry of nails scrabbled above our heads. Blinded by the glare from the candles, only shadows swirled amidst the diamond ceiling, but a trail of ash floated down.

Lilyanna pulled her silk robe tighter, flapping up the collar to obscure her bruises. "I don't usually hope for rats, but I do now."

"And if for some reason the wedding was cancelled and not due to your untimely death?" The prince had lied to me, to both of us, but that wasn't my primary concern. The look he'd flashed at Clement still haunted me. I didn't like being wrong, I'd given him the benefit of the doubt for the past few weeks and believed him to be innocent. But now I was unsure.

"It must happen. I need it too."

I leaned forward, dropping my voice to a whisper, "Why?"

She bit her lip. Her face shone wan in the orange flicker from the candles, bled of color. Every day over the past few weeks she became a little more drained, as if a vial of blood had been taken in her sleep.

"Gold mines are drying up." She kept her voice low to match mine. "People are starving, our alms are stretched painfully thin. The queendom is arranged so precious metals are our only resource. The same thing happened to emerald, ruby, sapphire, and silver, but once they merged with Prince Bellinor, the supplies were refreshed and the trade routes opened permanently."

"Because of the murder of their female heirs. They had no choice. Blackmailed into checkmate."

"If I marry him, I will have control. There's no other way."

"If you get that far."

She leaned back and shrugged. "You're such a pessimist." She held my gaze, her face deadpan. "You need to get laid."

It was so unexpected I threw my head back and roared, nearly toppling backward off my chair. My cheeks ached; my stomach tight as I tried to rein it in. Lilyanna hid her amusement behind her hand but eventually, she doubled over as well, knocking the counters to the floor.

"I think," I wiped my eyes, "the same could be said for Your Ladyship. Maybe then you'd get your priorities in order and stop chasing the crown."

She grinned at me. "I think we'll have to agree to disagree on that one."

"Yeah, okay. For now."

"But back to you. I've seen you and Clement flirting. You watch him all the time, when you're supposed to be watching me, hover near him, smile when he speaks."

"I do not smile. It's a sneer at his condescending, holier-than-the-Goddess attitude."

She stared at me, unimpressed.

"It's nothing." I made my voice strong and sure, but it was plain she didn't believe me. I stood and offered her my hand, pulling her to her feet. "Now off to bed. I'm sure we have the most enthralling game of checkers ahead of us tomorrow."

The collar of her robe flopped down exposing the roiling blue and gray skin of her neck. Her hand fluttered to her throat; what little color remained fleeing from her cheeks.

"It looks much better," I said.

She pursed her lips, dropping her hand from her neck and twirled the ring on her finger instead. "You'll sleep here again tonight?"

I sighed but nodded. She squeezed my hand, and I followed her into the bed chamber, climbing into bed next to her. The silk sheets were cool and smooth, as innocent as I once was. She really was going to be the death of me. Where had my detachment gone? It's what I prided myself on, or at least Siobhan did. Hadn't she spent years pushing me around the queendom like a checker piece, never able to forge even a semblance of a relationship? Maybe she thought I was too far gone, that her constant manipulation had finally seeded within me.

First, Clement managed to worm his way in as I couldn't stop thinking about him, and now, Lilyanna.

Maybe that would be *her* downfall.

My eyelids were heavy, an eternal yawn building in my throat. As much as I needed it, I'd never let myself sleep. Terrible things happened when I did.

CHAPTER EIGHTEEN
THE HIGHEST POWER

I WAS RUNNING THROUGH THE MOORS.

Climbing sloping hills and rounding rocky tors as the castle dwindled in the background. Grass clawed at my legs, pebbles embedding in my bare feet. The air was stale. Where was the fresh breeze? The scent of purple heather, the acidic twang of the peat?

It didn't matter, I was leaving.

My body was thrust left, and my foot sank into a deep pit, my ankle snapping. Icy air seeped into my skin, crystals solidifying like diamonds on my clothes. A dull ache radiated up my leg, spreading in a fiery circle.

I kept moving.

Another thrust. This time as if a rope had been coiled around my waist, snapping taut and severing my momentum. I glanced behind. A winding cord, glistening in the moonlight like an umbilical cord trailed behind me. It snaked over the grass, looped the gray wall, and slithered up the central parting right into the claws of the castle gargoyle.

I fumbled to rid myself of it, hands slipping and sliding over the mucus. The gargoyle tugged, and I flew backward, landing heavily on the frozen ground. Inch by inch it dragged me back toward the wall.

My magic sputtered. I fought to release it, clawing at the cord, but it dangled just out of reach.

The line slackened, and I pitched forward, moist moss smearing across my lips and coating my tongue making me gag.

I turned. Right behind me a saber speared into the line. My eyes flew up the silver blade and over the diamond hilt colliding with Siobhan's. She wore the sapphire tunic of the castle guards with black trousers, her blonde hair raked into a neat bun. She tsked, her full lips curving in mock disappointment.

I was running away, but I'd failed. I'd barely made it a mile, and she was on me.

She looked over my head and nodded at the two figures who stood barely feet away.

Burlap sacks were knotted under their chins, their faces smothered, but their necks elongated, pulled back and fully exposed. One male and one female, the clothing as familiar as the press of their arms into one another for comfort. It was a stance I'd seen for years with a pang of happiness.

My Collectors.

My chest constricted, my heart thumping against my ribs, unable to pump fast enough.

The air tickled past my ear, warm and powerful. The gust hit both people at the same time. Identical, deep gashes sliced across their throats, red smiles leering at me in the darkness.

I shook my head, slamming my fists into my eyes trying to rid myself of the images. The Collectors had died once already on my watch. They were my responsibility—my failure. The slashes carved themselves onto the inside of my eyelids, replaying again and again, the skin everting like ruffled pages, blood seeping down, down, down...

Siobhan tugged the saber out of the cord, and it snapped taut. I flew backward, hurtling toward the wall. Grass sliced through my hands as I clawed at the earth, the gray stone and jagged sparks of diamonds looming behind me.

I spun around and kicked. The surface of the wall cracked, spiderwebs fracturing like a sheet of ice. The cord jerked me forward, my shoulder slamming against the stone. A shriek emanated from deep inside me. I kicked out again, my foot plunging through the jagged shards and into frigid water.

A howl pierced to my core.

It wasn't mine. It wasn't me screaming. I wasn't here.

I wrenched away, slipping the cord down my legs. The tension flew away, and I plunged backward into a chasm where the wall had been.

Ash fell around me, cobwebs and dust floating in the air. I landed on a threadbare mattress, shaking the dream or illusion away, but this wasn't right either. Rusted springs and ripped goose feathers poked into my back, trying to spear into my flesh. The night was thick and the room windowless.

I crawled from the mattress, blindly feeling rough wooden floorboards before immediately hitting a wall. I edged around the perimeter, hitting wall, wall, wall. Reaching up, the ceiling hovered inches above my head hewn from the same gnarled wood. I sank into a corner, barely able to sit. Where was I?

A candle flickered across from me. The red taper melted, drops congealing like blood down its side. Cold forms danced on the walls behind the light, bony fingers, sinewy limbs, all twisting toward me as the flame advanced.

I pressed back into the wall. The wood creaked, releasing a rotten, mildew scent into the air. I slid my hand down my thigh looking for the knife. All that remained was a faint divot left in my skin where the holster should be. A similar indentation marred my wrist where the bangle had been.

The candle pressed closer. Everything in the room reduced to an inky void as I opened my mouth to scream, but my throat seized like wax had been poured down my mouth and sealed it shut.

A light female giggle sounded.

I loosed my breath, hands balling into fists. I swiped for the candle, intent on ramming it down her throat instead. This was no nightmare.

Siobhan held it aloft, her cherubic face swimming into view. "Did I scare you, child?" She chuckled again. "I only wanted to remind you that I'm always here. In your dreams, in your life, in your wildest fantasies..."

My ankle throbbed. I reached down to rub it and caught the outline of soot-stained fingers branded upon my flesh. "What've you done?"

"Oh, Tam. It was not me. How could you accuse me of such a crime?" She reached forward and ran a fingertip down my leg. Her touch was warm, petal-soft, and achingly familiar.

I hated what she did to me. The comfort she gave always lingered but never erased the memories. If anything, the trauma was accentuated, and her role as savior cemented. As she lifted her hand, an inky shadow followed in its path, leaving my skin beneath unmarred.

"The spirits in this castle answer to the highest power, child."

I tucked my leg back underneath me, cursing the cold that returned. "Will they answer to me?"

She giggled. "You really are my favorite, yes?"

I swallowed my retort. "So, it's spirits that live within the walls?" I asked instead.

"Yes, my dear. The walls, the ceiling, every liminal space within the castle. I'm surprised you can't see them."

I glowered at her, not in the mood for her condescending tone. My ankle throbbed.

"No?" she asked. "Well, it's for the best. If they decide to appear for you, you'll see the whites of their eyes first emerging in the gloom, then the wispy shape of their human form. By that time, it's far too late and one of two things would have happened. They're ready to listen to you and bend to your will like you do to me." She giggled and tugged at a loose strand of my hair.

I jerked backward. "Or?"

"Well, or you're one of them. The latter looks a much higher possibility at the moment. Haven't you wondered where all those missing village women ended up? The bumps in the walls, the falling ash..."

I swallowed, trying very hard not to think of all the times I'd touched the ash.

"Anyway, onto more joyful subjects. Beautiful work with the Sheriff.

Although, once again, the Collectors were sorry to have missed you. I thought bringing you back to your hometown would loosen your fonder memories, but anyone would think you were deliberately avoiding them?"

I pursed my lips but said nothing.

"Tut, tut. Well, at least I get to spend some quality time with you. Much earlier than expected too."

"They're okay though, right? You haven't harmed them?"

"Of course not. You're the only one who can harm them now. We're all relying on you. Such a fun weight of expectations settled on those perfect shoulders."

"Why didn't you come when I called for you?"

She flicked her hand as if batting away my irritating question. "I must not have heard, I am incredibly busy, my dear."

I held in my groan. She would've known, I'd even opened my veins to spill a drop of magic to summon her. She would've felt it like an elastic pulled tight around her soul, or whatever lived in its place. I took a steadying breath, it was time to broker the deal. My intestines writhed deep within me. It felt as though they snaked up into my chest and squeezed my heart. *Thump*. I swallowed, willing my voice to be strong. "I've paid my debt, though. *Yes?*"

The candle guttered as she heaved a sigh.

I forced the sarcasm down and tried again. "I want to make a deal."

She backed away, lowering the flame until she merged with the twisting shadows. "I'll think about it, child." She paused. "Meet me at the Red Blush tomorrow night and we'll discuss the details. Sounds awfully risqué, don't you think?"

"Wait! Don't leave me—"

The candle snuffed out, leaving a meager trail of crimson smoke suspended in mid-air. *Goddessdamn her!*

I crawled around the room hitting the walls and pushing at the ceiling. Was I *inside* the walls? In between floors perhaps? Please let there be no bodies in here. My knee caught on a rough board and pain seared through me as my flesh sliced open. Warm blood seeped down my leg.

I pummeled the wood, splinters embedding into my fist. It gave way beneath me, widening a small crack between the floorboards. Digging my nails into the grooves, I wrenched them back until I could fit through the opening and drop down into the dark room below.

A cool, sharp blade dug into my throat. I raised my arms a millimeter to shove it away, but a voice growled, "Stay still."

Someone fumbled in the gloom. A glass shattered, a few small trinkets clattering. Finally, flint was found, the blade never wavering from my throat. My raging pulse vibrated down it, the *swoosh* of my carotid forcing itself around the solid obstruction. One slip and I would be dead. At least it would be to a human and not to the spirits slinking through the walls.

Single-handed and clumsy, the flint eventually caught and a taper lit. "Tam?" The curve of the saber shone in the candlelight, its sparkling pommel grasped by familiar hands, but he didn't move the tip from my neck. "What. The. Fuck."

"Eloquent, my friend." I moved the blade aside and it fell slack between us. Rubbing my neck, I cataloged the injury to add to all the others I'd sustained that night. "Do you sleep with that under your pillow, big boy? No wonder you don't have many nighttime companions."

"Is that what you're here for, Tam? Because women don't usually just fall from my ceiling." Clement put the candle on a small dresser beside a narrow bed and sagged back into the messy covers. "There's a door, you see. For next time."

I laughed. Or tried to, but it came out a strangled whimper.

He patted the mattress beside him. "Tell me."

I hesitated until my ankle throbbed in warning. Why not? Sure, he had an actual mausoleum above his room, complete with a mattress and terrifying lack of escape, but maybe he didn't know it was there.

Or maybe he had never used it.

"Did you really try and save that woman?" I lowered myself next to him, my thigh touching his.

He nodded. "I did slip her a knife, but I was too late. She didn't manage to use it."

"Are you in trouble?" My fingers twitched. I'd barely have to move them, and I could rest them upon his leg, offer comfort, show him that my heart stuttered when I thought of him taking the blame. This was all my mess.

"Not yet." He patted my leg instead, fingers gently squeezing before he returned his hands to his lap. "The prince doesn't mind the odd mistake. In fact, he loves playing games. He's surrounded by us guards all day long, never challenged. That's why he likes taunting you."

I groaned.

"So, tell me." He nodded toward the ceiling.

"I was dragged up there. One second, I was dreaming, riding the moors. My happy place." A fleeting moment of embarrassment tripped my tongue, and I quickly moved on. "And then I woke up in your guest coffin." I pointed upward.

"I told you not to let him touch you." His voice was strained and low, a mix of sympathy and frustration.

"What? The prince didn't do this. It was the castle." I shuffled back upon the bed, dragging my injured leg up and nestling it atop the downy covers. How come he got fine wool, and I just had threadbare burlap or Lilyanna's murderous silk sheets? "Look."

He reached for the taper, looping his finger through the diamond handle and brought it to my leg. The ash mark had gone, but a circlet of bruises remained, vomit-colored skin churned into thin marks outlining bony fingers. My ankle beneath was a similar color and the size of his fist. Blood ran in a smeared trail from my chafed knee to mid-shin.

He lowered his face, gently cradling my foot, stroking my skin. The pulse in my ankle intensified, spreading as tingles up my thighs. My breath caught as his lips brushed over the marks, and my entire body crackled with sudden energy.

He raised his head, gaze locking with mine. "What're you wearing?"

Heat prickled my chest, and I tugged the tunic down my thighs, the dark fabric barely covering the lacy panties underneath. "We aren't issued sleepwear," I muttered. The guard's shirt I found was for a much more petite woman than me.

He grinned and despite myself, I grinned back. He gently lowered my leg back to the covers and my smile faded. His touch lay embossed upon my skin, a small patch of soothing calm amongst the broken.

"I don't know if I can keep doing this, Clement." I choked out the words. "The Sheriff...I didn't do it, but I was involved."

He remained still, listening patiently, but I couldn't go on. My heart swelled. He was too good for my burden. He shouldn't be condemned by my secrets as well. I never tried to find out what happened to my bounty after I'd tagged them. I made a point of never asking, of fleeing the city as soon as it was over, and not only because I couldn't face the Collectors. I couldn't face what I'd done.

"You should leave, Tamara," he breathed.

"Don't call me that." I pushed myself up, but he grabbed my hand and tugged me back beside him.

"Tammy? Tamlin? If you don't tell me, I'm sticking with Tamara because it suits you."

"Stick with Tam, then you won't need to hurt yourself by thinking about it too hard."

He chuckled. In the candlelight, his rugged face looked soft, dark eyes kind. A curl of pressure formed in my stomach. What I would give to tell him everything.

"You need to leave the castle. I've told you before, but—"

"I'm not going without Lilyanna."

His fingers laced with mine, his skin rough and calloused, but he fit perfectly around me. "Leave her and go. It wants you first, and I can't stop it." He squeezed my hand.

First? A shiver raced through me. "I need Lilyanna out." I forced my voice to be level. "I can take care of myself."

If he knew the truth, that I was after the prince, after everything he'd given his life to protect...he wouldn't be here with me trying to save me from the castle. I'd be thrown in the dungeon and left to rot.

He raised our joined hands and pointed at the ceiling. "Can you?"

I rolled my eyes. "I'm going back to bed." Hefting myself up, I gingerly tested my ankle. It would hold. Clement watched me hobble to the door, his face a blank mask. I paused with my hand resting on the carved diamond doorknob. "Could you do me a favor?"

He rose and strode to the door, his naked torso silhouetted by the candlelight. He scooped me into his arms and without a word passed into the freezing corridor outside.

"Actually, Clement." My suddenly fogged brain was acutely aware of his hand gripping my thighs, and his permeating scent of pine that flushed into my nostrils with every shallow breath. Oh dear, was I seriously smelling his neck? "This wasn't the favor."

"I know." The creaking floorboards under his feet melted seamlessly into the hard stone of the main castle. The walls lightened to a charcoal gray as fissures of moonlight stole into the corridor. "But you never would've asked, and I'm not about to watch you limp around in circles for the next few hours as you get lost finding your way back."

I threaded my arm around his neck, hovering my fingertips over the stubble that coated his jaw. Would he like it if I touched him? Would he close his eyes and nestle into my palm? Or would he use my weakening as another excuse to force me to leave?

It seemed like mere seconds before he was carefully setting me down outside Lilyanna's door. His hand remained on my elbow, his chest square in front of me. "What was the favor?" His breathing was labored. Was it just from carrying me, or was he as affected as I was?

"Can you babysit for me tomorrow night?" I tipped my head toward the room.

He nodded. "What are you doing?"

I stepped away, the air chilling between us as his body heat leeched from mine. I twisted the handle and slipped part way into the lounge.

"I have a date with the devil."

CHAPTER NINETEEN
THE DEVIL IS IN THE DETAIL

I WAITED UNTIL THE LAST POSSIBLE MOMENT TO TELL LILYANNA.

Clement's knock sounded at the door, and she grabbed my arm before I could open it. "What's happening?" she hissed.

"Clement's looking after you tonight, Your Ladyship." I freed my arm from her clutches. "I have an errand to run in town."

She folded her arms across her chest, rumpling the cream nightgown. "I don't trust him."

I sighed. He rapped on the door again. "Just a minute, Lilyanna's naked."

She hit me. "Tam, listen." She pointed at the door, punctuating each sentence with a jab of her fingernail in his direction. "You ended up trapped in *his* ceiling. *He* found you wandering the corridors at night after you reportedly heard a noise—"

"I did hear—"

"And *he* just happened to be awake to rescue you."

"Look." I lowered her arm and rubbed her shoulders. "I trust him, okay?"

"With my life?"

I rolled my eyes. "You're so dramatic." I moved toward the door. "Just drag something in front of the bedroom door if you must. He'll only be sitting outside bored all night, not planning your grisly murder."

As I opened the door for Clement, Lilyanna slammed into her bedroom. I shook my head and waved him in. He brushed past me, the faint scent of pine swirling behind him. I breathed in deeply and fought to control my pounding heart. "Thanks for doing this. I'll owe you, I guess."

"I know, that's why I'm doing it." He grinned, but his smile faded as he kept my gaze, his dark eyes intent on mine. "Are you armed?"

"Yes, but it won't do any good."

He nodded. "Yes, you have proven to be useless at defending yourself so far."

I swatted at him, accidentally leaving my hand a beat too long on his toned chest. "Are you offering to teach me?"

I felt every inch of his sliding touch as his hand moved from my shoulder down to the tips of my fingers. He chuckled, interlacing his fingers through mine, tugging me deeper into his chest. "Oh, there's a lot I want to teach you."

My body fired to life, blood zinging through my veins.

"Go. I'll see you later. I won't leave her." He released my hand, gripping my shoulders instead to turn me around and gently pushed me toward my room. "You can trust me, Tamara."

"I know."

The Red Blush was easy to find.

Scribbled upon the thick windows were the words I had seen the other day: *women only*. The heavy oak door creaked open, and I stepped into a wide passageway filled with pink-tinted mist. The air was sweet, perfumed with a heady mix of honey and excitement.

I hung my cloak upon a small nail in the wall, picked up a mask from the shelf and studied myself in the hallway mirror. The porcelain rested cool and smooth upon my skin, conforming to the shape of my face, riding the curve of my upper lip. Pink and red cherry blossoms wound across the pale surface with delicate buds of glitter adorning the center of each flower, the green in my eyes enhanced by the small leaves.

I shouldn't still be thinking of Clement and yet, I knew he wouldn't be able to resist if I showed up in his room wearing nothing except my cloak and this mask. Even his deep-set sense of duty would be cast aside for one wild night.

I shivered, brushing the thought away. If Siobhan caught a whiff of my attraction, however slight, she would pounce.

I followed lipstick red arrows on the walls to the end of the corridor and down carpeted stairs. The hazy mist increased, swirling around my ankles, lapping at my thighs, coating my senses in a warm, enticing aroma. My heart rate slowed, my muscles loosened as I drew a deep breath and surrendered myself to it.

I opened the door marked 'lounge' and wandered toward a corner booth. Silk pillows padded themselves around my body and I leaned my head back upon the diamond-stitched wall. I sighed. A moment of peace.

"You look ravishing tonight, my dear." Siobhan breezed into the seat beside me, placing two large glasses on the table. She wore a blood-red mask, with horizontal eye holes and two gnarled horns twisted upon the top.

I reached for the drink, inhaling a thick aroma of cherries and spicy cinnamon. "And you've chosen your natural form." I sipped at the drink and groaned, gulping half of it down. I shouldn't let her know me this well, but sometimes there were benefits.

"Here, let me." She dabbed at the corner of my mouth, wiping a droplet with her finger. "Such a shame to go to waste, no?" She sucked the moisture into her mouth, her slitted eyes ice blue and captivating. I preferred the dark depths of Clement's.

I turned back to survey the room. Women lounged on overstuffed chaises or leaned against the bar with drinks in hand. Ornate masks accentuated plump lips, soft jawlines and long, elegant necks. Serving girls flitted in and out, swishing their hips in flowing silken robes, sometimes brushing against a thigh, or sliding a warm hand down an arm.

I set my empty glass down, my body tingling as relaxation seeped into my heavy muscles.

Siobhan flicked her hand, and another two drinks arrived. She spoke a few whispered words to the server who giggled and nodded toward an adjoining room. As she turned, Siobhan carefully watched every sashay of her hips beneath the cream silk.

I sipped, hoping that despite the lightness of my mind, I'd still be able to form coherent demands. "Have you considered my request?" I swirled my drink, focusing on the clinking of ice against the glass.

"Perhaps we should visit the balcony next?" She pointed to where the server had indicated. "There are couches, swings, pillows, whatever you prefer. The mist clings to the floor of the stage below to obscure the view of the bashful, such as yourself." I rolled my eyes. "It may be an altogether more persuasive experience, especially when we have such heady matters to discuss, no?"

"Maybe next time." I plucked the cherry from the glass and rolled it around in my mouth, coating my tongue with the sweet syrup.

"I have all the time in the world, my dear." She flicked her hand again and the server reappeared with a small china bowl piled high with fat, glistening cherries. The red juice sloshed, rising and trickling down the sides.

"I found the Sheriff." I flicked my gaze to her. My stomach twisted at the intensity of her stare, the sickly concoction in my stomach lurching. I took another drink, pushing the cherries aside. "So, now I have a free one again…a spare…a favor?" I hit the bottom of the glass again, tipping it up so only ice crunched into my mouth. Another reappeared before me.

She shifted closer, her thigh pressed against mine. Nausea welled, a clammy fog creeping up my spine. Finally, she turned her head away and a cool rush of air relieved me.

"No," she said.

I tried to lurch to my feet, distant anger calling to me, trying to propel me toward the exit. She tapped my leg, the pressure featherlight, and my body slumped back into the cushions.

"I don't want to do it. I need to get out of there." My throat tightened, my glands threatening to swell. I swallowed, blinking furiously as I ordered my body to behave. How many lives would be ruined? Lilyanna's, Clement's? And I still didn't know if the prince was guilty.

Her hand remained on my leg, her slim fingers tightening around my thigh. "The prince is important, my dear Tam. That's why I gave the job to you, no?" She reached for my drink and molded it into my limp hand. "He's impenetrable, like you've probably already discovered. And there's this infernal aura of goodness around him, it layers on the guilt. So many others have succumbed."

That could explain why my magic faltered around him, why I was so conflicted whenever I neared. Though, I would never dare admit that to Siobhan. Had he played me like all the others? My chest heated.

She raised my hand, forcing the glass to my lips. "Drink, my dear." I swallowed another mouthful, unsure whether it would stay down. "Good girl." She patted my arm and slid her hand back onto my upper thigh. "But you're heartless, aren't you? You get in, get out, don't ask questions, and move on. Like I said, the Sheriff was a particularly impressive find."

The serving girl returned, and Siobhan shook her head, waving her away with a clipped, "Go wait for me on stage. Be ready."

She resumed focus on me. "I do so hope there is not another reason you are reluctant to complete this task? Say, a distraction?"

I slowly shook my head. A muffled buzzing rattled around in my mind. *She will never let me go.*

"Where was I?" She leaned closer, her hot breath fogging my mask. A sticky drop of red paint bled from the cherry blossoms, clinging to my chin and running down my neck. "You are loyal to your Collectors because it's their life hanging in the balance, not yours. *Yet.* So yes, you must complete this mission and perhaps afterward, you can request a small leave of absence?" She drew back and rose, straightening her mask.

"There are other places like this scattered up and down the country. We could see them together, Tam. Just say the word."

My stomach churned again. I put the drink on the table and rested my forehead in my hands.

She patted me lightly on the head and placed a heavy coin purse next to me. I turned to squint at the lacy white tag that dangled from a garter strangling the neck of the sack. *For a job well done. With Love. S. XX.*

I grabbed the money and staggered to my feet.

The chill evening air cut into my drunken haze. It was so dull and plain, flavored with nothing except the lingering scent of rain upon stone. The walk to the castle took forever. The gargoyles greeted me first, protruding from the walls as they loomed over me with gnarled fingers clawing for my flesh.

Lilyanna should be okay. She was wrong about Clement. He was a good man. He took his job seriously and would guard her until I returned. Even if he was involved in the other grisly deaths, I'd now discovered the secret lair above his room, so he couldn't use it. That was logical thinking, right?

I hovered under the fangs of a large demon. Its eyes sparkled like shattered glass, drops of rain oozing from its bared teeth. One alighted upon my hand. It sizzled, dim red smoke smelling faintly of roses wafted from my flesh.

Lilyanna would be asleep in bed.

I leaned upon the stone wall, and it shifted beneath my hand. A crack barely wide enough to creep through emerged before me. The scent of roses became overpowering, gusting through the crevice as if luring me back. My feet swayed, hands clutching at the rough stone for balance. I forced myself through the hole, ignoring the tugs and scratches as if the creatures living in the walls were trying to trap me midway.

I broke through into a passageway and heaved a breath. I was in the servant's corridor, barely feet from my own private door. Was the castle warning me? Or maybe helping me get to Lilyanna as fast as possible?

My heart thumped. A spurt of adrenaline chased the wooziness from my legs.

Moving quickly, I passed through my lower room and staggered up the winding staircase. I thrust open the door to the sitting room and almost impaled myself upon Clement's saber. I lurched backward, arms pinwheeling at the top of the open staircase, and Clement dropped his sword to grab my cloak, tugging me toward him.

"What are you doing?" he hissed.

"Is she alive?" I pushed away, beelining for her door.

He grabbed my shoulder and swung me back to him. "Of course, but she's going to wake up screaming if you barrel in there like that."

He reached for my face, his hands skimming my cheek as he lifted the mask. He turned it over in his hands, the porcelain surface completely white except for delicate red letters embossed upon the forehead. *'Three weeks to go. If you want out, as you surely know, the name you must say and the debt you will pay.'*

I snatched it back and threw it into the hearth. The fire roared, green-tipped flames incinerating the mask within seconds. Clement's mouth hung open, the question obvious on his lips.

"In a minute." I stumbled toward Lilyanna's door and fell. Somehow, he moved much faster than I did, his body dulling my impact which otherwise would have left me crashing right through her door.

He steadied me, hovering his hands inches from my arms in case I wobbled over again and quietly turned the doorknob for me. I peered past, clawing at the doorframe for balance. Lilyanna slept soundly, the silk covers flat, her golden hair unbound and unruffled.

I let out a burst of laughter, and he quickly shut the door. I clapped my hand over my mouth and sank to the floor.

"Did you not trust me?" Clement slid to the floor beside me, his arms hooked over his knees.

"Of course I did." I shuffled closer, leaning my head on his shoulder. I took a deep cleansing breath, inhaling the scent of pine that lingered on his skin. "It's the castle I don't trust."

He nodded.

"Thank you for doing this." I reached up and kissed him on the cheek. His stubble tickled my skin, sending shivers of pleasure down my body. He turned to me, his breath heavy, his eyes hooded. I leaned into him, meeting his warm mouth with my own, threading my fingers into his hair to pull him closer.

His tongue parted my lips, roving around my mouth to taste every inch. His kiss was different to every one that had come before. For a moment I lost myself, forgetting to be distant, forgetting to keep that one piece of my soul apart. He tugged me onto his lap, my thighs spread wide around his hips. He ground against me in slow, sultry pulses, hardening fast, and oh, the sound that he coaxed from my throat. I wanted to tell him everything, to have him tease every confession from my lips with his clever mouth, but I couldn't. We were still working against each other, our goals opposite.

"Clement," I whispered. He murmured an acknowledgement, his kisses moving down my chin, my neck, his teeth nipping at my collarbone. "I want you, but you can't stay afterward."

He pulled away with a short bark of a laugh. "You're forward today. First, you don't trust me to look after Lady Lilyanna, and now, you're thinking of excuses to kick me straight out after you're done."

The buzzing resumed in my brain, heat redistributing to my cheeks. "It's just the sleeping part. Not the sex. Afterward."

He took my hands in his and cocked his head slightly. Then he pinned me with his dark gaze. "Why?"

"Because that's when things happen."

His thumbs stroked the delicate skin of my wrist while a small smile curved the edges of his mouth. That same mouth that still glistened, smelling faintly of cherries and vodka. "Okay, Tamara. So, number one" —I wrinkled my nose at the edge of laughter in his voice—"we are not going to sleep together because you are *very* drunk."

I opened my mouth to protest but ended up nodding in agreement.

He laughed, kissing me softly on the cheek. "And two." He kept his face close, his eyes heating, breath caressing my lips. "When it does happen, it'll be somewhere private. Somewhere where I can take my time. I'm going to touch every inch of your body. Kiss and lick and nibble my way, explore you...fucking devour you." I realized I wasn't breathing and gasped in air. "I'll find the spots you love the most, the sensitive areas that make you writhe and moan and beg me for more, and I'll push and tease and play until you come so hard you forget where you are, who you are. You forget everything."

My heart thrummed, my body milliseconds away from claiming him right there on the floor. I shifted against his rigid length, causing his breath to catch. "I want that now."

He leaned closer, brushing past my lips to bestow a chaste kiss upon my other cheek instead. "Tell me why you're here. Let me help you."

I rolled off his lap and slumped next to him. He tugged the thin duvet I'd piled upon the chaise down and tucked it around us. Sliding his arm across my shoulders, I drooped into him, defeated. There were some parts to my story I could tell him without endangering either of us.

"I grew up on the outskirts of town, this is the first time I've been back since...well...when I was younger, I couldn't sleep one night. There was a raging storm catapulting branches against the house and slamming the window shutters against the glass. It felt as if the whole world was about to crumble.

"So, I crept into my parents' bed and nestled in between them, cocooned within the warm goose-down and fell into such a deep sleep I didn't wake for almost a day. I never slept in. We were up at dawn and awake until dusk, working on the small farm, but that night, it was late afternoon by the time I finally crawled out from under the covers. The clouds hung low and heavy in the sky, the sun obscured, so for a while I thought it was dawn.

"But the smell." I shuddered, and his fingers stroked circles on my arm, keeping me tucked closely beside him. "I knew what clotted blood smelled like and the acrid ammonia of spilled urine that infiltrates your sinuses. Before I even looked, I knew. I'd slept through everything."

I sighed. "Anyway, it was always the same. If I let my guard down, it was always at night that things happened. My money stolen, my bounty nabbed. I was stabbed once. Okay twice." His hand tightened on my arm. "But it never happened when I slept alone because you don't truly sleep. Your senses never turn all the way off. And then here, the other night, I fell asleep with Lilyanna and woke up in that mausoleum you keep above your room."

"It's not mine." He bent and kissed my hair, gently pushing my head back upon his shoulder. "And why are you always in danger?"

I gripped the edges of the duvet, slowly ripping the threads beneath my fingers. "I was roped into a deal with the devil. It wasn't mine to make nor mine to refuse. My life was tied into those of two others, the Collectors. They were saved from death and allowed a second chance at life, but they must collect the bounties I find." My eyes drifted closed as his fingers stroked through my hair, my grip on the duvet weakening. "If a Collector or their bounty hunter fails or is caught, the Collectors die, and the hunter takes their place. So if I fail, I become a Collector and am then at the mercy of another. Simple."

He gently untangled my fingers from the covers and held my hand within his. "Might be simple, but it's not fair."

I snorted an agreement. We remained in comfortable silence, my breath deepened, matching the sonorous rhythm of his.

"Why are you here, Tamara?"

"For the Sheriff." I yawned. "I was supposed to have a free ride with his capture but then was given another job." The lie came easy. I'd already told him more than anyone before. Only Siobhan knew the intricacies of my deal, the story of my life so far, and that was because she orchestrated it all. "But I can't leave Lilyanna here." Over the years, I'd found that the best lies were always laced with the truth.

Clement murmured his agreement, resting his chin atop my head.

My stomach churned. Bile laced with sickly cherries inched up my esophagus. What I would give to tell him everything, to have him help me get to the prince and complete my mission. But he'd never agree. His whole life had been protecting the prince. He knew the risks of working in this castle, he knew what really lived and breathed in the walls more than he let on.

"I don't feel well," I whispered. "You should go now."

He shushed me, keeping his head pressed atop of mine. "Try and sleep. Nothing will touch you while I'm here, Tamara."

"Don't call me that," I mumbled.

The room spun around me as my eyelids slid closed. But with every loop, I nestled closer into his embrace, tucked tightly against him. *Don't go to sleep*, echoed in my churning body, fading with every ricochet until I passed out.

CHAPTER TWENTY
OMENS

Nothing happened that night.

No handprints, no creepy giggles, no abductions. That said, I was basically unconscious and could have been dragged down to the gates of Hell themselves and not awoken.

Clement snuck out early, presumably resuming his position with the prince. He kissed my hair softly, but I pretended to be asleep, foggy memories of what I'd said to him threatening to resurface along with the cherry concoction churning in my stomach.

I moved along the stone walls gently tapping each join, scratching my nails down the chalky mortar until Lilyanna's door whispered open. She studied me with her hands on her hips, blonde hair in its usual wild morning state, but still beautiful. I'm sure I looked like I'd been dragged through the walls and partied all night with the gargoyles.

"Nothing happened last night because Clement was here." She stifled a yawn, pulling the cream robe around her. "And he controls *them*."

I rolled my eyes at her, pausing mid-tap. "It's not him. If it's anyone, it's the prince. When is it ever the loyal, humble, and dare I say it, very sexy, servant?"

She scoffed. "This time."

I grunted and resumed my search for vents, peep holes, or anything that shouldn't be there. "I did have an epiphany last night though."

She plopped down on the chaise, swung her legs up, and nodded.

I held her gaze. Both of us were too astute, too suspicious by now to glance at the ceiling or indicate the hearth, but a silent message of agreement passed between us.

"So, perhaps we should venture out into the city at some point. We've been cooped up here for weeks. Some fresh air would do your complexion a world of good. If we go through the servant's door at night when the kitchens are empty, there shouldn't be a problem."

She laughed. The natural glow that had filled her cheeks a few weeks ago was now replaced by a pale matte. "I think that's a great idea."

"I'll need to fix," I waved generally in her direction, "all of that first."

"You're the worst maid I've ever had, you know that, right?"

I curtseyed and went to retrieve the hairbrush. I'd barely finished taming the unruly mess when a smart rap came at the door. I went to open it, finding the prince, flanked by an unimpressed Bryn, and Clement with a wicked sparkle in his eyes.

"Good morning, Tam," the prince said.

I nodded and ushered him inside. Clement walked through with him, keeping his body between us like a shield, barely managing to fit abreast. I sighed at him and the corner of his mouth twitched in response. He glanced his finger down my hand as he passed, sending warm currents through me. *Goddessdamn him.*

I left the door open, content to have a quick escape route if Clement mentioned a word about last night.

"Lilyanna, my love." The prince walked to where she perched daintily on the edge of the deep purple chaise. He kissed her hand. "You look beautiful, as ever."

She smiled coyly, and I gagged. She stifled her snort of laughter by reaching quickly for a glass of water from the small end table.

"I've come with something I hope you both shall like." The prince moved back toward me and held out his hand. "Come sit with us."

My blood froze.

"Everyone always acts so formal around me, but I like you, Tam. You're real." He raised his hand again. "Come."

I raised my arm robotically, but Clement grabbed my wrist.

The prince straightened. He and Clement were evenly matched, both medium height and lean with every muscle perfectly carved. Or so I had discovered when I straddled him last night. My blood began pumping again. He barely needed to touch me, and in my mind, I was already sprawled naked in his bed.

"Clement." The prince's voice was light, but the warning was clear.

Clement's fingers dug into my flesh, the bangle trapped between his hand and my wrist bones. Did he think I'd use it on the prince? And if so, why did he bother giving it to me?

Silence sectioned the room, all of us trapped in our own parts. Clement's gaze plummeted to his shoes, but his jaw clenched, his body firmly blocking mine.

"So, my dear." Lilyanna jumped up, her voice light and melodic despite the ashen face and frown she tried to conceal. "What news did you have for us?" She hooked her arm around the prince's elbow, and they returned to the chaise.

Clement unwound his fingers, and I tugged my arm back, rubbing the sore skin with a glare at him. He steadfastly ignored me but let out a shaky sigh. His chest deflated, and his taut body relaxed. I stalked to the opposite end of the room and folded my arms over my chest.

"Well." The prince too seemed slow to recover. "You both said you were in need of some fresh air. To get out of the castle."

I blinked in surprise. Lilyanna's smile faltered; the words too perfect a match to what we'd just said to be a coincidence.

"That would be lovely," she managed. "What did you have in mind?"

He looped his arm around her shoulders, and they settled back into the plush buttoned upholstery. "A tour through my city, *our* city. My people are excited for the upcoming royal wedding and want to put a face to the wonderful descriptions that have been circling about you. I think they do not yet believe you are real, my dear."

She smiled and rested a hand on his chest, angling her body into the crook of his. But her leg jiggled.

Clement shot me a warning glare, knowing the words floating through my mind. *They really just want to see that you're still alive.* I smirked at him. Even from across the room, I could feel his sigh in response, and my chest tingled as the air warmed me.

The prince glanced between us before clearing his throat, drawing attention back to himself. "And then I have a surprise for you. Something that I know you will love and should put your mind to rest. Have Tam help you get ready. We'll depart in an hour."

The town had caught wind of Prince Bellinor's *spontaneous* idea to take Lilyanna for a tour. We stuck to the long, central street, walking so slowly, I kept tripping over Clement's boots. Lilyanna was wedged between the prince and Clement, with Bryn on his far side.

People spilled out of the crushed houses lining up alongside the cobblestone path to wave, cheer, and shout gratitude at him. All the upstairs windows were flung open despite the heady chill, and those who couldn't see on the streets were waving banners or flapping scarves, anything they could find to catch his attention.

No matter how hard I scanned, there were no scowl-faced people standing with arms crossed and feet planted, cursing his presence. Nor furtive figures, pressed back inside the alleyways, plotting some kind of retribution.

It hadn't been like this that day at the market. He'd almost gone unnoticed. I hoped Lilyanna didn't believe in the sham.

Her face turned as she caught sight of a young girl jumping up and down at the side of the road. She waved back. It was cold enough that I'd persuaded her to wear a knitted scarf, wrapping it gently around her sore throat, the bruises completely hidden. The only sign of her discomfort was in the hesitancy with which she turned her head. She smiled widely at the small girl, her eyes crinkling, cheeks lifted, but the light didn't fully evolve in her face, sparking but not catching.

Good. She wasn't sure either.

The prince turned back to see that I followed. I dipped my head, willing him to focus elsewhere, my skin crawling.

My magic chose that moment to stir.

"A word, Your Highness." A wizened man stepped forward, his back bowed, hand clamped around a cane. A hunk of crystalized diamond made up the tip, its multiple facets glittering in the sickly sunshine. "Your imposed clamp down on magic use has been highly successful." He tapped the cane on the ground at the end of every sentence. "The people are also very grateful for your tolerance. Your ability to forgive and send those who are guilty out of the walls for a second chance has not gone unnoticed.

"That murder," he shuddered, the cane vibrating against the ground, "was one of the worst these townsfolk have ever seen, that I have ever seen. And to befall my very own inn! Generations. It has been in my family for generations, and nothing of the sort has happened like that before."

The Sheriff forced his way back to the forefront of my mind. Splayed on the bed, body painted in red and black slashes.

"Yes," the prince said, "it was by far the worst crime we've ever had. I pride myself on keeping this town safe. Two of the men rounded up for magic use were not involved, so they were released, but you can inform the townspeople and visitors to your establishment they are quite safe. Nothing of the sort shall happen again. My investigators are close to capturing the culprit."

The innkeeper nodded. "It was more than fair, Your Highness, and far more lenient than the queens would have been."

The prince chuckled. "Don't let them hear you say that. We all have our spies and theirs are everywhere, even this far north."

The man ducked his head again and returned to the crowd. The prince tightened his grip on Lilyanna's arm, and she flashed him a small smile. He turned from the main street down one of the alleyways. The crowd dispersed, doors closing, windows snicking shut as life resumed its efficient bustle behind us.

He recounted the town's history as we walked, from the very first stone placed in the wall to the expansion of the maze of alleyways. I closed in, waiting for a natural pause so I could tug Lilyanna aside to discuss what I needed to say to her, before we returned to the listening walls of the castle.

Every time I opened my mouth, the prince would steer the conversation again, or head down an intersecting street. He knew I wanted her alone, and I knew he was playing with me. My hands balled into fists.

He chose that moment to round another corner, his face angling briefly to mine. The smirk on his lips made me want to punch him. Was he trying to get back at me for favoring Clement? We'd come so close to kissing at the moon festival, but there was an edge to him. The Sheriff tried to warn me, my magic had tried to warn me, even Siobhan may have been telling the truth.

I stomped after them, boring holes into his back with my glare.

Finally, a lull in conversation. I sped up to force myself between them so I could tug her back to walk with me when Bryn stepped across my path scanning the street around us, completely severing my momentum. She didn't even look at me, whipping her head back around so fast, I was surprised her immaculately coiled bun didn't unravel. She set off again, forcing me behind as the alleyway narrowed.

I groaned and kicked at a loose stone.

"Why are you sulking?" Clement fell into step beside me.

"I'm not sulking." I glared at him, unable to fix my face in time. "I'm trying to talk to Lilyanna."

"You talk to her all day, every day." His hand fell to the small of my back and he leaned in closer, a wicked grin curling his lips. "Talk to me."

I should have ignored him, should have pushed past the guards and grabbed Lilyanna. He was such a distraction. My body was hyper-aware of his every move, his warm breath, his featherlight touch against my back. My mind emptied.

He nudged me. "Tam?"

"Are you going to have another evening off before the wedding?" My skin flushed as I imagined sitting with him in the Diamond Nightingale, squashed into the corner with our knees touching, sipping ale while we both tried not to focus on the lure of the rooms upstairs. "I'd like to go with...spend time...you know, just us." I kept focused on the cobblestones, willing myself not to trip as my legs threatened to collapse. What was he doing to me?

"Not before the wedding, no." He watched my face fall. "I'll make it up to you, though." He hesitated, focused on the others rounding the corner ahead. The instant they disappeared, he grabbed my elbow and flattened me against the hard wall. He lunged, taking my mouth in a fierce, claiming kiss.

He pulled back, breath mingling with mine, his body still poised against me. "Do you feel better, now?"

Air rushed out of me in an incoherent mumble.

He grinned. "Good, let's go."

He pushed off and strode away quickly.

"What? That's it?" I tripped over my own feet in a hurry to catch up, stumbling after him.

His eyes flashed; his voice low. "That is nowhere near *it*." He winked and rounded the bend.

The others had stopped at the end of the maze of alleyways, a wide street opening before them. The prince scanned me, his gaze lingering on my flushed cheeks before tracing the rapid pulse of the jugular down my neck. He frowned before glaring at Clement, who stepped into his regular position at his shoulder without a word, hand falling to his saber.

I trailed after them again, content with bringing up the rear as my mind remained firmly back in the alley with Clement. Was I just a fun distraction for him as well? He kept telling me to leave, that he'd help, but not once had he suggested going with me. That was for the best though, surely? I couldn't have him endangered by my lifestyle, and if Siobhan caught a whiff of my attraction, he'd conveniently end up as my next mark. That was exactly the kind of retribution she would love. I touched my mouth, the imprint of his lips lingering, and my heart squeezed. No, it was better this way. We shouldn't let it be anything deeper.

Incense swirled into my nostrils, and I jerked my head up. A slender cathedral towered above; its spire lodged within the gray sky. The large double doors were flung open, a walkway of sheer diamonds glistening like ice led to a circular vestibule.

The temperature plummeted as I stepped inside. Once my eyes adjusted to the dim light, I scanned the room. Circular stone benches four deep spread around a central altar. A large wicker casket, jarringly out of place amongst the stone, rested in the middle. The place was empty.

My feet dragged as I followed the others. My life had been spent chained to the devil, not the Goddess. Would she be able to sniff me out? Perhaps summon thunderclouds of lightning to rend the air, cracking down to split the very stone beneath my feet and bury me under a pile of rock. Siobhan would not save me unless it benefitted her.

Lilyanna squealed, the sound ricocheting in the quiet. I jumped and flung my hand over my chest. She turned sharply to the prince, her eyes bright, her golden braid flying over her shoulder. "Is this the surprise? To have the banns read?"

He nodded. His lips were pressed tight and his smile forced. Was he nervous? Maybe he was worried about retribution for keeping that woman after the priestess had deemed her free of magic, only for her to die. Good.

On cue, the priestess emerged from the far recess of the chamber. Today, she wore her shimmering veil with the diadem nestled in her gray hair. Her robes were still black, the diamonds glistening like slime. At least you knew what you were getting from this side of the divide. There'd be no teasing, no flirting, and certainly no rendezvous in the Red Blush.

Flanked by his two guards, the prince moved to the right side of the altar. I hovered behind Lilyanna on the left and the priestess took the center.

"What's going on?" I hissed.

"Quiet, Tam." She swatted her hand at me. "This is important."

The priestess began to chant, and the wicker basket trembled.

"Lilyanna, what is—"

She half-turned, keeping her voice to an irritated whisper. "This is it. It will cement the match. When released, the patterns they make are omens for happiness, prosperity, fertility."

"When what is released?"

She shushed me again and focused on the now jerking basket. A muted hiss filled the air.

My skin prickled. I raised my gaze from the altar and slammed into the emerald eyes of the prince. The rest of the room fell away, a furrow of silence connecting us. The corner of his mouth twitched, plunging my stomach into my feet.

Did he know Lilyanna was having doubts? That she spent every free second following some superstition or other. She couldn't just let fate dictate her path for her, she wanted to make sure she'd done everything she could to win the Goddess's favor. If she made it to the actual wedding, she'd have gone further than any of the others.

The lid slid off the basket and tumbled to the floor. My attention snapped back to the altar, breath rushing into my stagnant lungs. How long had I been trapped in his stare? I breathed deeply, reining in my pounding heart.

Three emerald snakes slithered out of the basket. They wound upward, swaying to the melody of the priestess's chanting. I inched nearer to Lilyanna who had pressed so close to the altar, I suspected she could hear the sound of each individual scale rustling over each other.

The chanting stopped and the snakes paused, their lengths stretched vertically as if suspended from an invisible pulley in the ceiling.

The priestess nodded toward Lilyanna.

"Dear Goddess," Lilyanna said, her voice eager and strong, "we have gathered here today to ask for your blessing. What knowledge can you bestow upon us as to our future marriage?"

The snakes held still. I glanced at Clement who'd paled, his knuckles white on the hilt of his saber. Bryn seemed not to be faring any better, her body tipped back, neck extended as she put as much distance between herself and the snakes as she could.

The prince still watched me, but I didn't dare meet his gaze again. My skin froze wherever his eyes alighted.

One of the snakes swiveled, its red eyes coming to rest on Lilyanna. She leaned further forward, her fingers gripping the edge of the altar as her body quivered in excitement. "I'm ready, Goddess," she whispered, "show me."

The snake lunged. Long, white fangs flicked forward, driving for Lilyanna's face. I shoved her sideways, grabbing the snake in mid-air, my fingers tightening behind its head. It whipped its body back and forth, rough scales colliding with my arm. Furious hisses scorched the air. I scooped the lid from the floor and shoved the snake back into the basket, squashing the other two in with it. The snakes immediately calmed.

Even the priestess regarded me with a wary look, her hands scrunched into the fabric of her veil.

I let out a long breath and wiped my hands down my trousers. Nobody moved.

The prince cleared his throat. "Where did you learn how to do that?" His face tightened, the vivid color in his eyes dulling back to a dark green.

"Oh, don't sound so disappointed, my dear prince," I said. His lip curled. "I grew up on a farm." I shrugged, glancing at Clement. "The snakes were useful, they ate the rats. But they're still wild animals, and if they got too close to the chickens, I'd have to move them. It took only one bite and agonizing gangrene in my arm that had to be cured by magic, to learn how to handle them properly." I looked at Clement again. His face was still pale, but a sloppy smile spread as he listened. My chest heated.

Lilyanna gave a small sob, and I gathered her to me. "It's okay." I stroked her hair. "Let's go back." She nodded, keeping her face pressed against my neck. She took a deep breath and straightened.

The prince circled the altar, quickly inserting himself between us and took her arm. She gave me a wistful glance but molded herself to his body.

I walked on their heels, ready to swipe her back to me if she needed it.

"Lilyanna, my dear," the prince angled her further from me, "you shouldn't put so much stock in those old-fashioned rituals."

She sniffed; her words breathy as she tried to regain composure. "They always come true. It's a direct message from the Goddess. She was telling us not to proceed with this union."

"Don't be absurd." The muscles in his neck corded. "It's like Tam said, they're wild animals—"

"I believe it," I piped in.

Clement swooped in front of me, nudging my shoulder.

"They're wild animals," he continued, moving to block my view. She sniffed again, her breath catching. "Look," he snapped, "I wouldn't have taken you if I'd thought it would upset you this much." He took a deep breath, and I burned daggers into the back of his head wishing my magic could leech into the air and penetrate his thick skull.

"No, no." Lilyanna straightened, subtly increasing the gap between their bodies. "You are quite right. You must forgive me, I'm just a little shaken."

We stopped outside the main entrance to the castle, both guards on duty ducking their heads as they swung the heavy door open. The prince kissed Lilyanna's hand and stepped back. The moment he let go, I bounded up the stairs and took her arm. Clement's hand narrowly missed my sleeve as he tried to stop me.

"I still have some errands to run, my dear," the prince said. "Why don't you go inside and settle. I'm sure Tam is dying to get some alone time with you."

I narrowed my eyes at Clement, flinging my irritation toward him instead. He widened his eyes innocently, but his lips twitched.

"And later perhaps, we will all go and do something to erase the memories of this morning." He retreated to the bottom step, both guards moving to his flanks. "For the fayre is in town, my dear. Tonight, we shall all go."

CHAPTER TWENTY-ONE

FAVORS AT THE FAYRE

Everything was the same.

It was as if the fayre had been picked up whole and transported across the queendom. I drank in the fresh air as I absorbed the tender music, appreciating each and every hue of colored light. I hadn't spent long with the company, popping in and out to read tarot whenever it suited me to covertly study a mark, but every time I returned, it felt like coming home. The whiff of magic called to me, singing through my bloodstream and igniting a power I should never have unearthed.

It was ironic that the prince allowed this magic into his city. If he'd borrowed those stupid divining rods from the priestess, they would be zinging all over the place. I pushed the thought far from my mind and allowed the atmosphere to warm me to my marrow.

Clement walked a few paces behind Lilyanna and the prince. He kept me by his side, his hand on the small of my back. He'd relaxed significantly since the spat in the castle, and I leaned into him, eagerly absorbing every discarded comment.

"When I was a child," he said, "the fayre would come every few years. It would always be exactly here," he waved his hand in the air, "and there was never any warning. We lived outside the city walls, about a half day's walk, but me and my sister would sprint the whole distance." He chuckled, his eyes lighting up. "We would be exhausted when we got there, but the smells, the sounds, the excitement would fuel us. We'd do every game, visit every single stall, camp outside until our mother dragged us home again or the fayre packed up."

"What was your favorite?"

"Oh, we didn't have a favorite. Magic, fire, contortion, axe throwing…Although, the one thing we'd always get was cotton candy. A huge rainbow cloud of the stuff. It never ran out either. That's what it felt like anyway. I only ever reached the white stick when I was on the verge of puking."

I ran my hand down his arm and tentatively laced my fingers with his. Why was I shaking?

I cleared my throat. "When was the last time you came?"

He grinned at me, squeezing my hand. "Probably before I took over my sister's position as head guard. She was promoted down South to be part of the queens' protective service." He shrugged. "I never would have been gifted this position otherwise. We come from a rural hamlet in the mountains. No gossip, no drama, just a solid work ethic." He sighed. "I had pretty fucking difficult boots to fill. She was…*is* highly decorated."

We stopped as Lilyanna tugged the prince over to a stall, coming to stand just behind them. She seated herself on the low bench, the creaking sign above the stall advertising 'the future'. I smiled. This seer was far more practiced than me. Her deck was worn, the black and silver pattern marred with white lines. She probably didn't need to resort to cracking scents with her knees or cheap magic tricks.

She turned over the Lovers card immediately. The prince slid in beside Lilyanna and hooked his hand around her trim waist. Good. If she were doing a true reading, listening to the spirit world and not psychoanalyzing the body language of those in front of her, maybe she'd produce a real warning. Then Lilyanna would be ready to listen to me later when I proposed my plan to get her out of here. The banns disaster weighed heavily on her shoulders and even she couldn't ignore all the signs stacking in the opposite direction.

"Let's get some candy," I said to Clement. "They'll be fine here and it's just over there." I hooked my thumb behind us knowing how many strides it would take, the exact arrangement of sweets on the stall and the precise position of Candyman's hands looped into his suspender belt.

"They'll rot your teeth."

I rolled my eyes. "Who cares? My soul is already rotten, what's a little more?" I tugged him gently, and he offered no resistance, a tender smile widening under the ever-lengthening beard. "Besides, it reminds you of your childhood and me of more *interesting* times."

We paused in front of the delicious array of sweets, the scent of warm sugar drenching us.

"With a man?" he asked.

I grinned and turned away, my hand hovering over the crinkled white bags.

"I seem to remember that it was toffees you simply couldn't resist." Candyman plucked a bag from the pile, tossing the top cube into his mouth. He winked at me. "On the house, Tam."

I pretended to fan myself, dabbing at my cheeks and chest.

"Have you slept with everyone in the queendom?" Clement hissed in my ear.

"Oh, don't pretend like you haven't." I blew a kiss at Candyman and turned, stuffing toffee into my mouth. I offered him the bag as we walked back, and he gingerly took one, eyes narrowed. "I know firsthand that you have a filthy, *filthy* mouth, my friend."

He choked on the toffee, spots of color darkening his cheeks.

I pressed my hand to his mouth. "Don't apologize." I ran a finger over the contour of his lower lip, mopping up a line of burned sugar. "I can't stop thinking about it." I sucked my finger, the trace of toffee and him dancing on my tastebuds. I held his gaze and watched it heat as he closed the gap between us, his face lowering.

Bryn cleared her throat, elbowing Clement for good measure. Reluctantly, he straightened and took up his usual position, hand resting on the sparkling hilt of his saber.

Lilyanna rose from the bench in front of the tarot reader, and I swooped, linking her arm and whisking her off down the aisle.

"What did she say?" I asked.

"That my path was complicated and dangerous. That there were other ways to achieve my goals." I grinned at her, and she bumped me with her hip. "Stop it, Tam. I know your opinion."

"No, no. Tarot, I believe. Well," I popped another toffee in my mouth and rattled it around my teeth as I spoke. "I believe in most of these so-called omens actually. You've enlightened me as to the ways of the North."

She laughed. "I don't believe you."

"It's true." I emptied the rest of the bag into my mouth, humming with pleasure as the caramel and treacle melted on my tongue. "The bad ones, I believe straight away."

"You only believe in it if it suits your purpose."

"True, my friend. Very true." I steered her to an open patch behind the main line of stalls. "There's a wonderful fire show down here. Marianne is an old friend of mine and if you want, we can be part of her performance."

To her credit, she didn't balk at the idea until we stood in the center of a worn patch of grass with unlit tiki torches carved with ogres, dragons, and witches leering at us from every angle. "I feel like we're in a cult circle," she whispered. "Is this safe?"

I shrugged. "I've never actually been part of this act before. Although I used to feel the scorch of the flames from way down there."

She swallowed and gathered her long jade skirt, cinching it tight around her legs.

"But when the fire starts, it'll be safe to talk."

Marianne addressed the crowd gathering in front of us, dropping into an exaggerated bow for the prince. Clement stood behind him with arms crossed and a scowl etched onto his face as he stared at me. How did he always know what I was planning? My lips curved at the sight of him.

"What you're about to see is of course dangerous, exciting, and completely fucking reckless." Marianne grinned, shooting two fireballs from her outstretched palms. They roared over the crowd and circled like boomerangs, trailing sparks and crackling like lightning.

"I wonder who paints the flame-retardant herbs onto her hair when I'm not around," I said. Marianne liked to style red and yellow spikes atop her head, shaving the sides for a more dramatic appearance.

"I'm more worried about her puffy sleeves," Lilyanna replied.

Marianne waved her hands, silencing the crowd. She produced a small onyx box from her pocket. Carefully, as if it would detonate any second, she rested it in the center of her cupped hands and blew. A sharp gust of wind blazed through the clearing, ruffling the crowd's hair and billowing Marianne's flared trousers like sails.

A small sphere of fire ignited in her outstretched palms, and she tossed it into the air, a mighty golden dragon unfurling with a bang. It opened its wings, beating the air, causing the wooden signs of the local stalls to swing and creak wildly.

The dragon screamed, flames gushing from its mouth. Each of the torches around me and Lilyanna whooshed to life, the flames rising higher and higher, reaching toward each other until we were in a molten birdcage.

The dragon screamed again, circling us, brandishing its forked tail.

Marianne cracked her neck and popped her knuckles, the sound magnified so a shudder ran through me. "Shall we rescue some damsels in distress?" she called. The crowd roared in approval.

It was beautifully serene inside the flaming cage. Marianne had set it to crackle gently like a log fire in winter, perfuming the air with a mild wood smoke. The heat roared outward, causing the crowd to shy away, but inside our little cocoon it was perfectly comfortable.

"We should use your engagement as an excuse to leave," I said.

"I don't think I—"

Marianne dodged past the dragon, narrowly avoiding a tongue of flame. She snuffed out one of the bars, dragging her hand down the flame to the torch at the bottom as easily as if it were a candle.

"You were almost strangled. By sheets, for Goddess's sake. And I found myself *inside* the walls. Inside!"

"You could still—"

"I'm only leaving with you, Lilyanna. Unfortunately, I kind of like you now, and I know you're better off alive than dead. No amount of gold-infused diamond is worth finding out about your grisly murder later. You know your family would agree."

She laced her fingers with mine as another bar dissolved. "My family sent me knowing full well what happened to the others."

She jerked her head back as Marianne leaped upon one of the bars, a spike of fire impaled through her torso. She ripped it out and snapped it over her knee, tossing the smoldering embers toward the crowd who scurried back, cheering wildly.

"But," she sighed, "I don't want to die."

"Good. So, we plan to go visit your family. Discuss wedding arrangements or post-marital visits or how many grandchildren they want, whatever is most believable, and we'll get the fuck out of here."

"Simple."

I nodded. "It's genius if you ask me." Siobhan had given me a bag of money and an expanse of ideas. I'd busy myself putting everything into motion and at the last moment, I'd whisk Lilyanna away and the prince and that Goddessdamned haunted castle would be none the wiser.

Clement though? My stupid heart ached already. I'd have to ignore it. It was just lust. Pent up, fully saturated, ridiculous feelings toward a man I hardly knew.

The second to last bar disappeared, the crowd obscured by a smoky cloud that serpentined toward the night sky. The dragon roared and dived toward Marianne.

"But the prince can't get wind of it. None of them can. We have to pretend like we're coming back," I said.

She squeezed my hand. "Then we can send for the prince. Perhaps he will come visit me, and we can live in the West instead. He could be trapped by that creepy castle as well. Maybe that's what the signs are saying, that our paths still cross, but just not here."

The last bar disappeared, and the crowd roared. Marianne spread her arms wide, and the dragon launched at her. They rolled across the ground in a large fireball until she managed to wrestle it back inside the small box.

She put the box in her pocket, stood and took a deep bow, the tips of her hair smoking. She turned and gestured for us to join her.

I put on my most sincere voice, hoping she wouldn't notice. "I've often thought that as well. Why else would he stay?" I painted a smile on my face and grasped Marianne's slick hand, falling into a bow with Lilyanna bent beside me.

The prince would not be visiting her because before we left, I'd finish my job. There was nowhere for me to run. Siobhan would *always* find me and that was worse than just delivering a small scratch. Perhaps it would be a welcome relief for him. If he were truly trapped, he could create a new life of freedom in the afterlife. Lilyanna would get over it.

The prince wasted no time in reclaiming her, and we moved toward the outskirts for the finale of the evening. Clement trailed behind them, his body pressed against mine, tugging me back and allowing the gap to widen. Bryn fell into step on the prince's left with a small shake of her head.

I pointed at her and raised my eyebrows.

"She'll be fine." He shrugged. "She owes me, anyway. She was stationed with my sister for years, and I know full well they took any chance they could get to sneak out together." He ran his hand down my back, tucking his fingers into the waistband of my leggings. "I don't know what you're planning, Tamara, but it turns me on watching you try and hide it from me."

"You really do have an active imagination, my friend. Is there not enough danger threatening the prince today that you're turning your attention to me?"

"My attention is always on you." He shot me a not-so-subtle grin before he grabbed my ass and swung me to the side. He backed me against the canvas of the last stall, shadows softly falling from the overhang and enrobing us in darkness. He turned me around, his hands slowly roving my front while he pressed up hard against my back.

The prince stood barely feet in front of us with his hand in Lilyanna's, illuminated in the multi-colored glow of the fairy lights. Their faces were upturned as the night sky erupted in dazzling streams of color and light and sound. Each firework carried a different essence—lemon, saffron, honey—the scents infusing the air as the giant aerial show began.

Clement's clever fingers wasted no time. He found my breast, tweaking my nipple until it peaked. I arched into him, his erection already straining against my lower back. His other hand slid down my stomach, tracing circles upon my flushed skin, his movements hurried but *so* persuasive.

In front of us, the prince stiffened. The tips of his ears reddened as the muscles of his neck went taut. Could he hear?

Clement's fingers teased open my waistband, gliding over the front of my lacy underwear. At the slightest pressure, an infuriatingly brief shudder of pleasure fired through me before he paused. He nibbled my ear, his breath warm and heady as he whispered, "Yes?"

The prince definitely knew. The forearm that encircled Lilyanna's waist corded; his muscles enhanced by the flashes of shadows as the fireworks faded.

And I didn't care.

I nodded, and Clement let out a muffled groan, his mouth caressing my neck. A pinwheel of gold screamed in the sky above us, shards of light piercing the shadows all around as he plunged his fingers inside me. My gasp was swallowed entirely by the noise.

Sweet melon scent infused the air around us, but I could barely sense it. My breath was shallow, head light with my every focus on his stroking fingers, the squeeze of my nipple in his other hand, the lapping of his tongue against my neck, the tightening coil of heat in my abdomen.

There was a lull as the last stars of gold rained down upon the crowd, but his hands kept moving, hips rocking against my back. Small ribbons of purple and silver leaped into the sky, unfurling into sleek dragons, the two colors writhing and winding around each other in a sensual dance. Lavender and lychee perfumed the air.

As the dragons rose, readying themselves for the final embrace, the coil inside of me snapped. Heat flooded my system, my body arching into his. He wrapped one hand around my mouth, muffling my cry while his fingers still worked, drawing out every last ounce of pleasure, until my body sagged against his.

He stilled against me, both of us watching the spots of color fade from the sky. A low hum pulsed from all around, the wooden stalls vibrating and the fairy lights tremoring. People murmured, casting eager glances up into the sky waiting for the finale.

The prince softly kissed Lilyanna's cheek, and she leaned into him, but the movement was stilted, his head turned for too long. His attention was still on us, but why did he care?

Clement slipped his hand out and brought it to his lips. I turned to him, his dark eyes hungry, pupils blown. "Beautiful," he whispered, slowly sucking his fingers, his mouth glossy and swollen.

My lips parted, a soft moan escaping and he kissed me deeply, his tongue claiming my mouth as his arm tightened around me again.

"My turn." He eased away, kissing down my jaw, sucking and nibbling on the exact point on my neck that sent me wild. I raised my head, extending my neck to present myself to him. One arm held me tight, his hand splayed on my stomach while the other freed his erection, pumping with strong, smooth strokes.

I giggled. What was wrong with me? I didn't giggle.

He smiled against my skin, his breath warm, tongue never ceasing as it swirled, tasting every inch.

What would happen to him when I got the prince? Would it ruin him? Could he come with me?

Fireworks screamed into the sky, exploding in blinding flashes of color, light, and scent. I gripped Clement's arm, tightening his hold around my stomach. His strokes were wild now, his body straining against mine.

He suspected I was up to something. He knew more than anyone, more than he should. If he found out what I was planning, would he stop me?

The air thickened, the final medley of patterns claiming the night sky. He bit down on my neck, his body collapsing against mine with a groan that was primal and dominating and Goddessdamn it, *so sexy*.

He pressed a kiss to my cheek and rested his chin atop my hair as orange-scented flares twirled to the ground around us.

Lilyanna turned to smile at me, her face aglow, eyes bright. I grinned back with both Clement's arms now wrapped casually around me. She turned back and snuggled into the prince.

She still believed he was good, that he was innocent, and I would try and save them both. She thought someone else was controlling the castle, but even if that was true, I had no choice.

My life wasn't the only one on the line.

CHAPTER TWENTY-TWO
TREASON

EARLY THE NEXT MORNING, WITH THE DAWN LIGHT SMOTHERED BY HEAVY CLOUDS, I slipped out the servant's door and cut through the city toward the stables.

The streets were empty, the cobbles neatly swept with fresh rain lingering on the bare washing lines strung between the houses. My worn boots produced only a muffled tread as I hugged the shadows, acutely aware that my progress could be tracked from the castle windows directly to the main gates down the arrow-straight road.

The coin purse in my cloak pocket jangled with every step. As always, Siobhan had been generous, and there would be no shortage of funds. I just had to cement the getaway and hoard enough supplies so Lilyanna and I could travel west in the fast-approaching winter. She'd agreed to go, but she didn't need to know the plans. I would tell her at the last minute, announce to the prince where we were going, and flee before the castle could crumble down around us, trapping us forever.

Maybe Clement would come with me, and I could keep him a secret from Siobhan, at least for a while. He could prove quite useful when Siobhan inevitably forced me out on a new bounty. He knew just enough to understand what I did, and so far, he wasn't disgusted or horrified.

He'd probably become quite accustomed to murder with all the local disappearances.

I smoothed my cloak, even though it made no difference to the wrinkled fabric. It would be strange not being alone. I could rest knowing there was always someone watching or turn and speak my mind when a random thought occurred to me, rather than muttering it into the thin air. I smiled, a faint blossom of warmth stirring within me.

Reaching the wall, I stopped briefly to chat with the woman at the gates. Dew clung like slime to the crystals embedded within the stone. The fresh country air whistled barely feet away, but even the wind was barred from entering the confines of the city.

"Morning, lass. Found what you needed in our fair city?"

"Almost." I withdrew a gideon from my pocket and tossed it to her. She kept her palm out, the single coin resting on her frayed gloves. I groaned and handed over another. "If I want to leave in a hurry, no questions asked, you'll be here?"

"Aye." She pocketed the coins. "I'll know. I'll be waiting."

I nodded and turned left. The path was empty, my footsteps echoing on the cobblestones. The small houses all faced inward, their tall stucco backs windowless, blind to the beauty that lay behind the wall.

Finally, the scent of sweet hay and rolled oats replaced the stale air and a warm glow emanated from torches sunk into alcoves along the stable walls. The building stretched long and deep with small rectangular windows hollowed into the stone. Occasionally, a velvet-soft muzzle would poke out or the swish of a tail could be heard.

I rounded the open barn doors and walked straight into the prince.

"Good morning, Tam."

I stopped short, recoiling from the front of his dark wool coat. "What in the Goddess's name are you doing here?"

"Tamara," Clement hissed. He rounded the prince, hovering in his usual position between us.

"Tamara?" The prince turned to me, a light shining in his blue eyes. A shiver crawled down my spine.

"It's Tam," I huffed.

"No, I like it. It suits you." His lips curved, his dimples popping. "I know so little about you."

My stomach flipped and heat crept up my neck. I glared at Clement who had gone rigid, his face drained of color.

"But that's why I'm here." He patted his thigh. "Come, I'll show you."

Come? I mouthed at Clement, but he ignored me, striding after the prince toward the back of the stables.

The last stall on the right stood empty, the heavy metal chain hanging limp at one end. The deep straw inside was flattened in the center with traces of steam coiling in the air, its occupant barely having exited. I ran my fingers over a carved plaque on the side that said, 'Siobhan'.

"Where's my horse?"

The prince chuckled. "Tamara, Tamara, Tamara"—I shot daggers at Clement—"so suspicious of my good intentions. I had her turned out this morning just before you arrived." He waved his hand in the vague direction of the moors beyond the wall. "I know that you only had enough for a few weeks lodging for her and as you will be a permanent fixture at the castle with my beautiful Lilyanna, I paid for an extended stay. You need not worry about doing any *alternative* jobs to pay for her anymore."

He was still smiling at me, his teeth pearly white with small crinkles lining his eyes. He was handsome but dangerous. Dimly, the magic stirred in my blood, seeping into my veins, unfurling itself to protect me.

When I didn't answer or offer my gratitude, he continued, "And of course, she would be far happier turned out to pasture."

And much harder for me to get hold of. I forced a smile. "That's kind of you."

Clement elbowed me, and I rolled my eyes. "Thank you, oh kind and noble Prince Bellinor." I bowed and Clement elbowed me again.

The prince threw his head back and laughed. The sound spurred my magic into teeming centipedes, frantically circling the length of my body. He clapped his hand on Clement's shoulder. "Leave her alone. I love having someone who will play my games."

As the prince stepped closer, Clement's hand snaked around my wrist, tugging me behind him. He drew a breath, preparing to give me a whispered lecture, but I yanked from his grasp and backed away.

"I need to go back. I have lots to do today."

"Bye, *Tamara*," the prince called.

My spine stiffened, my nails extending. I thrust my hands into my pockets and vowed to punch Clement the next time I saw him alone.

Fine. The prince knew. The castle had been quiet lately, but the spirits never rested. They must have overheard, telling him I was planning on taking Lilyanna away. Or was it me he wanted? Clement said the castle was after me first, that he couldn't protect me when it did, but it didn't matter. I was still going to win.

The stakes were too high.

I lay beside Lilyanna, my body jerking every time I felt myself succumbing to sleep.

All the fires were blazing, the windows permanently locked, but the spirits closed in. Every puff of air on my face, every tickle on my calf had me jumping out of bed and swatting at my body. Lilyanna slept through everything; it seemed to be her forte.

I stared at the bare patch of wall between the mute-colored tapestries. The stones merged, gray on gray, the cement bleeding into the monotone. Noiselessly, the bottom stone pushed outward, barely an inch but enough to draw my attention. Then the one above did the same. A line gradually formed. Below the ceiling, the ripple spread sideways in both directions in eerie unison.

It was a 'T', a sign. Were they coming for me? Warning me? I leaped out of bed and stumbled to the wall, barely able to keep on my feet. I ran my hands over the surface, but it was smooth. No cement flaked to the ground beneath, and the stones were cold.

I turned to check on Lilyanna, who remained fast asleep, her breath rhythmic and soft. Maybe the spirits weren't malevolent. Or not to me, at least. Siobhan was surprised I couldn't see them. Maybe my magic did more than I thought, and it connected me or kept me safe. She'd been careful never to tell me what else blood magic could do. She sidestepped my questions, always keeping me focused on the thing I was forced into doing with my *gift*.

Midnight stillness settled on the room. The night sky was abnormally clear. Even through the thick windows, the stars beamed. I threw off the covers and glanced one last time at Lilyanna to make sure she remained asleep and that the sheets lay calm before slipping from the room.

My cloak hung in its usual place, and I wrapped myself within its familiar folds. Closing the door to my room behind me, I rested my hand on the cold stone wall.

"I want to go outside," I whispered, "and not meet anyone." Nothing happened. I'd been very drunk the last time the castle opened up before me. Maybe I'd imagined it.

A gust of winter air blew down the corridor, purging the rose scent. I snapped my head up and moved toward it, following a route I'd never taken. My shoulders soon brushed the walls, my way chosen for me by the narrowing passageway. Every time a new fork appeared, the castle forced me toward it, as if it were squeezing me out.

Eventually, a set of stone stairs rose before me spiraling up into the darkness. "I wanted to get out, not go up," I hissed. Nothing answered. I turned around but the corridor disappeared, replaced by a bare gray wall.

My stomach churned, but I had no choice. Hugging the wall with my eyes glued to my feet and not at the ever-increasing drop, I climbed until I hit another door. I pushed against it, but something pressed back. I slammed my shoulder into it and squeezed through the small gap.

The wind tore into me, crushing me back against the door and sealing it tight. I fought for breath, my chest aching and my eyes watering at the sudden cold. I pushed toward the edge, my hood flying down and my hair ripping free from its bounds.

I was on the turret.

The wind raced around the crenels carved into the parapet, only ceasing when I leaned over the edge, pressing myself against the stone for shelter. The central street glowed faintly, illuminated by starlight. Lights burned in some of the houses, chimneys smoking, bats silhouetted against the sky.

A faint slam echoed behind me, but the wind tore the sound away before I could be sure I'd even heard it. I looked around. The turret was empty. I leaned back over the crenel and squinted at the horizon.

Beyond the wall, the moor stretched vast and wild to the south, unlit and untouched. I drank in a greedy breath, imagining myself out there, free of all responsibilities, carving my own path.

"Sleepwalking, Tam?"

I spun around, clutching the turret edge. "Where did you come from?" The door remained closed. How had he managed to sneak up on me?

The prince bestowed me with a smile. His chestnut hair was tousled, pink whipped into his smooth cheeks. He was unnervingly handsome even when he was playing with me. This time, I could feel his aura luring me closer.

"I fancied some air," he said. "We seem to have a lot of similar ideas recently, you and I."

The magic pulsed. This was my chance. He was alone, unprotected, unguarded. But how to make it look like an accident? I couldn't just scratch his eyes out or seduce him. He couldn't know what had happened, or I'd be dead as well.

"Yes, but at least I can dress myself." I motioned for him to come closer. "Let me fix that." One side of his lapel had turned up in the wind. I could smooth it out, catch the smooth skin of his neck with the edge of my nail.

The Sheriff's face swam before me, and I blinked it away, swallowing back the bile that laced my throat. *Not now. Focus, Tam.*

He glanced down. "You have been most useful since coming here." His eyes met mine. Tonight, they were black. Cold drenched my skin, the magic faltering at my fingertips. He stepped closer, and I ran my hand slowly up the velvet lining.

"I'm glad you're staying longer to be with Lilyanna." His breath washed against my face, making my stomach flip. I flattened the lapel and pulled away. The prince turned to look out over the city, his body hovering next to mine. "The castle likes you, Tam."

I stiffened. I should push him over the edge. Scratch him first, do both jobs at once. He was so close.

"*I* like you, too." His focus remained on the resting houses below, but his words were heavy.

I raised my arms, inching behind him. My heart thumped. So close. I was so close to being free.

The door slammed behind us, and I jumped backward as Clement barreled over. His feet were bare and his belt weaponless. He crushed me into a hug, his chest heaving before pushing me away.

Bryn materialized behind him, fully dressed and with not a hair out of place.

"Stay with the prince," Clement barked. She nodded and moved into position behind him.

Clement grabbed my shoulder, spun me around, and frog-marched me back inside. He waited until we were outside my door before unleashing. "What were you doing?" His eyes blazed. Gone were the small crinkles, the softness, the comfort. For the first time, I saw the true professional.

"I, well…it."

"You were alone with him." He lowered his face to mine, his breath hot, voice shaking. "Goddess knows what—"

"It wasn't like that. Don't be—"

He shook me with a growl of frustration.

"Stop it. Calm down." I pushed him away, but he held firm.

"You just don't understand. You don't listen!" His fingers tightened around my biceps.

"I do listen, I—"

"If you won't leave, then at least stay in there with Lilyanna, Tamara."

You'll be safe." His hands moved to my cheeks. The gesture should have been tender, but his whole body shook. With anger? Fear? Jealousy?

"It's not safe anywhere here." I deepened my breathing, forcing my heart to slow.

His thumb stroked along my cheekbone. "I can't do my job if I'm constantly worrying about you."

"And I can't do mine!"

I froze.

He frowned at me. "Your job is in there."

"Yeah, I know. It's just…I don't like being cooped up. I only wanted some fresh air." Would he let it go? He already knew more than he should.

He dropped his hands from my face, running them down my arms, never breaking contact until he gently held my hands in his. "If you wanted fresh air, you should've told me. There's plenty in my room due to the large hole you put in my ceiling."

My breath whooshed out in a snort of relief. I ducked my head, and he waited until I met his gaze again. "Please behave, Tamara. Just until the wedding is over."

I nodded. Guilt warred inside me. I'd do anything for this man, and I had no idea when he'd affected me so. When had he lodged himself within my heart?

But we were at odds. If I succeeded, at the very least, he'd be out of a job. Most likely, all the guards would be transported to the South to face trial in front of the queens and be hanged. Then what would I do? Continue onward wrecking people's lives?

No. I couldn't think like that. I'd get Lilyanna out, rescue her from this castle, then flee. See how long it took before Siobhan found me.

And Clement? My body sagged. He would have to look after himself.

CHAPTER TWENTY-THREE
THE MAGIC TOUCH

THE CASTLE LAY DORMANT FOR THE NEXT FEW DAYS WHILE ITS OCCUPANTS scurried about preparing for the wedding.

Despite this, I knew the spirits watched me and the walls breathed my whereabouts to the prince. Every corner I turned, he would be there, grinning like a cat toying with its prey. But I behaved myself, still warring with my guilt over finishing this assignment.

Clement stuck closer to me than to him throughout these meetings, never smiling, never fully relaxing. Dark shadows lingered under his eyes, his skin wan. He never spoke to me, never even tried to get me alone to explain the change in the prince's behavior.

He never uttered a single warning.

The wedding was fast approaching with barely a week to go, and if I were to believably abduct Lilyanna for the purposes of traveling back to the West to celebrate with her family and return in time for her to get married, we'd have to leave that night.

The castle was silent, watchful. Through the thick windows, the winter storm clouds were just visibly rolling in, distorted amorphous smudges of night-black, moss-green, and frozen blue.

I made my way toward the cloakroom situated by the kitchens. Inside was a single wooden chair and a low table with a spinning wheel already laced with thread. Matron pumped her foot upon the treadle, feeding cobwebbed strands into the mouth of the machine. A pile of thick, woolen cloaks heaped at her feet.

"I need two spare cloaks for me and Lady Lilyanna."

Matron continued to weave, the wheel cracking as it spun. "Can't, Tam." The thread bit into her fingers, blanching the skin. "The prince has ordered me to get everything prepared for the wedding. He wants all the holes patched, frayed trims smartened, fur linings added." The wheel spun faster, droning its sad lament. "He's having guests come this time. Wants there to be spares."

"Because it's the first time his fiancée has actually survived to the wedding day?"

"Now, now, Tam." She plucked at the thread tangled around the bobbin, strangling the string underneath. "You're new here, but the prince has been nothing but generous. That's why the people love him. The whole city is currently dancing around their kitchen tables with excitement." She pumped at the pedal again and the wheel restarted. "And he's particularly fond of you, for some reason."

"Don't I know it."

She shot me a sly grin. "I told you to keep your head down, go unnoticed."

"No, you said I was plain enough that he would never notice me."

She laughed. "Aye, that sounds right."

I sighed, hypnotized by the blurring spokes of the wheel. "So, no spare cloaks then?"

She shook her head. "Go ask the prince yourself if you want."

I grunted and backed toward the door.

We still had to go tonight. If we were fast enough, we'd get there before the snow hit and blocked the passes. We could buy food from the small hamlets on the way, swing by Clement's hometown and befriend his mother. I could offer her updates on her faithful son, and perhaps she would even tell me some of his childhood stories in return. I bet he'd always been such a stringent rule follower, even as a boy, though I'd love it if he did have a wild few years at some point.

When I returned to the room, Lilyanna's pacing was wearing a circle upon the thick rug in front of the window. "Good, you're back." She marched over and turned me toward the hearth. "The fire went out, and I can't get it started again." The air had chilled, her breath fogging as she spoke.

I shivered. The logs were piled high with the ends barely charred. There was no water, no breeze, no reason for it to have extinguished. I grabbed the flint and the poker, prodding and poking at the sparks until a cloying gray smoke wafted from it.

"Why is the smoke not going out?" Lilyanna choked, her hand over her mouth.

I leaned into the hearth and jabbed up the chimney with the poker. The whole shoot was blocked. Thick ash and sticky tar clung to the metal, eventually coming loose with a moist sucking noise, plunging in one giant gelatinous ball to the floor.

A glint of white caught my eye. I poked it gingerly, the tip chiming against the object. Bile rushed into my mouth, and I hurriedly sank it back into the mess before Lilyanna could see. A tooth.

I rocked back on my heels and grimaced. "You're going to need a maid to clean that up, Lilyanna." I swallowed away the nausea, forcing the emotion far from my face.

The flames finally caught, and the wood cracked happily as a rush of heat swarmed around us.

"Yeah, I'll ask the prince for one as a wedding gift." She tugged me to my feet and brushed the soot from my shoulders.

I leaned in close and whispered, "We go tonight. Meet me at the stables."

Her fingers didn't stop as she continued to flick the dust from my sweater. She nodded. "Go get cleaned up. You're barely able to look after me as it is. Now your mind is going to be stuck on what Clement will think when he sees you covered in dirt and stinking of smoke."

I shrugged and moved toward the door to my small room. "He'll probably like it."

She grinned. Our eyes locked again as I paused at the top of the stairs. "I'll be ready," she mouthed.

This was a terrible plan.

I ended up not even telling Clement, thinking it was best we just slip away. Once Lilyanna was safely out of the castle and within her city, I'd have to come back and finish the job as I'd not managed to find myself alone with the prince since the turret. Maybe I could persuade Clement to leave first and transfer down South. There was still time on my deadline as long as Siobhan didn't think I was running away and sent her hounds to chase me down.

I had no packed food, nothing for us to wear except the literal clothes on our backs, and I still had to find Siobhan—the horse—in whichever paddock she'd been exiled to and get her ready.

But it could still work.

The wind howled around the castle wall, its gargoyles swiveling on their perches, haunted eyes tracking my every move as I sidled through the servant's door. The night was freezing with thick, dark clouds obscuring the light. In the distance, the village glowed with a warm, heady aura that lured me in.

I ran my hand along the rough stone wall, its edges molding to my fingertips. I willed my heartbeat to soften and stop thrashing so painfully within my chest. What would Clement think? That I'd deserted him? Used him? Thrown him away like another casual acquaintance? It was too late to change how I felt about him, and far too late to tell him the truth behind my plan. I'd just have to squash my feelings of guilt far away inside and hope he forgave me one day.

I paused before rounding the corner and stepping onto the central road. The gargoyle towered over me, icicles dripping from its fangs as it inched toward my face.

I loosed my breath and strode into the open.

A single footstep crunched behind me, strong fingers ratcheting around my sleeve. I spun, yanking from its grasp.

"Tamara, Tamara, Tamara," the prince sighed. "Why do we keep meeting like this?" His face was drained of color, eyes murky in the gloom. No guards flanked him. No servants scurried by. It was just us.

Again.

"I'm going out." I pulled my thin cloak tighter around myself, my nails quietly lengthening inside the long sleeves.

"I know what you were doing." He leaned closer, the rose scent overpowering. But there was something underneath, something masked. Blood?

Two guards appeared from out of the shadows, both tense, both with hands grasping their sabers. Neither of them Clement.

"I think it's better that you stay inside for a while." He held out his hand. "Just until the wedding."

The magic burned inside of me, my fingers twitching, nails fully sharpened. I shouldn't touch him. That was Clement's warning, but was it for me or the prince?

I could complete both tasks tonight after all. Embed the trackers in the back of his hand, pretend it was nothing but a small scratch, and slip into the night when he turned away. But would Lilyanna be waiting? She should be here already, this was all for her. She'd said she would go.

Could *she* have told him?

I stifled a curse. The castle was manipulating me and so was the prince. It wasn't Lilyanna, she was innocent in all this. Something deep inside me trusted her, we'd spent too long in each other's company now to be anything less than allies. We were family.

The prince pressed closer, his hand still outstretched. The guards withdrew their swords, the curved blades slicing through the shadows as they pointed them toward me.

Slowly, I reached for him. As my skin pressed against his, cold drove through me and my magic recoiled, driving itself back deep within my soul. My nails forcibly retracted, sucking themselves inside my fingertips.

My ribs squeezed, my breath choked out in a strained gasp. He closed his hand around mine and tugged me toward him, his other arm encircling my waist. "Stay close and you'll be fine." He backed into the wall, the stone melting behind him. Fire burned in my lungs as I struggled to breathe, and the vise around my chest snapped another notch tighter.

I reflexively dug my other hand into his side, sinking into his flesh, but the magic stuttered. No release, no power.

The stone clawed against my face, tearing at my clothes and slicing my skin. The pressure increased, the edges of my vision darkening, but I kept my grip on his side, trying to force the magic out.

"Hold on, *Tamara*," he drawled.

We thrust through the wall, the stone snapping back into place behind us. My heart pounded, my head throbbing. I still couldn't breathe.

The prince pushed me back against the solid wall, its cold leeching through my cloak. He forced his mouth on mine, blowing air into my lungs, my breasts pressed into his solid chest. I gasped and shoved him away.

Something trickled from my mouth. I wiped it with my sleeve, recognizing the gooey feel of blood as it coated my tastebuds and pooled under my tongue. He'd bitten me. I bent over and retched while he patted me on the back.

"I thought you carried it. I saw the sparks at the festival, noticed the way the castle drew toward you. It took a while as my guards never let me close enough. Clement in particular has a fondness for you. But now, I know it's there. I taste it." He smacked his lips together. "It won't be so bad next time."

I straightened, turning around in the corridor, completely lost.

"You have new lodgings, my dear." The prince opened a small trapdoor, visible only by three black slashes in the wood that he inserted his fingers into. "Temporary, of course, but this way you'll be closer when I need you."

I spun around, wildly searching for a landmark I knew so I could run and find Lilyanna or Clement.

The prince leaped on me, arms encircling my chest and threw me down into the hole. I landed heavily, dust and ash billowing around me.

The trapdoor slammed shut and silence descended until a familiar groan sounded from the corner.

CHAPTER TWENTY-FOUR
HEART OF GOLD

I didn't know if I was in a dungeon, a cellar, or inside the floor.

The groan echoed, mournful and hoarse, coming from all directions at once. I scrabbled backward, clawing at the dirt floor with my hands and feet until my back pressed against planks of wood and the top of my head was squashed under a low ceiling.

Fumbling for my knife, I dragged it from the holster on my thigh and slashed through the cold air. The blade whooshed in the stillness, contacting nothing.

Siobhan. Her name stuttered on the tip of my tongue. She could control the spirits and could manipulate the entire castle, but I'd held out against her for almost twenty years.

She'd found me sitting alone in the small barn that day after the storm. I'd left the house, the smells, the atmosphere, and mechanically started my chores. The animals were grateful to see me. The chickens swarmed my feet, clucking impatiently for treats, and the three brown cows lined up next to the milking stool, lowing calmly.

I'd seated myself and dragged an empty pail closer, losing myself in the rhythmic *swish, swish, swish,* of the milk hitting the metal bucket, coils of steam rising into the air. Siobhan sat behind me on a bale of straw, gently stroking my hair. She didn't offer me an escape, nor answers.

It was never my decision to make.

Instead, she visited every week for the following year while I carried eggs and milk to the market, slowly selling farm equipment, animals, and clothing to pay my way. She bartered the deals, getting me grossly unfair prices.

I'd idolized her. I tried to rub pure lily pollen on my skin to emulate her scent and padded my hips and breasts to steal her curves. When the deal was finally struck, I was powerless to refuse as the Collectors had chosen me to save them from death. Then she'd transferred a thread of her magic, binding me to my role. I'd be successful for her; do any task she set and make sure I excelled at it. Every smile, every lingering touch, far exceeded the monetary payment. She became my only constant.

It took me many years to uncover the truth and finally see the bodies, crimes, and heartbreak left in our wake. By that point, I thought I was too far gone to save myself.

But I wasn't hers. And I wasn't ready to prostrate myself before her.

Something heavy and metallic clunked to the floor, vibrations rocking my body. Very slowly, it dragged toward me.

Another groan sounded, lower, harsher, *closer*.

I lashed out with the knife again.

My hand dragged through a turbulence in the air, igniting my entire arm. Something shrieked, rancid breath billowing into my face. The blade burned in my palm, and I threw it down, already smelling my seared flesh and feeling the slick drops of serum run down my fingers.

I lunged forward, grasping for the other knife I had stashed in my boot, but multiple hands cinched around my wrists, my ankles, my neck. I flew through the air, smashing down in the center, my face crushed into the dirt.

Freezing shackles snapped around my ankles and a chain dug into my flesh as it wound around my neck, connecting my hands and feet. Even when I lay panting and writhing and cursing on the floor, the bony hands lingered on my body. I knew the ash marks would be branding me with their touch.

The magic in my blood lay dormant, hidden deep within my soul. It knew that when detected, they would slash open my veins and exsanguinate me with hungry maws sucking and clawing for every last drop. The blood from that poor woman in the pit must have gone somewhere. Fed something. It sensed what the prince wanted before I did.

I lay pinioned until my heart forcibly slowed, the cold spearing into my resistance. The room remained pitch black, its darkness spinning around me whenever I tried to focus. Hours may have passed, or was it a day? My stomach growled, my throat barren. Did I want to die this way?

I couldn't do it. I shouldn't do it.

My jaw smashed together, shivers wracking my body. Only one person could save me.

"Siobhan?" It was a whisper, forced through gritted teeth. Something in my bones told me she'd come this time.

A circle of warmth enveloped me, her sweet lily scent curdling in the air. She stroked my hair, her lips pressed against my forehead. "You're ready, my love?"

I would never be ready.

"I want out. I'll join you, but I want the Collectors freed. I will not be responsible for their deaths."

"Once was enough, my dear, yes? That blame you set upon yourself has been carried around with you for an unnecessarily long time now." Her nails massaged my scalp. Tingles of warmth ran down my neck and loosened the rigid muscles of my back. "It's hindered many of my plans."

"Or give them another bounty hunter." I swallowed, leaning into her touch, despising myself more with every flush of warmth toward her.

"It's not your deal to make. They chose this life and the bond they signed is unbreakable. They were ripped from death's clutches with the caveat they repay by serving me."

"You could—"

Even in the darkness, her eagerness leeched into me as she hung on my every word.

"Yes, I could." Her hands loosened the chain around my neck. "But I won't."

Rage erupted inside of me. I threw my head back, narrowly missing her chin. I screamed and tried to right myself, but she hovered just out of reach, still bathing me in the temptation of her light.

"The Collectors are your responsibility, no?" She waved toward the shadows, drawing the spirits out. Sharp hands ratcheted back around my wrists, ankles, neck. Probing fingers sank deep into the grooves between my muscles and latched on. "But if you've had enough, you just need to say it. Tell me."

The chains tightened, my feet dragged closer toward my hands, contorting my spine.

"Aren't you tired, Tam?"

The pressure intensified. My shoulders were wrenched back to the point of popping, the joint creaking with every eked millimeter.

"No." It was a whimper when I wanted to sound strong and defiant.

"Such a shame." She tsked, sucking the sound through her lips. "Well, we have seen each other in situations such as this in the past, have we not? And you always find a way to slither through."

"Without your *help*," I whispered.

She tittered, her voice resuming its deadly, yet airily persuasive quality. My stomach flipped. If only the pain would intensify so I'd black out and be unable to hear what was coming.

"Unfortunately, I gave this bounty to you with the best intentions. Although nowhere near as fun, I have a number of equally qualified candidates lined up. They are literally chomping at the bit to get ahold of this assignment. And considering the…" She tugged on the chains and my shoulders screamed in protest, "imminent danger you find yourself in, it makes sense to bump up the deadline. Don't you think?"

Finally, the pressure on the chains loosened and I groaned, slumping back to the dirty floor.

"It may not seem fair now, my dear, but there's not really anything I can do about it. If you won't join me, you'll continue to work for me instead." She glided closer and began stroking my hair again.

"Don't you set the rules?" I jerked my head away, her fingers slipping through the tangled curls.

She laughed. "Well, yes, I suppose I do." She turned my chin toward her to kiss me on the mouth. It had been a long time since she'd kissed me, but my body remembered. I softened, barely a fraction, but she felt it. "You have until midnight on the day of the wedding to complete the bounty. Three full days should be plenty. Until next time, Tam."

Her warmth disappeared, the scent of lilies rotting in the dank air. I pulled at the chains, digging furrows in my neck, forcing my throat to constrict. I screamed into the darkness, hearing not even a muffled echo return.

Eventually, exhaustion won out and my eyelids fluttered closed.

As soon as I drifted off, the chains tightened, and I moved.

I remained rigid, the pressure around my neck loosening enough to allow shallow breaths. I was dragged face down across the dirt, dust and ash embedding in my nostrils, lining my sinuses, my throat, my lungs. My bound hands scratched against the ceiling, splinters giving way to rough stone.

I was inside the floor but travelling upward toward the new castle again.

My heart thumped and a brief flash of hope warmed me. Maybe Siobhan *was* giving me another chance. Small pockets of foggy light speared through holes in the floor, dimly illuminating the way. The spirits were still invisible, but they no longer touched me, even though their marks were burned onto my skin. Their touch lingered with every swallow and twitch of my body.

Should I scream for Lilyanna? For Clement? The smell of roses was overpowering again so I must be close.

The chains tightened around my wrists, catching the flesh between the links. I stifled a cry, keeping my body taut.

Suddenly, the floor disappeared, and I plunged headfirst. Before I could scream, I was jerked upward, my body hitting the floor, but my face left intact. I continued horizontally again, the stone above my head transitioning to wood planks as the air chilled.

I was in the old part of the castle and lower than before.

I thrashed against the chains, my heels connecting with the shaft, and my whole body jerked to a stop. The pressure on my neck tightened, squeezing air from my throat. I tried to claw at the chains, but my hands only twitched uselessly behind my back.

I forced my body to relax, to silently promise the spirits I'd behave but nothing came out.

The chain was tugged hard once more, and I was squeezed from the shaft, collapsing in a heap on the floor. They loosened just enough for me to drag in oxygen. I gagged and choked, wheezing in dust-laden air while I lay on the hard-packed earth, my body wracked, the blood stagnant in my veins.

Once my head stopped swimming, I wriggled into a seated position, wedged in the corner, my legs to the side and body twisted.

Torches crackled in sconces on the wall. Heavy chains looped from rings bolted into the corners and ceiling. The dirt floor was strewn with hay, mold and blood lying heavy in the air. It was enough to know that I wasn't in the pit. This was a different dungeon, and I wanted to be nowhere near it.

At the far end there stood a raised platform. Four diamond shackles gaped open upon the wall above. A faint outline like a golden shadow filled the wall, its hands and legs running directly through the shackles. A golden 'X' was painted where the heart would be.

Next to the empty space, four bodies were mounted like hunting trophies upon the wall.

The first was still recognizable as a woman. Tufts of ragged black hair draped a sunken face with wisps of clothes covering a skeletal frame. Sparkling diamond shackles cinched her hands and feet, a matching crown upon her head. Her chest was carved open, the skin everted, the muscles and ribs pulled back and skewered by large nails like a dissected butterfly. Her heart was a ruby. The guttering candlelight flashing across the facets gave her a heartbeat, swooshing blood across the surface.

I blinked, trying to clear my mind. But the corpse next to her with a silver heart also pulsed. And the sapphire beside her. The last one, only chalky bones and rusted nails, still had an emerald heart that writhed under the light as well.

My stomach churned, and I tilted my head back to stare at the ceiling, away from the haunted, empty eye sockets that stared straight at me.

I wish I hadn't.

The ceiling teemed. Darkness churned and scrabbled, forming limbs, flashes of an arm, curves of a waist. One of the figures jerked around, the dark void of its face staring directly at me. The whites of its eyes dripped into place like wax running down a candle. There was no giggling, no shrieking, but they were producing a low rhythmic pulse. Murmurs? Groans?

My mind absorbed the low hum, the magic in my soul crawling further into itself. I could understand it, feel it. It was an incantation.

And it called to me too.

CHAPTER TWENTY-FIVE
SPILLED SECRETS

THE CHANTING THRUMMED THROUGH THE AIR.

There were no words, just a rhythmic swell and ebb that I understood in my bones. As I relaxed, the teeming mass above my head calmed, lapping at each other like ocean waves, sliding into the spaces, constantly moving.

The pulsing hearts on the wall sank into the same rhythm. The silver, sapphire, ruby, and emerald winking sleepily.

As one, everything paused.

Then the prince walked in.

The incantation redoubled, the hearts trilling as fast as a sparrow's. Prince Bellinor wore long, flowing robes with diamond crystals woven into the thread. A sash around his waist captured a long, naked knife with serrated edges. The hood sagged across his face, but even beneath the shadows, his teeth gleamed too brightly.

"Good evening, Tam," he said. "Are you ready to play my game now?"

My heart thumped, nausea welling in my throat.

He walked toward me and ran his finger along my cheek. I shuddered, the chains clinking together behind my back.

"It took quite a while for me to claim you." He lifted my chin, forcing me to meet his keen gaze. "The spirits are blind until they are given the scent. You must know how contact magic works?"

I pressed my lips together, sequestering my emotions deep inside. Of course I knew, it's what I did, what every bounty hunter used, but each in their own unique way. Even Siobhan used it to keep tabs on me, but she preferred to mark me with her mouth, not her hands.

"Well, loyal Clement tried to prevent the inevitable, always getting in the way. He is far too good for the likes of us. I couldn't understand why you at first, but eventually I saw it." He knelt before me, his hand sliding around my neck to grip the chain. "I saw you." He tugged the links, my head snapping back, neck extended. He pressed his nose to my throat and inhaled deeply, my skin moist and clammy beneath his touch. "There's magic in you, powerful magic. And I want it."

His tongue carved into the groove of my throat, tracing the pump of blood up my neck.

I squirmed helplessly, my body bound by the cold iron.

"But you need to give it..." he pressed the knife to my heart, the tip biting into my flesh, while his mouth hovered above mine, "willingly."

"Get the fuck off me."

He tsked, rocking back onto his heels before standing. He tucked the knife back into the sash, patting it lovingly and walked to the far wall, admiring each hung woman with his hands clasped behind his back. The glow from their hearts bled light onto his face.

"These lovely souls," he continued to stroll up and down the raised altar, "all gave themselves willingly. Their spirits live on, encased in their precious metals. It's how their homelands flourish. Why the emerald isle never runs dry, why the Goddessforsaken southern wastelands still overflow with silver.

"Not all the families are content with this deal of course. Some insisted the bodies be returned, but once they leave the castle, the spell breaks, and the supply dries up. The sensible ones realize what I'm doing for them. I'm royalty, not a God. I can't control the weather, turn the tides, exile evil. I can't even control my own damned fate."

His hands dropped to his sides in fists while his body momentarily seized. He exhaled, regaining composure and lowering his voice. "But I *can* command the flow of wealth."

He stood in front of the shadow with the golden heart and faced me. Slowly, he lifted the knife and untied the sash, his gaze intense on mine. The black robe pooled on the floor, his body completely naked underneath. He dug the tip of the knife into his chest, not even a flicker of pain crawling across his face.

Blood trickled from the wound. He sliced upward, peeling the skin back from the glistening ribs underneath. A flash of candlelight hit his chest, the carved hole sparkling with the shine only diamonds produced.

I pressed into the wall. Awareness shivered through me, brushing my crown, my neck, my spine. The spirits from the ceiling clustered above me, sinking deeper down the wall, hovering barely inches away, but they weren't threatening me.

They were cowering.

"Well, Tam, now you know." He pressed the skin back, the rapidly clotting blood suctioning it closed. He prowled toward me with the knife held loosely in his hand. "Do you want to join me?"

I glared at him.

He sighed. "Well, unfortunately for you, I love this part even more than I do the wealth." He dragged the edge of the blade down my cheek, smearing his warm, clotted blood on my skin. "Which is why my own mothers banished me here in the first place."

I leaned as far back as the chains would allow, the freezing stone digging into my shoulders.

"Oh, come now." He flipped the blade, repeating the motion on the other side of my face. "The others will go easier on you if you cede. If you fight too long, it reminds them they didn't do enough when it was their turn."

The spirits above churned, but their hate wasn't directed at me.

"That woman you tried to save..." He smiled at my twitch of recognition. "Oh, I know everything, Tamara. It was valiant of you to try and release her spirit, but you really shouldn't have dragged poor Lilyanna down there with you."

He pointed the tip of the blade on my forehead and dragged it down, slicing through my eyebrow, lifting just enough to not sever my eyelids. I hissed through clenched teeth as a line of fire burned down my face. The edge of my lip gushed blood, spilling into my mouth and coating my teeth. I spat into his face, peppering him with flecks of spittle and blood.

He continued to smile. "At every turn, there you were obstructing me, preventing me from adding gold to my empire. There should never have been a wedding, it makes it that much harder for me to claim the next one. It does present a good face to the public, I suppose. Regardless, it's why I sent the spirits after you. I couldn't understand why it was taking so long. It must have been your kinship, your magic. They like power. Shame you're not as powerful as me."

He slid the knife down my face again. I bit back my whine, twisting the metal shackles around my wrists to distract from the burn.

He grinned and wiped his hand across his face. "No one likes a show-off, Tam." He dug the blade into my forehead again, in the exact same spot. "A little harder this time?"

My heart throbbed. My chest burned. I dragged in a breath, every muscle in my body taut and expectant.

The knife sliced deeper, scratching bone, a slash of red candlelight burned through my closed eyelids. I tried not to whimper but a choked sob escaped my lips. I dug my nails into my palm, pulling my focus from him.

The gold bangle clinked against the chains. If only he'd untie me.

"There was a swathe of magic in that room when we held that trial, far too much. The divining rods couldn't decide whether yours or mine was stronger. But after you left, they wavered toward that woman. Her magic was weak, mainly elemental, basic trickery." He scoffed. "But she harbored traces of blood magic, enough to keep me satisfied and strong for a while. You, though..." His smile widened. "Will last me for months."

A form flickered amongst the tangled mass on the ceiling. Was she here? Would she remember I'd at least tried to save her?

"Again?"

The spirits above held their breath, a brief pause in the swell.

I held still.

"Spill your secrets, Tam. Come and join my collection. You just need to say the word." The knife returned to the start. A spasm of pain vibrated through my face as the tip carved a groove in my skull.

I closed my eyes, focusing on the pounding pulse in my ears, the pressure in my palm as I slowly speared my nails in further.

"Tut, tut. Poor Lilyanna. How long do you think she'll last when you're dead? Well, not dead exactly. Perhaps I'll have you fetch her in spirit form, hold her down while I mount her on the wall with the rest of my collection."

Blood gushed down my face, welling in my eye sockets, gumming to my lashes.

Boom! Something heavy collided with the door and the whole wall shuddered. We both jumped. A frantic thumping followed, then a muffled shout. The prince stepped back, tugging the knife from my skin and brandished it at the ceiling. "Bring him in."

Don't. I willed them. *Don't open the door.* I knew who it was, and I didn't want him to be forced to watch.

The spirits' hesitation was brief. Short enough that barely three heartbeats passed, roaring in my ears, but it was enough that the prince noticed.

"Now," he spat.

The tension cleaved as quickly as it had come. A portion of the roiling mass separated and flowed down the walls, seeping through the grout.

A moment later, Clement shot through the door. He spun around, eyes wild, his movements frantic. Then he lunged toward me but snapped back, caught by invisible claws. "No! You need to—" His shouts were silenced as black vapor poured into his mouth. He pawed at his face, but his arms were pinioned to his sides, gripped by shapeless beings, his tunic tearing at the shoulders as he fought for freedom. Bruises puddled around his wrists and encircled his neck.

Eventually, he stilled and so did my heart.

The look he gave me cut to my soul. The fear, the regret, the guilt. My throat closed. My breaths carved from my chest as I offered him a small smile. I'd seen that look before. When desperation seizes control of your entire body, and you're plunged headfirst into inertia because there's so much you should do, so much you'll spend eternity blaming yourself for not doing. Yet, all you can do is look. To capture every last second before time changes for ever.

That was me twenty years ago staring at my parents' bodies. Inhaling the blood, seeing the particles of dust and smoke and life ebbing away. When I moved, if I blinked, I would fast-forward, my life reset.

"Not her," Clement choked as the bruise darkened on his neck. "She's..."

"Special, I know," the prince finished. "Don't you think she'll fit in nicely here with her attitude? Bound to serve me like the others." He knelt in front of me and speared the tip of the knife into my chest.

My whine was lost amongst Clement's muted screams. The spirits tightened their hold, more pouring from the ceiling to strengthen the barrier.

"And you'll still get to see her." The prince twisted the knife. Its edges scraped along my ribs, inches above my heart. "But she needs to agree. That's the only way it'll work." He leaned forward until his lips hovered above mine. "Now, where was I?"

Even if I could scratch him, I'd still die. The feeble tower I'd spent my life constructing would topple. The deal would be over, the Collectors would have their lives ended.

And Clement? I'd watched people I loved die when I could have stopped it. I'd lived with the guilt. I'd not do it to him. He didn't deserve that fate.

My hand shook as I forced my fingers to slide under the thick iron bonds and depressed the clasp on the bangle. The cold tip of the needle slicked out.

One of the spirits slithered down the wall. Ice prickled my back as it molded itself around me.

I'd never join the prince. I'd spent my life bending to another's will, and I wouldn't spend eternity doing the same.

A single bony finger inserted itself between the cuff and the needle, but it wasn't enough. I speared the needle into my wrist, locking it in place with the heavy shackle. The spirit's form shuddered against me.

Numbness spread like a void through my hand, up my arm and into my chest until my heart seized, and I slumped against the wall.

CHAPTER TWENTY-SIX
DUTY BOUND

I probably wasn't dead.

The bed was hard, the air smelled faintly of roses, but the covers were thick and soft and infused with Clement's scent of pine. Fingers ran through my hair, smoothing the mess in a rhythmic motion. I snuggled deeper and blinked my eyes open to see Clement's face pressed close, his warm breath mingling with mine.

"Are you dead too?" I asked.

"Not yet." He shifted up on his elbow with the rest of his body coiled around me, his hand splayed on my stomach. "You should be dead, though. What were you thinking?"

"Don't." I forced my aching body to roll, managing to tip slightly toward him before I gave up and settled on my back again. "None of that was my fault. It's not like I tied myself up in the dungeons."

He exhaled heavily. "I meant the bangle. I never would have given it to you if I'd have known you'd use it on yourself."

"Better than being awake."

He growled before kissing my cheek. "Fuck knows what I would've done, Tamara." The ache in his voice tugged on my soul. "If one of them hadn't..."

I nestled closer as he extracted my arm from the cover and held it up in the dim light. My shoulder screamed in protest, my hand waving back and forth as I squinted at it.

Clement cupped my forearm and massaged my wrist. "Here, see."

The shackles had cut deep, leaving the skin oozing and swollen. Mottled bruises spread down my arm like poisoned blood, but there was a small patch of skin where my arm met my wrist and the veins crisscrossed together, that was pure black. It was shaped like a finger, long and gnarled.

"One of the spirits inserted itself between you and the needle. It took most of the poison, leaving you just enough to pass out. Although, you've been unconscious for hours." His voice wobbled. "I persuaded Prince Bellinor to let you live, for now at least. The town doesn't know about the woman he killed after the trial and people have settled down again, but if they get wind of your murder before the wedding, it'll stir up their suspicions." He laid my arm down again and tucked the covers over. "It's all one big game to him, and he knows he's right on top. He'll enjoy watching you, seeing how you react now that you know the truth. He forced the spirits to increase their guard and focus on you, not Lilyanna. You're essentially locked down until then."

"But they're on my side?" I whispered. The hearth flared in the corner of his small room, but if they wanted to listen, they'd find another way.

"Not really. Some retain more resilience than others, especially the newer ones, but ultimately, they'll answer to whomever is strongest." He kissed my hair before laying his cheek on my head. "Which is probably not you."

"You're the second person to doubt in my abilities." I sighed and let him mold himself around my body. "But why did they save me?"

"It was only one. Maybe they knew you needed to be conscious, and it wasn't really saving you but allowing him to try again." He kissed my hair again, his breath warm and comforting on my scalp. "Or maybe they couldn't bear the thought of spending eternity trapped with you, so they decided to let you live."

I snorted causing waves of pain to fire through my body. "Don't make me laugh, everything hurts."

"Everything?" He pressed his lips to my forehead, smiling.

I snorted again and weakly hit him. "Don't."

"Okay." He settled back around me, his fingers massaging my shoulder.

The fire crackled softly, and snow fell gently against the small slitted window. His room wasn't much bigger than mine, but it was far cozier. He'd plugged the hole in the ceiling with wood planks and a thickly woven tapestry.

My body relaxed, and I almost slipped into sleep, only managing to jerk myself awake at the last second. I forced myself to sit up, my heart racing and stomach churning. "Clement, you should—"

"I'm not leaving."

"Then I won't sleep."

"You're ridiculous, Tamara." He patted the thin mattress. "Lie down."

For the first time, I studied his face. Dark circles hung under his eyes, his beard was tangled, the skin underneath sallow. I laid my hand on his, lacing our fingers together, ignoring the tremor that shook him. "Why do you do it?" It was clear that he didn't just want me out of this mess, he didn't want to be here either. I recognized someone bound to a duty they didn't want.

He pulled away and slid his legs to the floor. Perched on the edge of the mattress, he doubled over, his face buried in his hands.

"My sister was one of the original guards when the queens sent the prince to live up here. They handpicked our family because we had nothing, didn't personally know anyone within the city and couldn't be easily blackmailed." He spoke through his fingers, his voice muffled. "Her job was initially to keep him safe, but the longer he was here, the more bored he became, and he fell into his old habits. She ended up having to clean up his messes without the public catching on."

I forced my body to crawl across the bed. Every joint ached, every muscle depleted of energy. I knelt behind him and draped myself over his shoulders. He straightened, turning so our foreheads touched.

"It still wasn't enough. The prince made his own deal, falling further and further into madness and wealth. From the outside, this place turned around. In a few years, it was the richest municipality in the entire queendom. But you saw how."

I nodded. The skin on my face pulled tight with the movement, the edges of the long scab bisecting my eye caught and tugged.

"My sister was always brave. I looked up to her, yearned to be as strong as she was. She plotted against him, tried to save who she could, but as you know, the walls have ears. There's always someone watching." He leaned forward again, a sob wracking his body.

I kneaded his shoulders. Something had turned. I'd do anything for this man, to ease his pain, shoulder his guilt. And I didn't want to admit to myself why. I didn't need another weakness holding me back.

"Bryn told me most of the story. She was already here. She and my sister were lovers, they shared everything. She'd tried to reach out to me, to warn me when I came, but I was too late. The prince condemned her for treason and sent her South. She's not part of the Queens' Guard as I told you, she's locked in a dungeon somewhere with Goddess knows what being done to her." He shuddered. "She's alive though, because as long as I keep the prince alive and his secrets safe, she lives. Ten years is the deal for both me and Bryn. We have to serve that long and then she'll be released."

"I'll free her, we'll go together. I can get in anywhere."

He turned, dragging his hands across his eyes and faced me. "It's far too dangerous. If they find out they'll kill her, or you." He took my hand and pressed his lips to my knuckles. "I've been trying to protect you, Tam. Ever since I saw you, but you make it impossible."

"I don't want a protector. There are enough people in my life trying to control me, Clement. I want an equal."

"I'll never be your equal."

My breath caught at the sadness in his face.

"But..." I prompted.

"But?" He choked out a laugh. "But I guess I have other talents that could help fill the gap."

I ran my hands through his hair, savoring the silky tug on my palms. "I think that's a fair trade," I murmured, sliding my hands slowly down his face to twine strands of his beard around my fingers.

He leaned into my touch, a deep purr vibrating through him. "I know why you're really here, what your job actually is. You're after the prince. I don't know who sent you, but it's about time." He gripped my hands, a hint of a smile emerging beneath the dark beard. "You're just like my sister, Tamara. She would've faced an impossible task like this without a second thought. I love surrounding myself with strong women."

"Good." I squeezed his fingers, ignoring the spasm of pain up my wrists. "But?"

He swiveled to face me. "If you get him, I fail, and my sister dies. There won't be time to save her, but I'll help you. She would hate what I've become...how often I turned a blind eye. She'd want me to do the right thing."

He swayed. How long had he been awake? Watching me sleep, keeping me safe. "Lie down." I pushed him gently, and he settled on the thin pillow, leaving his arm outstretched for me to sink in beside him. I snuggled close, his hand caressing my hip, warmth blossoming through my skin. His eyes fluttered closed, chest rising and falling deeply.

"There's always a way," I whispered. "When you're friends with the devil."

The next morning, Clement walked me back to Lilyanna's room and told me not to leave without him. It was cute that he now thought I'd do whatever he said.

A small wooden table had been erected in the corner of the lounge with two benches tucked on either side. Bacon sizzled in the central pan with herbed potatoes and crusted bread. I seated myself opposite Lilyanna, who, by the looks of it, had made no attempt to tame her appearance over the past few days. At least she was uninjured. And alive.

She studied her food, poking at it half-heartedly with a diamond fork. Did she blame me for not getting her out?

I loaded my plate with as much food as it could hold and stuffed myself, barely pausing to suck in breaths. When my stomach threatened to send it all back out again, I leaned back with my hands folded across my distended abdomen.

"Is this where we eat now?" I pulled a glass of water toward me. Droplets condensed on the outside, the cold a welcome relief for my tender skin. I rolled the glass over my face.

"Until the wedding, I think." A lank curl of hair drooped over her face, and she made no attempt to brush it away.

I held the cold glass to the tingling gash down my face. "In how many days?"

"Two."

The hearth crackled behind me. The ceiling lay still, its diamond stars dull against the stone. *Don't listen.* I sent the plea into the ether. Nothing answered.

"What's the prince's eye color?" I studied her closely, willing her to look at me.

"Brown?" She stilled. The tomato she'd speared with her fork oozed red slime, bleeding into the grease lining her plate. "Green, actually. Well, hazel then."

"Is that your final answer?"

She glared at me before dropping her gaze, her face melting a fraction. "And what's Clement's?"

"Black." I slid the glass down my cheek, resting it against my swollen lip. "And so is his hair. Right from the top of his beard, cutting down his chin and cascading down his neck. Then his chest is bare."

She peered up at me again.

"I know, I know. I expected him to be rugged all the way down. *But,*" I leaned forward, "it starts again just where that 'v' of muscle descends—"

"Stop! You'll make me blush." She grinned, a hint of life returning to her cheeks.

"Good." I rested the glass on the table and pinned her with my stare. "You need to pay attention, you need to really open your eyes and see—"

She leaped to her feet. Her hands dug into the table, body rigid as she leaned toward me. "Maybe you should be paying more attention to what's right in front of you rather than Clement's hairline!"

So, she did blame me. Fine. Screw the spirits. I lumbered to my feet, clutching the table myself, but for support. "I tried to get you out! How can you think that I'd leave without you? Look at me!" I gestured wildly at my broken body.

"I know you didn't leave me," she hissed.

I straightened. The words knocked from my chest as the truth hit. "You told him?" I couldn't keep my voice down, nor could I stop the chill seeping through me.

"I changed my mind. I couldn't go through with it. I have to stay; it's for my people. I still have faith that things will turn out as the fates predicted. I didn't mean for him to torture you, just to stop you from making me leave."

The fire flickered in the corner of my vision. Smoke pooled in the air, but there was no malice today. They were still listening, but they understood.

"He was going to kill me, Lilyanna, and he still will! Even if you manage to get him as far as marriage, he'll then kill you and hang you on the wall like the others. You're not special." I regretted the words instantly as they speared into her. "To him, anyway."

She nodded. "That's why you're here, Tam." She turned and headed back to her bedroom. "To stop him before he does."

I stared at the closed door in disbelief, the slam echoing around the room. She knew. *She knew*! She'd always known. She wanted me to do the job for her, pave her way to the throne. We'd been in each other's company day and night for weeks, and she never said a word. I trusted her. I delayed my own mission, put mine and the Collectors' lives on the line. And for what?

Is this what Siobhan feels like? When humans come crawling to her, begging, pleading, wheedling for a deal, for any small act of grace to make their lives bearable? No wonder she spends her days making them as miserable as possible.

I ran to the main door. The knob was ice cold and frozen shut. I rattled it furiously, my palm searing from the intense cold. I peered through the keyhole, but it was clogged with a gelatinous mound of ash.

I screamed and ran to my room, the spiral steps shuddering as I tore down them. My room was neatly made, the fire burning brightly, my cloak laundered and hanging on the back of the door.

I reached for the knob, my fingers gripping the diamond facets, but it too was bolted shut. I kicked the door, a warning spear of pain shooting up my back. The high window was rapidly being buried by snow, the light tinged gray and solemn. Sucking in air through my teeth, I stomped back up the stairs.

Lilyanna hovered in her doorway. She smoothed her nightgown, the creases springing straight back. "It's been like that for days." Her eyes flitted to the locked door. "And the snow is gradually burying us in from the outside."

The large, mottled window was half-smothered by snow, crystals of ice spiderwebbing up the pane.

"Should've thought of that before you betrayed me and condemned us both."

She clutched at the cream silk, scrunching it around her narrow hips. "I'm sorry. I really am."

"You should be." I pressed my lips together. I wanted to say, *Let's see how you like it when he has you in that dungeon.* But no matter how angry I was, I'd never let him do that to her. Instead, I said, "Why did you believe *I'd* be able to stop him?"

"It was the tea leaves, Tam. I knew before I came that you would protect me."

"That's ridiculous. What about everything that happened? The sheets? The fallen sconce? The banns?"

"I told you I believed in omens. I did waver, but I'm going to change the future of my entire people, and this is the only way to make it happen. I had to stay, and so did you."

I ground my teeth, my entire body vibrating with rage.

"We can do this, Tam. We're so close."

"We? You can bet your life on some dregs in a cup, but not mine."

Her face crumpled. I wanted nothing more than to keep screaming, to beat sense into her. Dimly, her words slotted into my thoughts, righting themselves with the truth. Could it still work? Had she seen me succeed? Goddess save me, was I about to stake everything on her stupid tea leaves?

I sighed. "I'm going to draw you a bath." I moved across the room, my body aching and tugging with every step. "You stink, Your Ladyship."

A sob caught in her throat, but she controlled herself. "So do you." Relief filled every line on her wan face, even though she couldn't bring herself to smile. "I'm getting married in two days, Tam."

"I know." I ushered her into the bathroom.

To a monster.

CHAPTER TWENTY-SEVEN
HAUNTED AND HUNTED

For the first time in weeks, I slept in my own bed.

Or tried to sleep given every minuscule shift of the mattress brought a new wave of pain to my aching body. Lilyanna glanced repeatedly at the expanse of white silk sheets in her own bed but stopped short of begging when she saw my mood.

The spirits were haunting me, not her. For now, she was safe.

The following morning, I leaned back on the buttoned chaise, watching the snow slap against the windows. Big, fat snowflakes and sometimes chunks of ice would break the monotony with a dull thud.

A sharp rap sounded from the door.

"I think it's your turn to get it," I said.

Lilyanna perched on the other end of the purple cushions, systematically pushing at her cuticles one by one with her thumbnail. Her smile was tight, but she rose without complaint. She smoothed the deep creases in her long skirt as she walked toward the door. She tentatively touched the diamond handle, her entire body stiffening as the cold speared into her hand.

The prince strolled in. He looked the same as ever, smile bright, hair tousled, clothes perfectly pressed in matching funereal tones. Two guards marched in behind him. Both were men. Bulky, sullen, and heavily armed.

"Up you get, Tam." He crossed to me, completely ignoring Lilyanna who cast a fleeting glance at the vacant corridor outside before one of the guards closed the door and positioned himself in front of it. He unsheathed his saber and dug it into the floor between his feet.

"Why?" I swung my legs to the ground, a dizzying wave of nausea firing through my body at the movement. I exhaled slowly, muffling the moan and burying my weakness.

The second guard detached himself from the prince's shadow and hovered at my shoulder. He slowly drew his blade, the metal clanging against the sheath and vibrating directly into my ear.

I swiveled to glare at him, but the prince moved toward me again, and I flung my attention back to him. "Where's Clement?"

"Oh, he's a little tied up at the moment."

My stomach twisted. Lilyanna tiptoed across the room; her slippers whisper-soft against the stone. She skirted the prince and sat on the raised arm of the chaise at the far end, her weight stacked in her legs as if she would bolt at any moment. She didn't look at me, choosing instead to resume picking at her nails, but her face paled.

The prince laughed. "No, seriously, Tam. My wedding's in two days. He has many chores to do, security details to plan. Hundreds of townspeople are coming."

I didn't know what to think. He looked like he was telling the truth, and I was so rarely wrong about people. My stomach shifted, pressing low in my belly.

"Hand over your weapons." The prince hooked his fingers into his waistband, his shoulders back, muscles loose.

"No."

The guard behind me gripped my arm and yanked me to my feet. He pushed me forward, and I stumbled, stopping myself from crashing directly into the prince at the last second.

"Unfortunately, Tam," he casually reached forward and lifted the hem of my sweater, his fingers brushing my thigh, "you can't be trusted not to harm yourself after that stunt with the bangle." He unbuckled the holster, grabbing the hilt of the knife as the leather strap uncoiled to the floor. "And we wouldn't want another accident like with that poor woman in the pit, now, would we?"

He raised the knife, hovering it above the gash on my forehead. Slowly he carved the air, following the line down to my lip. He jabbed it into my face, and I leaped back. My heart lurched, and the cut on my face burned as if he'd reopened the flesh all over again.

"I know you have more. You must've learned the castle has ears by now." He pointed the dagger toward my boots. "Hand them over."

The fabric lining slipped through my grasp as I forced my fingers to dig out the slim blades. I threw them at his feet, balling my hands into fists to sever the tremors. My chest heated and my throat tightened, but I kept his stare.

"Such a good girl now, aren't you?" The dimples popped in his cheeks as he smiled. "I must say, it's been a lot of work trying to tame you, but it has proven to be most rewarding." He ran my dagger through the air again, licking his lips.

I fought back a shudder as I relived the warm nodules of his tongue brushing against my pulse, his nostrils flaring as he dragged his face up my neck.

"I wonder what role you would be most suited to after the wedding. You have already had a taste of what my permanent consorts can do. They are even now jostling for position, carving out a niche for you amongst the hierarchy. Probably as we speak."

"Do I get a say in this, my prince?" Lilyanna kept her face smooth and her eyes soft. "Tam is mine after all."

He laughed, dismissing her with a wave of his hand. "No, no, my love. She is mine. I'll get you another one, don't worry."

Lilyanna quietened. She nibbled on her nails, her teeth clunking together every time she slipped. What would her plan be if I did die? She'd poured all her time and energy into getting here and then surviving. Why had she believed I could be the one to help?

I backed away and sagged onto the chaise. The guard behind me moved to collect the knives I'd tossed and pocketed them before sheathing his saber and resuming his position behind the prince.

"Poor, poor, Tam. Or should I say, Tamara. You do prefer that name, right? Or is it only when Clement whispers it into your ear." I looked through him, my body wilting as I sank deeper into the plush pillows.

Prince Bellinor's smile faltered. "Where's your fighting spirit today, Tam?"

I remained mute. The magic in my veins nulled, my core empty, my marrow sucked dry.

He shrugged. "Well, it doesn't matter. It's good practice for the coming days." He turned and headed for the door. "I'll see you both later. We've got an interesting afternoon planned, so rest up. I'll have my guards escort you to the banquet room when it is time."

The banquet room was the largest chamber in the castle. The marble floor was spiked with red arteries and glittering diamond veins. Multiple hearths lined the edges, all barren. When I stared long enough, faint tendrils would coil up and out like tentacles, slithering into the vaulted ceiling and disappearing.

Dozens of benches filled the space, crudely carved with thick fingers of ivy and stubby leaves. The aisle between lay empty, lined only by fresh candles with pristine wicks and arrow-straight tapers.

At the far end rose a dozen marble steps. Red and white roses perfumed the air, encircling wreaths of unlit candles leading up to a circular marble altar.

The large guard behind me shoved between my shoulder blades, and I forced my feet to shuffle down the aisle. Lilyanna moved next to me, tugging her sleeves down and shivering.

"It'll be warm on the day," the prince called from in front. "We must practice getting everyone in position." He halted at the end of the aisle, resting one foot on the bottom step.

My breath rushed out as I caught sight of the rigid shoulders and somber eyes of Bryn seated in the first row. She looked unharmed and unbound, but where was Clement? I swallowed and forced my lips to curve as I moved to slide in beside her.

"Not today, Tam." The prince gave me a toothy smile. "You'll be up here with me. Dear Lilyanna can sit and observe to make sure she has everything set for the ceremony." He extended his hand in a smooth and slippery motion, just as he had outside the castle when he'd marked me with his own magic. "It really is the best way to learn…" the large guards both stepped into position behind me, their boots clunking on the marble, "…from the mistakes of others."

I took his hand. My skin shrank from his icy touch, clinging to the fragile bones of my hand. He tugged me up the steps, turning to face me and claiming my other hand.

Awareness shivered through me. The spirits watched from shaded recesses, silent and unmoving, but their chant whispered to me, strumming through my bones, urging me to fight. I glanced at Lilyanna. She gave the barest twitch of a smile, her body tilted forward. I dropped my eyes to the floor.

The magic lay despondent in my veins, residue impeding my spirit. The hairs on my neck prickled, a wave of judgement and disappointment coming from the hovering presence above.

The prince stroked my palms with his thumbs, forcing me back to him. "This is where we will be bound for eternity, Tam." I stood numb, gazing at my distorted reflection in his polished boots. He turned his head, keeping a grip on me. "I do wish Clement and his dear sister were here to see such a successful match."

Lilyanna stiffened and a muscle pulsed in Bryn's cheek. She moved imperceptibly closer, her hand feathering the hilt of her saber and Lilyanna's breath deepened again.

"I'm sure you're glad his sister transferred, otherwise you'd have never met Clement, Tam." His thumbs kneaded my skin, cold and unwelcome. "We all know about your weakness for him. I must say, though, his sister would never have tolerated such disobedience. You'd have been kicked out on day one."

I ground my teeth but remained mute. If he was alive but trapped, I'd find him. The prince wanted me rattled. It was working, but I wasn't dead yet.

"I wonder how my lovely mothers are treating her?" His musing question hung in the air.

What I would do to wipe that smug look off his face. How long had Clement listened to his taunts? To imagine the depravities befalling his sister? At least my parents had been dead when I'd found them. I didn't have to wonder what was happening or what state they would be in if they ever returned. A dim fire sparked within me, but the magic stayed hidden.

How could I mark him without getting caught? His thumbs swirled across my frozen skin. He would be bound, unable to flee. No walls or spirits or blockade of sabers would be able to protect him. But if he knew what I'd done, he'd throw me into the pit and torture me for answers. Would he succeed before the Collectors arrived?

Maybe Siobhan would step in and kill me before I could reveal any information? Unlikely. She'd gag me herself and bite off my tongue if she had to. She'd let him punish me, hovering within sight but just out of reach. Always out of reach.

No. The next time I stood here, I'd be at Lilyanna's shoulder with hundreds of eyes on us, but it would still just be me and him.

He wanted to play, and the game wasn't over.

CHAPTER TWENTY-EIGHT
THE PROMISE

"Clement, where the hell have you been?"

He brushed past me and closed the door, setting the laden tea tray on the table.

"I've been scared to death worrying about you. Imagining you trapped in that box or splayed on a wall, but I've been locked in here unable do anything about it."

He kept his back to me, casually removing the teapot, saucers, and biscuits one by one, infuriatingly slow. Eventually, he turned to me and cleared his throat, brushing imaginary crumbs from the front of his uniform. "I know. I'm the one who did it."

"You *what*?" I stalked toward him.

He grabbed my shoulders and spun me around, shepherding me toward my room. I stopped on the top step, refusing to go any further, and he pulled the door closed.

It was tight and dark, the warm glow from the fire below barely tickling our feet through the metal staircase. His hands wound around my hips, his lips hot on mine before I could even collect myself.

I pulled my face away, keeping my body aligned against his with blood pounding through my veins. "I'm mad at you."

He grinned. It was such a wicked, wicked smile. "You seem very angry." He throbbed against me, pressed hard into my stomach.

"Clement." But it was a more of a whine, muffled by his mouth claiming mine again.

He kept his face close, barely allowing even air to pass between us. "I locked you in because I knew you'd try and escape." He kissed me lightly. "And I barely found you in time before."

"It doesn't mean you get to lock me away like a toy."

"Like a valuable treasure."

I groaned, and he pressed into me again, smiling through the kiss. Really, I was just pathetic around him, and I was right about him being a distraction. I tried to pull my thoughts together. "But where have you been? I thought you were..."

"Busy." He kissed me again. "I can't tell you yet. Just..." His breath sighed out, warm and sorrowful against my lips. "Keep fighting, okay? You can end this." He held me tighter, his heart thumping against mine.

"Tam?" Lilyanna's voice carried through the walls.

I pushed Clement away, but he held firm. "I'll stay with you tonight. Down here." He turned the doorknob, the light from the lounge spilling onto his face, highlighting the color in his cheeks. "The wedding's tomorrow, it'll be our last chance." He pressed a chaste kiss to my forehead before slipping a knife from his belt into my hand. I tucked it into my empty holster.

My stomach fell, the heat evaporating from my body. He knew what I needed to do and that if I succeeded, the last five years of his life would've been in vain. More than that, he'd be condemning his sister.

He squeezed my hand. "I love you," he whispered, before striding across the room. He collected the tea tray and nodded to Lilyanna who smiled at him before raising her eyebrows at me, then left.

I slouched across the room and grimaced at her. "Yes?"

Lilyanna drummed her fingers on top of the black velvet box she held. Her collarbone poked through the loose sweater she'd thrown on, creamy skin stretched tight on her face.

"What's that?" I asked.

She jumped, flinging her gaze to me as if she'd forgotten I was standing there. "The rest of the wedding outfit." She tapped the box again. "The crown, I think."

I pulled a face. The image of the blood-soaked crown still embedded in the woman on the dungeon wall raced into my mind. "Alright then, let's see what we can do."

I shepherded her into the bedroom. The wedding dress had been tossed onto the bed, waves of golden silk and ribbons spilling everywhere. I gagged, and she laughed. "I think it's beautiful."

"Of course you do." I reached for the box in her hands. "Give me that as well."

The hinges sprung open, revealing a golden crown sunk into a silk pillow. At first glance, it looked wet. The metal was carved into coils of ivy, sharp petals extended toward the sky. Diamond crystals rested atop the leaves, sparkling like dew drops. Would they absorb her blood when he dug it into her skull, shining red like the beating heart of the ruby woman? I snapped the box shut again and tossed it onto the pillow.

I clicked my fingers, and she dropped the robe she wore and turned around with a heavy sigh.

"I have no idea what I'm doing, Lilyanna." The dress seemed to have no end. It was all ribbons and silk in an amorphous mass.

"When have you ever?" She raised her arms, and I dropped the dress over her head, tugging and twisting it into position.

I stood back, hands on hips. "Is this the right way round?"

She shrugged.

Untangling the ends of the ribbons, I poked them through small sparkling eyelets and cinched her into an irregular lattice. It was probably fine. It wasn't like there'd be wedding portraits made when either she or the prince ended up dead the following day. Hopefully the prince.

I collected some pins from the dresser and gathered in the loose fabric sagging around her hips and chest. I should've noticed she wasn't eating well. Although perhaps a little guilt would do her some good, maybe even give her second thoughts about going through with this. My wrists throbbed in agreement.

"Ouch!" She flinched, batting my hand away.

"Sorry." I inserted the pin again, narrowly avoiding her flesh a second time.

"Are you thinking of Clement again? Or just punishing me?"

I put the head of another pin in my mouth, folding the fabric into a pleat. "I wasn't," I mumbled, "but I am now."

My stomach fluttered. We would only get one night together. He wanted to help me, but he'd never forgive me if his sister was hanged. Guilt like that irreversibly changes someone.

I inserted the pin into the fabric, creating a smooth contour around her waist and then circled to her other side.

As soon as the prince died, someone here would send a pigeon down South to the queens quicker than I could ride on horseback. Siobhan was the only one who could travel faster than the news. If I wanted any chance at saving his sister's life, she'd have to do me a favor. I shuddered, the pin narrowly avoiding Lilyanna's hip. Siobhan would be overjoyed to have me beg for her help, but I'd do it for Clement. I'd do anything for him. A flush of warmth swelled within me. Now he *was* officially a weakness, my weakness, and the thought didn't haunt me like it should.

"Why are you smiling?" Lilyanna slapped my hand away as I reached for the neckline. "You're going to stab me again."

"That's not why I'm smiling." I pulled the dress down, exposing more of her smooth, pale chest. Her ribs were faintly visible, and I chastised myself again. "I really am a terrible maid."

She laughed and took a step back so I could admire the full gown. I'd done an okay job. It was definitely the right way round and she had curves again. She twirled slowly, the buttery pleats of the full skirt swirling around her.

I nodded.

"You've never really been my maid, Tam." She stepped closer and wrapped her arms around me, her head pressed against mine. "You're my sister, my friend."

My throat tightened. The dormant magic finally bubbled up, spooling itself into my veins. So many people were relying on me. I needed to be strong, not just for them, but for me. It was my life too, and I was ready to take control.

"Okay, let's go eat." I broke from the embrace and headed to the lounge. "You're already dressed for dinner, so that saves me at least an hour."

She hurried after me, linking her arm with mine. She leaned close, her voice barely a whisper. "We can do this, Tam. I know we can."

A stream of ash fell from the ceiling in the far corner, the sound of scratching nails receding.

What was wrong with me? My hands shook, my feet wouldn't stop moving. If the spirits were watching me now, they'd think I'd lost it.

I took my boots off, then my leggings. Would he like this? Too forward? I put my boots back on.

Honestly, you'd think this was my first time. Maybe I should put the fire out and beg the spirits to drag me away so at least I'd have an excuse for looking frazzled when he finally found me.

I kicked my boots off again and strapped my holster back to my thigh just in case the spirits heard me muttering my plans out loud.

Soft footsteps echoed down the corridor outside. I leaped to the door, pressing my ear against the thick wood. My heart thumped in time with the footfalls, increasing in intensity as they neared. They paused outside my door and a key scraped in the lock excruciatingly slow.

I flung the door open.

Clement blinked in surprise, his mouth ajar with the key dangling from his hand. "Were you waiting for me?"

"No." I grabbed his shirt and pulled him in. Kicking the door shut, I pushed him up against it. "I've never waited around for a man or woman in my life." I tugged off his shirt, running my hands up his smooth chest.

"Mhm, I can see that." He cradled my face, kissing me gently. Too gently.

"Come on, I've had all day to think about this." My fingers hooked into his waistband.

"And I've had weeks." He removed my hands, but held onto them, his thumbs circling my palms.

"Fine." I pulled away. "What were you doing today? How long can you stay?" The skin under his eyes was stained darker and tension pooled in his jaw. My stomach fluttered. "How *are* you doing?"

The edges of his mouth quirked up.

"I'll do whatever you need to—"

"Turn that mind off, Tamara." He threaded his hands through my hair, gently tugging to raise my face to his. "I promised I'd make you forget everything." He pulled harder, his breath hot in my face, warmth rising through my body. He lowered his mouth, hovering over mine. "Everything except me," he breathed.

My reply was lost as his tongue pushed past my lips. He caressed my mouth, meandering, teasing, a faint taste of sugar lingering on my tastebuds. Goddessdamn him, I wanted to jump him straight away, but he kept the grip on my hair, stopping me from rushing.

As he pulled away, I whined. He tightened his fingers, tangling them in my hair, stretching my neck upward. His mouth roved down my face, my skin tingling at his touch. He suckled on my neck, his other hand loosening his trousers until they plunged to the floor, knives and saber clashing onto the stone.

Grabbing my ass, he tugged me into him. I gasped. He was already throbbing, straining against the thin fabric of his underwear. I reached for him, but he twisted, a seductive chuckle escaping.

"Clement," I growled.

He ignored me, tugging off my sweater and walking me backward until I fell onto the bed. He shed the rest of his clothes, before sliding down my chest, his mouth closing around one of my breasts. I arched into him, the sheer fabric of my bra clinging to my peaked nipple, warm and wet.

Sliding the knife from my holster, he ran the tip up my skin, pausing in between my breasts. With a grin, he sliced through the middle, and the fabric fell away. Cool air rushed my body. He took my other breast in his mouth and sucked, pressure firing through me. Coils of heat swirled through my lower belly. *Not yet, not yet!* I couldn't even control myself.

He lifted, and I half-sighed, half-groaned. He ran the blade down my stomach, tucking the tip just under my waistband. "These are my favorite—" But he ignored me, ripping the fabric and leaving me fully exposed.

The knife clanged onto the floor as he spread me wide, his hands gripping my thighs. His hot breath gave me little warning before his tongue eased inside me. I clutched the covers, my head thrown back, already so far gone.

His hands slid up my thighs, one resting on my hip to keep me pinned while the other circled my clit. His tongue plunged in and out mercilessly. I tried to rock into him, but his hand tightened, controlling the pace, keeping me riding the edge.

I gritted my teeth, unable to stop myself from spiraling.

Then, I fell. My back arched, and my hips bucked as the world exploded around me.

He kept the pressure, drinking me in, riding every last shudder until I slumped, boneless on the mattress.

Languidly, he kissed his way back up my body, settling me into his arms.

"I'm going to need a minute," I panted.

"Good." Moisture beaded around his mouth, shining in the flicker from the fire. "Because I'm still enjoying myself over here." He licked his lips before kissing me, the taste laced with salt and tang.

My libido stirred again. I rolled onto him, but he snaked an arm around my waist and flipped me, his thigh pressed between my legs. "I'm not done yet." He pinned my wrists above my head with one hand, his other tracing the line of my lower lip.

He met my gaze, his mouth quirking. "I'm all yours, Tamara." He spread my thighs wide with his knees, hovering tantalizingly close to my entrance. "And I promised to make you cum so hard you forget everything."

I mumbled something incoherent, unable to look away from the intensity in his deep black eyes. He was magnificent. Goddess above did I need him. Now.

He chuckled, his beard scratching down my face as he nipped his way to my neck. "I don't think you meant to say that out loud." His hand tightened on my wrists, my pulse bounding under his grasp. "But who am I to say no to you?"

He thrust inside me with one, deep stroke. His teeth bit into my neck with a primal growl that blended with my gasp. I locked my legs around his back, and he pushed deeper, stretching until I was deliciously full.

"Clement," I whispered, my voice needy and thick.

He anchored his arm around me while he plunged in again and again, his hips slapping against mine. His breathing became fast and ragged, moving faster, deeper. A dark thrill built inside me as pressure synched between us, increasing in intensity as our bodies fused.

I dug my heels into the slick muscles of his back, feeling them tense in a ripple along his spine which spread through into my core. His mouth found mine as we both released, our hearts thrashing together.

We lay on top of the covers, the gentle warmth from the fire licking over our bodies. The snow fell in an unbroken stream against the blocked window. The spirits were probably watching, which meant the prince was as well. But I didn't care.

Tomorrow was the day, and there was no person I'd rather spend my last night with.

I nestled into his warm body, my arm draped across his chest and allowed myself to sleep.

CHAPTER TWENTY-NINE
ALL'S FAIR IN LOVE AND WAR

THIS IS NOT HOW I PICTURED MY LIFE GOING.

I stood on the marble step below Lilyanna admiring the golden lattice crisscrossing her back. It was far neater than my first attempt, and her gown clung beautifully to the curves I'd created on her ever-dwindling figure. Her blonde hair was missing its sheen, her smile lacking the truth, and her posture was so stilted, she looked frozen.

The prince stood opposite. His dark suit hung perfectly on his lithe body, the diamond tie pin and matching crown twinkling in the thousands of candles which illuminated the banquet hall. Tonight, his eyes were gray, a fact I was sure of because he spent the entire ceremony looking straight through Lilyanna to pierce me with his smug look.

Every time my rage latched on to the roiling magic in my bloodstream, I'd have to look off to the side where Clement stood with Bryn. He would widen his eyes or shake his head, and I'd channel my irritation into digging holes in my palm. The magic wouldn't fail me this time.

My dress, which was embarrassingly sheer, clung to the curves I'd rather keep hidden. It was the same silvery gray as his eyes, but also a perfect match for the shackles he'd chained me with only days ago. The prince's thin lips twitched as my gaze sucked back to his.

The congregation was vast. Hundreds of townspeople lined benches and filled the walls, spilling out into the snow-laden courtyard beyond. If I wanted a subtle place to end things, this was not it.

The magic thrummed in my veins, pooling in my extremities, yearning for an escape.

As did I.

"We are gathered today under the benevolent eye of the Goddess to ask for her blessing." The priestess's gauze veil fluttered as she spoke. The diadem nestled into her smooth gray hair glittered in the candlelight. She gave no indication as to whether she approved of the match, nor of her opinion of the banns disaster, but she must know this could never be a Goddess-sanctioned unity.

"Prince Bellinor, heir of the queendom, and Lady Lilyanna, daughter of the people, you will both swear to uphold the traditions and customs of our fine country. Lead and be brave. Love and be generous. With the Goddess's blessing, you will be bound to each other for eternity, in this life and the next." The priestess lifted her head and raised her arms. "If there any objections as to why this match should not be cemented, either in this realm or the other, speak now."

Both Clement and the prince drilled me with identical stares, Clement's a warning, the prince's a challenge. I pursed my lips, willing the deafening thump of my heart to recede so I could concentrate.

The silence hung in the warm room, candles flickering noiselessly as the guests held their breath, refusing to move an inch.

The priestess lowered her arms and life returned to the room. She opened her mouth to finalize the blessing when the double doors to the hall were flung open. They cracked against the stone, the candles guttering in the rose-tinted air that swarmed inside.

As one, the entire crowd turned to the back. A ripple of excitement washed over them. My heart sank, the magic sputtering in my fingertips.

The queens had arrived.

I'd never laid eyes on them in real life but the resemblance to the prince was uncanny, in the perfect physical characteristics of one and the casual elegance of the other. Both were dressed in identical snow-white gowns with fur lined stoles and gloves. Pearls were strung around their necks and danced multi-colored hues in their crowns as the candlelight speared through. A gust of snow-spiked wind chilled the air.

I released a strained breath, adrenaline zinging through my system. All I needed now was for Siobhan to make an appearance, and I was completely screwed.

The queens' languid strides devoured the silence, the gap between us narrowing rapidly. Twenty guards marched after them, spears angled toward the crowd, polished boots ringing on the marble floor. They halted at the front, lowering their spears in unison with a solitary bang.

"Mothers," the prince beamed. His smile was all tooth, the same wolfish grimace he gave me.

Good, make him uncomfortable. Make him squirm.

"Carry on, carry on." The taller of the two queens with matching chestnut hair and eyes flapped a hand, dismissing him. "It's about time you finally made it up the aisle with no more unfortunate occurrences, my boy."

The prince's smile stiffened as mine widened. Clement glared at me in a clear warning.

"Don't let the small matter of our invitation being lost in another raging winter storm, which seems to only ever befall your fair city, keep you from delivering us a *live* heir."

The prince paled. His knuckles grew skeletal as he gripped Lilyanna's hand. She gritted her teeth, refusing to flinch.

"Continue," the prince barked.

The priestess nodded her head, the veil shimmering. Out of the corner of my eye, Clement stiffened and paled beneath the long beard. I could feel the change as well.

Dark shapes unspooled from crevices, filtering through the door jambs, rising silently from beneath the benches. The vaulted ceiling filled with their heavy presence, but today they were silent. No incantations, no curiosity, no rustling as they interwove. They were ready.

The gathered crowd shivered, rubbing arms along goose-pimpled flesh as they cast furtive glances at the dying fires and dwindling tapers.

The priestess raised Lilyanna's crown above her head, the gold glistening and moist. "With this matrimony, you are fated to serve the queendom, princess to all."

Lilyanna knelt upon the hard marble and bowed her head. Prince Bellinor took the crown from the priestess and pressed it into her hair, the golden spikes meshing with the blonde strands. Lilyanna pitched; one hand outstretched on the step above to steady herself and the other pressed to her chest.

I leaped forward and helped her to her feet. She trembled, her heart racing. I wanted to embrace her, to dip her head onto my shoulder and rip the crown from her hair with pointless murmurs until she calmed. But she was braver than me.

I unwound my arm from her waist and stepped back. She turned to face the queens, looping her hand through the prince's outstretched arm.

The spirits pressed closer, a chill cloud dripping down the walls.

They both knelt in front of the queens, heads bowed. Neither queen said anything. They remained swamped in their furs, content to watch the prince and Lilyanna squirm uncomfortably waiting for their verdict.

The crowd remained mute.

Finally, one of the queens said, "Stand."

The prince rose to his feet, dragging Lilyanna with him. "Well, mothers, as you have come all this way, I suppose you must join us for the celebration."

"The very least you can do, boy." The taller spoke again, flinging her comments over her shoulder as they moved together down the aisle, the prince forced to walk behind. Their guards closed in, but I wormed my way through, popping up next to Lilyanna. "While we are here, we will discuss why you have chosen to deal with inappropriate magic use yourself instead of following due process and sending the criminals down to us for testing."

"The credo states to send those that have been proven to carry blood magic within their veins, and we have had no confirmed cases within my city walls, Mother."

On reaching the end of the aisle, the queens halted, standing arm in arm. The crowd rapidly dispersed, benches squealing against the marble floor. The doors to the courtyard opened and the guests poured outside to await instructions while servants scurried around, transforming the ceremony hall into a banquet.

"That may be so, but we will perform some checks ourselves. Make sure no one is slipping through that fine net you cast. We know your fondness for certain types of justice."

The prince's lower lip blanched as his teeth crushed the soft tissue. "Do whatever you see fit." He turned away, glowering at any servant that passed too close.

The other queen watched him with interest, her nostrils slightly flared, chin tipped up. Her lips curved with a sincere warmth. My magic flared, cautiously unspooling toward her, darting in and out of my fingertips with an irritating tingle.

I hovered behind Lilyanna while the benches were cleared, the fires stoked, and long tables set up that hugged the edges of the banquet room. Plate after plate of sizzling meats, plump vegetables, and delicious sweets were brought out. Spices and herbs and sugar flavored the air.

The queens and the prince remained mute, the air toxic with unspoken words, while the guests filtered back inside as sensuous music spread over the room. Laughter and relaxation seeped into the lightening air as Clement slid in beside me, bringing with him a warm cocoon of safety. My shoulders relaxed, and my chest loosened as I soaked in his presence.

I edged closer, eliminating the gap between our bodies. How different my life could have been if I'd only met him sooner. I wouldn't be standing here, mere feet away from people who wanted to exsanguinate me. He'd have probably worked out his own deal to keep me safe and be enacting the strict rules set by Siobhan with infuriating precision. Although, then I'd have to find a way to rescue *him* from her clutches. At least this way it was only me who had to suffer.

Two ornate thrones were dragged out and the queens' guards lined up behind them. The butts of their spears rested on the ground, their postures alert and distrusting. Dressed head to toe in gray, they blended with the castle walls.

In contrast, the prince's guards spread out around the room, hands on their diamond saber hilts. They mingled with the crowd, snatching a few words of conversation here and there, picking from the laden tables, but they too remained focused on the prince.

I remained next to Clement, our arms aligned, the tip of my fingers brushing his. Outwardly, he was fixed on Lilyanna and the prince leading the crowd onto the clouded marble dancefloor. But his body hummed, aware and attuned to mine.

I focused on the ceiling. Why were the spirits so still?

Chills pimpled my skin and I shuddered.

"Because they know, my dear." Siobhan's voice sounded directly in my ear, her satin fingers kneading the small of my back.

I started, my heart hammering and heat flooding my cheeks.

"You've never worn something like this for me." Her hand circled upon the sheer fabric. "Something you're not telling me, Tam?"

"Nope." I dragged my attention from the spirits and turned to her. My jaw dropped. "What are..." *Goddess save me.* A diamond-encrusted chain mail suit clung to every curve. The spiderweb thin mesh twinkled in the candlelight. Underneath, only the skimpy outline of shadows covered her breasts and ran across her groin as if the spirits themselves were covering her modesty.

She giggled and bumped me with her hip. "It's not for you, my dear. At least not tonight." She waved her hand toward the dancing guests. Many faces were turned her way, a mixture of fear and lust and loathing adorning their expressions. "Although, I could spare one dance for my favorite."

I gently unwound her arm from my waist, cursing the brief flash of disappointment that chilled me. "I don't dance. Besides, I'm working."

She laughed. "Ah, yes. Midnight *is* fast approaching. There is barely an hour left. Shame, though, that you don't want to spend your final moments with me after all these years."

She pouted and damn me if my spine didn't soften.

"I bet you'd dance with him." She flicked her head to where Clement stood, arms folded, his attention firmly on me and not the prince anymore.

I shifted to block him from view, hurriedly burying my feelings. "He just...wants my help with something." I glanced at the thrones and lowered my voice. "In fact, I'm glad you're here. I have a favor to ask."

"Tam, Tam, Tam." She sighed theatrically, throwing her arm across her forehead and raising her voice. "That's all you want from me lately. Favors. Deals. When will it end?"

I clenched my fists. The queens tensed, their chins cocked, and ears pricked. They knew the conversations worth listening to.

"There's a woman that I need to free," I hissed. "His sister." I jerked my thumb over my shoulder. "She's in the queens' jail for treason. I'm going to try and reach her before they return and enact their penance, but if you could protect her for me, I'd owe you."

"You already owe me, my dear, and there's only one thing I want from you." She ran her fingertip up my bare arm. "Besides, you're already bound to a deal. I wouldn't want to overburden you." She hooked her fingertip under my chin, tugging me closer. "Kiss me and I'll think about it."

My back spasmed as I clamped down all my muscles. I leaned forward and kissed her with my breath held, not allowing the seductive lily odor to swirl into my mouth and nose.

She flashed me a grin, heading toward the swirling bodies on the dance floor. Before she slid onto the red marble, she turned back. "Oh, one last thing. As we're so close to the deadline and this evening promises to be so very fun, I have invited some close friends of yours a little early." My breath snagged in my throat. "It really is about time you caught up. Don't you think?"

I continued glaring at her retreating presence long after she was swallowed by the twirling fabric and glitter of jewelry. My mind whirred. I wasn't ready to face them. I didn't want to know what they would do. Would they apologize? Maybe dive straight into practiced excuses?

Perhaps they wouldn't even mention it, proud of transforming all our lives.

Or, if I failed, I'd get to relive their deaths all over again. Moving myself one step closer to Hell in return.

I needed a drink. Or to gorge myself on pastries.

My stomach growled and Clement edged closer, his mouth tipped up into a grin. Goddessdamn him, he was so distracting. As soon as he neared, I didn't even care about the food. All I wanted was to back him into the wall, disappear into the shadows and lose myself to him.

"Do you think you'll be able to spare *me* a dance before midnight?" His fingers stroked the back of my hand, the magic throbbing at his touch.

Midnight! The moon had fully risen, flashes of silvery light strobed the courtyard outside as dense clouds sped past and panic welled in my throat.

Clement nudged me.

"I don't dance," I snapped.

"Oh, I'm sure you do," the prince drawled. He released Lilyanna's hand, stranding her next to the seated queens. "This may be our last chance of a moment's peace, *Tamara*. Just you and me. Before our games begin again."

Clement pressed against me, his heart thudding against my shoulder. Icy tendrils crept between us. They bulged, forcing him away, burning my skin.

"Chop, chop, Tam." The prince backed toward the dance floor with his hand extended, every eye absorbed in tracking his progress.

"Don't," Clement pleaded. He swatted at the air, hissing in pain as his skin crackled. Black raced up his arm, the scent of charred flesh wafting from him.

"It'll be okay." I took a step toward the prince, my soul stretching as it tried to cling to Clement. "Do you trust me?"

"I don't trust anyone." He gritted his teeth and lunged through the dark barricade. "But I love you." He barely managed to kiss my cheek before he was flung backward and pinned against the wall by the spirits.

"That'll have to do then," I whispered.

My golden slippers made no sound as I stepped onto the dance floor. Clement's gaze was on my back, pricking the hairs on my neck. It was all I could do not to turn and run to him, burying myself in his arms.

Whispers swarmed through the crowd as they pressed closer to the edges, jostling for a better view. "His maid?" someone asked. "His whore," another answered.

The magic raged within me. My head swam, body wavering. Sweat laced my palms. I didn't want to touch him again, to feel his power seed within me.

The string quartet in the corner wafted a few tentative notes across the room. Couples paired up, none coming within feet of us.

The prince bent at the waist in a shallow bow, his gray eyes never leaving mine. His hand remained outstretched. He was going to make me take it, but he wouldn't break me.

I closed my hand around the prince's as acid burned in my throat. I needed to see Clement, for him to calm me, remind me, hold me.

The prince's arm coiled around my waist, dragging me close. He kept my back to Clement and winked over my shoulder, his grin widening before resuming focus on me. I didn't need to turn to know Clement's hand would be on his saber, his jaw tight, body poised to charge.

The music swelled. A perfect expanse of red-veined marble hollowed out around us as he forced me forward. I leaned back, my neck outstretched, my mouth tilted away from his rose-scented breath. Up close, even the perfume couldn't mask the aroma underneath. Rotten.

His arm ratcheted tighter.

I called to my magic, forcing myself to remain confident, to not think about every time it had cowered around him. It bounded through my bloodstream, gathering pressure with a pounding in my temples. I focused on my hands, channeling it through my body. It raced through me, tingling my arms and prickling the nerves of my wrist, but it shied away at the last second.

The prince's hold on me tightened, numbness spreading through me like a contagion. My foot slipped, my body weakening as my head swam.

A shadow fell over the courtyard through the open doors. As it lifted again, the moon hung central as if hesitating at its mid-point, the Goddess buying me a few seconds of extra time.

Midnight.

This time, I didn't call to the magic, I summoned it, forcing it away from safety and down through my body. It leaked through my pores, sticky black streaks running down the lines on my palm.

My nails extended, my fingertips burning. The magic rammed against my skin. I was stronger than the spirits, stronger than my magic, stronger than him.

My legs buckled, and I fell into the prince, my chest colliding with his, mouth inches away from his foul breath. I stamped hard on his toe, simultaneously raking my nails down the back of his hand.

He grunted. His hand reflexively tightened on mine to support my weight, dragging me upward and shifting me from his foot.

The magic thundered through me, pressure releasing in a split-second with a gasp flying from my lips.

He didn't even blink. His eyes remained intent on mine, surprise and even a flash of pleasure crossing his face.

"I told you. I don't dance." I wriggled from his hold and smoothed down my dress. Aware that all eyes were on us, all conversation severed.

A solitary drop of blood splashed onto the marble. He hadn't even noticed.

But the spirits had.

CHAPTER THIRTY
THE COLLECTION

CLEMENT APPEARED AT MY SIDE IN AN INSTANT.

Black slashes were carved into his neck, his tunic torn at the shoulders, the skin underneath charred. He ducked, dragging me to the floor and covered my body with his.

The candles all extinguished with one invisible gust, the moonlight in the courtyard suddenly strangled by the dense clouds. Darkness choked us.

Screams erupted from all sides. Bodies stampeded toward the exits, panic thick in the air. Spirits swooped from the ceiling, tearing at Clement's back. Penetrating ice-cold spears ripped into my exposed flesh, sizzling my skin. He rolled to cover more of me, squeezing the air from around my body and forcing the spirits to recede.

Heavy bolts thumped across the main doors. The fear grew, the guests now fleeing for the courtyard.

"Behind the altar," he hissed in my ear, "there's a passage." His body rocked as the spirits swarmed. He dug deeper, pressing me further to the ground as he bit back the pain.

"Lilyanna! I can't leave her."

"She wants to be here. As long as she survives the night, she'll be fine."

Somewhere in the distance, the prince yelled an order for the spirits to find me over the churning mass of people. One by one the fireplaces blinked back to life, congealed gray smoke dissipating.

"We need to go now. I'm not arguing with you, Tam."

Bony fingers locked around my ankle. I kicked out, hitting nothing but a dense cloud of pressure. It yanked me backward, and I slid out from under Clement.

He grabbed my wrists and dragged me forward. My leg stretched, my tendons extending. My ankle bones ground together in the spirit's grip. Clement pulled harder and my leg shot free. He dragged me to my feet, his arm encircling my waist.

We raced toward the dark altar, the candles swooshing to life behind us, the light biting at our heels. The shadows soared overhead, forced into the corners and away from the heat.

My slippers slid on the stairs, but Clement kept his grip until we rounded the altar. He flung open a trap door in the marble. "In. Now."

Stale air belched from the pitch-black shaft, and I opened my mouth to argue, but he kicked my legs from under me and threw me into the opening.

Seconds later, he collapsed in the dirt next to me and the lid slammed shut above. Mold and ash swirled into the air.

"Move. They'll chase us." He shoved me forward, the passageway barely high enough to stand. The walls clutched at me, rending holes in the sheer fabric of my dress. We descended sharply downhill before snaking left then right. Small eyes in the wood panels allowed brief glimpses of familiar rooms and snatches of perfume, smoke, or decomposing scraps.

I was in the walls. Again.

Clement kept pushing me forward, his shoulders stooped, his breath panting against my neck. "We'll go out through the sewers. The spirits can't leave the castle. If we keep moving, they may not catch us."

"May?"

He barked a laugh and shoved me harder. "I'll get you out, I promise."

"And you?"

I slammed into a wall, Clement colliding with me. "Sorry," he mumbled. "This way." We moved to an opening on the left, treading more carefully as the ground levelled out. The temperature dropped with every step.

"I can't smell sewage. Are you sure this is the right way?"

"These old tunnels don't work anymore. The prince keeps them open so he can sneak in and out of the castle. They spit out just inside the boundary, underneath those large gargoyles. It's barely ten yards to the street from there."

So, that's how he'd snuck up on me. "I hope Lilyanna's okay." The guards would have surrounded the prince, and the Queens' Guard protected his mothers, but who would be with her? I'd spent weeks caring for her and now abandoned her to whatever Fate had laid out for her. "Maybe the prince doesn't know what happened. We could still try and leave the normal way."

"The spirits would have told him. The castle is going to lock down any second. Keep moving."

The prince's voice echoed through the tunnels in a distorted whisper. "*Tamara*. Oh, what a scene you've caused at my wedding. You can't run, you know. You can't hide from me in my own home."

"Keep going," Clement urged.

A puddle of moonlight swirled gray in the darkness shone up ahead. He pushed me forward, his hand never leaving the small of my back. As my toes touched the light, a metal gate slammed down. Clement piled into me again, crushing me against the rusted bars. The earth shook. Dank mud and dust and cobwebs rained down from the ceiling.

The prince's laughter echoed around us.

"Ignore him." Clement gently moved me aside, then grabbed the bars and shook, achieving nothing except an eerie rattle. "Damn it!" He took my hand and spun down a smaller tributary. "This fucking way then."

Up ahead another gate slammed down. He cursed again and dragged me back the way we'd come. He paused at a fork, frustrated breaths loud and raspy in the stillness. The middle was the way we'd come, the right sloped gently upward in the vague direction of the new castle, and the left plunged downward into pitch black.

"We go up," I said. "We need to get out."

"No." He strode toward the left tunnel. "The deeper we go, the less control the castle has. Then we need to head south to reach the gates. Where's that compass he gave you?"

I tugged up the hem of my dress, revealing the slim holster that I'd turned inward so the bulge wouldn't be present against the sheer fabric. I'd have much preferred to have worn my knife, but as the prince made me wear this revealing dress, I wouldn't have been able to hide it, so I'd made do with the solid metal compass thinking I could bludgeon someone with it.

I flipped open the gold lid and rapped it against the stone wall. The needle quivered, emanating with a slight phosphorescence. It spun clearly toward the small engraved 'south' and Clement's dark, miserable tunnel that went further down.

I planted my feet and folded my arms, but he'd seen the result.

"Please." He gripped my shoulders, lowering his face to mine. "Trust me. I promised I'd get you out, and I will. That's the best way." He kissed me gently, his manipulative tactics rewarded when my body softened.

He tugged my arm, and I grudgingly fell into step behind him, one hand fisted in the back of his tunic. He waved his arms in front of him, sleeves swishing in the darkness. I crept after him, picking my feet up high, my spare hand trailing along the hewn dirt wall.

The tunnel rapidly closed in on us. Clement's shirt stretched in my grip as he doubled over, squeezing himself forward. Musty droplets sprung from the ceiling and oozed onto my skin whenever I brushed against the walls.

How easy it would be for the castle to squash us right now. To bury us down here amid tons of rubble. Would it mean our spirits would be trapped too, or would it be enough of a burial to allow us passage onward?

In answer, the castle groaned behind us. The floor trembled and the walls inched closer. Rocks and earth sprung loose, pelting us, before tumbling downward into the never-ending pit.

I flung my arm over my head, closing my eyes as dust stung my corneas, tears streaming down my cheeks. Clement barreled onward, tugging me out of the tunnel and into a circular vestibule.

Slivers of moonlight pierced the darkness, fogging as it hit my breath. The rusted rungs of a ladder scaled the wall in front. Behind us, the rocks ground to a halt, carefully layering themselves in an impenetrable barrier like maggots feasting on an open wound, leaving no skin untouched, blocking our retreat.

I stepped backward, away from the ladder and a blinding pain seared through my skull. Crushing pressure slammed into my temples, my vision darkening. I stumbled forward again, and the tightness vanished.

Tentatively, I eased backward. The pressure returned, but this time, it morphed into dozens of voices. The words merged into an incoherent chant. I focused on the rhythm, opening my senses, allowing my mind to accept the intrusion.

Go back.

Clement studied the ladder with his arms crossed and feet planted, completely oblivious. He turned to frown at me.

I moved forward, the pressure around my skull releasing once more and the sound vanished. I wiped my face, gasping and gesturing toward the wall. "We should go back. They want us to go that way." My finger shook as I waggled it toward the ladder. "Not up there."

"We can't go back. We need to get out."

I moved in front of him to reclaim his attention. "No, but—"

He shushed me, motioning for me to stay behind him. I stomped alongside him and glared until he sighed. "You can't trust them; they still obey him. Wait here, I'll go first. Check that it's safe."

The blocked tunnel behind us quietened. The rocks had plugged the gaps, and the dust settled as if it had been present for hundreds of years. Creeping veins of diamond glistened in stray shards of moonlight.

A light, tempting breeze seeped down from above.

I scoffed. "No way. I'm not staying here by myself."

I moved for the ladder, but Clement grabbed me, my feet dangling in the air. He spun and settled me behind him before turning back and climbing the rungs quickly. The ladder screamed, grinding its teeth under his weight.

I scurried up behind him, too close to react to his muffled warning.

Cold hands latched around my wrists, my ankles, my neck. My back hit the ground with such force that my spine was only spared from shattering by the carpet of snow. I tried to scream but icy tendrils squirmed into my mouth, snuffing out any sound and blocking my air.

I gasped, thrashing under the invisible weight. I dragged in oxygen through my nose, my nostrils flaring, breaths not enough to smother the rising panic.

Clement was immobilized against the wall. The gargoyle hovered over his head, its gaping maw spitting a single pointed icicle that inched toward his face. His hands were flattened to the castle walls, legs pinned. His eyes bulged as he fought, my name dying on his lips.

The prince stood in the open. His hands outstretched, vibrations thrumming through him. "The spirits only listen to me, Tam. Valiant effort though."

Slowly, the snow beneath my back crackled. The slivers of ice meshed together, hardening into a stretcher. My body moved. The castle looming higher above me.

I tried to claw at the ground, to dig my heels into the ice, but my muscles seized. The castle walls shifted before me, grinding open to reveal a passageway. Rose, blood, and rot smothered me.

My feet were dragged inside. The pressure of the castle popped my joints, squeezing the fluid from between my bones. The prince walked slowly toward me, his palms still lifted skyward, his mouth murmuring words I couldn't hear.

I should be screaming for Siobhan, pleading for my life, but the only name on my lips was Clement's.

Our gaze met and he kept it, holding it steady as my body was swallowed by the wall. The pressure wrapped around my chest, entombing me in darkness. If it closed behind me, I would never get out.

I opened my mind as I'd done in the tunnel. Let the pressure filter inside but not swamp my senses. The garbled voices returned, the chanting rhythm equalizing with my pounding heartbeat.

Let me go.

My body stopped moving. The invisible bindings around my torso slackened, the tendrils wrenched from my mouth. I scrabbled to my feet, clawing at the narrow opening. It still held me, sucking me deeper. Hands fisted into my dress, pulling and slipping until they held skin. I burst out of the wall, the pressure lifting, my lungs finally filling and collapsed against Clement.

He lifted my face and kissed me with such passion, I lost my breath again. "Fuck, Tamara, I thought…"

"I know." I clutched at his tunic, keeping his body safely pressed against mine.

"I don't really think we have time for that, do you?" Siobhan materialized beside the prince. Her chain mail suit tinkled faintly as she turned to him. "Nice to make your acquaintance. A wonderful wedding, Your Highness. What a shame you didn't beg me for your deal all those years ago, or we'd be in quite a different situation right now." She tapped a long nail over his heart. "Tut, tut."

She clicked her fingers, and the gargoyle shuddered to life. It clambered down the stone walls and toward the prince who remained frozen. It stretched out its arms, a bat-like membrane flapped taut and encircled the prince. He roared, woken from his trance and thrashed against the bindings.

"We can't have you spilling our secrets before the collection now, can we?" Siobhan reached toward him. The prince squirmed in the gargoyle's unbreakable grip. She forced open his mouth and tore out his tongue. It flopped onto the cobblestones, twitching as blood pulsed out. The prince's cry was lost amongst the gargling choke of blood pooling in his mouth.

I stared at his tongue, remembering the feeling of it tracing the lines of my neck, forcing its way inside my mouth. My stomach lurched.

Siobhan flapped a hand at us. "Off you pop, my dear."

Clement grasped my arm, gently shaking me back to the present. We turned together, only making it twenty yards before ice spiderwebbed beneath our feet, cracking the ground. The gate loomed above us, a rift between the castle's magic and freedom.

Just outside the castle grounds, two strangers halted. Between us, the spirits hovered, forming a black cloud. It pulsed, its tendrils sucking in the surrounding air, gathering more of the darkness.

Through the black mist, the strangers' features were blurred, but my heart squeezed. The man wore the same silver spectacles he'd always worn, the lenses so thick his jade green eyes were magnified. His hair curled, messy and artistic, a well-worn path visible through the center where he'd run his hand through it.

The woman wore what she always did—an old cream blouse and blue overalls. When it was hot, she'd flap one of the straps down and roll up her sleeves, but she'd never take it off.

Where were their weapons? Where was the magic? Why was the air not filled with gunpowder snaps and flashes of power?

The woman rolled up her sleeves and cracked her neck, lowering into a crouch. The man stood behind her, his hands hidden within deep pockets, his wiry body wound like a spring. They both leaped over the threshold.

The spirits swarmed toward the couple.

"Go!" Clement shoved my shoulder. "They're distracted, go now."

I couldn't tear my eyes away as the roiling darkness descended on them. Clicks, scrapes, screams spun into the air. How long would they be able to hold them off?

The spirits slipped into a whirling tornado, encircling them. Dark streaks broke off and lunged inside, shrieking, the air clouded with drifting ash.

I couldn't leave them to die.

The spirits' chant filled my mind, urgent this time, desperate, but there was an edge of sadness. It swamped me, prickling my skin, tugging at my soul.

Stop! I screamed at them.

They hesitated. The black mass flickered.

The Collectors passed through the swarm, advancing toward the prince, but the thread linking me wavered. The pressure increased, removing my control and the spirits flashed back into motion. Siobhan had vanished, but the gargoyle still gripped the prince, and he was reclaiming them. Blood trickled over his lips and down his chin, soaking into the membrane that enclosed him. His mouth moved in a silent command focused on the spirits.

No.

I wrestled back control. Sweat ran in a line down my back, my entire body rigid. I forced their chant to calm, binding them to the rhythm of my heart, making them mine.

The Collectors reached the prince. The man withdrew a hatchet from his waistband, bringing the butt down upon the gargoyle. It shattered like glass upon the cobblestones. The woman caught the prince, tugging his head back to expose his neck. The man flipped the ax around and sliced down the prince's neck. His blood didn't spurt but trickled slowly, congealing into sludge as it hit the cold air, steam hissing into the night.

The connection between the spirits snapped tight like reins. The opposing force eradicated.

Go rest.

With the prince dead, they'd be able to return to haunting the castle, waiting for another master. Until then, they could be in peace.

The Collectors held their positions, watching the blood drain from the prince, his struggles ebbing.

"Go!" Clement pushed me.

Fires ignited in the courtyard beyond. Guests clattered toward the exits carrying flames. The telltale march of the guards led the charge, their pace determined, hunting for the prince.

I kept staring at the dying prince, at the Collectors fixated on their task.

Clement lunged toward me, but I sidestepped, spinning around to watch again. "Go now, or I'll throw you over my shoulder like a bale of fucking hay."

The woman's eyes lifted to mine. Eight years of happy memories flooded my mind, but I couldn't do it. I couldn't forgive them. I backed away slowly with my palms raised as Clement advanced, unable to rip my eyes from the scene.

"Fine," I snapped.

He grabbed my hand and spun me around, dragging me down the central street. The shops blurred as we ran, their windows dark, signs blank and flapping in the wind. My feet were leaden, the fear barely outweighing the guilt at abandoning them.

"They're your Collectors, aren't they?" He kept my hand gripped within his, my only anchor in the rising panic.

"Yes." I glanced behind, but he tugged me onward, my legs barely able to keep up with his long strides.

"And you know them well."

"Yes," I panted.

"But you haven't forgiven them for binding you into their deal?"

I kept my eyes fixed on the straight road, the gate barely visible in the distance. "No."

He veered left, towing me behind him down zigzagging alleyways. Ice glistened between the cobbles. My feet slipped as they skimmed the ground, barely able to land before Clement urged me onward.

Finally, the glow of the stable lights emerged around a bend.

"Who are they?" He halted, still tucked inside the alley. He poked his head out, whipping it back and forth across the street before searching the sky above.

"My parents." I doubled over, my hands on my hips, trying to wheeze silently.

Clement froze. He bent down and scooped my chin in his palm, making me straighten. He wagged a finger in my face. "We'll talk about *that* later."

I groaned.

"Come on. Quietly."

I rolled my eyes. *Quietly*.

The stables were silent. Torches guttered along the aisle, casting dancing shadows into the stalls. The wind screamed outside, tearing around the sturdy walls, unable to find a way in.

"My horse has been turned out. I need to go find her." I shoved my hands under my armpits, biting back a shiver.

"No, she's not. She's in here." He nudged me forward, leading me to the end stall. "I had her brought in and tacked." He undid the heavy chain, gently lowering it to the straw so as not to make a sound. "And I prepared these." He hauled two stuffed saddlebags from the corner. "It's all the stuff you tried to collect. Clothes, food, and a few added items." A faint blush rose on his cheeks, and my throat tightened.

He extracted my cloak and boots, throwing them toward me, before turning and attaching the bags to the saddle. He handed me the reins.

"Thank you." I swallowed. The horse nudged my neck, her muzzle velvety soft against my frozen skin.

Clement backed against the wall and folded his arms across his chest. He nodded, eyes falling to the floor.

I led the horse down the aisle, her feet clopping in the stillness. As I reached the street outside, I turned. "Well, what are you waiting for? Hurry up, grab a horse and elope with me."

He threw back his head and barked a laugh, diving into the adjoining stall to pull out an already tacked black gelding. He joined me, grinning. "I was waiting for you to ask nicely."

"You'd have been waiting a while." I grinned back, my heart expanding.

We led the horses quickly toward the gates, hugging the shadows. Clement positioned himself on the outside, sandwiching me against the stone wall. His gaze never stilled, flitting between the skies and the surrounding houses.

"Are we going to get through the gates?" I whispered.

"I thought you knew everyone in the queendom?"

The woman at the gates sat perched on her three-legged stool, half-hidden in the gloom. Her hand rested on the lever with the gates open beside her just wide enough to slip through. She kept her attention on the long street before her, eyes focused on the castle churning in the distance. She didn't say a word as we crept past.

We slipped through the gate, and it immediately creaked shut behind us. We mounted our horses and faced the expansive moorland beyond. The chill air tore through my hair, reawakening my body, purging the lingering scent of roses and refreshing my soul.

"Where to?" he asked.

I tugged out the compass and watched the needle adjust. "South." I urged my horse onward; her hoof falls light on the frozen grass. "To rescue your sister."

Hope flashed across his face, followed by fear, then pain. He let out a shaky breath and my chest squeezed. "Why?"

"Because I love you." Even as I uttered the words foreign to my tongue, I knew I meant it. I'd do anything for this man, even if it meant I'd never be free.

He smiled at me, his dark eyes bright, and I grinned back.

We urged our horses into a gallop, tearing into the rising night.

Thank you for reading! Did you enjoy? Please add your review because nothing helps an author more and encourages readers to take a chance on a book than a review.

And don't miss more from N K Brown coming soon. Be sure to visit nkbrownauthor.com

Until then, discover A GAME OF FALLEN STARS, by City Owl Author, S.E. Berkeley. Turn the page for a sneak peek!

You can also sign up for the City Owl Press newsletter to receive notice of all book releases!

SNEAK PEEK A GAME OF FALLEN STARS
BY S.E. BERKELEY

The sun sinks behind the meadow's large hills, the last of day disappearing from the kitchen window. It's one of those breathtaking sunsets that reminds Ethan why he chose to spend his sabbatical out here in Parkfield, California.

But instead, Ethan is trapped inside, talking to his mother. Not that he has much of a choice. The weekly call is mandatory, the terms carefully negotiated with her after a very long session with his therapist. It would be nice to take the call on the porch and watch the stars wink into existence, but the kitchen is the only place he gets reliable cell service. So, he's stuck.

He checks the kitchen clock and his heart plummets. He is two minutes and forty-five seconds over the allotted time, and she shows no signs of stopping. Which means it's up to him to end it.

Ethan keeps his sigh silent, eyes closing briefly. Trying to end these calls is always tricky. There are two wolves warring in his mind. One snarls at him, *Be a good son, she only has you,* and the other snaps, *Maintain healthy boundaries, these are not healthy boundaries, my God, you moved out here for this exact reason.*

Well, not the *exact* reason. Sure, making it difficult for his mother to hop on a train to see him was one benefit of spending his time in Parkfield. Because Parkfield, where there are more coyotes than people, is absolutely isolated. Nothing but deer, raccoons, and the occasional boar family. And cattle. Lots and lots of cattle.

His sister, Andrea, had painted a beautiful picture of him getting out of San Francisco and being only a short distance away from her. His therapist warned him he was running away from his problems instead of dealing with them. She was right, but the idea that Andrea had put into his head sounded like paradise.

Speaking of which, Andrea glares with a judgmental arch of her brow. She mouths, "Hang up."

He glares back at her. Like it's that easy.

She points at the phone, and he tilts it away from his ear to hear her harsh whisper. "Do it. I did not hook you up with this place for you to cave like a little bitch. Come on, Ethan. Grow a pair."

His jaw clenches, but she does have a point. His sigh is audible now. His mother has yet to take a breath, and the energy required to interrupt her and instigate hanging up still hasn't manifested. His therapist would be disappointed in him. If she was here, she would remind him that he needs to end the call before his mother—

"And how's your hair?"

—starts criticizing him.

He leans on his forearms, and his shoulder-length brown hair falls into his face. He usually ties it back in a man bun or half up, but he didn't have the care to do that today. There's a pause as he searches for the patience to answer his mother's superficial question. All he comes up with is a bland, "Manageable."

Andrea smirks at him. "Should've listened."

He nods. When she's right, she's right.

His mother's disapproving hum is straight out of his childhood when she adds, "I'm surprised you haven't been written up at work."

"Mom, I'm on sabbatical. I have no work rules, that's the whole point of this break." His patience falters and out slips a mumbled, "And, no one fucking cares." Blessedly, she doesn't hear.

He eyes the fridge. If he hangs up, he can drink his beer. That's his deal with himself. A little incentivizing. God, won't that cold one be lovely...if he can just get off the phone.

"Well, Mary Anne said at her son's tech company they..." He starts to tune her out again. If he wanders out of the kitchen, the call will drop. A simple solution to his problem. But she will call back. Repeatedly. And if she gets too worked up, she might do something horrific like visit. He shudders.

Ethan watches the clock, his mother's voice a muted echo in the back of his mind. It's one of those analog clocks, and it's stylized to match the kitchen's "rustic chic." Ethan couldn't care less about what kind of chic it is, but he does appreciate the movement of the second hand. It gives his eyes something to settle on while he waits.

It's a miracle his mother hasn't passed out yet. She can easily set the record for longest stream of consciousness without breath. It's impressive. Annoying, but impressive.

A sneered "your therapist" from his mother penetrates Ethan's wandering mind. He snaps his head down to glare at the granite countertops, his shoulders rounding. "What?"

"I'm telling you, baby, they want to stuff you full of useless big pharma poison. What's the point of a therapist if you're still being all mopey like this? You don't need a therapist, Ethan. You're the most put together man I know. What you need is a wife. And kids. Theresa's son was just like you but then he—"

Ethan scrubs his face, frustration bubbling in his chest. It's always the same, and nothing he says will make a difference. He tried. He really did. He dated. They were all nice, but every partner sensed the same thing: Ethan is stagnant. And they left him to flourish with others.

As for having kids, well, he'd rather die, something his mother would gladly assist with if she ever found out about his vasectomy.

Andrea cracks open one of his beers and envy sweeps over him, his throat drying. She takes an extra-slow sip. He flips her off and mouths, "Ungrateful." She gives a satisfied "ah," tilting the bottle toward him. "If you had a spine, you could have one too."

"Have you tried calling Jenny?" His mother asks.

His gaze slides to the fridge. Out of all his exes to bring up, she chooses his college girlfriend from nearly two decades ago?

"Jenny is now happily pregnant and married." To a woman, for God's sake. "Remember?"

His mother's disappointed "hm" prickles his insides. "It's too bad. She was a delight. Much better than what's-her-face. You know. That last one."

His anger spikes, his gaze on the chrome fridge door hardening. He knows she remembers Taylor's name. His mother made it very clear to everyone involved how much she hated Taylor.

A tornado of emotions swells in him—shame, sadness, anger—all building, making his stomach twist. He cracks his neck, eyes closing, trying to breathe the discomfort away, but it stays, coating his insides.

Andrea's harsh voice cracks through the roaring in his ears. "Ethan. Hang up."

His lips thin. She doesn't understand. It's not that easy.

"Ethan."

The warning in her voice makes it worse. His jaw clenches. His mother's disappointed tone sets his heart pounding faster, the beats hammering in his ears. "It's funny how you mention Jenny's little family." He feels his stomach lurch as he clutches the phone harder. "It could've been you if you hadn't messed it up."

He sucks in breath, eyes snapping open. His phone is gone, his hand smarting from where it's suddenly been ripped free. Andrea glares at him, her voice hard. "Ethan, breathe."

His breath trembles, some of the chaos in his mind ebbing. Only some. Not nearly enough. He forces in a second breath.

Andrea adds a soft, "Should I get the Ativan?"

His jaw clenches again. "No." Shame. Guilt. Fear that his mother might've heard her. It starts building again. It gives him the incentive he needs—he can't do this anymore tonight. "Give me the phone."

Andrea scans him carefully before handing it over. He holds it up to his ear. Relief hits him. His mother didn't even notice, still prattling on about God knows what. His voice is harsher than he intends, and he would curse if it wouldn't make it even worse. "Mom, I have to go."

Her tone instantly goes defensive. "Go? What do you mean go? It's only been thirty-two minutes! And you don't answer my calls or text—"

"Mom, I get shit cell service here. There's nothing that can be done about it." God, he does love that. It was the selling point, really, for moving out here. Shitty cell connection. Bad internet. Easy excuses that allow him to ignore his mother, and the rest of the world. When he had packed, he'd dedicated two suitcases to the books he had thought about reading for the last decade.

"Can't you do something about it? You work in tech! You're an engineer. Can't you just figure it out?"

"Yeah, it doesn't work like that. I'll call you next week." Maybe. Probably. But his therapist would be so proud if he didn't.

"Ethan."

That tone. It prickles the back of his neck, and he stretches again. He forces his voice to be perfectly smooth. "Please, Mom. I'm really tired. I'll try to do better. Promise." Empty words that make his insides curdle.

"Okay, baby."

He releases a silent breath. "Thank you. Goodnight, Mom. Love you."

"Love you too. Be safe out there. You know how horror mov—"

He hangs up. It was that or another ten minutes of fear mongering to try to get him to come back to the city.

Andrea eyes him, and he can detect the anger simmering in her. He wasn't lying about the exhaustion. It hits him like a wave, and he leans heavily on the countertop. She searches his face, choosing her words. "You're iced out again."

His jaw ticks. "My face?"

She nods slowly. "She makes you do that, you know that, right?"

He doesn't want to talk about this. It's a familiar argument and not just with Andrea. Unwanted memories surface, making his heart hurt. They still feel raw, and he knows without needing a mirror that it makes his face "ice out," as Andrea likes to call it. His face is perfectly smooth, not a hint of emotion, not even in his eyes. Taylor hates it...or, hated it.

He stretches his neck one more time, forcing himself to straighten. "I'm fine." He's only constantly haunted by the best relationship he's ever had, one that he ruined. With momentous effort, he stomps down all the feelings and memories. He forces a smile, a carefully practiced one he's perfected. "Now where is my promised beer?"

It doesn't fool her. Fifteen years his junior and Andrea can read him like a well-loved book. Teenage Andrea would've called him out on it, but adult Andrea lets it slide. She flashes her own dazzling smile. "Coming right up!"

She flings open the fridge. "Hello, lovelies. Come to mama." He feels his lips twitch. Pulling out his favorite IPA, she tosses him a playful smirk. "And an iced mug, because you *fancy* tonight."

That twitch turns into a genuine smile, one that washes away his fake one. It's small, but still a smile. He accepts the frothing mug. They clink their drinks together, and he takes a hearty gulp. "Oh fuck, that hits the spot."

Andrea's lip curls. "You have froth on your nasty-ass beard."

He wipes it with the back of his hand. It has gotten rather overgrown lately. Usually, it's trimmed down, but he can't bring himself to care since going on sabbatical—before that even, if he was being honest.

Andrea takes a swig of her bottle. "What happened to the grooming kit I got you? You know, with the wash and balm and—what was it? Oil?"

He scratches at his beard, and she slaps his hand. Her lip curls higher. "That's disgusting."

He shakes out his stinging hand. "First of all, ow. Rude. And yeah, I have it with me, and I'll have you know I wash this beautiful beard every day. I just need to trim it."

"And your hair too while you're at it." He rolls his eyes and she scowls. "Don't give me that! Look, just a touch. I'll even do it for you." She nails him with a harsh look. "You used to look like one of those thirst traps on social media." The judgmental sweep of her gaze rankles him. "Now you have people wondering if you're homeless, and not in that 'oh, but maybe he's secretly a millionaire' kind of way."

He runs his hand through his hair. "It's not that bad! Look." He gives his beard a tug, using his fingers to measure. "It's not even that long."

"Yeah, but you're screaming *unkempt*." She points at him. "No one wants to fuck unkempt."

"Oh, yeah." Sarcasm and anger drip from every word. "A real pressing issue out here in the middle of fucking nowhere where the only person I interact with is my sister."

"There is a whole town—"

"Population eighteen."

She raises her voice to speak over him. "A *whole* town that would be interested. But you're screaming 'is he an off-season movie star or is he homeless' and—"

"I thought it was millionaire?"

"*Trust* me, Ethan." She points her beer aggressively at him, and his mouth shuts. "You want to land on the 'not homeless' side."

Silence stretches. Ethan decides his sister has used up her welcome. The rocking chair on the front porch is calling his name like a siren, and one overbearing woman already kept him from its loving embrace for the sunset. He'll be damned if the other takes up anymore of his evening.

Andrea's hazel eyes sweep him again, and Ethan's dark gaze meets hers defiantly. Both siblings take after their father in every way except for the eyes. Andrea inherited her mother's, while Ethan's deep-set dark ones mirror their father's. The only things Ethan got from his mother are a funhouse selection of behavioral disorders.

Andrea looks away first. She runs her hand over her hair, smoothing along the buzzed sides to grip the shock of longer hair on top. She straightens, the breath she was holding rushing from her. "I just want you to be..."

"Happy?"

"Ideally. But I'll be satisfied with at peace. That's why you're out here, right? Work was burning you out. The city wasn't serving you..." Her hand wraps around her beer again. "I don't care what your mom thinks. You have some soul searching to do, and going home now and just being miserable there isn't going to work. It hasn't been working for a long time."

He nods, gaze dropping. She's right, just like all the other times they've had this conversation. He's been pretty fucking blessed all his life. Got in with a tech startup right before it took off, catapulting him through the ranks and landing him a nice VP position where he does very little programming and a lot of paper pushing. The money is great. His investments, retirement, company stock...it would make the average millennial weep. Hell, he even purchased a large condo in the city before the housing market bounced back. And yet, he still feels the suffocating oppression of ennui. He just doesn't get it. He should be happy.

He takes a fortifying swig of beer. "I know." His fake smile is back. "I'm okay."

Her eyes narrow, but she drops it. Her empty beer bottle clatters in the recycling can. "I should head out."

He nods. "You good to drive?"

"Bitch, please. It was *one* beer. I could drink you under the table."

"Yeah, don't remind me, or I'll be forced to lecture you about my concerns with your level of drinking."

Andrea's gasp of outrage drowns out the creak of the porch door swinging open. "How *dare* you. I'm fine." She starts mumbling as she stomps out. "Sexist bullshit. Just because I'm a woman, I can't win a drinking contest? My liver is an overachiever!"

He walks her out to her car. Well, his car. His old truck, from before he bought his brand new souped-up one as a present to himself for his thirty-eighth birthday. With no marriage prospects and no chance of a "whoops baby," he didn't see the point of having such a thick savings anymore.

It had made him feel better. For a second.

Andrea hauls herself into the truck. "Night, Ethaniel!"

He smiles fondly at the nickname she bequeathed him when she was six. "Night, Andy. Drive safe."

The headlights flash and he's alone. Slowly, he makes his way through the cabin until every light is clicked off. Finally, there is nothing but blissful darkness. Grabbing another beer from the fridge, Ethan steps out onto his porch and sighs as he eases down in the old rocking chair.

Andrea was right in setting him up in this place. When she heard that one of the ranchers, her friend Lisa, built a vacation rental on their acreage, she immediately used her copy of his credit card, without his permission, to lock the place for the first two months of his sabbatical. He forgave her impulsive spending of his money once he saw the place.

The small cabin sits nestled between two massive hills on a large, grassy meadow with lots of oak trees and no light pollution for miles. The first time he beheld the night sky in all its glory, it felt like he was gazing upon the quiet splendor of heaven and his mind went quiet.

And yet here he is. Far away from both the corporate life that was eating him alive and the overstimulation from the city, and he still feels like absolute shit. It's downright aggravating.

He rocks in the chair, his eyes steadily adjusting to the darkness. It's a lovely evening, the kind he dreamed of when Andrea first texted him photos. The grass of the meadow takes on a light blue hue under the full moon. His eyes slide up to the twinkling stars, abundant and beautiful with a billowing stretch of cosmos. The knot of tension within his chest finally loosens and his head rests against the weather wood. It's everything the city isn't, and it helps quiets the frustration within him.

This is why he's here. The peace. Fleeting, hard-earned peace.

The scent of sweet dry grass and rich cooling soil fills Ethan's lungs as he breathes deeply. The way they blend with the crispness of night always settles his mind. It's better than any aromatherapy he's tried. His beer is empty, but he cannot bring himself to stand. The light creaks of the chair and the chirping of crickets are all he needs in this moonlit serenity.

Moonlit serenity that is steadily growing brighter.

Ethan's brows furrow. "What the f—"

The world explodes. His eyes burn under the oppressive brightness. His chair topples sideways, and he crashes to the ground hard, arms covering his head. The Earth shivers, tectonic plates shifting angrily.

Ethan pants, not daring to move while the earthquake rumbles all around. A cacophony of crashes from inside the cabin deafens him. The dishes he left on the counter shatter on the floor. Furniture topples over and decorative knickknacks rain down. He can hardly think of the mess he'll have to clean as he covers his head and waits.

Slowly, as the Earth settles, he dares to uncurl, his arms hesitating before lowering from his head. His hand brushes against the sharp edge of his smashed beer bottle that now lies on the ground next to him, and he flinches from it.

In the middle of the field, below the massive hills, is a giant glowing crater.

A wave of sickness washes over him. Suddenly, the isolation with terrible cell service no longer feels like paradise. Instead, the cold talons of fear sink into his mind at the possible pending death sentence of it all.

Maybe he should've listened to his mother's warnings.

He racks his memory for every science class he's ever taken to figure out if asteroids usually glow a light pinkish-purple. He wants to say no, and his brain unhelpfully suggests that if this is an alien of some sort, none of what he learned in high school science class applies.

He swallows thickly, trying to calm himself and think. He needs his gun.

The door is jammed from the house shifting with the earthquake, but he forces his way inside the house. Every shadow becomes a creature lying in wait to snatch him. Every creak of the floorboards is a monster slithering up behind him. His creativity offers horrendous combinations of abduction and slaughter to agonize over, his skin crawling with the creeping horror of it all.

He shakes his head violently. He needs to focus. Plan. And not become a plotline of *The X-Files*.

His numb fingers find the light switch and flick it. Nothing. He uselessly tries a few more times before pulling out his cellphone for the flashlight. The illuminated room is a mess, his interpretation of the sounds during the earthquake proving to be accurate, with furniture overturned and debris strewn around the small place. Cleaning up would have to wait though.

With a steadying breath, he carefully steps around the mess toward his gun locker. The time he spent shooting with Andrea and her friends is about to come in handy. He loads his Mossberg pump-action and cocks it swiftly, the *crack-crack* helping to soothe his quaking nerves, and steadies his hands.

He hesitates to consider the merits of searching for a bigger flashlight, but there isn't a need for one. The ominous purple light glowing outside is plenty to see by. With one last deep breath, he slides his phone into his back pocket and exits the house.

The light from the crater has changed. Instead of a bright, steady, lavender glow, it has begun to emit flickers of luminescence. The dry grass under his boots crunches until he reaches the soft upturned earth. He blinks, squinting down into the hole. It's much shallower than he expected, with a massive orb of light taking up most of the impression in the earth.

The light flickers again, and the outline of something small and crumpled in the center burns into his retinas. In the span of Ethan's slow intake of breath, the light takes on an opalescent hue. It's like the air is coated in mother-of-pearl, but it morphs, dances. The gun in Ethan's tight hold sags, his pupils dilating. Whispers of the world hum, the soil beneath his feet erupting in fresh sprouts. Wildflowers peek up before blooming, shedding, wilting, and starting over again from the seeds. Endlessly, over and over, the cycle of life coils and unfurls before him.

His gun falls to be cradled by the lush grass.

Ethan steps into the crater.

The light is losing its blinding quality, and he can clearly see the shivering form in the center.

His knees sink into the soft earth, the whispers becoming louder. Something is not right. Fear, not of what he is seeing, but of the wrongness of the form in front of him, blooms in his chest. It is leaking. He reaches out, touching it. He expects his fingers to burn, but instead a vibrant hum echoes within him. Unable to stop himself, he rolls the form over, its soft body falling into his lap.

A pulse echoes through the valley, the grass lying flat.

Ethan's eyes flutter, the mass of opalescent air circling. His chest jerks as his heart throbs. Pleasure, unfathomable pleasure, burns through him. His voice is gone, his mind is gone. The world glows and the air shimmers. His arms tighten around the form, and it shifts beneath his hands—but he cannot see. All he knows is this wondrous light glowing within him, consuming him, and he falls into the sensation joyfully.

The world sucks inward, the aura around them shooting in, and Ethan gasps, an echo of the same sound beneath him.

Just as quickly as it began, it ends. Only a few seconds pass, but it feels like an eternity. Ethan blinks, the night sky slowly becoming visible again. He wavers, limbs suddenly weak. Confusion makes his brain feel hazy, and his stomach rolls.

He needs to lay down, maybe have some water, but he definitely needs to get out of this hole first.

He looks down at the thing in his arms and jolts. Blinking up at him is something he can't quite comprehend. It looks human, but its skin radiates light with the same opalescent lavender sheen that he saw from the crater before. Ethan hisses in a breath when he sees a head wound, a nasty one, the mysterious being's skull nearly concaved on the upper right side of its forehead. White, shimmering liquid flows from the gash to drip down to the soft earth below, the soil sucking in the liquid greedily.

He looks the creature up and down, a wave of sadness and empathy hitting him right in the chest. He can't abandon it, hurt and alone. Not in this cruel world. Ethan swallows thickly, his voice harsh. "It's going to be okay." He's not sure why he says it, only that the sense of absolute rightness hums within him when the words come out. "I'm going to help you."

Eyes blink open again, settling on his face. Humanlike, but with soft blue irises that almost seem white. So mesmerizing that Ethan finds himself lost studying the different shades within them, until he notices the pupils, his brows furrowing. The black depths reflect the cosmos above. Beautiful and mystifying at the same time. He feels himself sucked forward, his own eyes widening and his heart thudding painfully against his ribs. In a great feat of self-control, he rips his gaze away, his chest heaving with the force of his breaths.

Ethan looks around wildly to see if there is anything nearby that could offer an explanation. When he finds none, he tilts his head back to look up to the dark sky. The stars watch him silently and offer no answers. He looks back down at the creature unconscious in his arms and wonders, *What the hell do I do now?*

In the deep dark of the world, in the cold watery depths of the enraged Ocean, the pulse of life washes through the abyss. Life stirs. Starved hunger, glowing eyes, and echoing bioluminescence flesh.

Magic has finally landed.

So long have they waited. Too long. But the magic, the star, it is too far away. Much farther than what was promised by prophecy. The creatures wail, writhing in despair. Great bodies slash through the water, circling round and round, snapping great fanged jaws at each other.

The largest of them, his milky white eyes blind to all, lifts his wide head. Ancient, far older than he should be, he is the last of the secret keepers of the great sea. He remembers what his father told him, whose own father told him in the great chain of tales. Not all is lost. His webbed, clawed hand reaches into the rock and pulls out a small glowing pearl. Hope in a small, round token. So few when there used to be so many. So precious. But one must go, or all is lost.

He turns to the other that is waiting, silent, watchful. The pearl passes between them, for it is not the ancient one's place to enter the Great Game. He must stay on his rock and protect the last few pearls. The other, the Contender, curls his webbed paw around the precious drop of magic, his thick skin blocking the glow within.

The ancient one turns his blind eyes toward the surface far, far above. So far that the light does not even twinkle in these dark depths.

His throat works rhythmically, squeaks and whirls of sound coiling out to the Contender. "Go, brother. Find the fallen star. Feast and claim the prize. Do not fail for we both know…death is the only outcome." A whirl sounds in his throat, his claws sinking into the sacred volcanic rock. "Yours or his."

Don't stop now. Keep reading with your copy of A GAME OF FALLEN STARS, by City Owl Author, S.E. Berkeley.

Don't miss more from N K Brown coming soon, and find out more at nkbrownauthor.com

Until then, discover A GAME OF FALLEN STARS, by City Owl Author, S.E. Berkeley

A Life-Changing Encounter with Magic, Romance, and Danger

Ethan is drowning in corporate burnout and heartache. Seeking escape, he retreats to the peaceful isolation of Parkfield, a quiet town in central California, hoping to heal. But his sabbatical takes an unexpected turn when a mysterious creature crashes into his front yard—Star, a being of pure magic, stranded in a world devoid of it.

With no memory of who—or what—she is, Star longs to become human. She forms a human body to live in and, with Ethan's help, starts navigating this modern world. But the closer they get, the more their chemistry intensifies, leading to a heated pancake-making lesson and a flirtatious game of pool. As passion simmers, their fragile connection is put to the test when an ancient sea monster attacks their cabin, narrowly sparing their lives.

Suddenly, they find themselves trapped in a cosmic horror's twisted game, with Star as the prey. As they flee, hunted by both mythical creatures and a shadowy secret society, Ethan and Star race toward San Francisco for answers. But time is running out. If they don't survive, Star's magic will be consumed by a brutal hunter, gaining unimaginable power.

Ethan faces an agonizing choice: run and protect the woman he loves, or fight against impossible odds to save her and stop an ancient evil from rising.

Please sign up for the City Owl Press newsletter for chances to win special subscriber-only contests and giveaways as well as receiving information on upcoming releases and special excerpts.

All reviews are **welcome** and **appreciated**. Please consider leaving one on your favorite social media and book buying sites.

Escape Your World. Get Lost in Ours! City Owl Press at www.cityowlpress.com.

ACKNOWLEDGMENTS

This novel was born from two things, a phrase 'it's fun to be the bad guy, until you develop a conscience,' and a magic trick (as featured in chapter 1). The rest gradually evolved into a hot mess of a draft as I've never been one for planning, which is why my critique partners Sheena and Nikki and my long-suffering developmental editor Kathryn are so valuable. Thank you now and thank you always for being so supportive and for your help in forming a proper story out of the chaos.

Another heartfelt thanks to my editor at City Owl, Lisa Green, who took a chance on this dark fantasy, adding my little book to her amazing list and gifting me my first ever Publisher's Marketplace announcement! In fact, the whole team at City Owl Press have been wonderful and held my hand throughout this entire process.

Lastly, thanks to Jericho Writers and their Ultimate Novel Writing Course program which gave me the tools I needed to craft multiple novels and the confidence to send them out to publishers.

ABOUT THE AUTHOR

N K BROWN is a veterinarian and proud mother of three. Originally from Stratford-Upon-Avon, she now lives outside of Boston.

Finally ready for the career change she always wanted, she joined Jericho Writers and is an alumni of their Ultimate Novel Writing Course. She loves to write in the SFF genre usually with a dark and speculative twist. An animal or two will usually pop up somewhere in my writing!

When not reading or writing or reading about writing, you can find her out on a long run, lost in her imagination (or a good audiobook) as she plans her next novel.

nkbrownauthor.com

ABOUT THE PUBLISHER

City Owl Press is a cutting edge indie publishing company, bringing the world of romance and speculative fiction to discerning readers.

Escape Your World. Get Lost in Ours!

www.cityowlpress.com

- facebook.com/CityOwlPress
- x.com/cityowlpress
- instagram.com/cityowlbooks
- pinterest.com/cityowlpress
- tiktok.com/@cityowlpress

www.ingramcontent.com/pod-product-compliance
Ingram Content Group UK Ltd.
Pitfield, Milton Keynes, MK11 3LW, UK
UKHW021833140426
5217IPUK00021B/1420